NEVER *FEAR -*

CHRISTMAS TERRORS

Heather Graham,
F. Paul Wilson
Thomas F. Monteleone,
E. McCarthy
Lisa Mannetti, Don Bruns

Connie Corcoran Wilson, Lee Lawless
Jeff DePew, Kristi Ahlers, Debby Grahl, Aidan
Russell, G. R. Linden, Liah Penn, Lisa Harris, Mathew
Kaufman, Richard Devin, Lance Taubold, Ed
DeAngelis, Elle J Rossi, Crystal Perkins and Jon Land

Discover new and exciting works by Invoke Books at
www.invokebooks.com

Print and Digital Edition, License Notes

DEDICATION

To Heather Graham and her incomparable annual Writers For New Orleans Conference where the genesis of this book was developed.

And to all of the contributing authors who were attendees at the 2015 Conference.

Thank you.

CONTENTS

A FAMILY CHRISTMAS TERROR

CHAPTER 1

Christmas Morning.
Upstate New York.
The Present.

On a perfect, white Christmas morning, the MacDonald family were all in the living room. Dan and Judy watched their three college-aged children opening the last of their presents. Their eldest, Jack, was a senior, and their twins, Nick and Nancy, were midway through their freshmen year. The grandfather, Joe, sat in his favorite chair, quietly enjoying the laughter and joking.

The perfect Christmas.

"Is everyone ready for fresh doughnuts and coffee?" Judy said, already on her way to the kitchen.

"Absolutely," Nick said. "I'm starving."

"You're always starving," Nancy said, not looking up from her cell phone.

"Well, can you blame him?" Dan said, rising. "That's all I've been smelling for the last hour. I think I'll go help your mother, make sure she puts enough powdered sugar on them." He winked at the twins and went to join his wife.

"Hey, we missed one," Jack said. "Over there in the corner." He got up from the floor, pushing his way through the mounds of festive, discarded wrapping paper.

"It's probably for me," Nancy said.

"Right," Nick said. "You got enough. You always get more than anyone."

"That's because I'm a girl. I need more things."

Jack walked over to Grandpa. "Here, Grandpa, you open it. It says: *For the MacDonald Family.* So, my dear sister, it's not for you."

Nancy made a moue in mock disappointment. "Open it, Grandpa."

Grandpa tore the paper off, revealing a colorful paperback book. *Never Fear—Christmas Terrors.* He turned it over and read the back. "Huh. Who would send us something like this?"

"Santa?" Nick asked.

"It was probably you," Nancy said. "You would probably think it's funny." She punched her twin in the arm.

"Ow, that was hard." He rubbed his arm. "Let me see it, Grandpa." Nick took the book, then riffled the pages. "You know... it's not too long, and we've got all day. Maybe we should read it. It'll be like spooky stories on Halloween, but instead it'll be Christmas."

"Like that Christmas song," Nancy interjected. "Something about 'Scary ghost stories and tales of His glories'—"

"The song is called "*It's The Most Wonderful Time of the Year*," Jack interrupted. "I was thinking the same thing."

"I don't know if that's a very good—" Grandpa started.

"Yeah, why not," Nancy said, ignoring Grandpa's protestations. "What's the first story called?"

"*The Ghost of a Christmas Past*."

"I do like ghost stories," Nancy said, reaching for the book. "Let me read the first one."

Nick begrudgingly gave her the book just as Dan and Judy made their way back into the room with doughnuts and hot coffee.

Jack grabbed a doughnut, saying, "Mom, Dad, we got this book of Christmas horror stories and I thought it would be a great idea if we read them out loud."

"I don't know..." Judy said, setting the tray down.

"It'll be all right, Judy. A little scare never hurt anyone. Lighten up." Dan set his tray down next to hers.

Judy looked at him doubtfully. "Well, maybe just a couple." She picked up her mug and sat on one of the couches beside Dan.

On the couch opposite them, Nancy said, "Here goes...

THE GHOST OF A CHRISTMAS PAST

HEATHER GRAHAM

The lambs had been slaughtered. Blood poured from their painted mouths—once white-washed and serene. Rings of blood surrounded their tender necks.

The Three Wise Men had fared no better; rings of paint—or whatever substance had been used to create the illusion of blood—dripped down their necks and onto their old Judaic tunics.

Nothing had been left in sacred peace—Mary and Joseph were chopped into mass sections of wood, all splattered in red as well. The infant's bed of straw lay in so many bloody bits of pulp and gore that it was almost impossible to tell what it had been. Camels had also gone the way of the axe—some kind of staged blood covered the entire scene like the remnants of a hard red rain.

"Lieutenant Marin, have you ever seen anything like it?" Captain Declan Craig asked, staring at the wooden carnage, a fierce frown cut into his features.

"No," Dakota Marin said, and she never had. But, then again, she'd come up from the City of Miami—where axes were more often used on living people than on wooden images. She imagined that this had been done by someone of a different belief, perhaps, furious that Christmas was being given so much play. And to be honest, she did find this bloody, pulpy destruction of wood to be more disturbing than some of the flesh and blood horror she'd witnessed in five years in Greater Miami.

Then again, the small town of Hanging Tree, Florida, had a reputation for the weird. Historically, a mysterious offshoot of the Caribe tribe had once lived in the area—and their shamans had made this a place where war parties were planned—and where they had been wiped out by another mysterious tribe. Then, the Spaniards had arrived in Florida in the late fifteenth century and their missionaries had come across from the coast to die at the hands of unknown assailants. After the Spaniards, the English had created a settlement nearby—and brought their evil-doers here—to be hanged from the giant old oak that sat just beyond the sacred burial ground that surrounded St. Marks, the now non-denominational church that was the largest in town. Supposedly, when the wiccans, paganists, or witches had lived here, there had been another outcry and one poor woman had been dragged out in the middle of the night to be hanged—at the hanging tree, of course. She had supposedly screamed about being possessed by a devil, and—as all good legendary victims should—she left behind a curse.

Naturally, those who had been hanged had joined with the demons in the forest. Sometimes, it was said that unlucky lads and lasses had disappeared here—other stories stated that gruesome remains had been found along forest paths—and the gravestones that had already cropped up around the church which had been originally been Catholic, with construction having been begun in the late 1600s.

Florida had officially become an American Territory in 1822 and the Americans had come, eager for land. It really was beautiful land, north of Ocala, east of Tallahassee, near such picturesque places as Micanopy and Gainesville. The land actually rolled here; oaks and pines still grew on rich land, horses and cattle were common along with good old Florida grapefruit and oranges. The Seminole Wars had brought bloodshed and havoc, only to be followed by the Civil War—and a skirmish just before the battle of Olustee that had left all dead.

Come the twentieth century, a group of psychics had moved in, and then, when one of their number had met with a gruesome end at the hands of something described as what might only have been a forest beast, they had declared the area far too active to be borne by such sensitives, it had been taken over by a colony of wiccans. The wiccans claimed that there was a curse on the land— and that the devil must be fed. There were those, of course, who never noticed the curse. Through it all, some hardy farmers, ranchers, and townspeople had held on. Today, it was just a typical small town with some interesting historic buildings and some ugly new ones.

And outlying areas with horses, cows, and fruit trees. It was very popular at Halloween—and enterprising citizens had gotten together to create "Haunted Hanging Nights." These days, however, the crime tended to be Bernie getting mad and belting Jez at the local dive bar, Seven Trees, when he got too carried away with his karaoke and dented the microphone, or when Mrs. Firestone called the cops, locked in her bathroom, because her husband had threatened her with a beating for changing the channel on the television. Christmas season was upon them. That usually meant a nice flow of tourists who came to see the historic buildings all decked out with their beautiful lights, the historic church—and the Nativity Scene set up on the church lawn.

Dakota knew all this because the minute she'd received the invitation from the town's mayor, she'd hit up Amazon for every book she could find on the area. Quirky—and close enough to Gainesville, Jacksonville, St. Augustine—and even Orlando and theme-parkville—to make it an okay move.

She still had all her books, piled high on her desk at the station.

"Interesting enough for you, Marin?" Declan asked, turning to look at her skeptically. "I know after the big city, we've been a little mundane."

"Bizarre, certainly," she said. "I'm going to take it we're looking for teens from the local high school—or someone who is angry that a Buddhist statue, a pentacle, a

7

Star of David, or some other religious symbol hasn't been given equal space."

She forced a smiled. Declan looked like he belonged in a move about a Stepford-style town; he was strikingly handsome, like a beach boy who might have cruised Miami Beach—tall, blond, tanned, and nicely muscled. He believed that, no matter how polite and respectful she tried to appear, she believed that she'd wound up working in this hick-cracker town like Mayberry and that he wasn't even as bright as a Barney Fife, or perhaps even something as pathetic as a cartoon creature like a Deputy Dawg.

She really wasn't sure what she thought as yet. All she knew was that she'd come out at the wrong end of a situation with Brendan Howell in Miami; she'd been the newbie—he'd had a nice long reputation on the streets and, apparently, no other female co-worker had gotten the nerve to complain about him. All she had known was that he appeared innocent before the powers that be—and she'd be the one to get the boot. When the offer had come from Hanging Tree—at a very nice salary—it had seemed a prudent idea to accept it. She'd been hired as Declan's second in command and it was a small force—there were only six more officers, two for each of three daily eight hour shifts.

They were all lovely people—but she wasn't sure she'd have wanted to be on a major Miami drug sting with them. They'd be far too polite to the Uzi-wielding pushers they were trying to take down.

At that moment, Pastor Frank Waterford came hurrying out of the church, shaking his head, his distress apparently in his ruddy cheeks, waddling speed, and wide eyes. Frank was okay—a religious man who didn't go fanatic on anyone and gave sermons that simply encouraged nice, polite, and kind neighborly behavior. He did, however, love Christmas—and the Christmas apparel that adorned the church as the season drew near. In Hanging Tree, the townspeople decked out the graveyard, placing Christmas wreaths and ornaments on their family tombs. Slightly weird, but kind of nice, really.

"This is awful, just awful!" Pastor Frank said, folding his shaking hands before him as he reached them—and looked over the "blood and guts."

"Yes, Pastor, and I'm so sorry," Declan said.

"I wish—I so wish there was something to be done!" he said. "The sheer destruction—but that's not it! It's what they've done. This is so wrong. Why, God and Christ and the Holy Ghost must be looking down on us in tears!"

If God cried, Dakota thought, it was over the real blood and guts humanity liked to shed. But she quickly said, "Pastor, we'll find out who did this. Probably kids, but, it could be what's considered a hate crime as well. We will get to the bottom of it."

He looked at her very sadly. "I don't think so, Dakota." No one in the area called Declan Captain—they certainly weren't going to call her Lieutenant Marin. The only one who did was Declan—and always with a certain tone.

"There's going to be a witness somewhere," she said. "Someone who saw something; or, perhaps, someone walking around with a bunch of fake blood all over them."

Pastor Frank looked at Declan and shook his head sadly. "We'll never be able to replace them. But, they knew that, didn't they? They've been waiting. And now, they've done it."

Shaking his head, he turned and headed back into the old Gothic church.

"They? He knows who did it?" Dakota asked Declan.

Declan kept his eyes steady on her. "He thinks it was done by the devils in the woods."

"What?" Dakota asked, incredulous. Frank was a minister! How could he believe such a thing?

"Everything bad in this town is blamed on the devils in the woods," Declan explained. "I guess we should be happy that this time, they tore apart mannequins instead of people."

"Please don't tell me that you believe that devils live in the woods—and that they hurried in with hatchets to tear up this Nativity scene?"

He shrugged. "Let's go see what we can find out."

"You're not going to set this up as a crime scene? Fingerprints, footprints, some kind of clues? I see a cigarette butt over there."

"You got an evidence bag? Bag it. You won't get footprints—rained heavy about six this morning. Fingerprints—you won't get any of those, either."

"Because devils don't leave fingerprints?" Dakota asked sarcastically.

He shrugged. "Because county forensic crews won't come in here with their expertise when its wooden objects that have been massacred. No—you just won't get any. Whoever did this wore gloves."

"And you know that because...?"

"There's a tuft of material caught on that lamb's ear," he said. "Bag that, too, if you will deputy. And then, we'll head over to the Seven Trees Bar."

Declan pointed across the quiet country road that stretched before the church. Ironically, the ramshackle building facing the church was a bar—a shanty bar, actually voted the number one dive bar in this section of north central Florida.

"Great. If we have a witness, it's going to be a drunk," Dakota murmured.

Declan looked at her and cocked his head to the side. "You said you wanted a witness. Besides, the bartender and waitresses don't get plastered. And Officer Cary Conklin has the graveyard shift and likes to ticket or arrest the drunks at night so most people come with a designated driver— believe it or not—even in this hick town."

Dakota hunkered down for the cigarette butt and then headed to the lamb to do the same with the bit of fabric. She realized that he was watching her as she did so. She flushed slightly as she rose; there was nothing licentious in the way that he watched her. Not like the way the bastard had in Miami. No, this was different. He studied her—as a mathematician might study an interesting equation.

As they walked across the street he asked, "What the hell are you doing here, Dakota?"

"Working," she said.

"Yes, why are you working here?"

"It pays well."

"Oh, that's bull. Yeah, the pay is good. You would have made detective in Miami. You're twenty-seven. Great record. Killer body, perfect nose, lips—eyes. Oh, sorry, not trying to be sexist or offensive. I just really want to know what the hell you're doing here."

"What are you doing here?" she countered.

He paused. "I'm here to catch the devils," he said.

"Oh, please," she murmured.

"I'm from here," he said simply.

"And you never wanted to go anywhere else?"

He was silent, stopping as they reached the opposite side of the street. She wondered if he'd shrug again and keep walking. But then, to her surprise, he offered her a crooked smile and said, "I'll show you mine if you show me yours."

"Okay. Mine is a fucking octopus of a man who everyone thinks is the Second Coming," Dakota said flatly.

"Figured something like that."

"And you?"

He paused again for a long moment, and then shrugged.

"Fifteen years ago, give or take a day or two, I was a student at the University of Florida. My girlfriend was driving down here to meet my sister, Linda—my twin, actually. Linda and Marissa were friends and that's how Marissa and I met. Anyway, Marissa had come down—right about this time of year, they had done some Christmas shopping together—and then she'd left my folks old home and headed back to Gainesville on a bright, beautiful morning. We were both due to come back for the holiday in a week. But, Marissa left that day and..."

"And?" Dakota asked softly.

"It's a drive that should have taken about an hour and a half. She never showed up."

"What—what happened to her?"

"Her car was found in a pond just the other side of the woods behind the church. Marissa was never found." He hesitated then. "One day, I will find out what happened to her."

"You never mentioned a sister—a twin," Dakota said.

"Because she left after Marissa disappeared. My parents were gone... Linda left. She had to forget. I couldn't."

He turned toward the bar. Dakota ran after him quickly. "Declan!"

He stopped.

"Anything might have happened to her."

"But, it didn't. There are devils in the woods," he said.

She stared after him, disbelieving. Then she ran to catch up.

The bar was truly rustic and looked like an old, decaying fishing shanty. That had not deterred the proprietors from the spirit of the season. The front door was festooned with a huge wreath and loaded with decorations. A cheap plastic Santa waved hello from one side of the entrance while cheerful plastic elves played on the other side. It was daytime, but dozens of strings of colored Christmas lights sparkled from rakish, anywhere—anywhere hanging around the windows, from the roof, and over whatever foliage ringed the place.

Declan opened the door to the bar. And then he froze.

"What...?" Dakota asked, trying to get past him.

He was solid. The best she could do was look over his shoulder.

There were body pieces everywhere. Blood everywhere.

But, this time, it hadn't been wooden mannequins that had been hacked to pieces.

And it wasn't stage blood.

Flesh, blood, bone, and brain matter was splattered everywhere.

And it was real.

"Time to call in the county," Declan said. "And every damned forensic expert they have."

*

Before they had even entered the bar, Declan was on the phone with a representative from the Alachua County Sheriff's Department and the Florida Department of Law

Enforcement. Despite appearances, they had to enter to assure themselves that all were dead, even though ambulances were on the way. The bartender lay behind the bar—no way to help him. His neck had been so seriously sliced that the head was nearly severed. What appeared to be a young woman—shapely legs emerged from a battered torso by one of the rough wood tables—looked upward with one eye. Her face had been so severely slashed she looked like a Halloween ragdoll. Four customers had been in the bar: two at a table, two at the bar.

All had met similar fates. It was tricky to assess the room and avoid the pools of blood.

"Look," Declan said, and pointed, indicating an old mirror over the bar.

She looked. Someone's blood had been used to write a message on the glass.

Merry Christmas, Hanging Tree. Old St. Nick is coming—for you!

"I guess people do come to hate small town life, huh?" Declan murmured.

Dakota swallowed. Even at Metro Miami-Dade, she'd never seen anything like this.

"You know these people?" she asked.

He nodded. "Gus Farley, bartender. Good man—intended to retire to the Keys next year. Lou Troy and Mitch Robinson at the bar. Old-timers—just like Jerry Simms and Mel McCarthy, the guys at the tables. I didn't know the waitress; she just came down here, kicked out of school, University of Florida, up in Gainesville. Name was Kerry

Reed, I think. Poor thing. God!" he exclaimed suddenly, betraying a moment's deep emotion. "What the hell."

She saw that his fists were knotted at his side and that he was straining to fight his emotions and his rage. "What the bloody hell, who the bloody hell...?"

The tinny scent of the blood was getting to her, too. She felt her stomach roil. This was the kind of sight that called upon everything in the human heart—it was a scene that hurt, and she was grateful that she had been in town only two weeks and yet to know its inhabitants well at all.

The devils in the woods! She thought.

No devil had done this. A human hand—*a human hand they could catch!*—had done this.

And yet... how?

How had these people all been taken down? Had none of them fought back?

It was while she was pondering the question that Dakota thought she heard the sound of a sob. Soft, like a child's cry.

"Someone's in here, somewhere!" she said.

And—trying to make sure that she didn't slide across the blood slick floor—she hurried around the bar. There was a door there, ajar now. It led, she quickly discovered, to a storeroom and office in back.

At first she saw nothing. She moved forward right before Declan nearly plowed into her back, having followed in her wake.

There was a desk across the room; she hurried around and looked beneath it. And there she saw the child.

It was a little girl; she was perhaps ten, with long blond hair. She was curled into herself under the desk, shaking and crying.

"Hey! Hello," Dakota said, reaching out a hand to her. She had dealt with survivors before, but it wasn't her forte. Most homicide detectives would tell anyone that dealing with the dead was easier than dealing with survivors. The dead needed justice. Survivors needed help and empathy.

This survivor was a child. What did she say? *It's all right? It wasn't all right. How did she even get the child out of there without bringing her past the scene of all the carnage?*

Declan was right behind her; he quickly hunkered down to talk to the child. "Sweetheart, hi, I'm the local police chief. And this is Dakota—she's a police officer, too. Were you here with someone—like your mom or your dad?"

She girl just trembled. Declan reached out to him. She hesitated, and then took his hand. He looked at Dakota. "Your jacket?" he asked.

"Yes, yes, of course," she said, quickly removing the jacket. She handed it to him. "I'm going to get you out of here; this is going to be over your head for just a minute, okay?"

The little girl just stared at him. She was a beautiful child, wide blue eyes, platinum blond hair, and an angel's face.

Declan eased her out from under the desk, draping the jacket over her head so that she wouldn't see. He hurried out and Dakota followed him.

By the time they were outside, sirens were screeching. A man named McSween introduced himself; he was a lead detective with the county. He listened to Declan's report on their strange discoveries. Forensic crews and a medical examiner had arrived; they were moving with admirable speed. McSween promised to secure the scene and collect all possible forensic evidence to get going on the investigation. "Not to be offensive," McSween, a tall, slim man with a sympathetic manner told him. "I don't mean to imply—"

"You wouldn't be implying anything, McSween," Declan told him. "We don't have the facilities you have. I'll get this girl down to our office and see if we can't find out something from her."

"The kid is probably in shock."

"We'll see that she gets to child services—maybe they'll have doctors who know how to get to... to talk. To tell us something. I'll start on the locals—seeing if I can't get something."

"Good then; you know your town here; me, I know bodies," McSween said. "And, as soon as it's... decent, we'll talk to the kid."

"Her parents?" McSween asked.

"I don't know," Declan said. "She doesn't belong to any of—to any of the victims in the bar. I know them all."

Dakota turned away from the bar, glad that a host of out-of-towners had arrived to make all the proper moves. She saw that a county M.E.'s wagon was among the arrivals.

Declan was already moving across the street. She ran after him.

He headed to their car, emblazoned with the town logo—an image of a great oak and the words, Hanging Tree.

As she reached the car, she found it sadly ironic that choir practice had apparently begun at the church. Someone was singing *Joy to the World*.

*

The shifts at the station ran from eight in the morning to four in the afternoon, four in the afternoon to midnight, and midnight to eight, with Declan and Dakota straddling the hours, usually from about nine to six or seven at night, later when needed, or any hour when needed.

When they arrived at the station with the little girl who wouldn't talk, Chancy Buell and David Lassiter were on duty; they naturally knew what had happened already and that the county detectives were on it.

The station, too, seemed garish at the moment—though it had been warm and festive when she'd left, Dakota realized. A tree was in one corner, loaded with ornaments, and a fine star topped it off. Streams of fake holly lined the windows. And here, too, playing softly, was a Christmas carol. Here, *Deck the Halls.*

Chancy Buell was nearing retirement; she was a small woman with iron gray hair, a gentle manner—and the ability to scare anyone into good behavior when pushed. Small—but mighty, Dakota had decided. She'd seen Chancy propel a few hulking football players into the holding cell, barely raising the tone of her voice.

But, seeing the child, Chancy immediately turned into grandmother mode. "What have we here? What a darling child. Honey, where's your mommy?" she asked gently.

The little girl just shook her head.

"Have they called child services?" Chancy asked Dakota. Declan had already headed to the coffee pot where he was deep in thought, pouring himself a cup.

"We got her out of there; country folks had just arrived," Dakota said. "I'm sure that McSween—the county detective—had done so, but, I'll make sure."

"Phones are out," David told her, shaking his head. "Old lines and old wires. You'll need to use your cell."

"Phones are out?" Declan said sharply, turning to look at David.

David was young; he'd just transferred over from the Gainesville department. With wild straw colored hair and a big hulking body, he really did make the perfect small town cop. He was unerringly polite at all times.

"Yep—tried to patch into you just as you came back. One of us was about to walk over, but we knew both of you were on the scene, and ..." His voice trailed. Either he hadn't wanted to add more confusion to such a scene, or, he simply hadn't want to see the awful gore, not when he didn't need to. County detectives were always called in on murder.

"I'll use my cell outside," Dakota said.

"Yeah, get someone here," Declan said, heading out before she could do so.

"Where are you going?" she called, hurrying after him.

"Whoever it is—*whatever it is*—is out there. I'm going to find the devil."

"There is no devil in the woods!" Dakota shouted.

"I'll get our little princess some hot chocolate, how about that?" she heard Chancy say. Chancy apparently hadn't heard Declan's insanity. "Then," Chancy continued, "Maybe we can talk and find out who you are and where we can find your mommy or your daddy. And you can tell me what you want for Christmas, little princess!"

Dakota continued on out and let the door close. She pulled out her cell—it was hard to get cell service inside, the building had been constructed of heavy brick during the eighteen-hundreds—she noted with aggravation that Declan was heading in much the same direction from which they had come. The town had a square—and the church and the graveyard and then forest sat across the expanse of the square while the bar was across from the church at the end of the square.

She dialed the division of child services at county and watched Declan go. He was headed back the way they had come, but he hadn't bothered with the car. He was walking fast—quickly eating up the half mile or so to the church.

But he wasn't heading to the church. He was heading to the graveyard—and the hanging tree.

He couldn't really believe in devils!

Child services answered; Dakota identified herself and gave the situation. She was passed around a few times and finally spoke with a man who gave her an address in Gainesville and asked if an officer was available to bring the child to them.

Chancy wouldn't mind; Dakota assured the woman they bring the child. None of them was equipped to deal with the little girl who had to be traumatized out of her mind.

She had to take charge. Someone around here had to stay sane.

Walking back into the office, Dakota saw that now both Chancy and David were hunched down by the little girl. They'd gotten her to talk.

"What do you want for Christmas?" Chancy asked.

"Toys!" the little girl said.

"We'll just find your mommy and daddy," David said.

Her eyes filled with tears. She screamed; a terrible scream.

"Oh, dear!" David said.

Chancy picked her up and held her near and rocked her. She looked over the little girl's head, hoping Dakota had information for her.

"They've asked us to bring her to them," Dakota said.

"I'll go," David and Chancy offered simultaneously.

"We should both go," David said. "If she... if she panics in the car, she could hurt the driver."

"Makes sense," Dakota told him.

"But, where the hell—sorry! Heck!—did Declan go?" Chancy asked.

"Don't worry; the town is crawling with law enforcement," Dakota said. "I'm fine; you two go."

Chancy held the little girl; Dakota tried to smile as she saw the angelic face over Chancy's shoulder. The little girl offered her a tremulous smile back. For a moment, the Christmas lights in the office seemed to catch in her eyes and they glowed.

Poor kid.

With them out of the office, Dakota sat at her desk. Had Declan suspected that the killer—or killers—had headed into the forest? He shouldn't have gone off alone. But, now, she was the only one at the station. She sat down at her desk and drummed her fingers on the hard wood and felt frozen for a moment.

She'd never expected anything so horrible here.

County was on it; officers with high tech and plenty of ability!

She picked up one of the books on her desk. *The Curse of Hanging Tree.*

She hadn't bothered with the book yet; she'd been looking at real histories and tourist catalogues.

It had been re-printed by some entrepreneur who, according to the title page, had found the diary at Hanging Tree. She started to flip through the pages. The book was supposedly the diary of a young woman who had once lived in Hanging Tree, somewhere around 1830. Dakota started to flip the pages, and then found herself reading near the end.

"Eleanor Grigsby disappeared last night; her mother is frantic. She tells a strange tale about a girl taken a decade before. That girl, I know was Mary Easton; Mary, they say, ran off with a soldier. I don't believe Eleanor did the same. She was my friend; she told me that she was haunted by memories of Mary! But, you know this town. They say that the devil in the woods has been there since time memorial, changing shape, becoming what it chooses. Only when one cries out to the spirits of goodness and the hanging tree is burned to cinder will the devil die, for its power lies in the terror of those who died there. If they do not find Mary soon, I will burn that tree to the ground."

Dakota turned the page. It was the end of the diary—an epilogue said that the author of the diary, Charlotte Anderson, had disappeared one night and never been seen again.

"Oh, bull!" Dakota said to herself, pushing the book aside. And yet, she couldn't help but feel a strange chill. Ridiculous. It was a beautiful Florida December—the day temperature was seventy-five; at night, it fell to the sixties.

And Chancy's iPod was still playing gentle tunes: *Oh, Holy Night*.

She tried to log into her computer; the Internet, like the phones, seemed to be out.

Swearing, she rose and headed out the front door. She was going to call Declan and find out just what the hell he was doing.

But she never even drew her phone from her pocket. Down the street, closer to the business section of downtown—as it was!—she heard a tremendous commotion. Then she saw that people were running toward the police station.

"What, what?"

"Come, come quick!" A man called. "There's been an accident! A terrible accident!"

She started to run. Whatever had happened was down, way down.

On the street that led to I-75. The path Chancy and David would be taking to get the little girl to Gainesville.

People were all out of the street—leaving their business and homes behind to gape in horror.

Dakota ran past them all until she came to the dead center of the town, the circle where they had raised a giant Christmas tree.

And then she saw. The official police car with the Hanging Tree logo was now in the tree. And the car and the tree were burning ferociously. She heard sirens from the fire station; there was a rush of county cars from the scene they had left that morning.

And there was... fire.

She burst her way through with the firefighters who tried to push her back. As they fought the blaze, she felt her stomach sink, felt a pain that squeezed around her heart and tore at her lungs.

David and Chancy. She could see, even as the firefighters pushed her back, even as others arrived, the charred bodies of David and Chancy.

There'd been a child in the car. Now, they wouldn't have to wonder where she had come from; they wouldn't have to wonder what she'd seen.

"Oh, dear God!" she breathed.

Someone was next to her; someone from county. Someone saying that she had to get away; county would manage everything. She had to find her fellows from the town; she was going to have to tell them the terrible truth.

Someone had an arm on her shoulder. Someone was trying to lead her away.

Someone else was trying to get her to drink something. Whiskey.

Whiskey wasn't going to help.

She shook them off; she was the town's police lieutenant.

Declan. Where the hell was Declan? Two people he cared about were dead, and...

Finally, not even sure how she really got there, she was back at the station. She stood in front of it, trying to reach Declan on her cell phone. He didn't answer.

She remembered then that child services would be looking for someone to arrive with the little blond girl.

"Dakota! You all right?"

She turned. It was Pastor Frank. He looked horrible; he obviously knew that his day had gone from the bizarre to the tragic, that people had died, that they'd been brutalized just as the figures in the Nativity scene. And he knew about the accident.

She nodded. "I'm okay, Pastor. I'm just trying to call child services." She choked on her words. "A little girl was in the car with Chancy and David and..."

"There was no child in the car, Dakota," the Pastor said. "No child."

"Yes, there was! That's why they were driving the car, they were taking her to Gainesville."

"Dakota," he said gently. "They've just—they've just gotten to the bodies. There were two people in the car. Just two."

She swallowed. The world seemed to be spinning.

She kept picturing the little girl, the beautiful little girl. Toys! She had wanted toys for Christmas, but didn't all children want toys?

And yet those eyes of hers...

That smile.

She was going crazy. Declan's belief in devils in the woods had made her mad.

"I'm fine, Pastor Frank. I need to reach out to fellow officers. I..."

She turned and walked back into the station office. She saw the book where she had left it on her desk. She walked back over to the book and slammed it shut.

She had to find Declan.

She checked her service weapon; she was armed, her gun was fully loaded. At the very least, there was an insane mass murderer out there somewhere! Even if the town was swarming with seasoned officers from the county...

She left the office unmanned. She didn't know if the second shift would come in or not; she didn't care. She started out to find Declan.

Then she hesitated. David had still smoked. He also kept a good lighter—one that was filled with butane. Wincing against her own stupidity and thinking that the deaths that morning and those of her two friends was making her numb and stupid, she nevertheless got David's lighter—and his supply of butane. Then she headed out.

Night was falling. Apparently, the second shift hadn't come in.

Maybe they were dead, too. Maybe Declan was dead, maybe she was heading toward her own death...

No. There was sanity in the world. She could still see all the county cars.

Yes, the town was crawling with law enforcement.

She headed across the square and started running again. She should have taken the car... no, she couldn't have taken the car. It had exploded. With David and Chancy in it.

With no angelic little girl.

She reached the church but veered around it, heading for the graveyard and the hanging tree and the forest beyond.

It wasn't until she'd almost reached the tree that she dead stopped. There was someone there. Someone sitting on one of the marble sarcophagi toward the rear—it was that of a soldier who had died in World War I. Old and beautiful, inscribed...

It was the child. The beautiful little girl. She sat there sobbing.

Impossible.

Before she could reach the child, she saw Declan. He was walking from the woods, looking weary and frustrated—and self-absorbed. Then, he apparently heard the crying. He stopped and saw the child.

"Hey, little one! What are you doing here?"

He started to walk toward her.

"Stop!" Dakota shouted, and Declan did so, looking at her with surprise, as if she'd lost her mind.

Quite possibly, she had.

"Don't! It's her—she's the devil in the woods!" Dakota said. Oh, they would lock her up, certainly. There was a child—one who had witnessed terrible deeds, one whose parents might have been dragged out and killed in the woods or met their fate somewhere else nearby...

The girl cried harder.

"Dakota, what the fu—"

"It's her!" Dakota said.

And then, the child changed. She seemed to grow and alter almost imperceptibly until she was different, entirely different; she was a beautiful young woman.

"Declan, help me, oh, please, my love, help me!"

Dakota saw Declan's face change. She saw the way that he looked at the woman.

"Marissa!" he whispered. He started walking to the young woman.

Dakota had never run faster. She streaked past the girl, running so hard and fast that she bore Declan down to the ground. "No! She's the devil in the woods!" she cried.

This was so sad, so sad and bizarre! He believed—she did not! And yet...

"It's Marissa, Dakota—don't you see? I didn't help her then, I wasn't here! I couldn't stop what was happening. And now..."

He was a powerful man. Even now, he wouldn't hurt her, though. He firmly set her aside, ready to go to the woman. It was as if...

As if she had gotten into his mind!

"No!" Dakota cried. But he was moving; he was approaching the young woman who was smiling, who had a strange glint in her eyes. Her mouth moved as she looked at Dakota.

Ah, yes, coming for you next! Merry Christmas, Lieutenant Marin!

Dakota jumped to her feet. She needed help from the county guys! But they were too far away, they were running between the bar and the accident scene and she was in a graveyard in the dark with a man who had been mesmerized by what he saw as a sin in his past.

She felt the butane and the lighter in her pocket.

Not enough for a giant tree that was hundreds of years old.

And yet, she had nothing else. She ran to the tree as fast as she could go. She shot butane over a low hanging branch. Her fingers shook so badly she nearly dropped the lighter.

Finally, flame shot out. She glanced back. Declan was almost to the woman; the woman was reaching out for him.

At last, one of the branches caught flame.

She heard a scream; she looked back. The woman/child thing was changing again. She looked like an out of sync holograph, becoming a child again, a woman, another woman...

And Declan had stopped moving; he stood there, paralyzed, staring.

Dakota squirted the contents of the butane with great effort, running the flame of the lighter under the branches of the tree with all her effort.

She looked back. The *thing* was then moving toward Declan. She wasn't getting it to burn hard enough or fast enough.

She remembered the diary.

"Dear God in Heaven, help!" she cried.

And then, she thought, there were miracles. She saw Pastor Frank, first. He was running toward her with something in his hands... a torch! A burning torch. And there were others... the two missing officers from her own office, Mrs. Villiers, who ran the local coffee shop, Jerry Tremaine, a teacher at the high school...

They were all bringing fire! And they were singing! They were singing Christmas carols at the top of their lungs.

There was a host of people next to her. And, at last, the tree was ablaze.

Burning in the night. The heat was searing against her flesh. It was insane...

She turned. Pastor Frank took her into his arms, blessing her. County people were suddenly flooding around, too, trying to figure out what the hell had happened.

And then, looking at her with disbelief—as if she had dropped out of the skies from a shooting star—was Declan. He was shocked at first. And then he was trembling as he looked at her and said, "I told you that there were devils in the woods. And somehow, you saved me. I always thought I had to be here, to save others from the devils. But... you saved me."

*

There were times in the days that followed that she wondered if she'd been crazy herself.

The town had remained a mess. Their giant Christmas tree had gone up in the explosion with the car.

People had been killed at the bar; people who had been beloved.

The church was a mess...

And yet, in the days that followed, the church was cleaned up. A new tree was obtained—as well as a new Nativity scene.

The dead were buried and mourned.

By order of the mayor, they waited until county had done all that could be done to investigate the murders, and then the roots of the hanging tree were dug up and burned to cinders as well.

It was very strange.

The pastor said a lot of prayers.

The murders never would be solved; they would become part of the legend of the town.

That wouldn't matter; she and Declan wouldn't be there.

It was on Christmas Day that he came to her, knelt down before her, and told her that he had buried the past. He'd like a future. He'd been given a nice offer over in St. Augustine.

"Does that mean you want me to... come with you?" she asked.

And his smile gave her the answer she realized she'd wanted. So, they would go together. Now, he could leave the town. The next captain would not be so plagued.

They stood with the town at ceremonies at the church that night. They sang Christmas carols. Happy ones.

And they watched the display of fireworks over the square, fireworks that lighted up the woods—plagued by devils no more.

A FAMILY CHRISTMAS TERROR

CHAPTER 2

"That was creepy," Nick said. "I think I need another doughnut."

"Like you wouldn't have had one anyway," Jack added. "Garbage-can gut."

"Just wait till you're older and metabolism catches up to you." Dan patted his slight belly. "But these doughnuts are damn good. Is there more coffee?" He raised his cup and motioned to his wife.

"I'll get it." Judy stood up and moved to the kitchen.

"Hey, Mom?" Nancy called out. "I think you should read this next story. It takes place in Iceland. Didn't you and Dad go there a few years ago for your twentieth anniversary? And you're always saying you've got Nordic blood in you."

Judy came back into the room, coffee pot in hand. "But l have dinner to get started," Judy responded.

"The turkey's already cooking and we'll all help with everything else. Right guys?" Nancy glared at her brothers.

"Right, right," the brothers assured her.

"Okay, but just this one story." She took the book from Nancy. "I did love Iceland. Beautiful country. Beautiful people. Remember, Dan?"

"Uh huh," he said. "But you know what the most beautiful thing I saw was?"

"Me?" Judy asked coquettishly.

"Yup," was his simple response.

"Ewwww!" the twins chorused. Grandpa chuckled.

"Enough reminiscing, guys," Jack said. "And I thought the doughnuts were sweet."

Everyone laughed. Then Judy said, "Here we go. I hope there aren't too many bad words."

"We've heard them before, Mom," Jack said.

She began, *"Christmas Terrors In Olde Iceland..."*

CHRISTMAS TERRORS IN OLDE ICELAND

LANCE TAUBOLD

In ancient Iceland, Christmas began on December 12 and ended on January 6.

Their Christmas has many legends. These legends were told to the children throughout the years to make them behave. There is one legend that says on Christmas Eve the animals will be able to talk, but if they are heard by human ears that person will go mad. Another says that if you do not wear something new on Christmas, the evil Yuletide Cat will come for you and eat you, for it means that you have been lazy and have not earned enough money to purchase something new to wear.

The Cat is the pet of the hag Grýla and her troll husband Leppalúdi. They also have thirteen mischievous children, the Yuletide Lads, who have been known to visit unsuspecting Icelanders, one each day, beginning December 12, leading up to Christmas. They come at night, perform their mischievous deeds, and leave. Their acts are mostly harmless, but not so those of their mother, the hag

Grýla. If she comes to visit, it is for the most vile of purposes. It is said she will eat the flesh of bad children and that crying babies are her favorite delicacy.

Legends always have some basis in fact, for where else would they come from? What is truth? What is legend?

One Christmas in 13th century Iceland, on a small farm in the wilderness, Berglind and her family learned the truth of those legends.

*

"Do not eat that!" Berglind, the tall, blond woman said, waving her flour-covered hand at her eight-year-old daughter. "They are for later. You are such a bad child, Lilja. Grýla the hag will come and eat *you*, you naughty child. How many times must I tell you?"

"No, Mama, please do not say that." Lilja's eyes filled. "I will be good. I promise."

"Remember what happened to the neighbor boy, Gunnthór; all that was left were his shoes."

"Did that really happen, Mama? Leifur said it was wolves." The girl made small trails with her floured finger in the stone around the oven.

"Your brother is a bad child also... and a liar. Why are you two *and* Magnús such bad children? Why do I try? I hate Christmas. Only bad things happen." She put the next batch of half-moon cookies in the stone oven. "Where are your bad brothers?"

"They are out in the pasture, Mama. It is the first day of Yule, and Stekkjastur, the first of the Yuletide Lads, is coming and he will try to drink the sheep's milk."

"Yes, Lilja, the nasty Yuletide Lads *may* be coming. I am hoping not. It is good to prepare for them. Mayhap they will pass our farm this year. We do not have so very many animals." She checked the baking cookies and breathed in their scent. "Go and get your brothers," she added, calling after the already departing girl, who was donning her fur and boots. "But if those sheep are not hidden safely away, they get no half-moon cookies!"

"Yes, Mama, and I will tell them to get the cows ready for tomorrow when Giljagaur will try to skim the froth from the milk pails."

"Very good, Lilja. That is the nice little girl I know. And perhaps your father will also be home before Christmas Eve. He and your uncle said they would try to bring a candle for us all. And if work was good, maybe two. That is why they have been working so hard up in the north these past months, Lilja, to bring you bad children the gift of light. You, Lilja, I have hope for... But Leifur and Magnús I fear will never learn."

"I will be good, Mama. I helped you bake the half-moons. And Leifur and Magnús are not always bad. Sometimes they are nice to me."

"Run along, Lilja, and tell those boys to make haste." She turned and pulled the cookies from the oven. Perfect. "I have a bad feeling this Christmas," she said to the cooling cookies. "Snorri, please come home soon. I am afraid for our children. They cause such mischief, but I love them. Leifur and Magnús need their father. They cannot manage this farm without you. Magnús is fourteen now, almost a man, but he still has much to learn. Please come home soon."

Berglind often spoke aloud to herself. It gave her solace when she became worried. It made things not so quiet. The winters in Iceland could be still as death, and at Christmas time, death was always waiting at the doorstep.

She walked over to the hearth and sat on the wooden stool in front of it. "Oh please, I beg the gods to spare us this year. We have had enough tragedy. That evil hag Grýla ate my baby, Stenn, and her monstrous cat ate Snorri's poor brother, Torvild. We thought his boots were new, but he..." She began to cry, as she always did when she revisited that awful time. She did this only once during Yule, on the first day... remembered. Then locked it away.

She keened over their loss, calling out her baby's name. It had been fifteen years, but she saw the hag's cruel countenance like it was yesterday. She could see Grýla biting into her baby's raw flesh while he screamed and cried. She could hear the sounds of the flesh tearing loose, see the hag's mouth covered in her baby's blood. And she and Snorri could do nothing. The hag had frozen them in place with a spell. They were forced to watch, horrified, as the evil beast ate their child alive.

When she had finished consuming their little Stenn, when the last finger bone had been crunched up and swallowed, Grýla spoke, "Berglind and Snorri you *will* have more children." She'd coughed and spat and picked at her teeth before continuing her imprecation. "But if they prove not to be good and decent children, I will come for them—no matter their age. I will roast them on a spit, then my beloved husband, Leppalúdi, and I will eat them. Heed my words. I will be watching. I am always watching." Then she'd laughed maniacally, her teeth bared, dripping red gore—their baby's gore. Then she'd waved at them with gnarled, bloodied fingers and left.

It had been several minutes before they could move, sobs wracked from both of them, their faces sodden with tears.

Fifteen years ago. Berglind had thought she would never recover. Stenn had been their first child, and it proved to be many years later that Magnús was born and she learned to love again. Two years later, Leifur, two years after that, her Lilja. But the boys had been mischievous from the day they could walk, and when Lilja came along, they included her in their mischief. They terrorized the livestock, firing their slingshots and hitting them with sticks. Berglind sometimes thought she had spawned her own Yuletide Lads.

But they were her children. It would not—could not—happen again. She must do something. She had to protect her children from Grýla and her brood. Even if she had to sacrifice some of the animals, she would protect her precious family. "Oh why could I not have borne good and sweet children? Why am I cursed? Snorri, please come home soon."

She stored her memories back in her head, dried her eyes, and went back to the cooking area to tend to the lamb stew she had been preparing for their evening meal. The children would be hungry.

She carved brown bread and brought it to their small wooden table.

The door flew open.

The children were home.

"Mama, he was here!" Lilja yelled. "Stekkjastaur!"

"We tried to stop him," Leifur said breathlessly. "He was so ugly."

"And big," Magnús joined in. "Short, but big like a boulder. We could not stop him. He tried to grab Lilja, but we pulled her away—"

"But he drank the ewe's milk," Leifur finished. "He drank it all and then the ewe fell down on him. He giggled and gurgled and... and..."

"...and he scratched and kicked at the ewe." Magnús picked up the story for his frightened brother. "I made Leifur take Lilja away... but it was terrible, Mama. He killed the ewe. Blood was everywhere. I ran out. I could not stop him. He was crazed—"

"This is not good, my children. Stekkjastaur is mischievous but not evil, like his parents. I had hoped we would not see them this year. I fear it is an omen." Berglind patted Lilja's head. "Calm yourselves now and come and have your supper. Lilja and I have made half-moons for after, but you must eat all your stew and brown bread. You need to stay strong to help Father with the farm."

Lilja sniffled. "Why isn't Father home yet, Mama? Where is he?"

"Do not cry, child. He will be home soon, I hope." She added the last as an aside to herself. "Eat, children, eat. I will go and take care of the ewe. And tomorrow you will not wait so long to take care of the cows from Giljagaur. Promise me."

"We promise, Mama," the three said, going to the table and getting their spoons.

"Here is what we will do," Berglind said, resolve in her tone. "Tomorrow, before dusk, you two boys will leave out five buckets of milk in front of the paddock. This should appease Giljagaur. He may skim all the froth he wishes. I want you all inside for the evening. Darkness comes early this time of the year, so be sure to give yourselves enough time. Do you understand me?"

"Yes, Mama," the three intoned again.

Berglind's idea worked. The following evening, while the five milk buckets were cleansed of their froth, her children and the animals were safe. Her children had not been good, and her primary concern was the knowledge that Grýla could come lumbering down the hillside at any time. The hag could decide to take any or all of them and Berglind could not stop her. Every day the sense of encroaching disaster grew stronger.

The following two nights brought two more of the hateful Yuletide Lads: Pönnuskefill, the pan-scraper, and Thvörusleikir, the spoon-licker.

Berglind brought the children in early for supper both nights. They had their meal, and then Berglind set outside two dirty pans the first night and three wooden spoons the second. The loss of three spoons far outweighed the loss of her three children. If she could satisfy the Lads, maybe Grýla would leave them alone.

She hoped.

December sixteenth brought Pottasleikir, the pot-licker, and as she had done with the pan-licker, this time she left out two dirty pots for him to satisfy himself with. When she opened the door the next morning, there on the ground were her cleaned pots. In her mind, she was preparing for all of the Lads to visit them.

Askasleikir, the bowl-licker, would need to be dispatched somewhat differently from the other "lickers." He liked to hide under beds and grab a wooden bowl that had been left out by an unsuspecting victim. Since he would be coming into their house, she wanted the children to be with her. So that evening Berglind told the children that they would all share her bed.

"But Mama," Magnús protested. "I am almost a man. I do not mind so much sharing a bed with Leifur, but I do not want to share the bed with you and Lilja."

"Nor do I," Leifur hastened to add.

Berglind stifled their protestations. "This night you will do as I say. I do not want to hear one more word from either of you. Oh, why can you not obey me?" Her voice had taken on a high-pitched tone of desperation.

The boys pouted but remained silent.

"I like sleeping with you, Mama. And I do not mind Magnús and Leifur with us," Lilja said quietly.

"You are a good girl, my Lilja. May you always be so." With Snorri gone these past months, Lilja had been sharing Berglind's bed and not the small private area set up in her sons' room.

They ate their meal together. The boys still being somewhat petulant, remained quiet. Berglind and Lilja cleaned up afterward and gathered their bowls with the detritus from their stew.

The children positioned themselves in the bed, Magnús and Leifur on one side, Lilja and Berglind on the other, and before joining them, Berglind set the small wooden bowls from their supper on the floor at the foot of the bed.

"This is very pleasant, my children," Berglind said, hoping to ease her son's ill humor. "Soon you will all be too grown up to do this. Please, for your mama, let me enjoy this time with my children." Her voice caught on the last word.

Leifur put his hands on his mother's shoulder, saying, "Please don't cry, Mama. We will be good. I am sorry we made you cry."

"I am also sorry, Mama," Magnús was quick to add. "It is not so uncomfortable in the bed. It is not much different with you both than it is with only Leifur."

"Thank you, Magnús. I am tired tonight. I will be fine. Sleep now, my children."

Berglind slept fitfully, thoughts of Grýla and of their next night's visitor, Hurdaskellir, the door slammer, kept her thoughts active. She knew without a doubt the rest of the Yuletide Lads would be visiting them. Their family had been singled out. Additional thoughts of Snorri and his brother's return plagued her mind: Would they have done sufficient work? Would it have been enough to keep the Yuletide Cat away? They all must be wearing something new or the Cat would eat them. Had Snorri gotten them all something to wear?

All of these thoughts ran through her troubled sleep, and she unconsciously hugged Lilja closer.

When they awoke the next morning, Berglind collected the wooden bowls from the floor.

Licked clean. Askasleikir had mysteriously entered, done his mischief, and left.

Berglind sighed audibly.

"What is it, Mama?" a very sleepy-eyed Lilja said, rising from her cozy spot on the bed.

"Nothing, little one. But I am afraid none of us will sleep well tonight."

"Hurdaskellir, the door slammer, comes tonight," Magnús said and pushed away from the still recumbent Leifur.

"Ow," was Leifur's response. "Don't push me."

Magnús ignored him. "Mama, do you know why all the Yuletide Lads are visiting us? What have we done?"

Berglind gave a bone-weary sigh this time and strengthened her resolve. She sat on the edge of the bed; Lilja snuggled to her. "I never wanted you children to know this, but I fear that if I do not tell you, you will do something to cause even greater troubles."

"Mama, please tell us. You are scaring us." Leifur, fully awake, now moved into his mother and held to her close. Lilja mirrored him on her other side, and Magnús found himself moving into Leifur.

Berglind began, noting how fear could bring a family close together, all petty squabbling instantly forgotten, "Many years ago, before any of you were born, your father and I had a child, a boy—Stenn."

"Oh, Mama!" Lilja said.

"Hush, child. It was many years ago." Berglind thought for a moment, trying to figure the best way to tell the children without frightening them too much. "Stenn was a naughty baby, crying all the time, refusing to eat his porridge. As hard as your father and I tried, Stenn would not behave. Yes, he was only a baby, but there are bad children born into this world, and I fear he was one.

"Stenn was born the day before Christmas and on his first birthday, Christmas Eve, Grýla paid us a visit. It was a bitterly cold night. We had finished supper and were huddled by the hearth. There was a knock on the door and Grýla entered. She was gnarled and hideous, as the stories tell. Your father tried to stop her from coming in, but she used a spell and froze him in place. She cackled and rasped with an awful, wheezing voice. She came to me and reached for the baby. And when I tried to get up and escape her grasp, she froze me also. She took Stenn from my arms. In her gruff, crackling voice she told us that Stenn was a bad

46

child, and bad children could not be abided. She foretold I would have other children, and she would be watching us. If those children were also not good, she would come for them and take them as well."

Lilja was crying in her mother's arms. Leifur shook.

Magnús stared, unblinking. He spoke first. "That is why you are always warning us to behave, isn't it, Mama? But we do misbehave—all the time. We are bad children, just like Stenn."

"Not so very bad, Magnús," Berglind tried to reassure him. "Every child—"

"No, Mama, we are bad... at least Leifur and I are, and we are making Lilja bad also. Grýla took Stenn, didn't she?"

Berglind tried to stifle a sob. "Yes," was all she could say. She could never tell them the truth.

"Grýla is coming for us," Magnús said in a low, ominous voice.

Lilja wailed, and Leifur began to cry in earnest, clutching at Berglind so fiercely she grunted.

"Hush, children. Grýla will not come. Your father will be home soon. Everything will be fine. You will be good children now. I will make you pepper cookies on the morrow, but you must sleep now."

The children quieted after a few minutes and at last fell into a deep slumber. Not so Berglind. Her thoughts were occupied with Grýla and visits from the rest of her brood.

And Berglind's revelation did indeed change the children's attitude. The next day, as promised, she made pepper cookies, and the children behaved all day and gave no word of protest when it was time to retire for the evening, once again all in Berglind's bed.

And as expected, Hurdaskellir arrived with a flourish, banging and slamming doors till the wee hours of the morning. The children remained uncharacteristically silent through all the noise, causing Berglind to wonder that there might be hope still for her family.

Magnús decided on the following day, December 19, to make a game with the Yuletide Lads' visits with his siblings. That day, Lilja would prepare a pail of curds for Skyrgámur, the curd glutton, while he and Leifur would prepare a string of sausages for the arrival of Bjúgnakraekir, the sausage pilferer, the following night.

The children participated with much enthusiasm, and Berglind let them have their fun, knowing disaster might befall them at any time.

Magnús' ideas worked. The curds were gobbled up that night and, similarly, the sausages on the following evening.

"What do you have planned tonight for Gluggagaegir, the peeper, eh Magnús?" Leifur said while removing the empty string from the arch over their doorway where the sausages had hung for the previous night's Lad.

Magnús reached to the peak of the doorway and released the final strand. He tossed it to Leifur and said, "When Gluggagaegir peeps in our windows tonight, I have decided to leave out in plain view a couple of old toys of Lilja's that she no longer plays with. He loves any sorts of toys, old or new. There is a small drum and pipe I have selected for him." He brushed some snow from his blond locks that had fallen from the doorframe onto him, shook his head, and said, "Mama and Lilja are preparing biscuits for Gáttathefur tomorrow and that should satisfy him." He leaned in close to Leifur and whispered, "I told Lilja to sneak some extra pepper into the biscuits. We will see how he likes that!"

"Magnús, do you think that is right? Did you tell Mama?"

"No, but do not worry, Leifur. It is only a joke."

"All right. Magnús, do you think Father will come home in time for Christmas? I miss him."

"He promised to be home for the Thorláksmessa meal."

"But that's the day after *tomorrow*," Leifur whined.

"Father and Uncle Reynir will be here," Magnús asserted. "Do not cry."

"I am *not* crying," Leifur said, a large tear rolling down his cheek. "The cold makes my eyes water."

"You *are* crying. You are a baby, just like Lilja, always crying." And he pushed Leifur into a snowbank.

"You are mean, Magnús. *I hate you!* I hope the Yuletide Cat eats *you!*" He got up and ran into the house.

Moments later, Berglind came out of the house. "*Magnús!* I thought you were all going to behave! You are the eldest. You should know better. Finish up, then come inside and apologize to Leifur. And here I thought you were trying to be better children."

"We are, Mama, but Leifur is such a baby. I was only playing with him," he said and kicked the doorstep.

"Have not these last days shown the seriousness of this all? Did my story of Grýla mean nothing to you?" Her eyes began to tear.

"Yes, Mama, it did. I am sorry. I will apologize to Leifur, and I will let him leave out the toys for Gluggagaegir tonight. That will make him happy."

"Thank you, Magnús. That is how you should treat your brother all the time. You must all get along." She turned and went inside.

The next morning, the toys, which had been carefully set out by Leifur, were gone, and Berglind and Lilja were hard at work making biscuits.

"MAMA!" The shout came from outside, and Berglind, fearing something terrible had happened to one of her sons, bolted to the door and rushed out, yelling, "Lilja, wait here for me!"

"Magnús, Leifur... what is it? What has happened?" she said, rushing out into the yard, fear and anxiety in her voice.

Rushing from the snow-covered field, the boys called, "Mama, Mama! Look! *Look!* Over *there.*" The boys pointed off into the distance.

"I think it is Father and Uncle Reynir," Leifur said.

"It must be them," Magnús added.

Off in the distance, she noticed two forms trudging through the fields. "SNORRI!" she screamed.

An arm raised in the distance, hailing her.

She pulled the children close and squeezed them. "Children, your father is home. Home at last! Wait here for us." She sped off, slogging her way over the snow, and her husband and his brother hastened their pace to meet her.

They met halfway. Snorri dropped his pack in the snow and embraced his wife. They held close for a while.

"I have missed you, Berglind," Snorri said, not even trying to hide the emotion in his voice.

"I have missed you as well, my dear husband."

Berglind embraced Reynir. "And you, dear Reynir."

"Thank you, Berglind." Reynir's low voice conveyed his feelings as he returned her embrace.

The three made their way to the house. The cries of the children grew louder. "Father! Father!" When they could remain still no longer, the children rushed into the yard and met their father with the enthusiasm of youth. "We've missed you, Father. You have been gone so long. We have so much to tell you—"

"There will be much time for talk later. Reynir and I have traveled far this day. Let us get settled and warmed by the fire," Snorri said, ruffling Leifur's hair.

Magnús started, "But Father—"

Berglind gave him a stern look. "Please, Magnús, later."

Chastised, Magnús said, "Yes, Mama."

Snorri raised his head in the air and sniffed. "Biscuits?"

"Gáttathefur," Reynir whispered, his blue eyes darkening.

Berglind's own eyes grew wide. "Oh, Snorri..."

Snorri looked at her, concerned. "Is that who the biscuits are for, Berglind? The Yuletide Lad? What has been happening here?"

"Come inside. We have needed you so much. But we have managed." Berglind pushed open the door and ushered everyone inside. The children stayed oddly quiet.

The men divested themselves of the packs and outer clothing and positioned themselves by the hearth while Berglind and Lilja finished up with the biscuits.

Leifur sat on his father's lap and said, "Have you brought us gifts, Father?"

"Leifur, only good children receive gifts," Reynir said jokingly, taking a quaff of mead from a stein Berglind had given him. "Everyone knows what mischief makers you three are." He lightly cuffed the boy on the side of the head.

"Mischief making—" Snorri began but was cut off as Berglind thrust a small tray with hot biscuits in front of them.

"After we have eaten and the children are asleep, we will talk," she said, a shadow crossing her face.

"The Yuletide Lads have been here every day, Father," Lilja volunteered from the kitchen area, where she was enjoying her own hot biscuit with Magnús. "But we have been having fun tricking them." She took a large bite and filled her mouth.

"Berglind, is this true?" Snorri said.

She sighed heavily. "Aye, it is. We have only heard the Lads, not seen them. And they have been mischievous is all, not much of a bother. But now that you and Reynir are here, we will rest easier. Perhaps your being here will scare away the last two Lads."

"I hope what you say is true," Snorri said. A look of worry came over his strong features. He brushed a long blond lock from his forehead.

"What is it, Snorri? What is troubling you?" Berglind grabbed his arm.

"It is nothing. Reynir and I... It is nothing."

Berglind stared at him for another moment. "Tomorrow Ketrokur comes."

"The meat hook," Reynir interjected. "For St. Thorlakur's Day. You will have the smoked lamb?" He munched on his third biscuit and drank his mead, apparently content.

Berglind noticed how much the two brothers had grown alike, while only two years apart in age. Both were tall, blond, and broad. "I have an extra shank prepared, should Ketkrókur lower his hook down our chimney."

"Perhaps I shall lay in wait for him and pull *him* down the chimney, instead of his taking our meat," Reynir said, taking yet another biscuit from the tray and another long pull from his stein.

Normally a man of few words, Reynir seemed to be in a talkative mood, Berglind noted, then said, "No need, Reynir. We have plenty of lamb. Even enough to fill your big gullet. Although I may need to make more biscuits for tonight."

"Reynir laughed and took the remaining biscuit from the tray. "You might. They are quite good, a little peppery."

53

Magnús and Leifur exchanged a look.

"I like you, Berglind," Reynir continued. "You speak your mind. You are a good woman. And I trust you have enough hay in the barn for me to rest my 'big gullet' on?" He laughed again and finished his drink.

Berglind took his stein to refill it. "You will stay through Christmas and the new year then?"

"Aye, if you will have me?"

"Of course." She returned the filled stein to him. "But perhaps you should stay in the house."

"Berglind," Snorri said. "Are you worried Reynir will hear the animals talk on Christmas Eve? That is an old story to scare children."

"There are stranger things in this world, Snorri, as you should well know." Berglind had raised her voice. "Come now, it is time to eat. Children?" She made her way to the table. "Lilja, help your Mama with the food. Do you not remember what I said?"

"I am sorry, Mama," the little girl said and rushed to help.

That night the biscuits were taken—pepper and all. Magnús had seen fit to add his own extra helping to the additional mix Berglind had prepared before retiring for the evening.

And as expected, the following night, the Yuletide Lad known as the Meat Hook arrived and snagged the leg of lamb set out for him by Berglind. The appearance of Snorri and Reynir had done nothing to deter the Lad's visit.

Christmas Eve. Kertasníkir, the candle beggar.

And tragedy struck.

The children were being rambunctious that afternoon. Reynir had brought the family a large candle, something very rare in Iceland, and in high demand. He had paid quite the sum for it, and if used sparingly, would last most of the long winter. For this particular candle was made from whale blubber, Reynir told them, and when lit, smelled of the sea.

"Thank you much, Reynir," Berglind said that morning when she awoke to see the large candle sitting by the hearth. "Children, we will light it this eve and you may remain awake and enjoy its wondrous beauty. Your uncle is too generous and you must thank him appropriately."

"We will, Mama," the three agreed, ogling the amazing treasure.

That evening, the family sat around the candle and enjoyed freshly baked cookies and warm ewe's milk.

"Mama, will Kertasníkir come to take our candle?" Lilja asked, taking a bite of her third cookie.

"No, Lilja. He only begs for candles. He does not take like his mischievous brethren. Hush now, and let us speak no more of them. Enjoy your cookie."

After the cookies and milk, and the enjoyment of Reynir's generous gift, they retired to their beds. Reynir went to his hay mound in the barn.

A scream rent the night.

Magnús.

Outside.

Berglind and Snorri bolted from their bed and ran for the door.

"What is it, Mama?" a sleepy-eyed Lilja said, following behind them.

"You and Leifur stay in the house," Snorri said.

The parents grabbed furs and headed out the door.

They didn't have far to go. The full moon shone brilliantly, lighting the snow-covered earth. And there in front of them, naked, running in circles, was Magnús.

"Stop! Stop! Stop!" It was an endless, mindless chant Magnús screamed, his hands clutched tightly over his ears.

Snorri ran up to the boy and tried to grab him.

Magnús screamed louder and lunged away from Snorri and off into a stand of trees at the edge of the field and...

THUD! ...rushed headlong into the first tree. He hit hard, face first, and fell back violently to the ground. Still.

Snorri reached the boy and gently, then more agitatedly, tried to make him stir.

Nothing.

Blood seeped from a split in Magnús' forehead. It ran into the corners of his open and lifeless eyes.

Snorri's grief was overwhelming. He fell to his knees in the snow next to Magnús. A soft mewling sound came from him. He brushed the bloody hair from Magnús' forehead, then brought the lolling head to his chest. His eyes burned and the tears ran down his cheeks. "Magnús... my Magnús... my—"

Another scream.

Inside the barn.

Reynir.

Snorri scooped up his dead son.

Leifur and Lilja came running from the house, Lilja to Berglind and Leifur to Snorri. Berglind held Lilja close to her and yelled, "Leifur, no! Get back here!" Berglind didn't move, keeping her terrified daughter close to her, shielded from Snorri and Magnús. She was too afraid of what she was seeing to call out to Snorri and discover her son's fate. Reynir was in the barn. She stood there numb, unable to move, knowing only that she needed to protect her daughter.

Leifur reached Snorri. "Father, Father! I tried to stop him, but Magnús... he wanted to see if the animals really do talk. I told him if he heard them, they would make him insane. I *told* him!" He was gasping and crying. "Is Magnús all right, Father? Father?"

Snorri stood motionless, the lifeless body of his son draped in his arms.

Berglind could contain herself no longer. "Snorri, what is it? Is Magnús all right?"

"*AAAAGH!*" Another scream from the barn.

Snorri snapped out of his stupor. "Reynir. I must go to him. Leifur, stay here and watch your brother." He gently set Magnús down in the snow. Leifur sat down next to him, picked up his brother's cold hand, and held it. His eyes fixed on his brother's face. He neither cried nor moaned. His body began to rock back and forth and he played with his brother's fingers.

Berglind screamed, and grabbing Lilja, rushed to her sons. She dropped down opposite Leifur and pulled Magnús' head up to her breast. "Magnús, Magnús," she softly uttered, her tears falling on her dead son's white skin. "Why could you not obey me? Foolish boy. Foolish."

Lilja knelt next to Leifur in the snow and buried her face in his cloak, crying but saying nothing. Still playing with Magnús' fingers, Leifur mumbled, "He only wanted to hear the animals speak."

"*AAAAAHH!*" An agonizing scream tore through the night, chilling them all to their bones.

Snorri was at the barn. He threw open the door just in time to see the gargantuan Yuletide Cat close its mouth around his brother's head and silence him.

Snorri had heard the stories of the enormity of the Cat, but he'd thought they must be exaggerations. They were not. The Cat was pure white and the size of two of his largest cows. Its black eyes held malevolence and hate. It gave a vicious twist with its mouth and wrenched Reynir's head from his body. Blood gushed over the Cat's snowy muzzle and face.

It tipped its head back and swallowed hard. The lump, which was Reynir's head, vanished down its throat.

The Cat turned and glared at Snorri, blood dripping from its chin.

Snorri could have sworn it smiled at him before returning to finish consuming his brother. He backed out the door, feeling the gorge rise in his throat.

He couldn't contain it. The evening's stew and bile spewed from his mouth in a violent gush, covering the ground before him and his boots. He heaved several times, the Cat ignoring him, intent on its meal.

Snorri's knees buckled, stupefied by the horror before him. His knees sank into his own vomit, his head bowed low, hiding the unspeakable sight from his vision.

He turned away and stood, head still bowed, grief-stricken, and trudged away. There was nothing he could do for Reynir. His brother was gone... and so was Magnús.

He approached the remainder of his family, who knelt in the snow over the corpse of his son.

"Oh, Snorri what has happened? Magnús? Reynir?" Berglind looked imploringly at him, freezing tears and new ones covering her cheeks. Helpless. Hopeless.

"Father, Magnús wanted to see if the animals really talked on Christmas Eve," Leifur said. "I could not stop him." He still held Magnús' stiffening hand.

"They did speak, Leifur," Snorri muttered. "And he went insane."

"Reynir?" Berglind whispered.

"Jólaköttur, the Cat," Snorri choked out, the too recent memory causing him to heave once more.

Berglind gasped. "No... why?"

"He–he bought the candle for everyone in place of a new piece of clothing for himself, and... and..." He couldn't finish. The bile at the back of his throat yet again threatened to spew out. He collapsed in the snow over his dead son and sobbed.

"Oh Snorri..." Berglind wept harder for all the loss and for her husband's grief. The children wept silently with them.

Then...

A horrific cackling burst through the night.

Grýla.

The misshapen form of the aged-ageless hag came from around the barn. She went to the still open door and looked in. She nodded and made a gesture, summoning her "pet."

The enormous head of the Cat appeared. "Ah, my Jóla, I see you have eaten well." She cackled again and brushed at the gore hanging from the Cat's whiskers. "Oh, my pet, watch your step. It seems someone has had mutton for his meal that did not agree with him."

The Cat exited the barn and went off to the field. It sat and began to clean itself.

Grýla approached the grieving family.

"Ah, Snorri..." She cackled brightly. "Did something upset you?"

A soft moan escaped Snorri's lips.

"Father!" Leifur wailed, dropping Magnús' hand and throwing himself at him.

Snorri wrapped his arms around the boy and held him.

Lilja wrapped her arms around Berglind, mirroring father and son.

"Now, now, Berglind. I warned you many years ago. I foretold you would have more children, but they must grow up and behave. Be good children... or I would come for them." She gave a low laugh. Did you think I spoke falsely? For shame. Grýla always keeps her word." Another low laugh.

Berglind found her voice. "No, Grýla, I did not think you spoke false." She stifled back another sob. "They *are* good children. They cause no more mischief than any other child. Why us? *Why us?*" She could no longer suppress her sobs.

Grýla gave a long chuckle this time, revealing browned and violently jagged teeth. She narrowed her eyes at Berglind. "Why not?" She let her question linger in the air. The family stared motionless at her. "And I am nothing if not an honest woman who keeps her promises. Now here I am on Christmas—yes, it is past the midnight hour. It is Christmas. Look above you to the heavens. The light from the gods shines brightly tonight."

The family looked up, and indeed, the aurora borealis flicked and shone in a vibrant display like none they had ever seen before. Vast rainbows of ethereal lights covered the dark sky. A magical sight amid all this carnage.

Snorri spoke, pleading, "Grýla, please have mercy on us. You have taken Reynir and Magnús. Surely it is enough? The children have been behaving better. Leifur has been most helpful and takes care of his sister. Our Lilja helps her Mama prepare the meals and—"

"Enough!" Grýla snapped. Then slowly, an evil grimace formed on her face. "I can be a merciful woman. Since my Jóla has already eaten heartily..."

Snorri and Berglind let out the breaths they had been holding. "Yes, Grýla."

The hag continued ignoring them, "I am certain my pet's stomach only has room for one more, small... de-lec-table... child... *morsel.*" She gloried at the look in Snorri and Berglind's eyes as she slowly drew out each word, the last word being drawn out the longest, followed by a low malevolent cackle. She extended both gnarled hands to the children. "Come here, children."

"No!" Snorri and Berglind screamed and held the children to them hard.

"Yessss... come, children." Grýla's eyes grew even darker. She raised her bony arms higher, then paused. "Hmm... I seem to recall something similar to this the last time we met." Cackling again, slower, more pronounced.

Snorri and Berglind could not move. It was happening again... their baby Stenn... Magnús... Reynir... now...

"Come, children." Grýla's fingers beckoned, and the children left their parents' arms and were hypnotically drawn to her.

"No, no, no..." Snorri and Berglind pleaded.

The Cat approached from the field with a low growl of anticipation.

The children stood side by side. Waiting.

The Cat stopped before them.

Grýla reached up and began stroking the Cat's head. "Now, Snorri, Berglind, this is where I show my benevolence. You begged for mercy. Here is my judgment.

I will leave you one child: the boy, Leifur, or the girl, Lilja. Which will it be?"

"No, please. You cannot do this," wailed Snorri.

"You cannot make us choose," Berglind cried.

Grýla slowly nodded at the desperate couple. "You are right. That would be exceedingly cruel." A low, insidious cackling started at the back of her throat, then built to a crazed, high-pitched, hysterical laughter. "But I am cruel!" she screamed. *Decide! Decide!* Or my Jólaköttur will decide *for* you!"

It was too much for the parents.

"Save my Leifur," Snorri yelled.

"Save my Lilja!' Berglind shrieked.

Grýla's voiced boomed, silencing them, "Aaaahh, cannot decide?" she raised her arms above the children's heads and began to wave them back and forth.

Leifur and Lilja, both frozen in place, silent as tears ran down their cheeks, looks of horror and fear in their eyes.

"All right then, my pet. *You* will decide. Who will be the tastier treat, hmm?" Grýla continued to stroke the Cat's head. "The boy or the girl? Which will it be?"

The Cat lowered his face to the children, sniffing one then the other.

"Yes, my pet, smell them. Delicious, young flesh. My sweet Jólaköttur, you must choose. Choose *now*!"

The Yuletide Cat opened its enormous mouth...

...and bit down.

A FAMILY CHRISTMAS
TERROR

CHAPTER 3

"That was rough!" Nick said.

"How awful for that family," Judy said, holding the book to her chest.

"Yeah, sorry, Mom," Jack said. "You being a mom and all."

Judy said. "As horrible as the story was, it's only a story. Worse things happen every day in the news."

Jack jumped in, "But remember: basis in fact. All legends come from somewhere."

"In ye olde Europe," Grandpa said in his best old Irish lilt, "many of the Christmas stories are not happy. They believed in fear to help make their children behave. You should use your Google or one of those other fancy computer thingies, or maybe a library and research these old legends."

"Really, Grandpa?" Nick said.

"Yes, those legends—"

Nick cut off the old man. "No, Grandpa... I meant, you really know what Google is?"

"Of course I do." Grandpa held out his hand to Judy. "Give me that damn book; I'll read the next one."

He took the book. "Hmm..." rubbing his unshaven chin. "Now this one might be even rougher than that last one. *Carol of the Refugees...*"

CAROL OF THE REFUGEES

AIDAN RUSSELL

"Do not let go of my hand, Sabra. Do not let go." Her father held her hand and pulled her along the side of the building. A screech echoed through the narrow street as a rocket flashed by overhead, a shooting star with no accompanying wish. Sabra in turn held on to the hand of her younger brother, Fahim, the four-year-old squealing at her tight grip. She dreaded losing him in all the confusion. Mother and her older brother, Qadir, trailed behind them, but she would not risk losing her younger sibling. If any of them were left behind, the militants would give them one choice: convert or die.

The shelling had started earlier that morning. The first rounds fell among the city of Sahiliya's residential bazaar. The militants adjusted their artillery and mortar fire and resumed the bombardment on their intended targets: The small Army base and police station. With explosions tearing apart their position, the Army *jundis* and police abandoned their posts.

With the city defenseless and night falling, the militants advanced. That is when Father abandoned trying to start the old truck he had been hired to fix and made the decision to flee the city on foot. None of his three children questioned the decision. Fahim was too young to truly understand what was happening, but Sabra could read quite well for a nine-year-old and would often study her schoolwork on the floor in front of the television after dinner. The news reporters never had much good to say.

The Islamic State's advance into Iraq gained momentum every day. Sabra had watched the suffering of the Yazidi tribesmen trapped atop Mount Sinjar earlier in the year. She recalled the tear-soaked faces when many had been rescued from death by the Kurdish helicopters that had swooped down like angels from on high to take them away from that hell. Sabra wondered what her face looked like as her family fled a similar hell.

A sharp crack sounded behind them. The entire family ducked low, just in case the gunshot had been meant for them.

"I said do not let go," Father scolded, latching on to Sabra's hand again. She had not realized she had let go to cover up Fahim's mouth, to keep him from screaming.

"Where are we going? Surely they have taken the roads and train station by now." A line of black grease smudged across Qadir's forehead from where he had wiped his sweat away.

"We have to make for the river. It is farmland on the north side. They are too busy taking the city. We will be safe once we reach the farms." Father scratched at his short beard before peeking around the corner of the house they had taken cover beside.

Sahiliya's narrow streets offered them no room to run if they were to be spotted, but the streets crisscrossed and zigzagged, slowing the advance of the militants. The close buildings cloaked the streets in shadows, giving the family a bit of concealment and also hiding the ever-present trash scattered across the streets. Mother scolded the children every time they stepped on an empty plastic bottle, reminding them to watch their step, even though they could barely see the ground beneath their feet.

"The river?" Mother said. "How are we supposed to get across the river? Fahim cannot swim, and if we are not caught, then we will freeze to death or drown."

"I can swim with Fahim," Qadir said, "and I know a shallow spot. It is by the mosque, about a block away. That is where I would play with Mohammad and Haroun."

Qadir winced, realizing he had just reminded his parents about his skipping school to swim with a few other boys in the Euphrates. As bad as Qadir's punishment had been, his two Muslim friends had to make penance for their truancy as well as endure the Christianophobic imam's scorn. The few Christian families residing in Sahiliya usually endured a lazy indifference from their neighbors. The Sunni Awakening within Al Anbar a few years earlier had stymied the region's desire to see more bloodshed than they had already endured during the years of insurgency. This spared them the derision many Christians in Mosul had to endure. Sahiliya's current imam, however, did not believe much in a peaceful coexistence with non-Muslims.

"We will go there then," Father decided, leading the family on toward the mosque.

"Aziz." Father flattened against the wall as his whispered name carried over the chaotic din filling the streets. "As-salamu alaykum," a man said, stepping from the shadows.

"Wa-alaykum salam," Father replied, placing a hand over his heart when he recognized the man as Malik, their neighbor and one of the family's few friends outside the Chaldean Catholic community.

"Where are you going? It is not safe to be out, especially for you," Malik said. His own children peaked out from the gates of the mosque's courtyard, the family seeking shelter in the one place they knew would not be targeted by indirect fire.

"It is not safe anywhere. We have to get out of here," Father replied.

"You can still live here. The Daesh will let you live in peace so long as you pay the jizya."

"I will not pay another man so I can worship God. No, Malik, there will be no peace for us if we live under that black flag."

Malik nodded and placed his hand on Father's shoulder. "Wa alaykum salam wa rahmatullah."

"Thank you. And, please, look after my house. I hope we will be returning someday soon." Father grabbed

Sabra's hand and she reciprocated by grabbing her little brother's, Fahim's, hand.

Qadir took the lead and led the family down to the river bank and to the shallow spot. Father released his grip on Sabra's hand and, with his son, Qadir, began checking the depth of the water and scanning the opposite bank for militants.

Sabra zipped up her jacket, less concerned with the freezing cold water they were about to traverse than with protecting the one item she had taken the time to grab before abandoning their home, a Christmas card. Her uncle, aunt, and cousins had been granted asylum in Australia during the height of the insurgency. Their uncle knew nothing about dry-cleaning when he left Iraq, but that did not stop him from opening a successful and growing chain of shops. The front of the card bore a painting of the Nativity, the Holy Family kneeling beside a manger with a bright star dominating the sky. A picture of Sabra's relatives beside a Christmas tree had been slipped inside, and her aunt had scribbled a blessing of peace across the card's interior.

"Come on, Fahim," Qadir said, picking up his brother. The child whined as he rubbed his tired eyes. Qadir pulled the jacket hood over his brother's head to keep out the frigid wind.

"Come, Sabra." She wrapped her arms around Father's neck and he hoisted her off the ground. He groaned while carrying her. She was much bigger than the last time he had carried her, his age adding to the effort required to carry his daughter

Qadir unconsciously sucked in his breath, stepping into the gelid water. Sabra pulled herself tight against Father's chest, an extra precaution to keep the card safe. Mother muttered a prayer to Christ that they should cross the river as safely as when He had walked upon the waters.

Father began to shiver. The river water soon lapped against Sabra's toes and then crept up her leg until her bottom submerged. The water felt like needles. As the cold seeped into her legs, tears forced themselves from her eyes and she sobbed into Father's chest.

Father and daughter shivered in synchronized convulsions and it comforted her to know she was not alone in her pain.

"Shh, quiet yourself, Sabra. We are almost there, only a little farther. God has graced us with a calm current. Your brother's misbehavior and skipping school appear to have been a blessing so he could guide us to safety."

Sabra nodded and pulled herself as tightly as she could into what remained of her father's warmth while her mother prayed them to safety.

The sky erupted with sound, as if the stars were being ripped from the firmament. A pop resonated over their heads and Sabra forgot the numbing cold just long enough to lift her head and take in the dazzling golden orb of light drifting lackadaisically over their heads, an illuminating mortar round suspended by a tiny white parachute.

Shouts came from the city's riverbank. Sabra could not see the militants in the shadows, but she knew they saw them, knew orders were being shouted to condemn the family to death.

"Qadir! Run!" Mother shouted. Fahim wailed as sporadic gunfire cracked overhead, the shooters putting little effort into aiming at the exaggerated shadows the gold light of the illumination round caused. More shouts came from the riverbank and Sabra buried her face back into Father's chest, the cold long since forgotten.

"Do not look back, Qadir," Father shouted over the ruckus of combat and Fahim's cries. "Run for the trees."

A brief quiet overcame the militants on the riverbank, then a shout followed by an explosion. The rocket-propelled grenade sailed over the family's heads and tore apart a date-palm on the river's far shore. The tree's top collapsed as its midsection splintered, the base igniting with dull, orange flames that came to life as the gold illumination round hovering in the air extinguished.

"Keep going, run toward the flames," Father said, hoping the old adage about lightning striking twice applied to rockets.

The militants stopped shooting, the new darkness hiding away even the shadows upon which they had aimed. Sabra found herself sobbing once more, not from the pain of the river's freezing touch, but she could not help but think of her family being torn apart by blind gunfire.

The sky erupted with noise once more. The screech grew louder than the illumination round had been and

Sabra knew something even worse was coming for her and her family. She screamed into Father's shirt.

She felt the explosion deep within her chest a moment before all sound ceased, her ears failing to comprehend the noise barraging her senses. Date-palms simply ceased to be while men died by the handful. Far off in the night sky, an unseen angel had delivered its payload onto the Islamic State militants after the co-pilot had decided not to wait for authorization from CentCom headquarters to engage the rocket's position.

Father collapsed onto the dry land, clutching Sabra to his chest. Mother ran up and hugged them both, praying through the tears. Fahim cried for his mother and Qadir crawled to her side. The family sat atop fallen palm branches, clutching each other to confirm they still lived. Father was the first to join Mother in the Marian prayer she began, thanking the Holy Mother for delivering them from evil. Qadir joined his voice to that of his parents, and Sabra followed her brother.

The fear and rush faded away and the cold returned, soaking their muscles and bones as the water had done to their clothes. Beneath the date-palm's embers, the family began to shiver.

*

"My friend. My friend, you must wake up. Come on now, it is not safe."

Sabra squirmed and rubbed at her eyes. She forced Fahim closer, for his warmth as much as for her own. The four-year-old did not understand and squealed out a "no" as he pushed back against his bigger sister. She did not relent in her quest for warmth.

"Where are we?" Father asked the strange voice. "Have we made it Ramadi?"

"No," the man laughed. "You are a long way from Ramadi. But you have come far, and I do not think the *Daesh* cutthroats will find you any time soon." Sabra opened her eyes and saw the man pulling Father to his feet.

Despite the gunfire and explosions, Father and Mother had insisted they keep moving, partially to put as much space between the fallen city and themselves, but more to keep from freezing to death after their swim. They walked until Sabra could no longer stand, and Father had to drag her through the farm fields. With morning fast approaching, they curled up beneath a layer of palm leaves and fell asleep the moment their heads fell to rest.

"You poor children. Come," the man said, lifting Qadir and Fahim to their feet. He did not look at Mother and her, as it would do dishonor on himself and the family to help the women. It was the duty of their own family to help and cherish them. Many of the urban people did not adhere to the old customs so strictly, but Sabra could tell by a quick glance at the man's calloused palms that he spent many hours at work and prayer.

"Come, you all must be starved and freezing. My wife is cooking. I have not kept to my *zakhat* this year," he said, referring to Islam's pillar demanding he provide for those less fortunate. "It would appear God has sent you to make me holy once more. Come, break your fast with my family."

*

"So, when will Santa Claus bring you your presents?" the boy Mohammad asked.

"It is not Santa Claus who brings presents," Sabra answered. "The Three Wise Men bring us gifts, just as they did for Jesus when He was born."

"But if it is Jesus' birthday, why does everyone else receive gifts?"

"Because, silly, Jesus is the Son of God. There is nothing we can give to Him which is not already His, so he allows us to have gifts on his birthday instead."

"Oh..." Mohammad said. Sabra was glad she had paid attention during her church lesson. Mohammad had a hundred questions about the family's religion. Mostly, however, Mohammad asked about Christmas. He had seen a few American movies on television, but the American traditions did not well represent the traditions and customs of the Chaldean Catholic Church. Sabra suspected Mohammad was trying to find a way he too could receive presents. She would have given him a present, but she had nothing to give but Bible lessons.

"Sabra! Come!" Mother shouted.

"Mohammad! Wash up!" the boy's mother ordered.

The children scrambled to their families. Since Waleed and his family had invited them in, pre-dinner rituals had become disport. The families prepared the meal together, separated to pray in their own rites, then came together to share in Waleed's bounty. The Muslim hosts did, however, take a bit longer to pray their *salat* than the Christian guests did to say their simple prayer of thanks.

"When will we get to eat the *koleicha* you talk about?" Mohammad ripped a piece of bread off and shoveled rice and lamb onto the flatbread before the boy stuffed it into his face. Sabra had told him all about the sweets her family made every Christmas. In previous years, their neighbors and anyone who stopped by the house received a portion of the dessert. It was the one time they could stir up more than blithe indifference from those they encountered. Sometimes, their neighbors even smiled, and their friendly next-door neighbors, Malik and his family, counted the days before Mother delivered to them a hearty portion.

"We will see," his mother said. "There are still several days left before they celebrate Christmas and the market has not been open since the Army fled. If we cannot buy flour, Aziz and his family may not be able to make the *koleicha*."

"But what about the tree? Sabra says they put up a tree with lights and decorations," Mohammad whined.

"We cannot put up a tree," Mohammad's father said between chews.

"But why?" the child continued to whine.

"We have gone over this already, Mohammad. If we put up decoration for Christmas, we are inviting people to come and ask questions. If they find Aziz, Qadir, and Fahim hiding here, we are all in trouble. God has charged us to protect them. They are children of Abraham as much as you and I. We must keep them safe from the *Daesh* bandits."

"But I want a tree." Mohammad threw his bread and rice down.

"Mohammad," Father said. The boy looked up from his pouting to Sabra's father. "It does not matter whether we have a tree or *koleicha*. These are things created by men. What matters most, come Christmas, is that good people like your family are willing to help and protect poor people like my family. This shows true love, and this love is the greatest gift which has been given to us by Jesus Christ. If not for that gift, we would never have been brought together to celebrate in—"

The unmistakable sound of a truck speeding across a desert road crept into the room. The families had had one scare already, when an Islamic State patrol nudged its way along the river before turning back.

"Go," Waleed said. Father snatched up Fahim and grabbed Sabra's hand, running out the door into the small courtyard where Waleed's goats and sheep scurried.

Waleed, Father, Qadir, and Mohammad hurried to roll away two petrol drums from alongside the mud home's wall. Waleed had sheltered a fleeing family before and dug out the hiding place for them. That family had not stayed as long as Sabra's, though. They stopped, rested and resupplied off Waleed's kindness, and continued onto Baghdad. Father and Waleed, with the militants so close and patrolling along the river, thought it best to wait until the Army launched a counterattack. The Army never came.

The family crammed themselves into the dirty cavern dug beneath the house. There was barely enough room for the five of them. The cramped quarters did not bother Sabra so much as the fear of spiders and scorpions hiding in the hole as well. Those creatures could be just as deadly as the militants and did not care if they were Christians, Muslims, or Jews.

Their hosts rolled the petrol drums back into place and Mother began her prayers. Sabra prayed as well, asking God to send the truck past them, hoping it was nothing more than a farmer out running errands despite the warplanes sporadically circling the skies. The truck screeched to a halt outside the courtyard walls and Qadir clasped a hand around Fahim's mouth before the child could cry.

"*As-salamu alaykum*," Waleed said. Sabra heard men jumping from the bed of the truck and talking to each other. They rushed into the courtyard, sheep and goats bleating and scattering. "Be careful! You will chase my herd off. What is it you want?"

"Where are the others?" a man asked.

"What others?" Waleed said.

"Do you know who I am?" the man said, his voice deep and calm, just like Sabra remembered of her grandfather before he passed away. A moment of silence held between them, punctuated by the herd's continued cries. "I am Asadullah bin Bahdur." The name added to Sabra's fear. She did not know who he was, but one was not named "The

Lion of God, son of the Warrior" by a father intending to raise a weak and merciful son.

"Welcome to my home, Asadullah. How may I, a simple farmer, assist you?"

"I will ask again, where are the others?"

"And I will ask once more, what others?"

"You have two children and nine places set for dinner. You may be a simple farmer, but I suspect you know how to count."

A goat scurried up to the petrol drums, sniffing at the ground.

"I did not know how many you would be bringing for dinner," Waleed said, "so I had my wife set all the extra plates we had. Come, your dinner is getting cold."

The goat began stomping at the ground and bleating loudly.

"Shoo, get out of here," Qadir whispered. He tried to throw a rock at the animal, but he did not have enough room to move his arms.

"What is that animal so interested in?" Asadullah shouted. One of his men plodded toward the petrol drums. Sabra fought harder and harder to keep from screaming as the footsteps came close. Instead of coming from her throat, her fear forced its way from her eyes in a stream of tears. Mother pulled Sabra close to her bosom, a prayer to St. Michael the Archangel whispered on her lips. Sabra had not learned the prayer yet, but she tried her best to add her voice to Mother's whispers.

"I am here. Wait. I am coming out." Sabra reached out and grabbed onto Father's hand as he shouted and wormed his way out of the hole and between the barrels.

"No," she squealed quietly. "Do not go. Please." Father peeled her fingers away and crawled out of their hiding place.

"Show me your hands! Do not move!" the militant shouted a moment before dragging Father from the hole completely.

"Well, that accounts for one place setting. Where are the others?" said Asadullah.

"My family has moved on. I sent them ahead."

"Now why would you be hiding someone from me, simple farmer?"

"They were not hiding me. They took us in and fed us because we were hungry and cold. They were giving us charity."

"Why would you be in need of charity? It sounds to me like you were attempting to flee the Caliphate. Why would you be fleeing from the Caliph's rule? Do you fear God's law?"

Another moment of silence hung in the air, Father thinking carefully of his answer. He knew his children would hear his answer. They had not fled their home only to deny their faith now.

"I will not pay the *jizya*," he said.

"A *kafir*? *Abd-al Meseeh*," Asadullah said, accusing Father of being a "slave to the Messiah." "You have been hiding a non-believer?"

"Waleed did not know I am Christian. He merely did his duty by giving me charity."

"Why else would you need to flee unless you were a *kafir*? And why else would you hide a *kafir* from us unless you were an apostate. There is only one way to deal with these crimes."

A burst of gunfire ripped loose and Sabra screamed into Mother's hand. Mohammad, his mother, and brother screamed briefly and then went silent.

"...be our protection against the wickedness and snares of the devil," Mother continued to pray while smothering Sabra's screams with her hand. Qadir did likewise, one hand over Fahim's mouth while his other arm held the younger brother tight to keep him from flailing.

Father and Waleed shouted at the militants and Sabra heard them struggle with their attackers until the unmistakable sound of a rifle stock against a skull quieted Waleed.

"You bastards! God sees your crimes! He sees your sins!" Father shouted.

"No, *Kafir*, he sees our righteousness. He sees us punishing the non-believers and traitors for their sins. You feared the Caliph's laws? I will give you a reason to fear those laws. Bring me a knife," Asadullah commanded.

Father shouted and Waleed whimpered, then he screamed, then he fell silent. Sabra heard a torrent of blood splash into a muddy puddle. She gagged as Mother's hand kept her from ejecting the vomit rushing from her throat.

The bile shot back down her throat and she retched again, the warm fluid squeezing out between Mother's fingers.

"No!" Father struggled. Sabra could hear him fighting against the men holding him. He shouted and cursed like Sabra had never heard him before. "*Ayreh feek. Kess ikhtak!*" Father's curses and demeaning commentary of Asadullah's sister ended in his screaming. His scream lasted longer than Waleed's, the militants taking their time with the *kafir*. Soon enough, the screams died down and the same gush of blood declared Father's death as it had Waleed's.

Sabra stopped crying, she stopped trying to scream, and her brain stopped trying to think. It was as if she were asleep, unable to move or speak but unable to close her eyes. She could not pray everything she had heard was a bad dream, her mind too cluttered, too numb to wish she would awaken and be safely away in her bed on Christmas morning.

"Rahman!" Asadullah shouted. "Quit standing there like a fool. Go and check on the hole this *kafir* crawled from."

Qadir and Mother both cursed as footsteps stopped beside the petrol drums. The militant kicked the curious goat aside and groaned when he rolled one of the heavy barrels aside. Fahim's weeping pried Sabra from her emotionless trance.

She looked up and saw a young man, a pathetic attempt at a beard spotting his cheeks and a Kalishnokov rifle slung over his back, looking down at them. The man's eyes were tired, not from too little sleep, but from seeing too much of the worst mankind could offer in too few years.

"Please," Mother whispered to him, clenching her hands in prayer. "Mercy." The man paused, the consternation plain in his eyes. He did not have the look of someone capable of killing.

"There is no one here. It is empty," the man called back to Asadullah.

"Come, Rahman. Let us go then. The *kafir* said his family has moved on. We may still be able to find them."

Rahman put a finger to his lips. Then he stood and ran to his leader's side.

The family waited until the truck had sped off. Qadir crawled from their space first and helped Mother to her feet before pulling Fahim out from the dirt. Sabra, her senses recovered, crawled under her own power from beneath the house that had once been their sanctuary.

A soft scream grew within Mother's throat. She ran beside Father's corpse and collapsed. Qadir cursed, throwing rocks at the goats lapping at the blood-soaked mud. Sabra covered Fahim's eyes, but could not tear her own sight away from the scene before her.

Waleed and Father both lay in the blood-soaked mud, their heads resting on their chests, their eyes closed restfully, but their mouths still twisted in agonizing screams. It took a moment for Sabra to recognize Mohammad, his brother, and the mother's bullet-strewn bodies cluttering the home's doorway. The cold, emotionless trance fell over Sabra once more and she pulled

Fahim closer just to make sure he was still real, to make sure he was still alive. As she did so, she felt the Christmas card in her jacket press against her skin. She had lost her father, but she still had her family.

"Sabra. Fahim. Come on. We have to go. Gather what food and water you can. We still have to make it to Ramadi just like Father wanted." Qadir was the man of the house now. He could not take a moment to grieve. Father would look at him with shame if he put his own emotions before the well-being of his family. Qadir grabbed Mother's hand and helped her to her feet. Sabra pulled at Fahim, leading him into the house, stepping over Mohammad's corpse, refusing to look into her friend's eyes for fear of vomiting once more. She grabbed an empty flour bag and threw the remnants of their meal and a jug of water into it.

The younger siblings emerged from the house, stepping back over Mohammad's body. Mother still knelt over Father, her eyes closed and her lips moving silently. She finished her prayer, pleading to God for the salvation of the man who had raised her three children, and stood.

"Qadir, lead us."

*

After two days, they exhausted their food, so they rejoiced when they stumbled upon the Army checkpoint that morning. Three soldiers stood behind a barrier of sandbags and concertina wire. Clouds had rolled in shortly after their arrival, trapping the day's heat, so not only did the family get to drink purified water from bottles instead of drinking river scum, but they sat together in safety without shivering.

"I see the truck now," one soldier said. "They will be here soon and you will all be on your way."

The family smiled. Sabra had no idea how Mother could go on after seeing Father's murdered body, but she insisted Qadir lead them onward. Though Qadir was head of the family now, he could not disobey his mother.

The Army truck pulled up to the concertina wire and both doors opened. The driver and passenger hopped out with their Kalishnokovs, while another man jumped from the covered back. None of the men wore uniforms, which confused Sabra.

The passenger greeted the Army corporal with a hug. The man wore running pants, sandals, and an ammunition chest rig over a soccer jersey. His beard was close cropped and he wore a red-and-white checkered *kefia* scarf around his head.

Two soldiers coaxed the family to their feet, taking Sabra and Fahim by the hand and leading them to the truck. Sabra looked back at Qadir, an expression of unease on her brother's face. Why did the soldiers not wear uniforms? Why had they come from the west when Ramadi was to the east? As Sabra and Fahim climbed into the back of the truck, the black and white *shahada* flag of the Islamic State hanging in the truck's bed answered her questions.

Qadir did not hesitate; he made Father proud. He punched the militant guiding him to the truck right beneath the chin. Had Qadir been bigger, it would have knocked the militant out. Instead, the militant recoiled for a moment then thrust the Kalishnokov's muzzle into Qadir's forehead.

The militant in the truck with the two younger siblings grabbed both their arms while another shoved Mother into the back of the truck.

"We will find a use for these ones, for sure. They will cook and clean or serve as comfort." A militant handed over a stack of dinar bills to one of the soldiers.

Qadir screamed and lunged at the militant; Mother screamed for her son. Sabra shielded Fahim's eyes once more. Qadir pulled at the Kalishnokov rifle while the soldier pushed the boy away, not wanting to lose his money as soon as he had earned it.

A knife flashed overhead and Mother screamed. Blood shot into the air from the laceration in Qadir's chest. More blood followed as the militant ran the blade across the teenage boy's throat. The blade was dull, so the militant had to press hard against Qadir's neck before sawing his way through the muscle and blood vessels of his neck. Qadir's head fell back, exposing the deep gash and the musculature of his throat.

Sabra could not turn away. Mother scrambled for her son, trying as she could to reach the boy, with the futile hope she could save him. The soldier swung his rifle up with a crack and Mother fell limp into the truck's bed.

The militants and soldiers argued for a moment, but Sabra did not comprehend anything they said. She could not turn away from the sight of her older brother lying in the sand, his head flopped at a sharp angle from his neck. The dry, sandy road drank up Qadir's blood. Sabra continued to hold a hand over Fahim's eyes. Her brother bawled; snot and tears soaked her palms. She still could not turn away. One of the militants hopped into the back of the truck and it turned back west into enemy territory.

Mother awoke by the time they reached the Islamic State compound: a large clump of buildings in the middle of the Al-Anbar desert with a shared cement wall enclosing their perimeter and a large courtyard with several cars and pick-up trucks parked in an asymmetric motor pool.

A cheerless sky greeted Sabra when she stepped from the canopied bed of the truck, the clouds ready to weep when she could not. Fahim grabbed at Mother's leg, his tears exhausted and his eyes red with grief. Mother swayed, her head still pounding and her senses muted after having a rifle butt beaten across her temple.

The truck's driver walked over to a man who stood in the courtyard's center looking over a notebook and watching the other militants scramble about. The driver motioned to Sabra and her family, or what was left of it. The man shut his notebook and came over to inspect the three of them. Sabra pulled her jacket tight around her to keep out the cold wind as much as the man's malicious gaze. The jacket pocket still held the Christmas card. It reminded her that she still had a family. It reminded her that her Savior was coming. It reminded her to hope.

The man grabbed Mother by the hair and pulled her face close to his.

"Mama!" Fahim screamed, clinging to her leg. Tears returned to his eyes.

"No," Sabra said to herself. She ran to the man and pulled at his belt to get him away from Mother. Father and Qadir had already been taken from her. She could not lose Mother as well. That would make her the head of the family, and she was much too young to lead even Fahim.

The man swung a backhanded fist at her, splitting her lip and nose open and sending her tumbling across the sand. Sabra blinked back tears and strained to regain her senses so she could comprehend the muffled voices in her ears. The harder she strained to come to her senses, the more severe the pain became. Rather than rushing to Mother's aid, Sabra bawled into her jacket, curling into a ball on the ground.

"Where did you come from? Where were you going to?"

Sabra recognized the man's voice. The voice did not bring back memories of being back home or going to school. The voice reminded her of Father's severed head. Sabra looked up and instantly recognized the young man standing off to Mother's side and the wicked man growling into her ear. It was Rahman, the militant who had saved their lives at Waleed's home.

How could she think that? Rahman had not saved them. If he had wanted to save them, Father would still be alive. He stood by and let an entire family be slaughtered. He had not saved them. He had simply done nothing.

"Please, stop. You are hurting me," Mother said through ragged gasps and tears. The man put a hand around her throat and stroked at the graying streaks in his beard. He wore military fatigues, unlike most of the militants, and kept a pistol on his belt while the others carried Kalishnokovs.

"If you are not a *kafir*, then why will you not answer me?" The man threw Mother onto the ground. Sabra knew the voice then. She remembered the way Asadullah had called Father a *kafir*. "She is obviously a *kafir* or an apostate. Prepare her." Two men came forward with strips of cloth and bound Mother's hands and blindfolded her. She screamed and one of the men punched her to silence the noise. Sabra hid her eyes and continued to sob into her jacket. Fahim screamed for the woman who cared for him until a militant came and carried the boy off.

After a minute, Sabra looked up from her crying. Rahman stood still, watching Mother's pain, and Asadullah completed his prayer. Asadullah dropped his pistol-belt to the dirt as he approached Mother. He continued to undo the belt to his fatigue trousers while one of the militants holding Mother pulled down the thin wool legging she wore beneath her dark blue *abaya* dress to keep warm during the winter.

"What are you doing? Stop. Please! Why are you doing this," she cried, straining to be free of her bindings.

"Why am I doing this?" Asadullah said. "God wishes it. You do not believe in the words of the Prophet, Peace Be

Upon Him. It will bring you closer to him and to God for our flesh to be made one."

"No. Stop. Stop!" Sabra retreated back into the sanctuary of her jacket, shielding her eyes from Asadullah undoing his trousers and lying down on top of Mother. Mother screamed and the militants standing around laughed.

Sabra's face became wet with tears and blood as her nose ran. She shook with fear, grief, and cold. More than any of those feelings, Sabra hated herself for her helplessness. A single punch had incapacitated her with pain. There was no way she could help Mother. The men were twice her size and had guns. There was nothing she could do. So she prayed.

"Our Father in Heaven, hallowed be Your name..." It was the first prayer she had been taught, so the easiest for her to remember. Mother eventually stopped her screaming and Sabra lost track of how many times she recited the prayer. Asadullah quickened the cadence of his thrusts, let out a long groan, and finished.

The militants' leader stood and dressed himself. The others undid Mother's binds and left her an exhausted heap of limbs sitting in the cold sand. She pulled the skirt of her *abaya* close up between her legs to hide her shame. Asadullah began another prayer session and Mother began her sobs anew. Sabra began to pray again, a new prayer, thanking God and Christ that her mother still lived. Mother began to pray, but her prayers were meant to counter Sabra's own.

"Please, God, let me die," Mother wept as she crawled in the dirt. She stood and turned her face to the cloud-covered sun. "Kill me, God!" she screamed. "Let me die with my shame!"

A gunshot answered Mother's prayer.

Smoke drifted from the chamber of Rahman's rifle, the young man's eyes wide and frightened. Mother's chest exploded outward with a brief spray of bright red chunks. Bone splintered and her body fought quickly to abate the damage. It was too late, though. Her body had abandoned the fight by the time she fell to her knees. A dark puddle soaked her already dark *abaya*, turning the blue to black. Mother's eyes fluttered and she fell into the dust from which God had made her.

Sabra howled.

She needed Father and Qadir. They would know what to do. Father and Qadir were always calm when times were rough. If they were here, she would not have to worry. She could turn to her brother and her father to fix whatever was wrong, or at least they would hug her and give her a kiss until the pain passed, but Father and Qadir were dead. And so was Mother.

The militants had forgotten about Sabra when they turned their attention to Mother's defilement. One came over and picked her up. She did not fight. She hoped they were taking her to her death.

Sabra fought back her tears for a moment. She could not die yet. Fahim still lived. If she died, Fahim would be alone and there would no longer be a family. She had to live, and so did Fahim. They were all that remained of Father, Mother, and Qadir. The two of them had to live so the family could live.

They took her into one of the buildings, down a hallway to a steel door. One of the militants undid a padlock on the door. A wave of odors assailed Sabra's nostrils as they pulled the door open and dragged her inside. They dropped her into the middle of the dirt floor and left, locking the padlock behind them.

Sabra was not the only one sniffling in the room. Fahim snorted and clung to a woman dressed in a black *abaya* with a white *hijab* wrapped around her head. She looked to be Mother's age but with soft, hazel eyes. Four other children sat in the dirt watching Sabra. They ranged from half Fahim's age to a handful of years older than Sabra, all boys.

"Come, child, everything will be okay. Come. Your brother needs you," the woman cooed. Sabra pushed away on the dirt, backing herself against the steel door.

"No, do not be scared. Fahim, what is your sister's name?"

"Sabra. Sabra." Fahim reached for his sister. Sabra looked at the woman. The woman seemed just as scared as she was. She looked to her brother reaching toward her for comfort. Sabra led the family now; she could not let her brother be scared. Father and Qadir would never let her be scared and she could not disappoint them. They were watching from heaven. Sabra ran over and embraced her brother, who let out a torrent of tears and weeping, his hands clutching at her jacket.

"Sabra, you must be thirsty. Let me get you some water." The woman grabbed a small cup and dipped it into a tall metal can originally used to store cooking oil. Sabra gulped down mouthfuls of the cold water, never having realized how thirsty she was.

"I am Madihah," the woman said, refilling Sabra's cup and wiping the blood from Sabra's face with the skirt of her *abaya*. "They keep me here so I can be the mother to the children they bring. I know I cannot replace your mother, but I hope we can learn to trust each other. We are all we have now. God has given us hardships, and now he has given us each other."

Madihah handed Sabra the cup and the girl hesitated, unsure what to think of the possibility of a new mother. No, no matter what, she and Fahim were family. They still belonged to Father, Mother, and Qadir.

"You are Chaldean, yes?" Madihah asked. Sabra glanced up at her, wondering how she knew their secret. "Fahim told me you are Christian. Your holiday is tomorrow, yes? I forget what it is called. Can you tell me?"

"It is Christmas. Is it really tomorrow? I forgot." Sabra pouted. How could she have forgotten Christmas? She had waited all year for that day. Father, Mother, and Qadir would never have forgotten.

"Yes, I think it is. The twenty-fifth, yes?"

"Yes," Sabra said.

"Then tonight is the night. I am sorry, young one, but I do not think we will be eating any *koleicha* tonight. Just rice, I think. I do not think our guards will be making us any special treats for dinner. It is just another day to us, I am afraid."

Several men shouted outside and Madihah and the boys jumped to their feet. They gathered around the water can, taking turns to wash their hands, faces, and feet. Once washed, Madihah led the boys in facing the wall away from the room's entrance, and then in reciting the litany and in the kneeling motions of the evening *salat*, the fourth of the five daily prayers.

Fahim crawled into his sister's arms and the siblings watched their Muslim cellmates offer reverence to the Almighty. Sabra wondered how they knew in which direction Mecca lay. She did not know which way was home or even where they were anymore. The steel door rang out, struck from the other side, and brother and sister jumped with fright.

"Why are the two new ones not praying?" Rahman shouted. "Do they not know what happens if they do not complete their *salat*?"

"Forgive them, friend," Madihah said, rushing over to Sabra and Fahim. "They do not know how to pray. I will teach them. They will finish the *salat*. Please, do not tell Asadullah. I beg you."

"Finish you prayers," Rahman said, walking away.

Madihah led the two into the prayer huddle.

"I hate him," Sabra said.

"Shh, you must not say that. Rahman can seem cruel at times, but it is only a show for the others. He is kind to us and will help us with whatever we need."

"He killed our mother."

Madihah did not respond.

"He shot her right in front of me."

"Quiet, Sabra. Do not think about it. It is time to be with God. Repeat after me and do as I do. God is most great."

Sabra and Fahim repeated Madihah's words and bowed with her. "In the name of God, the infinitely compassionate and merciful..." Sister and brother followed the example of their new guardian. They finished the ritual and Rahman returned, his eyes fearful once more. He dropped a plate of rice with a stack of flatbread onto the ground in the room's center. Then he bowed out of the room, afraid to look into Sabra's baleful stare.

"Would you like to lead us in prayer now, Sabra or Fahim?" Madihah said, waving a hand over their simple meal.

"We do not know any Islamic prayers. We should not have even said your prayer with you. Jesus will be mad at us for not saying his prayer."

"Oh, sweet child. It is not like that. Our prayers are not enemies. We are all children of the same God. We just choose to worship the Almighty in different ways. You believe Jesus is the son of God and in your Trinity. We believe in the words of the Prophet, Peace Be Upon Him. I am sure you and your brother showed your father and mother love in different ways, but they still loved you both. If we creatures are capable of that, then how much more so is God?"

"But your religion started this war. The men who killed my family are Muslims. They are the ones ruining our country." Sabra turned away to hide her tears. She was tired of crying and wanted to stop, to be strong in front of Fahim until he was old enough to be the family's leader, but she could not stop herself.

"This war and these countries are not God's doing, child. They are the creations of men. This war exists because men have lost sight of what God wants of us and are thinking only of themselves.

"God knows your pain, child. Remember when Jesus was born? When King Herod wanted to kill Him and Mary and Joseph had to flee with him to Egypt? You and your brother are not much different from Jesus now, and God knows it and He loves you all the more because of it.

"You did not think I knew that story, did you?" Madihah smiled. "Come, pray with us." Madihah guided Sabra back to the plate. Her stomach growled, and she knew Fahim would be even hungrier, so she did not resist. She knelt beside their supper and folded her hands together.

"Our Father in heaven, hallowed be your name—"

"Rahman!" Asadullah called from down the hallway, his shout interrupting their prayer. "Rahman, what is this? Who were you calling? The Army? The Americans? Who did you call?"

"No one, Haji! It is not my phone. I do not know what that is. You know I would not betray us. I even killed that woman for you," Rahman squealed.

"You killed that woman to end her suffering. You killed her because you pitied the *kafir*. And do not lie to me!" A sharp smack rang out from the door's other side and Rahman yelped from Asadullah's assault. Madihah gathered the children together in the far corner of the room, afraid Asadullah's wrath would breach the steel door.

"Kaliq saw you on the phone and then you hid it behind the armory room. You lie, Rahman. You have betrayed us. You are in league with the enemy. You are an apostate."

"No, please no. Listen to me," Rahman pleaded.

"Bring me a knife," Asadullah said.

Sounds of Rahman's struggles against his captors crept under the cell's door. "You cannot do this. You have no proof. Call the phone. Asadullah, please, have mercy! Let me explain. No. No!" Rahman's scream lasted only a second before blood seeped into his severed windpipe, gurgles and coughs trying to push the liquid from his lungs.

Madihah wept for the jailor who had shown the children and her mercy. Sabra stared at the steel door, her jaw clenched and her eyes dry. She would let God decide if Rahman's good deeds outweighed his sins.

"Our little dog probably told his master we have new prisoners. Bring me the two *kafir*," Asadullah ordered.

Sabra grabbed her brother and ran behind Madihah and the other children. She had to keep Fahim and herself alive. Qadir, Mother, and Father were watching. The family depended on her.

Two militants fiddled with the padlock on the door, apparently unfamiliar with the keys Rahman had carried.

Sabra hugged her brother tight, burying his face in her chest and leaning her face into him, kissing the top of his head. She felt his body pressing their uncle's Christmas card against her. If they killed her, she would not die alone.

The militants undid the padlock finally and the door began to squeal on its hinges. Then they paused.

Sabra did not hear the sound at first, her breathing hard and her pulse pounding in her ear. She felt the noise before she heard it, a quick, staccato drumbeat keeping cadence for a cavalry charge. It had been many years since she had heard that sound. She was probably Fahim's age, maybe even younger, the last time the Americans flew a helicopter over Sahaliyah.

The militants turned and shouted. Children were of little importance to them now. Men were coming. Dangerous men with guns were coming to kill them. The militants rushed from the room, pausing only to reaffix the padlock.

Madihah hugged the six children in her charge together in the corner. The militants' shouting grew louder along with the beating of helicopter wings slicing through the air. Gunshots echoed, thunderclaps signaling a coming storm. The scream of helicopter engines drowned out every other noise, and billows of dust clawed beneath the steel door and floated down from a small hole in one wall. Then the helicopters rushed off and the rattle of gunfire returned.

Sabra could not understand any of the shouting. Some was Arabic and some was foreign, but none of it made any sense to her. The gunfire began to die away and the foreign shouts overtook those in Arabic. A militant within in the room beyond theirs shouted, only to be silenced by three gunshots. The whole building shook, the bullets passing through their target and playing out a percussive note upon impacting the cement walls.

A moment of quiet followed the militant's death, then the sounds of feet shuffling from outside the door. Fahim and the others cried out. The door rang like a gong, struck from the other side. Sabra waited, greeting whatever came through the door: death or salvation.

The door rang once more and swung open, colliding against the wall as the top hinge came loose from the doorframe. The shapes of two men, pure, white light emitting from their weapons and helmets, rushed into the room. Madihah hugged the children tighter.

"*Left side clear,*" a foreign voice shouted. Sabra had seen enough television to know he spoke English but could not understand the words.

"*Right side clear,*" the other voice replied. It spoke English as well, but the accent was familiar. The man was Iraqi, Sabra was certain of that, but she was not sure from what part.

"Baz!" the foreigner called out to the Iraqi. "*Get her and the kids up. We need to get them counted and out of here.*"

"*You got it, boss.*"

The foreigner lowered his weapon and shut off the light on his helmet. Spots filled Sabra's vision. She blinked to push them from her vision. She looked up at the foreigner. He was taller than anyone she had ever met. A red beard spilled over the chinstrap of his helmet, and calm, blue eyes greeted her from behind a pair of clear protective glasses.

"*It's okay,*" he said. "*You're safe now.*" Sabra nodded, having no idea what he had just said.

*

Baz held the smallest child's hand, leading them from the room, with the woman bringing up the rear of the hand-holding train. Sergeant First Class Emerett finished checking the room and turned to the door when he saw two children still sat in the corner. The boy shook and clung to the girl. She stared up at him. He could not tell if the look was one of suspicion or wonderment.

"Come on you two, we have to get going. You don't want to stay here." He picked the boy up and released his rifle to take the girl's hand. They were the same ages as his two children back home, so he already had plenty of practice juggling squirming masses their size. These two were much lighter though, which told Emerett all he needed about their hunger.

He fell in behind Baz's trail of children, and they halted at the building's entrance. He released the girl's hand for a moment, hoping she would not run off, to press the button on his radio's push-to-talk.

"Em and Baz are coming out with six civilians. Still taking them to Viper 55?"

"Roger, Em, Viper 55 is the transport bird. Objective is secure, so you're good to move," a voice answered in his earpiece.

"Copy that, Broadsword 6. We're on the move. Let's go, Baz."

His Kurdish teammate led the way through the courtyard and out the east gate to where the Blackhawk helicopter had landed after they fast-roped into the courtyard. Baz stopped at the door and gave instructions to the children and woman to make sure none of them wandered off and lost their heads to the tail rotor. Then he gave Emerett a nod and ran headlong to the waiting Blackhawk.

Baz grabbed the children and handed them off to the door gunners. He instructed the woman to make sure the children stay seated or else they might fall out. He relieved Emerett of his two burdens and they both hopped in and hooked in their safety tethers to keep from falling out themselves. A minute later, the crew chief gave the pilots a thumbs-up and the helicopter lifted off the ground and turned east.

Despite the winter night being cold enough to freeze the water in his CamelBak's drinking tube, the short operation had him sweating. The years in Group had not been kind, and moving fast while carrying heavy loads was not as easy as when he had tried out for Selection the first time. Emerett rolled his sleeves up to his elbows, as much to let a draft in as to get that "operator" look.

The girl he had carried crawled over to him despite the woman's rebukes. She grabbed his hand and pulled his arm to her, studying the crucifix tattoo on his right forearm. She looked up, delighted, and said a few words while pointing to herself and the boy he had carried.

Emerett could not hear her over the engine noise and would not have understood what she said anyways. He spoke Tagalog and Pashtu and the little Arabic he did know was of little use.

Baz saw his predicament and scooted over to the girl, leaning in close so she could hear him. The girl shook her head and cupped a hand against Baz's ear. He nodded and pressed his push-to-talk.

"She is Chaldean, a Christian. She likes your tattoo," Baz said. Emerett gave the girl a nod and she turned back to Baz. Baz nodded, but the smile waned from his face. He paused for a moment before translating.

"They killed her whole family. The little boy is her brother and they are all that is left. Fuck these ISIS pigs, man."

Emerett looked at the girl, unsure of what to say. He put a hand on her head, hoping she could feel his empathy. She smiled and reached into her jacket pocket, pulling out a folded piece of paper and handing it to him. He looked at it and saw a Nativity scene on the front. Inside, a family stood around a Christmas tree, Arabic script written across the inside. The girl turned back to Baz and he smiled while she spoke.

"She says 'Merry Christmas.'"

Emerett smiled. He zipped open one of the dozen pouches on his plate carrier and pulled out the trail mix he had packed in case the mission took longer than planned. He handed it to the girl and returned the Christmas card. She smiled and handed the snack to the woman so they could all share. Then she showed the card to Baz.

"What does it say?" Emerett said into his radio.

"Peace on Earth and good will toward men. God bless and Merry Christmas."

A FAMILY CHRISTMAS TERROR

CHAPTER 4

"Holy crap!" Jack said.

"Yeah, that story should have come with razor blades," Nick muttered under his breath. "Any more doughnuts?"

"I could use a shot of brandy in my coffee." Dan raised his mug to his wife.

"Way ahead of you, sweetheart."

Nick looked sheepish. "I don't suppose you'd spare a shot for your favorite son?"

"Oh brother," Nancy said.

Judy gave her younger son an uneasy look.

"C'mon, Mom," Nick entreated.

Dan said, "Why not? Nobody's going anywhere today. Drinks are on the house!" He waved his hand with a flourish.

"There's the Irish in ya," Grandpa said to Dan.

"Are you imbibing as well?"

"Have I ever said no?"

"Not that I can recall." He cleared his throat. "I think I would like to try my voice on the next story." Grandpa handed him the book just as Judy came back, brandy bottle in hand. She laced everyone's coffee but Nancy's, who had put her hand over her mug.

"I don't really like brandy. Give mine to Nick," Nancy said. "Do we have any cherry vodka?"

"Alright! Merry Christmas, sis!" Nick raised his mug to her.

"I hope you aren't like this at college," Judy admonished.

"Of course not," Nick was quick to assure. "I'm only nineteen, besides."

"Uh huh." Judy's skepticism was apparent.

"So, Dad, what's your story called?" Jack broke the awkwardness.

"Uh, it's called, *The Night Is Freezing Fast*. Oh, I know this author. This should be good."

THE NIGHT IS FREEZING FAST

THOMAS F. MONTELEONE

"Oh damn!" cried Grandma from the kitchen. "I've run right out of shortnin' for my cake!"

"Are you sure?" asked Grandpa. When his wife cussed, she usually was very sure. He eased the Dubuque newspaper down from his face and peeked at her through the kitchen door.

"'Course I'm sure! And if you want a nice dessert for after Christmas dinner, you'll get into town and get me more shortnin'!"

"What's 'shortnin'?" asked Alan, ten years old and always asking questions at what always seemed like the wrong moment.

"But it's a blizzard goin' on out there!" said Grandpa. "And it's Christmas Eve to boot."

"What's 'shortnin'?" asked Alan.

"Rolf, if you know what's good for you, you'll get into that town and get me my shortnin" Grandma used her tone of voice Alan had learned long ago meant no foolishness.

Grandpa must have noticed it too because he said, "Oh, all right."

Alan watched him drop the newspaper and shuffle across the room to the foyer closet where he pulled out some snow boots, a beat-up flapdoodle corduroy hat, and a Mackinaw jacket of red and black plaid. He turned and looked wistfully at Alan, who was sitting on the rug watching the Baltimore Ravens play the Kansas City Chiefs on TV.

"Want to take a ride, Alan?"

"Into town?"

"Yep. 'Fraid so."

"In the blizzard?"

Grandpa sighed, stole a look toward the kitchen. "Yep."

"Okay. It sounds like fun... we don't get snowstorms like this in L.A.!"

"Fun?" said Grandpa, smiling. "Oh yeah, it'll be great fun. Come on, get your outerwear on, and let's get a move on."

Alan ran to the closet and pulled on the heavy, rubber-coated boots, a knit watch cap, and scarf. Then he shook into the down parka his mom had ordered from the L. L. Bean mail order place. His first encounter with cold weather had been a great adventure, a great difference in his life.

"Forty-two years with that woman and I don't know how she..."

"What's shortnin', Grandpa?"

The gray-haired man had just closed the door to the mud porch behind them. He was muttering as he faced into the stinging slap of the December wind, the bite of the ice-hard snowflakes attacking his cheeks. There would be roof-high drifts by morning if it kept up like this, he was thinking.

"What? Oh... well, shortening is butter or oleo, or even cooking oil, I think. Whatever it is, it's for making cakes." Grandpa stepped down to the path he'd shoveled toward the garage. It was already starting to fill in and would need some new digging out pretty soon.

"Why do they call it that? Why don't they just call it butter, or margarine?" Alan had already lost interest in the question, even as he asked it. The hypnotic effect of the snow was captivating him." Do you get storms like this all the time, Grandpa?"

"'Bout once a month this bad." Grandpa reached the garage door, threw it up along its spring-loaded tracks. He shook his head and shivered from the wind-chill. "And to think your mom and dad are cruising the Caribbean! Hard to believe, isn't it?"

"I'd rather be here," said Alan, shaking his head. He smiled, obviously immune to the shrieking cold and the missile-like flakes. "This is going to be the first real Christmas I ever had!"

"Why? Because it's a white one? Grandpa chuckled as he walked to the door of the 4-wheel drive Cherokee and slowly climbed in.

"Sure," said Alan. "Haven't you ever heard that song?"

Grandpa smiled." Oh, I think I've heard it a time or two..."

"Well, that's what I mean. It never seems like Christmas in L.A. even when it is Christmas!" Alan jumped into the Jeep and slammed the door. "Boy, Grandpa, it's really coming down, now..."

As his grandfather backed the vehicle from the garage, swung it around and churned down the long driveway toward Route 14A, Alan looked out across the flat landscape of the farm and the other farms in the distance. There was a gentle roll to the treeless land, but it was lost in the wall of the storm.

In fact, Alan couldn't tell where the snowy land stopped and the white of the sky began. When the Cherokee lurched forward out onto the main road, it looked like they were constantly driving smack into a white sheet of paper, a white nothingness.

It was scary, thought Alan. Just as scary as driving into a pitch-black night.

"Oh, she picked a fine time to run out of something for that danged cake! Look at it, Alan. It's a regular white-out, is what it is."

Alan nodded. "Jeezoowhiz, how do you know where you're going, Grandpa?" The first twinges of fear were creeping into his mind.

Grandpa harrumphed. "Been on this road a million times, boy! Lived here all my life! I'm not about to get lost. But my God, it's cold out here! Hope this heater gets going pretty soon."

They drove on in silence except for the crunch of the tires on the packed snow and thunk-thunk of the wiper blades trying to move off the hard new flakes that filled the sky. The heater still pumped chilly air into the cab and Alan's breath was almost freezing as it came out of his mouth.

He imagined they were explorers on a faraway planet an alien world of ice and eternally freezing winds. It was an instantaneous, catapulting adventure of the type only possible in the minds of imaginative ten-year-olds. There were creatures out in the blizzard great white hulking things. Pale, reptilian, evil-eyed things. Alan squinted through the windshield, ready in his gun turret if one turned on them. He would blast it with his laser cannons...

"What in heck?" muttered Grandpa.

Abruptly, Alan was out of his fantasy world as he stared past the flicking windshield wipers. There was a dark shape standing in the center of the white nothingness. As the Cherokee advanced along the invisible road, drawing closer to the contrasted object, it became clearer, more distinct.

It was a man. He was standing by what must be the roadside, waving a gloved hand at Grandpa.

Braking easily, Grandpa stopped the Jeep and hit the button that lowered the side window a bit. The blizzard rushed, slicing through Alan's clothes like a cold knife as he looked the man standing in the storm. "Where you headed?" cried Grandpa over the wind. "I'm going as far as town..."

"That'll do," said the stranger.

Alan caught a quick glimpse of him as he pushed into the back seat. He was wearing a thin coat that seemed to hang on him like a scarecrow's rags. He had a black scarf wrapped tight around his neck and a dark blue ski mask that covered his face under a floppy-brimmed old hat. Alan didn't like that not being able to see the stranger's face.

"Cold as hell out there!" said the man as he smacked his gloved hands together. He laughed to himself, then: "Now there's a funny expression for you, ain't it? Cold as Hell.' Don't make much sense does it? But people still say it, don't they?"

"I guess they do," said Grandpa as he slipped the Jeep into gear and started off again. Alan looked at the old man, who looked like an older version of his father, and thought he saw an expression of concern, if not apprehension, forming on the lined face.

"It's not so funny, though." said the stranger, his voice lowering a bit. "Everybody figures Hell to be this hot place, but it don't have to be, you know?"

"Never really thought about it much," said Grandpa, playing with the heater controls. It was so cold, it just didn't seem to want to work.

Alan shivered, uncertain whether or not it was from the lack of heat, the words, or the voice of the stranger.

"Matter of fact, it makes more sense to think of Hell as full of all kinds of different pain. I mean, fire is so outrageous, don't you think? Now, cold ... something as cold as that wind out there could be so ...subtle but be just as bad, right? The man in the back seat chuckled softly beneath the cover of the ski mask.

Grandpa cleared his throat and faked a cough. "I don't think I've really thought much about that either," he said as he appeared to be concentrating on the snow-covered road ahead. Alan looked at his grandfather's face and could see the unsteadiness in the old man's eyes. It was the look of fear, slowly building.

"Maybe you should ..." said the stranger.

"Why?" said Alan. "What do you mean?"

"Well, it stands to reason that a demon would be comfortable in any kind of element as long as it's harsh, as long as it's cruel."

Alan tried to clear his throat and failed. Something was stuck down there, even when he swallowed.

The stranger chuckled again. "Course, I'm getting off the track we were talking about figures of speech, weren't we?"

"You're the one doing all the talking, mister," said Grandpa.

The stranger nodded. "Actually, a more appropriate expression would be 'cold as the grave'..."

"It's not this cold under the ground," said Alan defensively.

"Now, how would you know?" asked the stranger slowly. "You've never been in the grave ... not yet, anyway."

"That's enough of that silly talk, mister!" said Grandpa. His voice was hard-sounding, but there was a thin layer of fear beneath his words.

Alan looked from his grandfather to the stranger. As his eyes locked in with those behind the ski mask, Alan felt a burst of acid in his gut, an ice pick threatening his spine.

There was no staring at the stranger. There was something about his eyes, something which seemed to lurch violently behind them.

A dark chuckle came from the back seat.

"Silly talk? Silly?" asked the stranger. "Now what's silly and what's serious in the world today? Who can tell anymore?! Missiles and terrorists! Vampires and garlic! Famine and epidemics! Full moons and maniacs."

The words rattled out of the dark man and chilled Alan more deeply than the cold blast of the heater fan. He looked away and tried to stop the shiver which raced up and down his backbone.

"Where'd you say you was going, Mister?" asked Grandpa as he slowly eased off the gas pedal.

"I didn't say."

"Well, how about saying right now?"

"Do I detect hostility in your voice, sir? Or is it something else?" Again came the deep-throated, whispery chuckle.

Alan kept his gaze upon the white-on-white panorama ahead. But he was listening to every word being exchanged between the dark stranger and his grandfather, who was suddenly assuming the proportions of a champion. He listened but he could not turn around, he could not look back. There was a fear gripping him now. It was a gnarled spindly claw reaching up for him, out of the darkness of his mind, closing in on him with a terrible certainty.

Grandpa hit the brakes a little too hard, and even the Cherokee's 4-wheel drive couldn't keep it from sliding off to the right to gently slap a bank of plowed snow. Alan watched his grandfather as he turned and stared at the stranger.

"Listen, Mister, I don't know what your game is, but I don't find it very amusing like you seem to and I don't appreciate the way you've dealt with our hospitality— especially on Christmas Eve."

Grandpa glared at the man in the back seat and Alan could feel the courage burning behind the old man's eyes. Just the sight of it gave Alan the strength to turn and face the stranger.

"Oh, yes... is it that time again? I'd forgotten..."

That made Alan feel even more weird. How could anyone forget it was Christmas?

"Just trying to make conversation." The man continued in a velvety soft voice. It seemed to Alan that the stranger's voice could change any time he wanted it to, could sound any way at all. The man in the mask was like a ventriloquist or a magician, maybe.

"Well, to be truthful with you, Mister, I'm kinda tired of your conversation,' and I'd like you to climb out of here so my grandson and I can be on our way in peace."

The eyes behind the mask flitted between Grandpa and Alan once, twice. "I see..." said the voice. "No more silly stuff, eh?"

The stranger leaned forward, putting a gloved hand on the back of Alan's seat. The hand almost touched Alan's parka and he pulled away. He knew he didn't want the man touching him. More acid churned in his stomach.

"Very well," said the dark man. "I'll be leaving you for now ... but one last thought, all right?"

"I'd rather not," said Grandpa as the man squeezed out the open side door.

"But you will." Another soft laugh as the stranger stood in the drifted snow alongside the road. The eyes behind the mask darted from Grandpa to Alan and back again. "You see, it's just a short ride we're all taking ... and the night ... well, the night is freezing fast."

Grandpa's eyes widened a bit as the words drifted slowly into the cab, cutting through the swirling, whipping cold wind. Then he gunned the gas pedal and the engine raced. "That's enough of that crazy talk, Mister. Have a nice day!"

The Cherokee suddenly leaped forward away from the strange man. Looking back, Alan could see the stranger quickly dwindle to nothing more than a black speck on the white wall behind them.

"Of all the people to be helpful to, and I have to pick a danged nut!" Grandpa forced a smile. He looked at Alan and tapped his arm playfully. "Nothing to worry about now, boy. He's behind us and gone."

Alan nodded. "He was creepy, wasn't he?"

Grandpa grunted, kept looking at the snowed-up road.

"Who you figure he was?"

"Oh, just a nut, son. A kook. When you get older, you'll realize that there's lots of funny people in the world. Some funnier than others."

"You think he'll still be out on the road when we go back?"

Grandpa looked at Alan and tried to smile. It was an effort and it didn't look anything at all like a real smile.

"You were afraid of him, weren't you boy?"

Alan nodded. "Weren't you?"

Grandpa didn't answer for an instant. He certainly looked scared. Then: "Well, kinda, I guess. But I've known about his type... almost been expecting him, you might say."

"Really?" Alan didn't understand what the old man meant.

Grandpa looked ahead. "Well, here's the store..."

He eased the Jeep into the half-plowed parking lot of Brampton, Iowa's only full-scale shopping center. He ran into the Food-A-Rama for a pound of butter while Alan remained in the cab with engine running, the heater fan wailing, and the doors locked. Looking out into the swirling snow, Alan could barely pick out single flakes anymore. Everything was blending into a furiously thick, white mist. The windows of the Cherokee were blank sheets of paper, and he could see nothing beyond the glass.

Suddenly there was a dark shape at the driver's side, and the latch rattled on the door handle. The lock flipped up and Grandpa appeared with a small brown paper bag in his hand. "Boy, it's blowin' up terrible out here! What a time that woman has to send us out!"

"It looks worse," said Alan.

"Well, maybe not." said Grandpa, slipping the vehicle into gear. "Night's coming on. When it gets darker, the white-out won't be as bad."

They drove home along Route 28 which would eventually curve down and cross 14A. Alan fidgeted with the heater fan and the cab was finally starting to warm up a little bit.

"Grandpa, what did that man mean about a 'short ride' we're all taking? And the 'night freezing fast'?"

"I don't rightly know what he meant, Alan. He was a kook, remember? He probably don't know himself what he meant by it."

"But you said you were kind of expecting him ..."

"Oh, I was just thinking out loud. Didn't mean a thing." Grandpa pretended to be concentrating on the road.

"Well, he sure did make it sound scary, didn't he?"

"Yes, I guess he did," said Grandpa as he turned the wheel onto a crossing road. Here we go, here's 14A. "Almost home, boy! I hope your grandmother's got that wood stove hot!"

The Jeep trundled along the snowed-up road until they reached a bright orange mailbox that marked the entrance to Grandpa's farm. Alan exhaled slowly, and felt the relief spreading into his bones. He hadn't wanted to say anything, but the white-white of the storm and the seeping cold had been bothering him, making him get a terrible headache, probably from squinting so much.

"What in—?" Grandpa eased off the accelerator as he saw the tall, thin figure standing in the snow-filled rut of the driveway.

"It's him, Grandpa." said Alan in whisper.

The dark man stepped aside as the Cherokee eased up to him. Angrily, Grandpa wound down the window and let the storm rush into the cab. He shouted past the wind at the stranger. "You've got a lot of nerve coming up to my house!"

The eyes behind the ski mask seemed to grow darker, unblinking. "Didn't have much choice," said the chameleon-voice.

Grandpa unlocked the door and stepped out to face the man. "What do you mean by that?"

Soft laughter cut through the howl of the wind. "Come now! You know who I am ... and why I'm here."

Suddenly Grandpa's face turned pale, his eyes became vacant and empty. He nodded his head quickly. "Yeah, I guess I do, but I never knew it to be like this."

"There are countless ways, said the stranger, who was no longer unknown to the old man. Now excuse me, and step aside ..."

"What!" Grandpa sounded shocked.

Alan didn't know what was going on, but he could detect the terror in his grandfather's throat, the trembling fear in his voice. Without realizing it, he was backing away from the vehicle. His head was pounding like a jackhammer.

"Is it the woman?" Grandpa was asking in a whisper.

The dark man shook his head.

Grandpa moaned loudly, letting it turn into words. "No! Not him! No, you can't mean it!"

"Aneurysm ..." said the terribly soft voice behind the mask.

Suddenly Grandpa grabbed the stranger by the shoulder and spun him around, facing him squarely. "No!" he shouted, his face twisted and ugly. "Me! Take me!"

"Can't do it," said the man.

"Grandpa, what's the matter?" Alan started to feel dizzy. The pounding in his head had become a raging fire. It hurt so bad he wanted to scream.

"Yes you can!" yelled Grandpa. "I know you can!"

Alan watched as Grandpa reached out and grabbed at the tall thin man's ski mask. It seemed to come apart as he touched it, and fell away from beneath the droopy brimmed hat. For an instant, Alan could see or at least he thought he saw nothing beneath the mask. It was just an eye-blink of time, and then he saw, for another instant, the white angular lines, the dark hollows of the empty sockets.

But the snow was swirling and whipping, and Grandpa was suddenly wrestling with the man. Alan screamed as the man wrapped his long thin arms around his grandfather and they seemed to dance briefly around in the snow.

"Run, boy!" screamed Grandpa.

Alan turned toward the house, then looked back and he saw Grandpa collapsing into the snow. The tall, dark man was gone.

"Grandpa!" Alan ran to the old man's side as he lay face up, his glazed eyes staring into the storm. "What happened? Grandpa! Oh Jeez!"

"Get your grandmother ... quick," said the old man." It's my heart."

"Don't die, Grandpa ... not now!" Alan was frantic and didn't know what to do. He wanted to get help, but he didn't want to leave his grandfather in the storm like this.

"No choice in it," he said. "A deal's a deal."

Alan looked at his grandfather, suddenly puzzled. "What?"

Grandpa winced as a new pain lanced his chest. "Don't matter now ..." The old man closed his eyes and wheezed out a final breath.

Snowflakes danced across his face, mixing with the first tears, and Alan noticed that his headache, like the dark man, had vanished.

A FAMILY CHRISTMAS TERROR

CHAPTER 5

"Dad, you were right, I didn't see that ending coming," Jack said.

Nancy said, "I like the way you read that, Daddy. It was really scary."

"You're such a baby," her twin sneered.

"Be nice, you two," their mother said. "It's Christmas.

"Fine," Nick said. "Hey... can I have some more brandy?"

"No."

"Please." He held up his mug to her. "Just for the next story."

"C'mon, Judy," Dan said from the couch. "It's Christmas."

Judy rolled her eyes and relented. "That's it, though."

"Thanks, Mom. You're the best."

"And put some more coffee in there. You're not your Grandfather." She pointed to the pot on the table.

"How did I get in this?" Grandpa said and sipped. "But as long as you're pouring..." He proffered his mug.

"Thank God Christmas is only once a year," she said and poured. Then, as an afterthought, poured into her own mug. "What the heck, if you can't beat 'em..." She took a healthy swig. "Go ahead, Dan. What's next?"

Dan glanced at her mug and said, "This one's called *The Gift That Won't Stop Giving*."

THE GIFT THAT WON'T STOP GIVING

LISA HARRIS

> *"A Holly Jolly Life"*
> *Blog post from Holly Marshall*

Dear Readers,

I'm especially excited about the upcoming holidays this year, mainly because I've finally managed to find my dear hubby the perfect gift! I simply can't wait to see his face when he opens it. I don't want to give too much away here – he does sometimes read my blog – but I will be sure to update you after my Christmas break and give you all the juicy details!

Speaking of the break, I'd just like to remind you that this will be my last post for the next two weeks, during which I'll be enjoying time with my friends and family. I have tons of fun activities planned to do with the kids, and C. and I are hosting a grand holiday party at our home.

At this point in my holiday preparations, the finishing touches have been placed on the decorations, the gifts are all wrapped and under the tree (thanks to C.'s gift being delivered earlier today), and most of the shopping for party food and decorations has been done and stored away. All that's left to do is enjoy each day as it comes, and I hope that you will be doing the same.

I'll leave you with my deepest, heartfelt wishes for you for a Merry Christmas and a Happy New Year,

Holly

Holly Marshall could barely contain her glee as she raced to open the door for the FedEx guy. She actually let out a childish squeal when she signed for the package and snatched it from his hands. His truck hadn't even left the driveway before she was ripping through layers of cardboard, tape, and bubble wrap. When her hands touched the smooth cold stone, she shivered with anticipation. She extricated it from its wrappings and held it up to admire it. The ancient Mayan mask smiled back at her, its gleaming, vacant eyes staring at her. She held it to her chest, thrilled that she had finally managed to find the perfect gift for Chris.

She wasn't bitter about the fact that her husband always seemed to know just what to get her—well, maybe she was. But that was beside the point. She'd noted his recent passion for all things "Ancient Indian" and had run with it. When she'd found the relic on eBay with a $145

"Buy It Now" price, she'd assumed it was a replica. But further inquiry had confirmed that the seller did indeed hold a certificate of authenticity stating that the mask dated back to 6th or 7th century Tikal. In the photographs it seemed in pristine condition, and she could already picture it hanging in a place of honor on Chris's office wall at the bank. She'd pounced on the screaming deal before anyone else had a chance to figure out the real value of the prize.

Now, clutching it to her chest, she felt a strange sensation, a flicker of dread, but she laughed off the notion and set to work rewrapping the box with Christmas paper. She placed it underneath the tree and artfully rearranged all the red and white packages to resemble a display straight out of a Christmas magazine.

She couldn't shake the vague feeling of anxiety she'd felt when holding the mask, but she didn't have time to think about that. Now that her shopping was complete, she needed to photograph the fully decorated living room for her final holiday blog post before taking the next two weeks off to focus on spending time with her family. The kids would be out of school and Chris would be home the Thursday and Friday before Christmas Eve. She still had a party to plan, but she'd taken care of most of the arrangements weeks ago, and only had a few last-minute preparations to see to.

She opened the door to the impeccably organized hall closet to retrieve her camera, and was startled when she heard a crash coming from the living room. Upon returning, she saw that the huge family portrait from the fireplace mantel had inexplicably tumbled to the floor and the glass from the frame lay in tiny shards, strewn across the hardwood floor. Bursting into tears, she headed into the kitchen for the broom and dustpan.

*

Chris was just wrapping up his last appointment when Carol, his assistant, poked her head in the door. "Need anything, sugar?"

"Uh, no. We're good here, Carol. Thanks." She was a real hottie—all blond hair, curves, and legs, but her terms of endearment were starting to set his teeth on edge. He was "Honey," "Babe," "Darling," and now, apparently, "Sugar" far more often than "Chris," or more appropriately, "Mr. Marshall." She was outside the boundaries of professionalism, clearly, and he would need to set her straight. Right after Christmas, he promised himself. After all, she'd been a lifesaver to him these past few weeks, working late right alongside him, seeing to his every need. It seemed almost cruel to reprimand her now. No, he'd wait until after the holidays, when business would be slower.

The long hours were beginning to wear on him. That, and the emotional wear and tear of handling cases for so many of his friends and acquaintances. They all came to him for help when they got overextended or just plain couldn't make ends meet. Especially in the weeks leading up to Christmas. He seemed to be seeing people at their most desperate, and he hated it. He did everything he could to help them all out, sometimes taking risks he knew he shouldn't. But that was one of the advantages of being the senior loan officer. He was at liberty to make those kinds of decisions.

He was saying his goodbyes to Mr. Wise when he felt the vibration of his cell phone in his pocket. He waited for the other man to round the corner before glancing at it. Three missed calls, all from Holly. Something must be up. He hit the callback button and waited for her to pick up.

"Chris! Oh my God, Chris! It's S-s-s-snowflake!" she was crying hysterically.

"What? What's going on, Hol?" the hairs on the back of his neck stood on end.

"Snowflake! She got run over!" Holly blurted into his ear.

"Stay put. I'm on my way home." He grabbed his coat as he reached for the door, hanging up the phone as he did.

"Carol, I'm heading out early today," he snapped as he passed her desk.

"Something wrong, Sugar?"

"Nothing to worry about. Can you close out everything here?" he begged.

"Sure thing. I've got it all under control. See you tomorrow," she cooed. Her voice followed him to the elevator, grating on his spine, causing him to punch the button harder than ever.

*

When Chris arrived home, he found his little family all huddled around the body of their miniature poodle. Snowflake appeared to be sleeping, but when he looked closer, he could tell that she had stopped breathing. His six-year-old daughter, Belle, sobbed as she stroked Snowflake's fur, and his ten-year-old son Nick knelt stoically by her side, patting Belle's back reassuringly. Holly cried silently, watching her children say their emotional goodbyes to the family pet.

She looked up at Chris, seeing the questions in his eyes. She shook her head slowly and stood up to embrace him.

"It's okay," he whispered, wrapping her in his arms. He stroked her hair and she wept softly into his shoulder. "What happened, Hol?" "I went out to get the mail and when I opened the door, Snowflake came running out like something was chasing her. She was yelping like she was scared to death, and she just darted out into the road. Some asshole was coming down the street—you know how fast they drive around here——and he just ran right over her. Didn't even stop. She was already gone when I got to her." She sobbed the last few words, and Chris hugged her tightly, letting her cry it out.

Later, they held a grim little funeral ceremony in the backyard, burying Snowflake under her favorite tree, then ordered pizza for dinner. Exhausted and emotionally drained, Chris and Holly tucked the kids into bed early, then retired for the night.

"I can't imagine what it's going to be like without her around here," Holly sighed, wearily climbing under the covers. "I mean, I knew she wouldn't be around forever, but I never thought she'd be gone so soon. It's so unlike her to take off like that out the front door. I wonder what got into her."

"There's no telling. That dog was afraid of her own shadow."

Chris replied, "But I'm sure going to miss her. She was the first animal that actually liked me." He switched off the bedside lamp, cloaking their bedroom in darkness. In minutes, they were both dead asleep.

Holly awoke suddenly from a dreamless sleep. What had wakened her? She listened intently in the darkness. There. There it was again. A faint scratching at the door. It couldn't be. But it sounded just like *her*! Was her mind playing tricks on her? She heard it again, only this time she could have sworn she heard the high-pitched whine Snowflake used to make when she wanted in.

"Chris!" she whispered loudly, nudging his shoulder. "Chris. Wake up. I heard something!" He groaned and turned on his side, facing the wall away from her.

She heard the scratching again a little louder, and her blood ran cold. Was it possible that they had buried Snowflake alive? But, if that was the case, how had she managed to find her way into the house?

Holly threw back the covers and jumped out of bed, bolting toward the sound. In the split second before she flung open the door, she actually allowed herself to hope that she would see the beloved pet on the other side of it, scratching to come into their room and snuggle in bed with them once more. But when she did open the door, she was greeted with nothing but the darkness of the hallway. Curious, she looked both ways, but again saw nothing. She checked the kids' rooms, then the bathroom, then finally wandered downstairs. She turned on the living room light, and a few seconds later she heard the faint sounds again. This time the noise seemed to come from the front door. Cautiously, she tiptoed to the door and turned on the porch light. Bracing herself, she opened the door slowly, then breathed a sigh of relief when again, she found nothing.

Shaking her head, she locked up, turned out the light, and headed back upstairs. Just as she reached the top, she heard the sound again, louder and more insistent. The hairs on the back of her neck prickled and she ran toward her bedroom door. She scrambled back under the covers and turned on the bedside lamp.

Chris stirred. "What's the matter, Hol?" He yawned.

"I heard something. I-I-I heard Snowflake. She was scratching at our bedroom door, and then the front door. I'm really freaked out right now!" The words tumbled out of her mouth.

Chris pulled her close and snuggled her down beside him. "Wow, you're really shaking, Babe. Hush now . . . it was just a bad dream. We've been through a lot today. Go back to sleep." He wrapped his strong arms around her and held her close, drifting back to his dreams. She knew what she'd experienced hadn't been a dream, but she let him comfort her and tried to go back to sleep. When she heard the scratching sound again, she began to cry softly, determined not to wake her husband again.

*

"Kids! Breakfast!" Holly called up the stairs. It was their last day of school before Christmas Break, and they were already running late. She just couldn't seem to get her act together since Snowflake's accident, and she hadn't gotten any sleep the last several nights.

"Oatmeal again?" Belle complained.

"You'll eat it and be grateful," Holly chided. "There are children in the world who would love to have a warm breakfast like this one. In fact—"

She was interrupted by a terrible tumbling noise, ending in a thud. She heard Nick cry out in pain and immediately feared the worst. She hurried into the living room to find her son lying in a crumpled heap at the foot of the stairs, his leg jutting out at an unusual angle.

"Oh my God, Nicky! Are you okay?"

"My leg hurts, Mom. It hurts so much!" He was fighting back tears, and her heart melted at the sight of him trying to be a tough guy.

"It's broken. Listen to me. I want you to stay right here, and I'm going to call an ambulance." Chris had already left for work, so as soon as she had the ambulance on the way, she dialed his office number, crouching next to Nick and rubbing her hand soothingly on his forehead.

"Chris Marshall's office. Carol speaking. How may I help you?" came the saccharine-sweet voice of her husband's assistant.

"Carol! I need to talk to Chris right away!"

"Oh, I'm afraid he's stepped out. Can I take a message?" Carol oozed insincerity, and it grated on Holly's already frayed nerves.

"No, thanks. I'll try his cell."

"Oh. Oops. I've got it right here. He must've forgotten it." The assistant snickered.

"Wow. Okay. Just... tell him to call me as soon as he gets back. Okay? It's an emergency. As soon as he gets back," Holly insisted.

"Will do, Sugar," Carol replied, then hung up the phone. Holly didn't have time to let the exchange get to her. The ambulance had arrived and she stayed by Nick's side to offer whatever comfort and reassurance she could while the paramedics carefully lifted him onto the gurney and into the back of the ambulance.

Before the ambulance had even left the driveway, Holly had strapped Belle into her booster seat and cranked the car, ready to follow Nick to the hospital. She tried Chris's cell, but was directed straight to voicemail. "Hey. It's me. Nicky fell down the stairs. I think his leg is broken, and we're headed to the hospital now. Call me as soon as you get this. Or better yet, meet me there." She hung up and silently prayed that her husband would get the message and come right away. She really needed his strength right now, because she was just about to lose her mind. Why was this happening now? All she'd wanted was a peaceful, relaxing holiday at home with her husband and kids, and now it seemed to all be going to hell in a handbasket.

Back home that afternoon, Holly fought back tears of anger and frustration as she busied herself settling Nick in and making him comfortable. She hadn't heard from Chris all day, and she'd had to watch her son suffer through the painful procedure of setting the bone and casting the bottom half of his leg over the knee. Thankfully, Diana had come right away to see to Belle, getting her to school and bringing Holly a tall mocha latte back to the hospital.

Diana Ramos was the sweetest, most caring friend Holly could have asked for. She was so warm and open, the eternal earth mother, and Holly knew she could count on Diana if ever she needed her.

Trouble was, Holly wasn't used to needing anyone. She usually had her life in order and under control, but lately, she couldn't seem to get it together. In fact, she was afraid she was finally falling apart. Every night since they'd buried the family dog, she'd been hearing sounds like the animal was scratching and whining to get in. When she'd tried to tell Chris about it, he'd been dismissive, saying she was having nightmares or suffering from stress. As a result, she hadn't told him about the shadows she'd seen dancing on the wall the previous night. She wasn't even sure how she'd describe what she'd seen. The terrifying figures seemed to be performing some sort of ritual dance, moving in time to a beat she couldn't hear. She tried to convince herself that there was some logical explanation for what she'd experienced, but in truth, there wasn't.

Determined to put it all out of her mind, she made Nick his favorite supper of grilled cheese and tomato soup and delivered it to him in bed. She helped him sit up and propped pillows behind his back before placing the tray on his bedside table.

"Mom?" he began.

"Yeah? What is it, son?" she asked brightly.

"I don't want Belle to get in trouble," he replied.

"What do you mean, Nicky? Why would Belle be in trouble?"

"Because she pushed me and made me break my leg," he answered matter-of-factly.

"What? Where did you get an idea like that?"

"I felt it. I was at the top of the stairs, and Belle pushed me. She made me lose my balance, and I fell and broke my leg." He seemed so sincere, and for a moment Holly wondered if it could be true. But no.

"No, honey. Belle was in the kitchen with me. I was giving her breakfast, and she was giving me grief about having oatmeal again. I was scolding her when I heard you fall down the stairs," she informed him. Stroking his face, she added, "I think that pain medicine they gave you might have made you a little loopy." She winked at him and chuckled, but noticed that the color had drained from his face.

"Mom!" he whispered intensely, "Something pushed me! It had to be her! She had to be there! Something pushed me!" he was trembling, and his panic-stricken face twisted with frightened tears. He was petrified, and when Holly pulled him into her embrace, he sat stiffly against her, his breath short and ragged, not responding to her attempts at soothing him.

"Oh, honey. It's okay. Shhh. It's okay. There's nothing to be afraid of. It was just an accident. You must have tripped. No one pushed you. It was just an accident," Holly cooed.

Nick pushed back to look at his mom. His eyes were as big as saucers. "I saw something," he choked. "Something in my room. Last night. I was scared, but I didn't think it was real. But what if it was real, Mom? What if it was real and it pushed me and it made me hurt myself? Mom, what if it was real?"

"What did you see, Nick? Tell me exactly what you saw," she whispered softly.

"I don't know what it was. It was a shadow or something dark. There were more than one. They were dancing. I couldn't hear the music, but they were dancing. I didn't think they could be real, but what if they were? If Belle didn't push me, it might have been them." His voice rose with panic again, and Holly pulled him in tight, rocking him and stroking his hair reassuringly.

"Hush, now. You're alright. You're safe. Nothing's going to hurt you. Mommy's here," she whispered over and over until he finally began to calm down. "I want you to try and rest. Lie back and close your eyes. I'll be right here."

She tucked him in again and smoothed his hair back from his forehead. She tried to mask her concern for Nick's sake, but every cell in her body was on high alert. Her son was experiencing the same things she'd been experiencing, and now it seemed he'd been hurt as a result of it. She had to do something, but what? What did people do when their nightmares became real? Where did you turn in a situation like that? And where the *hell* was her husband? He should be here, helping her, helping Nicky.

*

Holly trudged downstairs, exhausted. Nicky had finally gotten to sleep, thanks to the combination of painkillers he'd been prescribed and her reading a few of the Christmas story books she'd brought down from the attic a week ago. No matter how hard she tried, she couldn't seem to ease Nick's mind about what had really caused him to fall down the stairs, and he hadn't wanted to fall asleep for fear of having more of the strange nightmares he'd experienced the night before. It broke her heart to see him suffer.

She needed tea. Sweet, hot, chamomile tea to help calm her nerves and make her feel normal again. Just as she reached the bottom of the stairs, she heard what sounded like a drum beat—faint, low, and steady. "Damn kids," she thought, moving to the living room window to spot the car from which she believed the sound was coming. When she neared the living room, the sound grew louder, but she saw no sign of a car. She shook her head, willing the sound away, but it only came stronger. Then she saw headlights turning into the drive. Chris! Finally!

She rushed to the door, a swirl of emotions running through her mind. Where had he been? Why hadn't he called? Was he okay? Had something terrible happened to him too? She felt relief mixed with fear and frustration as she flung open the door to greet her husband.

"Where have you been?" she cried, wrapping her arms around him and squeezing tightly.

"I told you. We had the company Christmas party tonight," he replied, puzzled.

"You've been at a *party*? All this time? Why didn't you come home when you got my messages?" she asked in disbelief. "What are you talking about? What messages?"

"I left a message with your secretary and on your cell. Nicky fell down the stairs today. He broke his leg!" she countered.

"*What?* Is he okay?" Chris made for the stairs, but Holly grabbed his arm to stop him.

"He's all right. I finally got him to sleep a little while ago. Chris, what happened to you? Why didn't you call me back?" she pleaded.

He ran his hand through his hair, shock on his face as he glanced up the stairs. "It was a slow day, so Mr. White took a bunch of us in the loan department out for an early lunch. We wound up at this little karaoke bar and had a few drinks."

"Why didn't you answer your cell?" she asked again.

"I gave it to Carol this morning. She needed to get some contacts from it. I guess we both forgot she had it. It must still be on her desk."

"Carol, huh? What's going on there, Chris? I left a message with her this morning right after the accident. I told her to have you call me right away, and she said she would. Did she even *tell* you about it?" Holly's voice rose now as rage boiled up inside her. How dare that little blond bitch keep her husband from her!

"She never mentioned, it, no," he replied, deflated. "I really want to see Nicky for myself. I'm just going to poke my head in the door and check on him. I'll be right back."

"Don't wake him up!" she snapped.

Exasperated, Chris climbed the stairs two at a time. Holly watched him go, hearing the drums beat louder now. Her anger at Chris, at the whole situation, grew stronger with each beat of the drum. She no longer cared where it was coming from. She paced in time to the sound, waiting for her husband to return so she could rip into him. He was going to hear about this. And she was not going to allow him to patronize her. He needed to know what had been going on, and he needed to help her get to the bottom of it.

Chris descended the stairs, his shoulders slumped, his eyes red-rimmed. Seeing their son in a leg cast had shaken him, and he was kicking himself for having not been there. For kicking up his heels at the bar, and, later, back at the office during the Christmas party.

"Where's Belle?" he asked when he rejoined Holly in the living room. "And where's that beating coming from?"

"With Diana, to the first question, and I don't know to the second," she bit back. "What the hell, Chris? You just party with your secretary all day. You don't check in, even *once*, and she doesn't bother giving you an important message from your WIFE? And you're okay with that? Because I'm not!"

"No, I'm not okay—" he began.

"There's something else. You know I told you that some really weird things were happening ever since Snowflake died. Like me hearing her trying to get in. And seeing shadows on the wall. Well, Nicky's been seeing them too." The words tumbled out of her. She barely registered Chris's dumbfounded expression as she continued. "He thought Belle pushed him down the stairs this morning. I told him it couldn't have been Belle. She was right there with me, in the kitchen, when it happened. When I told him that, he freaked out! He started telling me about the shadows and how it must have been them who pushed him. No matter what I said, he insists he was pushed. Something is going on, Chris. Something awful, and you're off partying with your stupid secretary!" she finished on a high-pitched shriek.

"Whoa. Wait a minute. First of all, I had no idea all this was going on today. If I had, you know I'd have been right here. Second, there is nothing going on with Carol and me. She might be a little flirty, but I promise you, I have not encouraged her to be that way." He noted his wife rolling her eyes. It pissed him off, frankly, but he reminded himself of all the stress she must have been through today, for the past week, really, and he tried to exercise his patience.

"There must be some reason why she thinks It's okay to not give you my messages," she accused.

"Dammit, Holly, I don't know what to tell you. I don't know why she didn't give me your message. And I don't know what's going on with you and Nicky. He probably overheard you telling me about your nightmare and got scared too. I don't know. But I do know I don't deserve this. I don't need to be interrogated in my own home. I'm tired. It's been a long day for both of us. Why don't we just go to bed and talk about this tomorrow?" He reached out a hand to her, beckoning her to follow him upstairs. She hesitated, but in the end she took his hand. She was still fuming inside, but what was the point in hammering on him now? They'd figure it all out tomorrow.

"Wish those kids would knock it off with the drums," he mumbled, climbing the stairs. She agreed, though the sound seemed to be fading away.

*

Holly drifted into a fretful sleep, the worries of the day still heavy on her mind. She'd been so angry at Chris—to the point of rage, and she was having a hard time processing it. They never fought. That was one of the things that all their friends admired about them as a couple. It was so unlike her to just see red like that, but if she was being honest with herself, she was still more than a little miffed. She couldn't believe he'd been so dismissive about hers and

Nick's nighttime terrors, or that he'd suggested it was her fault that Nick was having these experiences. She'd been very careful not to mention anything in front of either of the kids, and she knew in her heart that it hadn't been because of her influence. All these thoughts and emotions haunted her dreams, and she tossed and turned until something suddenly woke her.

She lay still in the darkness, listening for whatever it was that had startled her awake. She heard the sound of drums the same as before, but there was something else. A shriek or howl of some sort that seemed to be coming from downstairs.

"Chris! Chris!" she hissed. "Wake up. Do you hear that?" "Hmm?" he stirred slowly, opening his eyes. "There's those drums again. I'm gonna call the cops. They're disturbing the peace." He sat up and swung his legs over the side of the bed, but the next sound he heard stopped him dead in his tracks.

The shrieking sound came again, louder this time, accompanied by an inhuman growl and the slamming of a door downstairs. Something *was* in the house! Realizing this, they both jumped out of bed. Chris grabbed the baseball bat he kept under his side of the bed, and Holly threw on her robe. Before they could even move toward the bedroom door, they heard another door slam downstairs, and then a clawing, thudding sound that traveled up the stairs. Holly screamed and bolted for the door. All she could think of was Nick, alone and vulnerable in his room with some monster pressing down on him, intent on doing God only knew what.

"Holly! Stop!" Chris reached for her, stepping in front of her with the bat. He flung open the door, and she darted behind him running for Nick's bedroom door. Chris stepped behind her, turning his back to her and toward—whatever it was. He followed her, backing toward her and Nick, the baseball bat poised and ready to do damage to the unknown person or creature that had invaded their home. As she opened Nick's door, Holly turned to glance over her shoulder. Seeing the gigantic shadow beast bearing down on them, she grabbed Chris's arm and dragged him into the room with her, slamming the door shut behind them. They heard the loud thud and felt the impact of a body crashing into the door. There was a high-pitched howl and then silence.

Breathlessly, both of them looked at Nick and were astounded to see that he was sound asleep. His expression was peaceful in his dreams, and it seemed as if he hadn't heard a thing.

"Did you see that?" Holly whispered, her expression one of sheer terror.

"What the hell was it?" Chris replied, gripping the bat so hard his knuckles were white.

"I don't know. Is it gone?"

Chris took a moment to catch his breath, then slowly opened the door to the hallway, peeking out through the narrow space. He saw nothing and heard nothing, not even the drums from before. Opening the door slightly wider, he carefully stepped out into the hall, looking both ways as he moved. There was nothing there.

Holly followed, silently pulling the door shut behind her. Her mind jumbled with a million dark thoughts, and she trembled from head to toe with the fear and adrenaline pumping through her body. She had to do something. Had to put a stop to whatever it was that was happening to her family. An idea began to form in the back of her head, fuzzy in the murky fog that was her present state of mind.

The mask.

All this chaos seemed to have started when she'd brought that mask into the house.

*

She grabbed Chris by the hand and led him downstairs to the living room. She clicked on the overhead light. Everything looked just as it always did—normal, peaceful even. Driven by terrible curiosity, she reached for the gift she'd so carefully placed beneath the tree just a few days ago.

"I think it's this! All these terrible things ... they started when I brought this into the house!" she said.

Chris took the box, a stunned expression on his face. He wasn't thinking clearly, the fright from moments before still fresh in his mind. He tore into the paper without even noticing what he was doing, scanning the room, reassuring himself that his little family was in no immediate danger.

When finally he opened the box and pulled out the mask, Holly could no longer contain the anxiety she'd felt from the start. "Oh my God, oh my God! It's this mask! Look at the expression! It wasn't like that when I got it, Chris, I swear. It was smiling." The mask now held a grotesque snarl where before its eyes had seemed vacant, its smile vague. The expression now was one of menace, its cruel purpose clear in the intense stare it aimed at whomever held it. Holly shivered, disbelief and terror coursing through her mind.

"It's incredible! Where did you get it?" Chris seemed enamored with the object. It was just the reaction Holly had hoped for when she'd clicked "Buy It Now," but it rang hollow in her ears now.

"I bought it on eBay." Realization dawned. "That's it! I've got to find that seller. Maybe he can tell us more about this thing and why it's ... haunting us, I guess," she rambled.

"Hmm," was the only reply she got from Chris. He seemed taken with the relic, so she left him to look it over while she hunted down the seller. She fired up the laptop and logged on to her eBay account.

She clicked to view her recent purchases, and there it was: a photo of the mask as she'd purchased it, vacant smile and all. Oddly, the seller's name was grayed out, and she couldn't click his name. Puzzled, she pulled up the advance search and entered in his seller ID. "The seller User ID you entered was not found," the search returned. And that was it. Just like that, the mystery man from whom she'd bought this curse was gone for good.

*

When Diana drove up the next morning with Belle in the car, Holly couldn't hide her relief at seeing her younger child happy and whole, nor her fatigue from lack of sleep from the night before. Still, she politely invited Diana in for a cup of coffee, and, sensing that something was very wrong with her friend, Diana accepted.

"Can I be honest, Hol? You look like hell. How's Nick doing?" The concern was evident in her voice. Diana mothered everyone, and she had taken Holly's little family under her wing soon after they had met at a coffee shop.

"He's okay. He was a little shaken up about what happened, but he rested well last night—which is really weird. And this morning he's been trying out his crutches. Doctor said he should heal completely." She tried to force a smile, but Diana could see right through it.

"What's up, Holly? Your eyes are bloodshot, and I'm not buying that everything is hunky dory. Did you and Chris get into a fight or something?"

"No! Well, yes, but I think we're past that. No, it's something else. If I tell you, you'll think I'm crazy," Holly responded, debating whether or not to share the whole story with her friend.

"Try me." Diana pulled her coffee cup closer and folded her arms on the counter, all ears.

"Well... it started a week or so ago. I bought this mask to give Chris—he's so hard to buy for, and he always gets me the most thoughtful gifts." She was stalling, but Diana was rooted to the spot, determined to hear her out. "As soon as it came into the house, strange things started to happen. One of our family portraits fell off the wall and shattered. It was really heavy, and it was anchored to the wall. I can't explain how that could happen. And then, you know, Snowflake got run over?"

Diana nodded.

"Well, that night, I heard her. She was scratching on the door and whining to get in. But when I looked, there was nothing there. And I've been having these dreams—nightmares, really. Or maybe it's really happening. I saw shadows dancing on the wall. Shaped like people, five or six of them. Dancing this wild, crazy, I don't know... tribal... dance."

"Wow, seriously disturbing, girl. But you know, sometimes stress can do funny things to us. It can mess with your mind. And you've been really stressed lately!" Diana encouraged.

"Right. And I thought that myself. But then Nick fell down the stairs and broke his leg. Which was bad enough, but yesterday when we got home, he told me someone pushed him. I tried to tell him no one could've done that—Belle was here with me—but I couldn't change his mind. He's convinced he was pushed. And... he told me he's been seeing the shadow dancers too. The way he described them sounded just like what I've been seeing. And the worst thing happened last night. Chris and I both heard and saw it. It was a shadow too, I think. Only it was more like a giant dog, and it chased us down the hall to Nicky's room. Neither one of us got a wink of sleep after that," she finished, taking a long sip of her coffee.

Diana was stunned. "That. Wow. I don't know what to say. You think it started when you bought this mask? What kind of mask is it?"

"It's an old, old Mayan mask. I found it on eBay for next to nothing. The last few months Chris has been obsessed with ancient Indian cultures, so I thought it would be perfect for him for Christmas. When I put two and two together, it must be the cause of all this chaos. I tried to find the guy who sold it to me, but it's like he's vanished into thin air. There's no profile for him on eBay anymore and no contact information. I don't know what to do. I don't know anything about curses, but I think that's really what we're up against. I just don't know what to do," she repeated.

"Let's see this mystery mask," Diana said, curiosity radiating out of her.

Holly led her into the living room, where Chris was again admiring the mask, staring at it with a faraway look in his eye. Diana leaned over his shoulder to examine the relic for herself. Her eyebrows knit together and a scowl darkened her countenance. She motioned for Holly to rejoin her in the kitchen.

"Okay, that thing is seriously spooky. I don't like the vibe I get from it," she said in a low voice, once she and Holly were alone.

"Me either. But Chris won't stop staring at it. I think he likes it, but it totally creeps me out, and I really think it's cursed. What do I do?"

"I just might be able to help. I know some people who may know some people," Diana offered.

"Yeah, that's right. You do dabble with the occult."

Diana chuckled. "I don't dabble, darling. I'm a witch. Wiccan. I don't do curses or any sort of dark magic. But like I said, I know some people who know worlds more about this stuff than I'll ever know, and it could be that they can help us find some answers." With that, she drained her cup and stepped around the counter to embrace Holly in one of her warm hugs. "Cheer up, Buttercup. It's going to be all right."

Holly smiled gratefully and saw her friend to the door.

"Oh, and Holly?" Diana turned back just as she was leaving. "Don't touch that thing. I don't like the way Chris seems so entranced by it. Just try to stay away from it until we can find out more."

*

Turning to go back into her home, Holly felt a sense of relief. At last, someone was on her side, and that someone was Diana Ramos, a force to be reckoned with. She'd find an answer to this problem or die trying, and it warmed

Holly's heart to know this woman was in her corner. She could relax and focus on taking care of her family.

She walked into the living room and was alarmed to see that Belle was sitting next to Chris on the sofa, her little hands running all over the surface of that awful mask. Diana had warned her not to touch it, so she was certain she didn't want her daughter anywhere near it. Her first instinct was to scold Belle and send her upstairs, but instead she picked up the shipping box she'd set aside the night before and walked over to the sofa.

"Honey? Why don't you drop your mask back into the box," she said with a calmness she didn't really feel.

"That's okay. I'm not done looking at it. It's amazing!" her husband replied.

"Please? I want to rewrap it and put it back under the tree. Come on, now. You need something to open on Christmas morning," she pleaded.

He looked up at her, frowning, but did as she asked and dropped the mask back into the box. She quickly folded the flaps in, being careful not to allow the relic to come into contact with her skin.

"Belle, you can help me. Why don't you go grab a roll of wrapping paper?" she chirped, a little too brightly.

"'Kay. What color, Mommy? The red or the white?" Belle hopped off the couch to do as her mom asked.

"Doesn't matter, baby. Whichever you like best," she responded. Surprised by her mom's uncharacteristic flexibility, Belle took off upstairs.

That evening Diana returned with a bundle of sage. She asked Holly for permission to do a ritual she called "smudging," which she said would protect the family from evil spirits. Holly agreed, and Diana lit the bundle, wafting the smoke around all the rooms of the home. Afterward, Holly felt a sense of well-being return, and for the first time in many days, she began to hope that this strange ordeal would soon be over.

She tucked the kids in early, reading each of them one of their favorite Christmas books. She then headed to bed herself, confident that she would be getting a good night's sleep for a change.

She couldn't have been more wrong.

Around 1:00 A.M.., she awoke again to a bizarre sound. It sounded like children's voices humming or singing. Panicking, she got out of bed and threw on her robe. She opened the door and listened for the sound. She heard it again, louder this time. It seemed to come from Belle's room, and the knowledge made her blood run cold.

She flung open Belle's door, dreading the worst, and yelped when she saw her daughter. She was standing in the corner of the room between the window and her closet. Beside her was a shadow figure, not much taller than Nicky, and the two of them were chanting something in an eerie singsong voice.

Chris appeared in the doorway, startling her, and she screamed again. Her heart pounded in her chest, and she listened closely to hear what her daughter and the ghost figure were saying.

"It's not going away," Belle sang, staring straight through her mother.

"What? What is it, sweetie? What's not going away?" Holly whispered. Her legs felt like wood and she couldn't move.

"It's not going away. You can't make it go away. It's not going away. You can't make it go away," her daughter continued to chant.

Then Chris joined the chanting, and with lead in her stomach, Holly knew what they were telling her. What the mask was telling her. It, along with its curse, was here to stay, and she was helpless to do anything about it. The smudging hadn't worked. Nothing would work. The thought both terrified and infuriated her.

She ran to Chris and grabbed him by the shoulders. Shaking him, she cried, "Chris, wake up! Snap out of it!"

"We're not going away. You can't make us go away," her husband responded.

Holly shrieked and, without thinking, slapped her husband's handsome face. He blinked, and instinctively, she slapped him again. "What the hell, Hol?" he shouted.

Immediately the chanting stopped and the figure by the window disappeared. Chris's eyes grew wide with fear. Holly grabbed his hand and pulled him to Belle's side. Their daughter's eyes filled with tears and she flung her little body into her parents' arms, sobbing hysterically.

"It's okay, honey. You're okay. You're okay," Holly murmured into her hair. Chris lifted their daughter up and carried her back to their room to spend the rest of the night.

When finally she calmed enough to go back to sleep, the couple moved to the window seat to talk.

"You really scared me, Chris. What the hell is going on?" she demanded.

"I don't know. I don't even know how I wound up in Belle's room. All I remember is hearing those damn drums in my dreams. I think I was having a nightmare. The next thing I knew, you were hitting me," her husband replied, clearly shaken by the experience.

"It's the mask, Chris. It must carry some sort of curse. Diana's looking into it, but we've got to do something about the kids. They can't be here with this going on."

"You're right. I'll call my mom in the morning. I'm sure she'd love to have the kids come stay with her for a few days before Christmas. She'll spoil them rotten."

"I really hate to send them away. I had so many things planned to do with them over the break. Are you sure she'll be okay taking care of Nick?" She couldn't see any way around it, and hoped Chris's parents would be up to the task of caring for the kids until they could figure this whole thing out.

"They'll be fine. I'll call in the morning," he repeated. "Let's get some shut-eye.

It tore Holly's heart to pieces, watching her kids get into their grandma's van, especially Nick, who tried hard to look tough and brave with his crutches. She hugged each of her children a little longer than necessary, and profusely thanked Chris's mother, Mary. Chris had told her he and Holly wanted a few days to themselves to finalize their

Christmas shopping and party preparations, and Mary had been more than happy to accommodate them.

The house felt incredibly empty after they left, and Holly couldn't help feeling a little bit sorry for herself. Chris spent the afternoon with his buddies at the country club, so she had plenty of time alone to process all she'd been through. She hadn't heard from Diana yet, and she wondered if her friend would truly be able to dig up a solution to this terrible predicament she found herself in. She sure as hell didn't know what to do about it.

*

In fact, she didn't hear from Diana for three more days. During that time, the drums and shadows continued to haunt her at night. Chris was barely speaking to her. She could only guess that the anger and confusion between them was a side effect of the curse, and she desperately needed things to return to normal.

When Diana finally called with news, Holly was barely hanging onto her sanity. She'd thought of destroying the mask, but some instinct kept her waiting—impatiently—for answers that may or may not come. Diana phoned on Wednesday afternoon to say that Fred at The Wiccan Way shop had a lead for her. He had connections through a few Internet forums, and had put out the word about the mysterious Mayan mask and the strange happenings surrounding it. There was no response at first, until finally, one woman had made contact saying that she knew of a medicine man from Guatemala that might have information that could help. This woman had given Fred the man's telephone number, and he had passed it along to Diana.

Exhausted, Holly hung up from Diana, feeling a renewed sense of purpose. She took a few deep breaths and gathered her courage. She sat down to call the man, praying that he could tell her how to end this curse once and for all. She was grateful the man even had a phone, living in Guatemala.

He picked up after just two rings. "Mr. Zacapa?" she queried.

"Yes?" came a distant, frail male voice.

"Mr. Zacapa! My name is Holly Marshall. I'm calling about a mask. Fred Bailey told me to call you. I'm having a big problem, and I need some help. Can you tell me what you know?"

"Slow down," Diego Zacapa replied. "My English ... not so good. First, tell me. What this mask look like?"

Holly described the mask, being mindful to slow her speech and enunciate carefully. The man listened, interjecting "si, si" once or twice, until Holly had told him everything.

"Yes. I know this mask. This mask cursed," he began.

"I knew it. Can you tell me more?" she breathed. "I appreciate any information you can give me—especially how to break this curse off of my family."

"Ah. Is not easy. This mask very, very old. Made by ancient artisan. One of my ancestors. He lived in little village. One day, my ancestor saw a vision. He saw many bad things to come. He told the village chief about this vision. Chief did not believe. He told others too. Chief did not like this. He wanted to sacrifice the artisan."

"Oh no! I didn't realize they—I mean—your people practiced human sacrifice!" Holly exclaimed.

"Not much. Only when necessary," Chief said. "If war is coming, we must sacrifice to war god. So my ancestor was chosen to sacrifice. He prayed to Buluc Chabtan, god of war. The god heard his prayer and curse mask, which artisan gave to chief to spare his life. Mask brought many troubles to village. Many people died, but not chief. He gave mask as gift to another chief. This chief's village suffered too, until they give mask away. And so it went for many years. One day mask disappeared. It was found again three years ago in cave in Honduras. In cave, with it, are bones of many men, women, and children."

Holly gasped. Why hadn't she researched this gift more carefully before hitting that "Buy It Now" button? "So, Mr. Zacapa, are you saying there is no way to break the curse?"

"There is one way. One way only. You must give mask to another. Your troubles end, but for other ... they begin," he replied. She couldn't help but note the sadness in his voice.

"Why couldn't I just destroy it? Wouldn't that break the curse?"

"Oh, no. No. If you break mask, curse stays with your family forever," he informed her. "I am sorry this trouble come to you. Now you must decide. Is not easy," he repeated.

After hanging up with the old man, Holly slumped to the floor.

How in the world could she knowingly and willingly pass along this evil to someone else? She melted into tears feeling very much trapped between a rock and a hard place.

*

When Friday evening rolled around, Holly's nerves were frazzled beyond repair. She'd pleaded with Chris to cancel the party, but he would hear nothing of it. She'd even reminded him that the spirits haunting them might decide to make an appearance for their guests, but he insisted that they go forward with the party as planned.

Ordinarily, Holly was the ultimate hostess. She thought of everything, and her guests never wanted for anything. She had done the lion's share of the party planning weeks ago, but there were always last minute details to see to. Between lack of sleep and worry over her moral dilemma, Holly couldn't concentrate on any of that, and she worried that she would disappoint their attendees. At the last minute, she had given in and hired a caterer at an exorbitant price and left the final bits and pieces up to the catering staff. All that was left for her to do was to sip a few pre-party cocktails to try and calm her jangled nerves.

By the time the guests arrived, she was into her third cup of liberally laced eggnog and beginning to relax. She welcomed their neighbors, friends, and Chris's coworkers with her usual warmth and poise, and the party was soon well underway. She circulated among the guests and kept an eye on their drinks and hors d'oeuvres, seeing that both were well supplied. *I'll be damned*, she thought. *That caterer was worth every penny.* She knocked back another cup of eggnog and grinned, satisfied that no one seemed to have noticed that she and Chris were barely speaking to one another. Almost no one, as it turned out.

As the evening drew to a close, she wandered into the kitchen to check in with the staff and see how supplies were holding out. When one of the girls asked where to take out the trash, she cheerfully offered to do it herself. She needed a breath of fresh air, anyway, and she made quick work of it.

Stepping out into the night, she heard the sound of women's voices around the corner on the patio. She thought it unusual for anyone to be spending time out in the chill, but was prepared to dismiss it until she heard one of the women speak her husband's name.

"I think Chris is getting really sick of dealing with her. She's been so clingy lately. So the dog died and the kid broke his leg? Woman up and deal with it! The kid's leg will heal, and they can get another dog. No big deal." It was Carol's voice. Holly would know it anywhere. She'd come to loathe it in recent days.

"I don't know. That's kind of harsh, don't you think? Either one of those things is terrible, but having both of them happen at the same time, and right before Christmas . . . I'd be stressed too. Maybe Chris should cut her some slack." Holly didn't recognize the second voice, but she appreciated the woman's words nonetheless.

"I'm just saying. If he were my husband, he'd never have to worry about any of that. I'd keep him happy every day, in every way, if you know what I mean." Carol's voice began to fade as the women headed back inside through the back door.

Enraged, Holly flung the trash bag into the dumpster and stalked back inside. She made her way into the living room and found that people had begun collecting their coats and saying happy goodbyes. The party had been a success in spite of all their troubles, and inwardly Holly congratulated herself on pulling off what had seemed impossible only a day ago.

She plastered on a smile and exchanged Christmas wishes with the exiting party-goers. Still fuming, she couldn't wait for Carol's turn. She was really going to give the woman a piece of her mind! Chris stood beside her, oblivious to the drama about to unfold, yet still icy cold toward her. But Carol hung back, obviously trying to be the last to leave. That was fine with Holly, who never liked to make a scene.

Then, as the last group of people parted, Carol made her way toward the door, smiling coquettishly at Chris. Impulsively, Holly leapt in front of her, and, not even knowing what came over her, she spoke sweetly to the other woman. "Carol! Before you go, Chris and I wanted to give you a little something just to say how much we appreciate your help all year long." She reached beneath the tree and grabbed the box. Turning to hand it to his assistant, she noticed Chris's eyes grow as large as saucers. He shook his head frantically, but she calmly looked into the other woman's eyes. "We hope you like this small token of our gratitude. Merry Christmas!"

"Thank you. And Merry Christmas to you, too, Hol— Mrs. Marshall. Mr. Marshall," Carol sputtered. She took the gift and quickly headed out the door.

As the final strains of *Have Yourself a Merry Little Christmas* drifted out of the sound system, Chris and Holly stood arm in arm in the doorway, waving goodbye to their friends, and more importantly, to the curse that had nearly destroyed their family.

"There goes your Christmas gift," Holly said. "From now on, you're getting a subscription to the cheese-of-the-month club," she joked.

"I love cheese," Chris said. "And I love you. Let's go get the kids first thing tomorrow." And with that, they closed the door and, feeling lighter than air, they headed for bed where they slept peacefully through the silent night.

A FAMILY CHRISTMAS TERROR

CHAPTER 6

"This is awesome!" Nick slurred.

"No, it's not. That story was sick. Would someone really do that to someone else?" Nancy scolded. "Are you drunk? At one in the afternoon?"

"Hey!" Nick said, sitting up then slumping back. "I'm just tired, 's all."

Judy shook her head. "I knew I shouldn't have given you that last drink."

"He'll learn," Dan told her. "Experience is the best teacher."

"I know, but I don't want him to get sick on Christmas. He'll ruin dinner."

"He won't get sick. Will you, Nick?" Dan looked meaningfully at Nick and held out the book. "You read the next one."

"I'll be fine," Nick said, opening the book. He hiccupped.

"Oh Jesus. Give me the book." Jack snatched the book away.

"Hey—*hic*—I can do—*hic*— it," Nick fell back on the sofa.

"You're such a loser," Jack hissed.

"I'll—*hic*—read the next one—*hic*—"

"Hold your breath," Judy said.

"Yeah, like for an hour," Nancy stage-whispered to Grandpa, who guffawed.

Nick looked at them. "You're not nice—*hic*—either of you."

Dan had had enough. His hand tightened on his mug. "Jack, just read the goddam story."

"Okay, Dad. Calm down." He looked at his mother, who was studying her hands, and then turned back to the book. "*The Little Helper*." He glared at his younger brother. "Guess it's not about you, Nicky boy."

"Shut up—*hic*—and read."

THE LITTLE HELPER

E. MCCARTHY

He sees you when you're sleeping. He knows when you're awake.

Grace Boggs rubbed her eyes as she walked down the hall of the psychiatric ward of Charity Hospital, the Christmas song blaring over the PA system. It was a jarring and ironic jingle in a wing where half her patients were paranoid. All she needed was a single patient to stop and listen to the cheerful lyrics about Santa stalking and she was in for a hell of a night. She'd been working this wing for twelve years and she knew the drill. Christmas was infused here for the morale of the staff, not the patients, many of whom never seemed to notice that suddenly there was an explosion of garland and blinking lights after every Thanksgiving.

Walking into Mr. Jefferson's room, she assessed him. He was standing in front of the window with his eyes closed. He wasn't a patient who needed to be restrained, merely locked in. He had been brought in for wandering onto a playground in his bathrobe, touching the back of the heads of several small children, trying to access their brains, per his explanation. "You okay, Mr. Jefferson?"

He turned, but didn't open his eyes. "Go away."

"It's time for your medication. Can you open your eyes for me?" Despite a constant weariness after the dozen years on the job, Grace still cared about her patients somewhat. She just didn't have a lot of energy left for bullshit. It was two days before Christmas and she wanted to be at home with her vodka.

"No. If Santa thinks I'm sleeping, he'll come down the chimney. If I'm awake, he won't show and I have a thing or two I want to say to that fat fuck about what he owes me for the Christmas of '59, when he no-showed."

Running her tongue over her teeth, Grace longed again for a drink, but instead spoke in low and soothing tones to Mr. Jefferson, encouraging him to take his medication. Ten minutes later, she was back in the hallway, behind on her rounds, and pissed off to see the new hire, Maisey, sitting on her young and perky ass, blond head bent over.

"What are you doing?" she snapped, resenting Maisey's smile and pert tits. She had waltzed onto the ward only a week earlier, all bouncy breasts and backside, charming the doctors and patients alike, with an infectious laugh and a total lack of respect for personal space. She was a hugger and a thigh-toucher and Grace looked at her and saw not her own youth, but what she had never been. She'd never been particularly pretty or sexy or charming and Maisey reminded her of that fact.

"Oh, hi, Grace." Despite the fact that Grace's tone had been sharp, Maisey still looked up and smiled at her. "Look what I found in the storage closet in the empty Christmas tub! Why isn't this out? I think it would be fun." She held up a toy in her hand.

Grace's eyebrows went up. It was a skinny elf wearing a perpetual grin as annoying as Maisey's. He had on striped leggings and had the kind of figure Grace could only dream of— all long limbs and flat stomach. She knew what it was. The Elf on the Shelf, a marketing trend that had taken off in the last decade with parents who needed to outshine other parents on social media with all the creative ways they could display their family elf on the shelf. It was a bullshit made up tradition that merely gave parents one more way to lie to their children in the name of Christmas.

Not that she was cynical or anything.

"Why would we want to do that elf thing? We're already doing a Secret Santa gift exchange." Which was pointless. Every year someone gave Grace hand cream or a candle and every year she was forced to do the same for a co-worker. Just once she wanted to request her secret Santa get her vodka, but her love of the bottle was a heavily guarded secret. Secrets, secrets, everywhere.

"It's for the patients. I think they would get a kick out of it." Maisey stood up and pretended to make the elf talk. "Merry Christmas, friends! Let's sing some carols."

Grace had tried to hide her disdain of Maisey, but this time she couldn't prevent a snort from slipping out. "Are you serious? The whole point of the elf on the shelf is that he moves around while everyone is sleeping. Do you honestly think that is a good idea where half the patients are paranoid and the other half are afraid of their own shadow? There's a reason it was still in the storage closet—it's a bad idea."

"I ..." The blood drained from Maisey's face. "I just thought it would be fun."

Annoyed beyond reason, Grace snatched the toy from Maisey's hand and tossed it into a drawer behind the nurse's station where they kept their communal candy stash and Grace's Virginia Slims. "Just use a little more sense next time, honestly. Don't show that to any of the patients or I'll write you up."

She stomped away and went into Rose Litwinksi's room. Rose was only thirty-two but looked like she was twenty years older, mental illness weaving lines of worry and fear into her once smooth face. A veritable roadmap of mental illness. "Hi, Rose, how are you tonight?" Grace asked.

"The elf made me do it," Rose said, looking ashamed and embarrassed.

Now it was Grace's turn to furrow her brow. A shiver rolled up her spine. "Do what, Rose? What elf?"

But Rose looked away and smiled, a secret, sly smile. "Never mind."

Then Grace saw the dark stain at the waist of Rose's hospital gown, the blood spreading across her abdomen.

"The elf did it."

*

Maisey thought Grace was a grumpy old poop, bitter because she probably hadn't had a date since the eighties, and sex— never. The older nurse struck her as someone who needed a good pounding. Okay, so Maisey understood that the patients weren't exactly going to understand the concept behind the elf on the shelf, but if anything, they needed a little magic in their lives. They needed a voice of hope, a cheeky joke. It would bring some smiles, she was sure of it, and obviously someone else in the past had thought the same thing since the elf had been with the other Christmas decorations.

But whatever. Grumpy Grace had put the brakes on fun.

When she heard Grace yell, for a split second, she hoped the old bat had fallen, but then she felt immediately guilty. Grace wasn't that bad. Plus she was actually calling for help with a patient. So Maisey hot-footed it out of the nurse's station but the other nurse on duty, Patrick, waved her off.

"I've got it," he said. "Just finish your rounds, please."

"Okey doke." Maisey checked the board and started down the hall. She smiled at Sam, the man in his sixties who had been the janitor at the hospital for thirty years. "Hi, Sam."

"Hello, Maisey. What are your Christmas plans this year?"

Sam was the kind of guy who always smiled back, who made small talk, who asked Maisey how her day was and meant it. He was a nice person, so in short, the opposite of

Grace. Grace thought no one noticed she was sour or that she sometimes looked at her purse with a little too much longing. Maisey wasn't an idiot. She knew there was a flask in there.

It was clear Grace was a crank because she missed her boozing when she was at work.

"Oh, you know, just eating too much food." She laughed. "How about you?"

"The wife's family is coming over. I'm looking forward to ham and football games." He waved as he went on down the hallway.

When Maisey went in to Bob Davenport's room, she grabbed his chart off the door and started glancing through it. When she looked up she let out a shriek, totally caught off guard. Bob was sitting in a chair.

With the Elf on the Shelf on his lap. What the hell?

"Where did you get that?" she asked, annoyed. Was Grace messing with her? She wouldn't put it past the old bitch.

Bob just stared at her like he had no idea who she was or what she was talking about. He was young, only in his mid-twenties, so her age, but he looked like hell. He nervously tugged at his hair and he had scabs on his face from chronically picking. She immediately felt bad for snapping at him. He hadn't done anything wrong.

"Hey," she said in a more gentle tone, sinking down into a squat in front of him so they would be more at eye level. She tapped the elf on Bob's lap. "Where did you get this?"

Bob continued to stare at her, his pale blue eyes watery and vacant.

For some reason it made her so angry she stood back up, slowly. How dare he not fucking answer her when she was being so damn nice. Wasn't she sweet? Wasn't she cute? Everyone always said she was fucking cute. Why didn't Bob see that? Why couldn't he open his stupid slack mouth and answer her? She reached out and shook the elf in Bob's lap.

"Where did you get this?"

When he continued to stare at her, she felt the rage coursing through her, an actual chemical response. It invaded her limbs, shooting down into her hands so that the intensity of the anger had nowhere to go but out. Without being aware of intention, she lifted her hand and cracked it across Bob's face in a hard, loud slap.

The noise startled her and she jumped back. "Sorry. Sorry."

A single tear rolled down Bob's cheek and she felt shaky, guilty, shocked. Breathing hard, she backed up and out of the room. In the doorway, she realized she should grab the elf but she was so upset over losing control of herself she just left it. She wasn't the one who gave the toy to him. Whoever did could take it away from him. Turning on her heel, she quickly walked down the hall, heart racing. What the hell had just happened?

She went through the rest of her rounds on auto-pilot, trying to figure out how she had exploded so quickly. Her anger toward Grace was building as she felt like she was the only one who could have given Bob the elf. After thirty minutes, she went back to the nurse's station and impulsively yanked open the drawer Grace had tossed the elf into.

He was still there. Grinning up at Maisey.

She slammed the drawer shut.

*

Grace still couldn't figure out how Rose had gotten hold of a pen or how she had managed to break the skin with it. But it was exactly the kind of thing she didn't need going down on her shift. It had to have been one of the other nurses on earlier rounds. They must have dropped it. Mental patients were surprisingly cunning and no doubt Rose had scooped the pen up and used it to impale herself.

"Just when I think I can't be creeped out by anything they do, one of them manages to prove me wrong," Patrick said to her back at the nurse's station. "What the hell was that? Do you know how tenacious you have to be to stab at yourself with a friggin' ballpoint pen?" He shook his head. Patrick was tall, broad shouldered, sporting a woodsman beard.

Grace liked him well enough but she wouldn't cry if he took a new job. Her feelings about Patrick were ambivalent. But he did his job well and generally without complaint. She got along better with men than she did with women, always had. They saw her as a broad, a peer, not as a sexual interest, so there was no posturing, no bragging, no flirting. She wondered what Patrick would do if she told him she wanted to take him into the staff restroom and blow him. The thought amused her. She didn't, of course. She just thought it would be funny as hell to shock him. That would creep him out even more than Rose's little pen trick.

"There is no true normal here," she told Patrick. "But if you think about it, everything here is really routine, mundane. So when one of the patients goes beyond the usual ranting and babbling and accusations, it's unnerving. Just don't let it bother you. She'll heal. It wasn't a deep wound." It had just been fleshy. Rose had really hacked the hell out of herself.

"So what do we tell the doctor? I don't want my ass chewed, and I know I wasn't in there earlier today. Neither were you, right?"

"Only Maisey was in there on this shift," she said, with no small amount of triumph. "And then whoever was on for first shift. There is no telling." She eyed Patrick. "So I suggest we don't tell. Rose could have just as easily done that with her fingernail."

Patrick eyed her with disbelief. "I seriously doubt that. We can't just lie about it. No one is going to buy that."

"Then you're basically throwing Maisey under the bus."

"She'll just get reprimanded," he said, suddenly sounding doubtful. "Not fired."

"She's been here a week. Of course she'll get fired." Grace watched him out of the corner of her eye. He was wavering. He felt the urge to protect Maisey, clearly. So predictable. He would jeopardize his own job to protect a piece of pussy he'd never get to touch.

Fine by her. She thought it was stupid, but he was entitled to be stupid. She had no intention of lying about the incident. She had just been curious what his response would be and now she knew. He was an idiot.

"I don't know. I just don't think we should lie... it seems unethical."

"So don't." Grace reached over to the drawer beneath the desk and pulled it open to grab her cigarettes. The elf that should have been there, wasn't.

Damn it.

She slammed the drawer back shut and went outside to smoke, grabbing her winter coat with the flask in the front pocket. Just a little nip to get through the rest of her shift. Nothing more, nothing less.

He knows if you've been bad or good, so be good for goodness sake.

Grace shoved at the emergency exit doors. How the hell was that song on again? It was a playlist of what seemed like only four songs that repeated constantly and it was annoying. Outside snow was soundlessly drifting down in wet flakes and Maisey was crying behind the dumpster.

Grace sighed and knew she was going to have to give up her smoke break.

She immediately turned and went back inside before Maisey saw her and wanted to be comforted for who the hell knew what. Grace didn't do comforting.

Back in, she was barely two steps forward when the lights cut out. Patients started screaming. Grace's foot gave way, sliding through a wet spot, and she scrambled to maintain balance so she didn't fall.

The generator kicked in and the lights went back on.

What she saw made her wish they were back out.

Blood. All over the floor. A heavy trail of it, fresh, still wet and bright crimson, heading all the way down the hall. As if someone had been dragged the length of it while bleeding.

The door slammed shut behind her and she whirled around to see Maisey standing there, her face pale, cheeks damp with tears, snowflakes in her hair and dusting her shoulders. "What is that?" she gasped. "Oh, my God."

"It's blood. Help me figure out where it's coming from."

Without warning, Maisey glared at her. "Fuck you, no. I'm not doing it." She brushed past Grace and stomped off down the hall, rushing into the staff restroom.

What the hell was that? Totally unexpected and another time the behavior would have been distracting, but Grace barely spared a glance in Maisey's direction because this was a lot of blood. Enough blood that someone could be bleeding out and she could be getting fired. Grace wasn't going to let either happen.

Not on her shift.

*

Maisey stared at herself in the mirror, afraid she was hyperventilating. Her eyes looked wild, her skin tone splotchy and embarrassing. She still couldn't believe she had hit Bob and she had screamed at Grace. What was happening to her? It wasn't supposed to be like this.

Everyone thought she was just a pretty girl, but they didn't know her. She had secrets. Everyone had *secrets*. Even Santa had secrets, that judgmental old prick. Like he hadn't had an inappropriate thought or two about the elves? And that red nose had to be from years' worth of hard drinking. No one got a red nose from being jolly. Excessive smiling just created crow's feet.

The random thoughts whirled around in her head and Maisey felt scattered and crazy and alien. It was like she had been hijacked by someone else and they were controlling her thoughts and actions. She splashed water on her face and shook her head, like she could rattle out the weird thoughts, but they still teased at the edges of her consciousness, creepy visuals of Santa and Mrs. Claus, and a view of her own hands reaching out and choking the life out of Bob while he sat there slackly and took it, never fighting, like a total idiot...

Maisey let out a cry and grabbed her head. "No. Stop it. Just stop it." She didn't think like that. She didn't have insidious evil little dirty thoughts that were insulting, cruel, deviant. She didn't.

Yet she was.

Yanking open the restroom door, she decided she needed to go home. Something was wrong. She wondered if she were having an aneurysm or something. Could that do this to her? Make her feel violent and gross?

In the hallway she saw the blood again and her stomach turned. For a split second she thought she was going to vomit but she swallowed convulsively and managed to keep her bile down. Grace and Patrick were at the end of the hall, heads together, murmuring. Patrick was gesticulating wildly. Moving cautiously, so she didn't step in the blood, Maisey made her way to them.

"What's going on?" she whispered, feeling like she couldn't say anything in a normal voice. The hall was quiet, the Christmas lights that had been hung on the nurses' station blinking madly. The carols blaring over the speakers sounded tinny and harsh, forced cheer, a manic response to Christmas. The patients were quiet, drugged down for the night. Somewhere in the distance she heard a door open and she turned, scared, but saw nothing.

"I have no idea," Patrick said. "Look, this blood just stops here, right outside Bob's door, but he's fine. I've checked on him three times because I can't figure it out."

Maisey shivered. Why did it have to be Bob's room? She still felt guilty over hitting him. It had been such an unnatural reaction and she hadn't been able to control it. Not one bit.

"I'll go check on Rose. Maybe she got herself again," Grace said, shaking her head, her mouth pinched.

"What happened to Rose?" Maisey asked Patrick as Grace walked away. She rubbed her hands over her arms, unnerved. The ward had never felt eerie to her, but now it did. Ominous. The air wasn't moving and the piped in music seemed to grow louder and louder. There was a song about a happy elf playing now.

"She cut herself with a pen."

"Oh." Maisey looked at the smears on the ground, turning a rust color now as they dried. The abrupt ending at Bob's door made a shiver roll up her spine. "I'm going to see Bob." She needed to apologize.

"Maybe we should call someone," Patrick said, chewing his fingernail.

"Like who? The cops?" she said doubtfully. "What would we say?"

"I don't know."

He followed her to Bob's room, across the hall. "Maybe you shouldn't go in there, Maisey." He grabbed her arm.

She glared at him, yanking herself out of his grip. He couldn't touch her. She'd never fucking said he could touch her. "Get off of me."

Patrick blanched. "Fine. Do what you want."

She would. She pushed past him and went into Bob's room, distraught, hands trembling. There was a pounding behind her eyes and she wished she'd never taken this damn job. She was better than this. She deserved something better. Less... mental.

Bob was still in his chair. His eyes were fearful when he saw her come in, and oddly, it was a relief. Having him afraid of her was better than that terrible blankness he usually displayed. The lights were on, but nobody was home. That was Bob the majority of the time.

"Hi, Bob," she said softly. "I'm sorry for before. I don't know what got into me but it was totally uncalled for."

He stared. But then he turned, slowly, and looked to the right, before turning back, his eyes beseeching. He looked truly terrified. Maisey followed the direction he had briefly looked in and what she saw made her frown.

"Where did that come from?" she murmured.

It was the elf. Sitting on the edge of Bob's bed. Grinning away at her.

She leaned over, very, very close to Bob and searched his expression. "Did he do it?" she whispered, leaning her head just imperceptibly towards the elf. It was a crazy question. She knew it was.

But Bob's head went up and down, very slowly, before his hand reached out and he laced his fingers through hers, like he needed comfort.

"It's okay." She gripped his hand back. "I'll get rid of him."

"Or he'll get rid of you."

Goosebumps rose on Maisey's skin. Bob didn't speak. Bob never spoke. Yet his shaky voice whispered to warn her. His hand gripped hers so hard it was painful.

And she could have sworn she heard the elf laugh.

Grace paged Sam to clean up the blood. She wasn't going to touch it and it required appropriate pathogen removal. But to go along with the rest of her lousy day, he didn't immediately appear and she wondered what he was up to. Things were off kilter with Christmas Eve the next day. They were understaffed and for the love of all that was holy, if someone didn't turn off that damn music she was going to lose it. Lose it all over the bottle of vodka she craved like a hungry baby did a nipple.

"This is just BS," she muttered to herself, starting to feel like this had all gotten away from her.

Maisey came out of a patient's room holding the elf on the shelf straight out in front of her, like it had been pissed on. She brought it to the nurse's station and dropped it into the trash.

"What are you doing?" Grace asked her.

Maisey just shrugged. "I'm getting rid of it."

Grace was amused. So Miss Perky had lost a bit of her holiday cheer.

But then Patrick started yelling and she and Maisey went running. What they found made Grace's stomach sink. "Holy Jesus..."

It was Sam. He was in the storage closet right next to the back door. He was dead, eyes wide open. His chest had been torn open and there was blood all down his abdomen, his pants stained red. It was a shocking and brutal death and Grace backed up, afraid she was going to vomit. Maisey started screaming, a high-pitched hysterical shriek that harmonized with the holiday music still raging over their heads and it all collided into Grace's head, paralyzing her.

She breathed hard, in and out, grappling for the door to close it shut behind them, blocking them all from the terrible view of Sam.

Maisey turned to her and held out her hands, her eyes glassy and filled with shock.

"What–

A knife dropped from Maisey's hands, clanking down onto the linoleum floor, its blade stained. "I found it in my pocket," Maisey said. "I don't know how... I didn't do anything... oh, God." She turned and threw up all over the wall, hunching over, not even pulling her hair back.

Grace watched, horrified. Disgusted. This was wrong. All fucking wrong.

Maisey stood up and grappled at the doorframe, trying to hold herself up. Her face was tear-stained, makeup running, vomit splattered all over her uniform.

Not so pretty now, was she?

*

After the police left, and extra staff had been called in, and all hell had broken loose and settled back down again, Grace sat outside by the dumpster, ass on the curb of the driveway. She took a long swig off of her flask and passed it over. Following it with a long drag on her cigarette, she blew the smoke out as she spoke.

"You went too far, you know. There was no reason to kill Sam. I just wanted the blonde fired."

She didn't expect a response and she didn't get one.

"He was a nice man. A good man. The best." She was already buzzed. Her stomach was tight and before long she'd probably be tossing the vodka back up but she couldn't stop herself. There were tears in her eyes, blurring her vision. It was freezing outside and she wasn't wearing a coat, but the wind cutting through her felt fitting, appropriate. She needed to be jarred.

"You've got to promise me, you won't do anything like that again. Do you understand?" She reached back to retrieve her flask, ashing her cigarette into the slushy snow.

The elf winked at her.

Grace stood up on shaky legs, and once back inside, put him prominently on the countertop of the nurse's station.

"I love the Elf on the Shelf!" the cheerful temp nurse said, poking him in the gut like he was the doughboy. "OMG, I had one of these when I was a kid."

It was the last thing she wanted to deal with tonight. Her shift was over. She was going home to spend her Christmas Eve alone with takeout and her Smirnoff. But she didn't want to return to work and have to deal with Perky, part two.

She met the gaze of the elf. "I changed my mind."

"What?" the new nurse asked in confusion.

"Oh, nothing. I was just talking to myself." Grace smiled and grabbed her purse.

She whistled along to the Christmas music as she left.

He knows if you've been bad or good...

A FAMILY CHRISTMAS TERROR

"Oh, yuck!" Nancy said. "Didn't Aunt Jeannie buy Francie an Elf on the Shelf? I'll never get my kids one now. If I ever have any, that is. Ick!"

"I thought it was cool," Nick said. "Aaaand... "He waved his finger around his sister's nose.

She slapped his hand away. "Aaaand, what? Aaaand you're a dork." She poked him in the gut.

"Hey, that's not nice," Nick said, belching and rubbing his stomach.

"God, you're disgusting," Nancy said, turning away.

"Anyway... aaaand... I got rid of my hiccups. Which means now I get to read." He grabbed the book from Jack. "I don't know what it is about this book, but I can't wait to read the next story." He flipped to the next story. "Then again, maybe it's all the coffee I've had."

"Or the brandy," Jack added.

"Actually... I kind of feel like that too—as much as I don't want to agree with him. About the stories, I mean," Nancy said.

Judy made busy cleaning up some doughnut crumbs. Grandpa looked pensive.

Dan said, "Go ahead, read the next one. What's it called?"

"Oh! We know this one," Nick said. "*'Twas the Night Before...*"

"I have a feeling it's not the poem we know," Judy said. "But go ahead."

'TWAS THE NIGHT BEFORE...

RICHARD DEVIN

There was a tale of Old St. Nick.
A tale of doom, with a hypnotic trick.

The tale was too true for holiday cheer.
So tales were told for those who fear.

That tale was told and told again.
It was told so much that a legend set in.

A legend of holly and holiday cheer.
A legend of sleighs and tiny reindeer.

A legend of gifts and good girls and boys.
A legend of workshops and elfin-made toys.

A legend to deceive and mask away fears.
A legend now told down through the years.

A legend of Santa so gentle, so jolly.
A legend of good tidings, filled with such folly.

A legend unlike the fable of truth.
Where vampires fangs and blood are the proof.

So good tidings to tales of jolly old Nick,
Know the beginnings to the devil's old trick.

'Twas the night before Christmas and all that you know
Is not as it seems and never was so.

And Saint Nick is not the saint that you seek.
For he is not jolly nor ever so meek.

If he finds you, awake, not asleep.
'Tis blood, a child or soul's what he'll keep.

If an elfin ending is what you desire,
Then this St. Nick is sure to inspire.

A wonderland of toys and musty old tales,
Will serve for all time, for Nick never fails.

Legend – a tale told when the truth is too
unbelievable.

'Twas the night before Christmas, when all through the house
Not a creature was stirring, not even a mouse.
The stockings were hung by the chimney with care,
In hopes that St Nicholas soon would be there.

Steam spewed with a nearly deafening whistle from the old, rusted, heavy machinery as it drove the piston— hissing, lifting the hammer, releasing in a cloud, and smashing the hammer down onto a metal plate. Then with a great rumble, the cycle began again.

The workshop was filled with a cacophony of thuds, clangs, whistles, and bangs. Smoke filled sunlight streamed through small rectangular windows frosted over by the never-ending, frigid arctic air held at bay beyond the walls.

Scampering about the workshop, rushing from one of the massive machines to another, in a curious choreography of near collisions, squat elfin creatures scurried, hauling, pulling, plying, and maneuvering the toys that popped from the ancient machinery. They handed off the toys down a line of bearded, grease-covered elves in a game of "new toy" hot potato until they reached the decorating tables. There, the metal and wooden toys were painted, then glossed and trimmed and bejeweled, by younger elfin boys and girls.

Laboring elves pulled trolleys laden with newly made toys, down tracks in the flooring. When they reached the ramp leading to the loading dock, they clambered behind the trolley, pushing on it with short stubby legs that strained under the effort.

Trolleys and carts were haphazardly parked with their burdens of toys by the receiving dock, where slightly larger elves hauled the toys up to the dock and stuffed them into animal-skin bags trimmed with the fur of the once living creature.

Then, filled to near bursting, the bags were loaded into the back of a black sleigh that lacked any shine or ornate decoration. Worn, chipped, and dented, the sleigh faced two great metal doors. Scenes of high walled castles were depicted on thick, mammoth tapestries that hung from the top of the doors, and despite having been closed and latched with a rusted iron rod the size of a telephone pole, snow and wind managed to creep in at the corners where the doors met, leaving slight mounds of ice-crusted snow on the workshop floor.

> *The children were nestled all snug in their beds,*
> *While visions of sugar-plums danced in their heads.*
> *And mamma in her 'kerchief, and I in my cap,*
> *Had just settled our brains for a long winter's nap.*

Snow blanketed the fields and woods surrounding the sagging, ramshackle cottage that we called home. A fire burned and crackled in a corner of the only room. From a distance, the cottage and nearby barn—that was in only slightly better condition—looked charming dusted with snow. Smoke rose in a twisted column from the stone chimney, and tree-trunk fence rails bore a burden of windswept snow. It was a winter wonderland to the mind's eye. And hell to us who were its inhabitants.

The past growing season had not been fruitful. The less-than-normal rains meant fewer than normal crops. Most, we harvested and stored for the winter, keeping the two cows and donkey fairly well fed, but they were by no means fat. For me, Milan, my dad, Mickel, and my mother, Jenia, there was little food to spare. As winter had settled in, my parents rationed what we had in storage, making it last as long as possible by mixing it in soups and stews with the rarely snared bird or rabbit.

We made the cabin look the season as best we could. My dad and I felled a small, unshapely evergreen tree, and along with my mother, decorated it with bits of straw, an old bird's nest, and red berries found in the nearby woods. Then we set the tree upon a rickety table, placing both the table and tree near the fire nook, with a silent prayer that neither would go up in flames.

The tree was there, decorated and beckoning, but morning's break would find no gifts under this tree— despite tonight being the ending of the eve of Christmas.

> *When out on the lawn there arose such a clatter,*
> *I sprang from the bed to see what was the matter.*
> *Away to the window I flew like a flash,*
> *Tore open the shutters and threw up the sash.*

All were asleep. I stayed awake to tend the fire so that Christmas morning wouldn't find us all frostbitten and shivering. I stoked the fire with one log, not wanting to use up the dried kindling too quickly and force me to the outside and the windy, cold night.

A baying from the barn outside caught my attention and drew me to the window. I glanced toward the barn and fields, where not a creature stirred. Then a shadow in the night sky drew my eyes upward. There, the darkness of the sky nearly consumed the black, sleek sleigh that careened through the star-filled abyss, driven forward by creatures colored even blacker than the night. Had I not seen it with my own eyes, I would have mistaken the sleigh that flew with such soundless speed for a moon shadow.

> *The moon on the breast of the new-fallen snow*
> *Gave the luster of mid-day to objects below.*
> *When, what to my wondering eyes should appear,*
> *But a miniature sleigh, and eight tiny reindeer.*

As the sleigh descended from the ebon sky into the moonlight, the driver and creatures leading it became clear, and the horrors of what they were became evident. They were eight-in-hand, yet not one was a horse or mule or ox, but a combination of all. They had horns that grew straight back from mule-like heads, curving down at the shoulders, with cloven hooves on long thin legs, backs that were strong and full at the loins, and a tail that looked like that of a rat's.

The creatures brayed as the crack of a whip sliced into their backs. They bucked in the air, tossing their heads, horns clashing, with the sound echoing into the night.

> *With a little old driver, so lively and quick,*
> *I knew in a moment it must be St. Nick.*
> *More rapid than eagles his coursers they came,*
> *And he whistled, and shouted, and called them by name!*

The driver, dressed in black fur with a cloak that undulated behind him, snapped the whip once again and called in a voice filled with malevolence to each of the

187

creatures pulling the sleigh. A guttural sound that no man could make or understand, he growled what to my ears I thought might be their names. As each creature was called, it responded with a snort.

> *"Now Dasher! Now, Dancer! Now, Prancer and Vixen!*
> *On, Comet! On, Cupid! On, Donner and Blitzen!*
> *To the top of the porch! To the top of the wall!*
> *Now dash away! Dash away! Dash away all!"*

Then with the whip twice as long as three men, the driver stood, pulled his arm back, and cracked the leather lead onto the backs of the creatures. They grunted and brayed like no animals on earth. A horrendous sound of terror descended upon my ears and heralded their arrival. Then a cackling and hiss from the driver could be heard above the creatures' cries. The sound sent an uncontrollable shiver throughout my body.

> *As dry leaves that before the wild hurricane fly,*
> *When they meet with an obstacle, mount to the sky.*
> *So up to the house-top the coursers they flew,*
> *With the sleigh full of toys, and St Nicholas too.*

The driver directed the creatures by pulling on a harness of leather embedded with nails, creating deep scratches in their darkened hides, where a black liquid oozed out. Scars blighted their sides and flanks, where harness and whip had met the creatures' bodies many times before.

And then, in a twinkling, I heard on the roof
The prancing and pawing of each little hoof.
As I drew in my head, and was turning around,
Down the chimney St Nicholas came with a bound.

The sleigh turned and dropped, heading straight for the cottage. It was out of sight for only a few seconds when I heard it light upon the roof. Snow, dust, and soot fell from the old broken beams supporting the roof, filling the interior with a curtain of particles. I quickly covered my mouth and nose with the sleeve of my shirt.

He was dressed all in fur, from his head to his foot,
And his clothes were all tarnished with ashes and soot.
A bundle of toys he had flung on his back,
And he looked like a peddler, just opening his pack.

Out of the dust and from the fire, a figure appeared. He was covered in soot and ash and it cascaded around him, falling from the black fur collar and cuffs of his cloak. The fire instantly flashed, nearly igniting the table and tree. Even though only one log lay in the hearth, flames burst forth as though it had been stoked full.

His eyes-how they twinkled! His dimples how merry!
His cheeks were like roses, his nose like a cherry!
His droll little mouth was drawn up like a bow,
And the beard of his chin was as white as the snow.

He hesitated, then caught sight of me crouched on my bed in the corner of the room. In the loft above, my mother and father slept soundly, unaware of the intruder. I pulled the blanket up closer to my shoulders, hoping it would help to hide me. His eyes gleamed a reddish glare and he scowled in my direction. His face was black with soot and a dark beard hung from his chin. He remained where he was, and his eyes also remained staring directly into my soul. After a moment, a slow smile spread across his face.

> The stump of a pipe he held tight in his teeth,
> And the smoke it encircled his head like a wreath.
> He had a broad face and a little round belly,
> That shook when he laughed, like a bowlful of jelly!

At first, I thought I could make out a pipe hanging from the corner of his snarled smile, but as he moved into the dim light cast by the moon coming through the window, it became apparent that it was not a pipe at all, but a long, twisted tooth that hung like the fang of an old hog. Then, while I watched with dread, a second tooth in the other corner of his mouth extended and snaked its way down till it met the length of the other. He cackled and stepped closer. As he did so, the flames in the hearth faded and the room grew suddenly cold.

> He was chubby and plump, a right jolly old elf,
> And I laughed when I saw him, in spite of myself!
> A wink of his eye and a twist of his head,
> Soon gave me to know I had nothing to dread.

The black fur collar and cuffs, along with the wide cloak that wrapped around him, gave him the appearance of some girth, and he stood taller than most men. As he closed the few feet between us, I could make out more of him: hands that were skeletal and a face that betrayed his many, many years. His skin was near gray and patches of it were bruised and rotting. I wanted to look away, but dared not. He took another step.

> He spoke not a word, but went straight to his work,
> And filled all the stockings, then turned with a jerk.
> And laying his finger aside of his nose,
> And giving a nod, up the chimney he rose!

He moved slowly, nearly gliding over the warped and worn floorboards. Not a sound did he make as he stepped closer and closer to me. I sat with the blanket pulled up tightly as possible, with my back flat against the wall in the corner of the room, where the small bench that served as my bed at night and for storage during the day had always been. I could not move.

Then he sprang. His body reached mine in the blink of an eye, and should I have blinked, I would have missed seeing him move at all. Suddenly, he was over me, leering at me. I was paralyzed in fear. I tried to yell for my father, but my dry throat would only choke out a strained whisper.

He cackled at me, then let a long hiss slip between the blackened fangs and his lips. He slowly moved down toward me, lowering himself as if he were a puppet on a string. I could feel the bristles of his fur cuffs as his hands reached for my head. They brushed my cheek, and if the circumstances had been any different, they would have tickled, but now they caused a deep chill to rush down my spine. He leaned in, pushed my head to the side, revealing the throbbing vein in the side of my neck. I tried to resist; I could not. As if possessed, I allow my head to tilt without resistance, exposing my neck to him. I could feel the hot breath on my neck, then the scratch of fangs on my exposed skin, tearing slowly across my jugular. And then they pierced. Scalding pain seared through me, and yet I did not move. I was in his trance, before falling into a nightmarish slumber.

> He sprang to his sleigh, to his team gave a whistle,
> And away they all flew like the down of a thistle.
> But I heard him exclaim, 'ere he drove out of sight,
> "Happy Christmas to all, and to all a good-night!"

I awoke, confused, panting, my lungs hungry for air. Darkness enfolded me. I tried to raise my hands but hit rough canvas. Reality began to settle in, and an image filled my mind's eye. I was inside the large cloth sack the monster had brought with him. I could now hear the wind and felt the occasional bump as the sleigh rose into the night. Then, just before I went unconscious again, I heard the unmistakable sound of his cackle.

I was not alone when I woke. There were others: another boy of twelve or thirteen, a girl nearly an adult. We had been piled in a corner of a room that was clearly a tinker's workshop. Machinery stood silent, and sawdust littered the floor, capturing little footprints from those who had worked the machines. It was dark and quiet and smelled of wood and grease and sweat. A calendar on a distant wall hung crookedly from a nail. Red marks were drawn through each of the days: day number 1 marked, day number 2 marked. And so were all the remaining days up to the 24th, the last day marked. The 25th remained unmarked. Christmas.

A small, thick wooden door opened near where the calendar hung. A figure appeared in the doorway and beckoned to us. "Come."

The girl stood and started moving first. The other boy and I followed.

As we drew nearer to the figure, I could see that he wasn't a man, but a boy. Not much older than I was. He looked into my eyes as I passed through the doorway and he whispered to me, "The story was wrong. He does not bring gifts... He takes them."

A FAMILY CHRISTMAS TERROR

"Wow," Nick said after he'd finished the story. "You don't think Santa could really be—"

"You still believe in Santa Claus, Nicky?" Jack ribbed.

"Not the real one, moron... but this one... I mean, hey, there are unexplainable things out there in the universe." Nick turned to his twin. "Look at us. We're twins. Same DNA. But I'm a boy, you're a girl. I'm good-looking, you're—"

Nancy punched him in the gut this time. "Don't even. I'll have you know—"

"Knock it off!" Dan stood up. "I'm getting —"

Judy jumped in, "I think that might be enough with these stories. Christmas is supposed to be a merry time."

Nick raised his mug. "Aw, Mom, I'm merry. Aren't you merry, Nancy? Jack?" He continued before they could answer. "Dad, Grandpa? Aren't you merry?" Again, he barreled on before anyone could answer. "See, Mom? We're all merry!"

Judy started, "I don't know... There's dinner..."

"I'll read the next one too. It's kinda long. One more." He was almost manic. "Hey! How about some eggnog, Mom? Yours is the best—with your special ingredient." He waggled his eyebrows. Badly.

"You know he means the spiced rum," Nancy muttered to Jack.

"Duh," was Jack's response.

Nancy looked up at him, shook her head, and went back to her phone.

Grandpa to the rescue. "You know, Judy, the boy's got a point. Your eggnog is the best I've ever had. And I consider myself a connoisseur."

Judy smiled hopefully. "Everyone want some?"

The five nodded eagerly. "Yep."

"Definitely."

"Yum."

"A tall one."

"All right. Start reading, Nick, but speak up so I can hear you in the kitchen.

"You got it, Mom. Ahem. *The Twelve Frays of Christmas...*"

THE TWELVE FRAYS OF CHRISTMAS

LEE LAWLESS

> *"And so now we have the promise of a New York that no longer festoons its capitalist mythologies with promises of social mobility, but rather a place where rich people can sell things to each other, and sometimes to slightly less rich people, without having to worry about too much else at all."*-Brendan O'Connor
>
> *"Nowadays people know the price of everything and the value of nothing." -Oscar Wilde*

New York City—December 13th
The First Day of Christmas.

As she leaned forward toward me, I wasn't sure if Clara smelled overwhelmingly like peppermint because I'd been skulling cocoa spiked with peppermint schnapps all morning, or if it was due to the foot-long peppermint pole she'd just been fellating on the mainstage. It was part of her act —"Mrs. Claws"—a Yuletide dominatrix thing where she stripped off a matronly dress and white wig to reveal a bandolier of candy canes, including the lucky long one that she'd so sweetly swallowed before disgorging it and tossing it to some weirdo in the crowd. She also had a whip made of tinsel, some strategically-placed snowflakes, and a strappy red leather outfit that wouldn't have kept her warm for two seconds if we were at the actual North Pole.

But we weren't at the North Pole, we were at the Pussycat Palace strip club, and she wasn't Mrs. Claus or even Claws and I wasn't really Santa, although my immaculately-fluffy red suit, droll little mouth, and snow-white beard are paid professionally to make people think otherwise this time of year. Namely, six days a week at Percy's department store in midtown, the plushest gig in town. I've been at it for thirteen years, and I rake in more loot than the real Santa would theoretically give out. I could be going to way better strip joints than the Pussycat Palace, but Clara's here, and on my watch, I don't want her dancing for any of these horny little elves.

A few of them were glaring over their expensive Times-Square-priced beers, trying to give me mean looks for hogging her time. Fuck them. This was *my* lap dance... or three, and none of them had the balls to start something with Santa. Anyway, Clara-Claws was by far the hottest one at the Pussycat Palace, and I was there enough times in my civvies for the elves to know to keep their dirty dollars away from those particular Christmas cookies while King Kringle—or even just regular old Sam - was in the house.

Clara shook her voluptuous South American ass, her G-string's single jingle-bell ringing merrily up at me as she twerked, and I tipped my Santa hat to the horny elves while flashing my famous dimples (of the poetic "how merry" fame.) The horny elves, mostly finance bros and midtown office drones, scowled. Fuck them, it's my lunch break. I'm off. Clara was mine, for now. Who cared I was still in uniform, I wasn't giving them any presents. Maybe I'd throw them the red and green Mardi Gras-style beads Clara-Claws had draped around my neck before the lap dance—the sole element that put me out of standard uniform.

I've even got the little round belly. I came by it honestly. I earned it. I sipped my beer.

Peppermint-infused Clara shook her snowflake-tasseled titties at me, making me want to suffocate to death in this greatest avalanche ever. Some of her red body glitter fell into the fur of my suit. Between that and the peppermint scent, I knew she'd be on my mind (and my Santa costume) for the rest of the day.

Fuck. The rest of the day. I had to get back to Percy's.

"Baby, I gotta roll," I muttered as the song—Elvis's version of "Blue Christmas"—came to a close. "Come by later."

"*Possible*," she smiled.

"I know that's your native word for 'yes'."

"*Possible*." She kissed me quickly, close-mouthed but deep-lipped enough to make my senses shut off for a second. When I came to, the lingering peppermint flavor hinted that it was time to retry reality. My ridiculous, day-drunk, midtown-mayhem version of it, anyway.

I watched Clara scurry backstage to reset her candy bandolier and "Mrs. Claws" outfit. I wished I could stay and watch her hit the pole again—both the stripper pole and that peppermint pornography.

My beautiful Bolivian bird. My partridge in a bare tree.

I paid my tab and sidled to the door, enjoying the darkened enclave of the room for a few seconds more. The majority of the ambient light was either from the stage strobes reflecting off of Christmas balls dangling haphazardly from the ceiling, or from the strands of multi-colored Christmas lights that purfled it. Both were left up year-round, regardless.

The door to the outside world opened a split second before I intended it to, making me freeze and readjust my eyes to daylight a moment too early. Two gangly frames entered enthusiastically. As my eyes refocused, I saw that it was two sailors, both of whom appeared young enough to still believe in me. Well, the fake me, what I represented. Even I didn't believe in the real me.

"Hos, hos, hos!" one of them chortled, raising a high-five, appreciating my absurd appearance here.

I smiled a smile that's a good deal wearier than the one I use professionally. It kills me to see kids like this out on deployments, cruises, whatever, during the holidays. I myself had had a few memorably unpleasant holiday seasons halfway around the world, way back in the day. But even if they weren't nestled all snug in their beds back at home, with ma in her kerchief and pa in his cap, at least they were here, a mere subway ride from a miracle on 34th street, instead of some Christ-forsaken jungle or desert or whatever current place where tinsel is an infidel abomination.

I returned the high-five, patted the other sailor on the shoulder, and tried to give my eyes the trademark twinkle as I made my exit.

"Be good, for goodness' sake."

*

Freight entrances make you feel like just another piece of cargo, which was almost certainly the reason why Percy's made me come into work that way. Even though I was their star this time of year, it was clear that was no reason for me to be thinking I was any more important than the shoes, shirts, handbags, coats, pants, dresses, and accessories that comprised the five floors of their year-round business.

I'd hauled balls across midtown in no time flat—people tend to make room for Santa, and my black "costume" boots were almost the same sort of standard-issue ones I wore back when I was tear-gassing through 'Nam—and made it up the freight elevator and through the "backstage" of the first floor with a full five minutes to compose myself behind the ornate cardboard gingerbread house that served as backdrop to my throne.

You're goddamn right I had a throne. Being a sixty-something, authentic-down-to-the-facial-hair Santa Claus buys you some executive privileges.

By design, I hadn't exposed myself to the floor of the store, but a quick peek through a trapdoor in my flat cardboard-gingerbread mansion showed a line of fidgety children and phone-finagling parents snaking through the store. The crowd was primed for show time. *You better watch out.*

Stretch, the obvious nickname of the dwarf who played my chief elf, had a small candy-cane clenched between his teeth like a cigarette. He was unloading a bag half the size of his body into a huge bowl held by a swiveling snowman, intended to be carted out for the impending merry mendicants.

"Help me out with this shit, Sam, they made me drag four of these fuckers up here today."

"What's the matter, Stretch?" I chuckled as I hoisted the economy-sized bag. "Come on, aren't these fun-sized? Like you?" I tilted the bag so that a flurry of individually-wrapped candy canes cascaded into Frosty's bowl.

"Fuck you, and fuck fun-sized," Stretch wheezed, readjusting a pointy latex ear.

"Fuck fun-sized?! Oh Stretch, what'd I miss?"

Stretch glowered. For a little guy, he sure could project a lot of anger. I sat down on a spare faux-snowbank and looked at him seriously.

"Management was lurking back here earlier, Sam, just before you left. Carnahan said something about there being no 'festive feeling,' whatever the hell that means. She was showing around some tub of shit who looked like he's been rotting in either middle management or McDonald's for the last forever. Had the Short Eyes, too, I swear he was scoping out the kids. Even creepier than that frosty execu-bitch Carnahan."

I rolled my eyes at the thought of my malevolent manager Candy Carnahan and her awful offspring Carson, both of them heirs to the Percy's fortune, but forced by family tradition to work for it. Candy's personality was the antithesis of her name, and Carson was the kind of guy who ate other employees' sandwiches in the break room despite (or because of) his family owning the empire. I knew he'd been transferred from the working on official business— something about stalking one of the makeup-counter girls via his access to employee records— but hoped he wasn't about to be plunked down as some sort of Santa supervisor.

I handled my faux-North Pole empire just fine all by myself. Well, with Stretch as my co-pilot.

I took a final, pepperminty hit of Rumple Minze 100-proof schnapps from my flask, then offered it to Stretch. He took it in both hands and tilted back with half his body.

"I wouldn't worry. You're never gonna get fired, Stretchy. Not only can they never find someone to compete with your talent, but it's always tough getting a replacement on... short notice."

"Ha, ha," Stretch muttered, wiping his lips. "You're gonna get a fun-sized fist in your face if you keep up with that shit."

"You seriously don't like that term?" I asked, standing and lightly brushing off the more overt clusters of Clara's red body glitter from my fur coat.

"Fuck yes," Stretch said. "And not just because I'm a horizontally-challenged person. 'Fun-sized' pisses me off. Don't tell me what size my fun comes in. And definitely don't tell me that size is SMALL."

"Fair enough," I said. "By the way, if Carnahan comes back, you tell her to sit back and watch as the festive feelings flow over me. She's delusional if she doesn't understand the magic."

Stretch shook his head and crunched off the end of his candy cane. "You're drunk, dude. And she is DEFINITELY gunning for some kind of change. Watch your jolly old ass, out there."

I assumed my most robust posture and gave a dry, sub-vocal pantomime of a hearty Santa laugh. Tipping open the small hatchway that led out to the Santa stage, I tousled Stretch's hair and dropped the red and green strands of Mardi Gras-style stripper beads around his neck.

"Frankly, my dear," I intoned, "I don't give a fun-sized fuck."

*

Someone once said that if we revealed all of our sins to each other, we'd laugh for the lack of originality. Children's Christmas wishes tend to move along the same lines. Video games, ponies, mom and dad to get back together, it's really all the same rehashed themes. I shouldn't feel bad about not really caring. Like many of life's greatest relationships, it's not like there's anything I can do to change things for these kids or their families, but being there to listen to them makes them happy, and maybe believe wishes coming true are possible. They feel like they got their day in karmic court. There's your festive-feeling magic right there, at least for the kids. That idea that hope, big hope, HOLIDAY hope, coupled with morally-relative good deeds, can transcend things. Hell, hope of that caliber doesn't come along every day. That's why we contrived this whole crazy season for it.

Weirder still, I actually used to believe it worked. I mean, I knew it was fake, but *trying* invites tremendous capacities for suspending disbelief.

I guess I just wasn't faking it as well as I thought anymore. I wasn't suspending any disbelief at all. Carnahan—Candy Carnahan, Executive Manager, stalked up to the stage twenty minutes before close, along with some flabby shape of a thing that appeared to be a melted human man with a cheap suit coagulated onto him. Fucking Carson. Stretch had been right, the landfill did give off a distinctly creepy vibe, and not just because he apparently treated himself like a landfill. Neither the walking trash-stash nor mother Carnahan looked or felt festive, or for that matter, happy. At all, possibly ever.

Disbelief was not being suspended any longer. It was quite clearly on the table, clear as Scrooge's Christmas goose, but with fewer intimations of a happy ending.

"Mr. MacSorley," Candy Carnahan clipped, in a tone more severe than her bob-haircut and angular pantsuit,

"Please explain to me why you've been imbibing spirits before interacting with our guests?"

A sheaf of security-cam photographs clutched in her bony, multiple-Tiffany-ringed hand clearly implicated me. Goddamn. They'd upped their camera game since last season.

"Holiday spirits, ma'am," was the only thing I could say. Surely this wasn't serious. I could tell by Carnahan's frenzied eyeballs that she was at least a pill or line in for each of the drinks I'd had today. "I apologize, but I don't believe there've been any complaints on my behalf."

"And we're going to keep it that way," her globular acolyte Carson wheezed. He proffered a pudgy hand that squashed like a piece of undercooked cake when I shook it. "I'll be taking over Holiday Operations for the remainder of the season."

I looked hard at Carnahan. He'd obviously never worked a serious day in his life. His pink, pudgy cheeks belied a youthfulness that his abject unctuousness was trying to smother inside its rolls upon rolls of careless consumption. He didn't look like a Santa. He looked like a slouch, at everything, ever.

"I'm sorry," I apologized again, not meaning it again. "I've held this position for over a decade. I'm skilled at my job and I feel this accusation deserves re-evaluation."

"Maybe you should re-evaluate it from the unemployment office," Mount Carnahan murmured past his nasty fat lips. "Goodbye, Mr. MacSorley."

NEVER FEAR

I served our nation through several of its darkest years, and I swear to you I have never seen a look of such arrogant achievement, even from our most fucked-up foes. I wasn't letting this go as easily as Carnahan Jr. had obviously let his personal standards go. I idly grabbed a fistful of fun-sized candy canes from Frosty's bowl, mostly to keep my hand from taking a swing.

"Well," I stated calmly. "It seems like negotiations are off the table. Like everything else that'd be on a table around you, you disgusting, slovenly waste of a biological process. Maybe you should head over to the makeup counter, and treat it like you would a buffet. Then you'd stand a chance at being as pretty inside as you are outside."

Candy, my former boss who now held no sway over me, and who had brought a Percy's security guard with her to protect against that fact, barked a horrified gasp.

Carnahan The Larger chuckled. His self-pleasure sounded as gross as he looked. "Ignore him, Candy. He's an old man whose ideas of respect and appropriate business don't conform at all to the modern world, and I feel sorry for him."

The security guard, himself no stick figure, pushed his girth in closer. I shrugged.

"I feel sorry for your *skeleton*," I said. Dropping the fistful of candy canes to the floor, not waiting to see which of the lardy party dived after them first, I turned and walked out the front door - whose politesse in opening, albeit automatically, was more kindness than I had felt the place had ever afforded me.

206

The Second Day of Christmas.

When I first got to the city, you couldn't walk down the block of 42nd street without someone shoving a spoon to your nose to try a sample, or some streetwalker shoving herself to your eyeballs under the same premise. Nowadays, it's all family fun and pedestrian thruways and costumed characters and conspicuous consumerism and fieldless bleachers to sit on and gaze out over the everything-nothingness of it all.

I'd preferred the dirt, for what it was worth. Too much light all at once makes you blind.

Even the hustle felt fake, as though everyone here was as much an actor as anyone behind the shining marquees. Or worse: if not an actor, an ad. Some people were both, in their designer outfits, costumed for the roles they felt they deserved in the world but never had to audition for, not anywhere outside their wallets at least.

Speaking of wallets, I spotted my buddy Marcos—well, the outfit that I knew contained Marcos—collecting cash from some tourists who had stopped to take a selfie with him. Marcos is a Times Square regular who cosplays as a famous children's television character whose name rhymes with Hellno. I always told myself I'd never get roped into the Times Square character game, but I knew Marcos and others of his ilk made a damn killing at it. Stuffing tourist bucks into a hidden furry pocket, he ambled over, his oversized character-head leering eerily at me.

"Ey bro," Marcos threw an arm around me but spoke low, waving and continuing to keep his allure to passersby on point. "What up yo? Did you for real get booted from Percy's?"

"That got out fast."

"Streets is buzzin' bro, you know that. Mariana heard from Clara mad quick."

Mariana was Marcos' girl, who slung drinks at the bikini bar over on 9th during this time of year. During the summer—the real sweet months for scratch—she and Clara had been among the famous Latina *desnudas* of City Hall's horror, working the pedestrian paths of Times Square in inexplicable infamy. Of all the afflictions and restrictions the city contained, the powers-that-be had decided that the legally topless women who inhabited this Times Square tourist oasis deserved to be vilified for making money with what god and/or glorious genetics had given then. In this financially ripe yet still socially seedy core of the Big Apple, it was perfectly acceptable to wear a copyrighted costume and swelter to death in the name of selfie-snaps and scratch, but government forbid you paint yourself up real pretty and dance skin-clad in the sunlight with some flyover-state folks whose idea of kicking back usually didn't go further than takeout pizza and an PG-13 rated movie.

Yes, I met and befriended Clara when she was a topless selfie-slinger in Times Square. Don't judge. She eventually parlayed that seasonal gig into her headlining show at the

Pussycat, and goddamnit, I could pull the same sort of thing...except in reverse weather, and, you know, dressed.

"If you're tryin' to pick up some Santa fans, you gonna wanna roll someplace else, bro," Marcos warned me. "These fuckin' *maricones* over here got all the game."

He bucked his hilariously-oversized costume head toward some twenty-something twats who weren't performing yet, but had a crowd circling around them. Four of them were non-descript chorus-boy types in red pleather pants, form-fitting lumberjack shirts, and elf caps. They were led by a shrimpy kid in skintight red jeans, a light-up Santa hat, noticeably-nice designer boots, an expensive-looking but thin red velvet jacket with white rabbit-fur liner and ruff, and an ironic "Santa suit" T-shirt. I gagged a little in the cold air.

They all seemed to be shills for some off-Broadway thing called *Santastic!* At least, that's what it said on the sign above the large pail their waifish commander set up next to his boom box, which made me wince as he cranked up cheesy-techno, holiday, background music.

"THAT'S the competition?" I asked Marcos. His slow nod but lack of reply made his gigantic furry head seem strangely somber.

"Santastic!" swung his skinny little arms over his head, attempting to induce the audience to clap to the beat. A smile any decent psychiatrist would define as "manic" ravaged his features as he twitched to the music.

"Hell-lloooo my Broadway beauties! Who's feeling pleasin', this holiday season?"

An unsettlingly bright cheer arose from the crowd. I shuddered inside both my robustly red fur jacket and the black trench coat I was wearing to obscure it. *This guy* was Times Square's biggest Santa draw?

"We are part of the off-Broadway production of *Santastic!*, a multi-holiday-themed musical EXTRAVAGANZA, and we are here to spread a little extra holiday chee-eer!"

The five broke it down boy-band style, doing a bunch of dance moves that I can't exactly name. Not breakdance stuff, just generic Broadway shit. The crowd ate it up. I'd seen more talent swinging around subway poles.

"Aaaaand, we are co-llec-ting a little something extra for the local AIDS shelterrrs!" He preened.

"No fuckin' way that loot's goin' to shelters," Marcos muttered. "Dude is pulling in hundreds every day, rollin' up in them Gucci kicks and rollin' out in a livery cab. Bullshit, yo."

"Is the real show any good?"

"How the fuck should I know? I get thrown fifty free tickets a week. I got better shit to see. I only catch shows if it's like, Henny Ibsen up in there." His costume-head's giant, lifeless black pupils sternly accentuated his point.

Santastic was playing a child's toy xylophone—badly—and humming on a kazoo as the crew did a few more half-assed dance moves. He threw a few handfuls of snowflake-shaped glitter in the air for effect as he went. Neither his moves nor manic music matched the bad background soundtrack. Yet, after two minutes or hours, or however much longer the endless-seeming abomination continued, the purses cracked and the tourists attacked.

I'd seen smaller crowds hounding major celebrities. Even the pigeons drew closer.

Marcos patted me on the back with one of his oversized costume paw-mitts. "I gotta get back to work, bro. Holler at me if you can't find a new gig quick, I got a spare Christmas Miss Piggy suit you could rock."

"Thanks."

Marcos stepped off toward a crowd of kids all wearing the same class chorus T-shirts, brandishing smartphones and cash money. I shrugged my black leather trench coat up around my furry suit a bit more, and wandered westward, timed out of Times Square.

*

I had a wad of singles that I had intended to dispense into various outfit-strings and orifices of Clara later that night, but as I wound my way out of Times Square, down 8th avenue past Port Authority, a few of them made their way into the jingling cups or outstretched hands of the grizzled old vets huddled under piles of dirty blankets, or wrapped in layers of military surplus clothes that were the perfect tragic dress code for their military-surplus existences. One guy I'd seen over the last few years, Sergeant Franklin, was already passed out cold, cradling a paper-bagged 40 like Jesus in the manger. I tucked a fiver into his camo cargo pocket and kept going.

Sure, that could have been me, but I'd always kept working. Rallied. Me sitting on the sidewalk doing nothing would be the real day the war was lost. I wasn't a loser. I was out of a job, out of luck, out of grace, and a little out of my mind, but I was not out of that winning spirit. I wasn't a believer in much, including in myself, but I wasn't a loser. Not after making it this far. Surviving. Not even if that survival was for apparently no reason.

Where but for the grace of my lack of God go I.

When I see all the old homeless vets, I can't ever bring myself to look at them directly in their faces, but I figure it's all the same, since so much of what we went through always keeps replaying in my mind. The good and the bad, all at once, sometimes changing places, depending on how I recollect it. The real good stuff always sticks, though. Watching the stars through gaps in the jungle canopy after the rain cleared. Handing out candy to kids who'd hound us in small towns. Handing out care packages of medicine or food to families that needed it. Yeah, long before I was this Santa, I was another one. It's just something that's in me, I guess. Unfortunately, I also gifted a lot of bullets.

I stopped thinking about it, at least as much as I ever stop thinking about it, and started thinking about what I was going to drink once I got to the bar.

Trooley's Tourist Tavern was a downtown staple that was perfectly obscured, unless you knew what to look for. The "tourist" part had been a joke since sometime in the '20s—it was strictly regulars now. Still, the bar itself was covered in varnished-over maps of old, hinting at adventures far and wide, if you could only manage to get up off the damn barstool. I'd taken my usual spot and usual drink, sipping a French Hens beer and tracing a map of the Venetian canals with my increasingly-blurry eyes.

"You got shat on," the bartender, Reli, informed me after delivering my drink and hearing my tale of holiday woe.

"As always, I appreciate your candor," I tilted my glass to her, then to my lips.

"No, I mean literally. There's pigeon shit on your shoulder." She wadded up some napkins and dabbed at a spot on my shoulder just beyond my line of eyesight. Reli was a good, observant bartender like that, full of help and facts. "They're a kind of dove, you know. Rock doves. Cool name. Not that it makes them any better in real life."

"They were everywhere in midtown today, flocking all around some *Santastic!* boy-band crap in Times Square. Must have hit me there."

Reli wrinkled her nose, not at the pigeon shit, but at the mention of *Santastic!*

"Ugh, I saw those hipster fucks on the morning show the other day when I was closing up," she growled. "As if Christmas needs to be any cheesier, now we have hipsters hawking it."

"I disagree with that term," I said in between sips. "I met some of the original hipsters around here, back in the day. I drank with Bill Burroughs a few times in the Village. That guy was more hardcore than any of these little twist-moustached twerps. He'd do..."

"...a shot of tequila for every beer you drank?" Reli finished my thought aloud at the same time I said it. She smiled sternly. "Yeah, you've mentioned it. But he's dead, and so's Kerouac and Cassady and Creeley and Ginsberg and all the rest of the cool kids, and now we're just left with these hand-me-down-'hipsters' who buy things up, fuck things up, and leave it to the rest of us to rinse and repeat."

"Sounds like I'm not the only one with this particular problem," I said, opening up the conversation. If anyone might have a good line on how to fix this insane issue, it might be Reli.

"Hell no. You wouldn't believe what some of these little trust-fund troglodytes are up to. It's bad enough that five of those snooty Obscene Caffeine coffeehouses have cropped up around here in the last year. Now they're trying to take over the bars they can't buy out. You should have seen the hipster herd at Shillelagh last night. They were fucking *finger painting.* Some thousand-dollar adult-preschool shitshow. Ridiculous."

"Shillelagh's way uptown, though. They're invading the Heights too?"

"It's a goddamn infestation of imbeciles. Padraig flipped his shit when he saw them pouring their wine into sippy cups and using the rocks glasses to mix their fancy paints. He told them to fuck off and go buy a gallery or a nursery if they wanted to do that shit, that this was a bar. They split without tipping. Fucking worthless weirdos."

"Surprised they haven't taken an eye to this fine establishment," I ventured. A dark look crossed Reli's otherwise pretty face. She sneered with a raised lip that'd put Elvis to shame.

"Oh, don't think that little snot from *Santastic* hasn't tried to bring that shit-show in here. Hells no. Not a chance I'll let them get their manicured claws on my family's bar. I don't know how they found us, but I made it clear they could go back to their precious coffee shop if they wanted to court cracked-out Christmas fans. That shit they do, it's supposed to be some schtick for charity cash, and they frigging half-ass it. That *Santastic* brat is the worst. I guess his dad's one of the main owners of the Obscene Caffeine chain, as if that makes him important or something just because they were able to tank a bunch of cool old mom 'n pop bars and put up churches of coffee capitalism."

"Obscene Caffeine? You mean those snooty places with the $5 cupcakes and the fake-barn wood everything?"

"Yeah. Because only the coolest of people can hang in their hipster hideout, and by 'coolest' I mean 'trendy-spendy.' God forbid they actually work on art, or improving anything about anything. His whole crew moves like they each drank a pot of meth-laced espresso, and they pull off the theatre thing about as well as middle schoolers putting on a self-made skit about dying chimpanzees. This 'special snowflake' shit has got to end, I don't care how many 'unique' bits of crap they buy or wear. Like it makes them automatically interesting, or something. For the one drink they stayed here, 'Santastic' tried to get Seany to give him some powdered sugar to lighten up his beard to look more the part. Said he could just mix it with some of his artisanal beard wax. *Beard wax*, Sam. What the christfuck."

"That's not particularly appropriate language for this season," I mock-chided her.

"Well, it's particularly appropriate for these losers. I heard that uptown they were acting all impressed that Shillelagh was 'authentic' and 'special' since they haven't got any TVs, but then they got mad when Padraig explained they didn't make mojitos, or frozen drinks, or anything with organic juice or 'herbal infusions'. He had to warn them twice about not going into the bathroom stall in groups of three in the middle of happy hour, staying in there blowing lines until people were pissing on the wall outside. Finally, he kicked them out after they wouldn't stop huffing some cotton-candy shit out of vaporizers and begging to hang up their fucking finger-paint art on the walls next to the framed book covers. They didn't tip him a dime, on a hundred-dollar tab. Trust-fund trash."

"Well," I muttered sarcastically, "Let's have a shot to never worrying about our love of Christmas getting tainted by the likes of them."

A whiskey bottle materialized in Reli's hand, and two full tumblers appeared in rapid succession. We raised them and she toasted.

"Fuck this season, and let those special snowflakes wreck someone else's halls with boughs of folly."

I clinked glasses with her. "Cheers. I hope they melt."

We skulled. I paid, then headed out.

As I walked outside, a lone pigeon (*rock dove?*) pecked at the snow-flecked ground by a corner embankment. Ruffling its grey and white feathers, it regarded me with either disdain or curiosity—it's hard to tell with pigeons— and made as if to fly in my general direction.

"Don't even think about it," I demanded.

It stared at me a second longer, pooped profusely into a snowbank, and then flew away, just another non-contributor who fed off the guts of this great city and then left just as quick, crass, and carelessly.

The Third Day of Christmas.

The reality of my situation hit me squarely in the face when I woke up the next morning still jobless. I remedied this affront with a hearty round of day-drinking. I bought three French Hen 22s and shored up on my couch, waiting for Clara to call and say she was done with work.

I was particularly mad that I'd gotten fired for drinking, and not for being a drunk. I'd put in effort not to be a mess, at least overtly. It's fine lines like these that keep me from being just another deadbeat in the streets. Being a drunk would keep me from being able to do *any* job, but drinking was what facilitated my survival of the job I'd had. I'd even bothered to hide the scent, slurping that disgusting over-proof peppermint schnapps. That was how committed I was to appearing normal, while knowing there was no reasonable way I could operate within the bounds of corporate workaday "normalcy."

Sure, it wasn't healthy. But at least half of the rest of the gainfully-employed world knows exactly what I'm talking about. Maybe not booze, but we all have our coping mechanisms that may or may not also be doping mechanisms.

I was an old pro at this, from way back. Even most of my time serving in Vietnam had been spent inside a pot cloud. I had basically no regrets—I had been good at what I did, maybe too good. Not that it ended up *doing* any good, but hey, we can't have it all.

The worst was thinking about it this season. Although I'd spent two hellish springs, summers, brutal monsoon seasons, and falls stationed there as well, it was the winter—well, Christmas, really—that stuck in my mind like a knife in the back.

The Special Forces teams had been training the Degar, the native mountain people, for months. Indisposed to helping out the Viet Cong, the Degar had quickly entered into an arrangement aiding us, and they'd been astoundingly helpful. Whether it was terrain issues for the best forward mobility, support as fighters, or (best of all) information on enemy movements, we were happy to have the durable, tenacious Degar along with us.

It had been an uneventful Christmas, right up until the trouble started.

The village had been a small one, nestled in the mountains. Barely even noticeable from the air, save for small wisps of smoke from cook fires. Under the jungle canopy in a clearing, there were small hutches made of sticks and fronds, with large rice barrels sitting outside. Typical stuff. One of the Degar soldiers, a kid in his teens, had been living there, and had reported up the chain to the Special Forces that V.C. had been sighted in the area for weeks now, and that they tended to terrorize the villagers for food. The intel hinted that particular division of V.C. were a far-flung faction and, as such, eradicating them would compromise a considerable tenet of their aggression in that area.

We'd made it to the village after an all-day trek, during which we'd sang Christmas carols, substituting bawdy or silly lyrics to amuse ourselves and staunch the nagging, nigh-fictional visions of silver bells and decked halls back home. Here the only chestnuts getting roasted were when we were nape'ing some V.C. balls.

We were halfway through a new parody I was pretty proud of—I fancied myself a musician back then, at least maybe for when I got home—and we'd been belting it through the chest-high grass that led to the village.

Rudolph the Red Spy reindeer
Had a very shiny nose
And ranted Commie prop-a-gan-da
That all the other deer opposed
All of the other reindeer
Were in favor of dem-o-cra-cy
They never let poor Rudolph
Crush oppressive bourgeoisie...

Charlie's artillery fire provided the bridge. Immediately we were taking cover in the grass, running for the tree line hither and yon, completely confused.

The V.C. hadn't just been dropping by there for food. They knew the place inside and out. We were at a complete tactical disadvantage, totally FUBAR.

I just don't remember how it happened. Maybe I do, or did, but I just... well, the details are hazy to the immediate recollection. Except one.

I'd managed to get completely lost in the tall grass when I'd ducked, covered, and ran, and ended up flanking the village. In the commotion, I'd snuck up behind a hutch and watched as four black-clad V.C. railed at the few villagers around a central fire.

A kid in a Degar uniform was being held by the hair. He seemed strangely calm, as though he'd already accepted his fate, but on closer inspection I could see he was dazed, probably from the massive, bloody wound on the back of his head. The V.C. jackass holding him was brandishing a hunting knife and screaming. It didn't take much to deduce that they had figured the kid for a snitch.

Without any delay, the V.C. bastard spiked one of the kid's eyeballs onto his knife. The villagers gasped in horror. The sound of bullets cascaded closer. The soldier raised the knife again—for what intent, I'll never know—and that was it.

I swung out from behind the hutch and shot the knife-wielding soldier plus the three V.C. flanking him, all in what seemed like one burst. I paused and picked off another two at the village's perimeter, allowing a few of my fellow soldiers to dash in and secure more of the area.

The kid who'd been knifed stood and staggered, admirably attempting hand-to-hand combat with a remaining V.C. thug who was armed with a machete. Unarmed but still quick on his feet, the kid took surprisingly accurate swings at the soldier in close quarters, stunting the other soldier's ability to swing the huge blade. It wasn't nearly a fair fight, though, as evidenced by the large swath of the now-monocular kid's arm the soldier managed to carve open in passing, taking off two fingers, shortly before I shot him down as well. The kid, still standing, was bundled off by the villagers, maybe to safety, but who knew. The term was relative, over there.

I had really thought I was being helpful. Useful. But who knows.

More V.C. were pouring into the village. Explosions, gunfire, and smoke became my world.

The rest is just a smattering of sensory input. There was more fighting. More screaming, more noise, more bullets. Orders to retreat, that an airstrike had been called in. No sight of the helpful Degar kid or any of his comrades, no warnings for the villagers.

I remember being back in the tall grass again, hundreds of yards out now, watching the fireball of foliage and former foes as the attack helicopters rained hell onto where the village had been. My mind, shocked and tired and at odds with everything I'd previously known as reality, defaulted to the seasonal soundtrack. I started humming to myself, from cracked lips that had somehow become bloody.

Hang a shining star upon the highest bough.

And have yourself a merry little Christmas, now.

*

The uptown A train clattered to a stop at its terminus below 207th street. Once above ground, I hardened all of my senses amidst the ubiquitous, slush-slinging snow.

Clara buzzed me up and greeted me at her apartment door, instantly making me forget the tundra-wide trek I'd endured to get here. Her skin was a perpetual color of caramel that insinuated she had a private stash of sunshine somewhere within, some radiance that was tanning her from the inside out, whatever the season, a tantalizing to-go tropicality that made her stunning in the warm months and scorchingly irresistible in this blasted winter.

She was hot in every way possible.

The coke was definitely a problem, though.

As I self-medicated with booze, Clara was fond of the blow. I didn't hold it against her; she'd been using before she even came to the states. And, compared to the pitfalls I'm sure her ecdysiast Pussycat colleagues dealt with, she seemed to have it in control. But as we drank the French Hen 22s and snuggled on her collapsing couch in that tiny, turn-of-last-century apartment, I hated thinking about how much better she could be doing, and I had to turn my head every time she'd unsexily huff up a pile of snow that could have put the sidewalk outside to shame.

To even things out, she lit a joint wrapped in a red-and-white-striped candy cane paper as she listened to me bitch about Santastic and his scene.

"You hate him because he *maricon*?" She did a limp-wristed sashay that any twink would have given his flat abs to pull off as adorably.

"I don't give a fuck who he fucks, that doesn't factor into any of why he's a terrible human being."

"But is porsoot of happiness, bebe, no?" She handed me the candy-cane joint. I took a cloyingly heady drag. The paper made my lips taste of peppermint.

"Well, the rest of us would be a damn sight more inclined to pursue our happiness if assholes like him didn't pursue theirs by fleecing us at every goddamn turn. And needlessly, no less. He's got plenty of money, but for some reason that makes him immune to the idea of ever actually perfecting a skill. That's not just lazy, that's actively being useless." I coughed and handed her back the candy-striped peppermint joint. "I don't know how you can stand all this peppermint crap."

"You no' like it?" Reclining, she sipped on the joint and slowly French-inhaled the smoke. I'd paint her like that, if I could paint.

"No, I can't just *not like* it. It makes me think of you."

She smiled mischievously. "Do a little bump with me."

What the hell, it was a snow day. I sprinkled a snowflake's worth of blow onto the crest of her breast and (*laying a finger aside of his nose*) rode it into my face like a champion skier slamming into the first powder run of the day. My heart got tight in my chest. I groaned as I pulled back.

"No good, bebe?"

"Good. All good," I wheezed. "You just make my heart stop, beautiful." I forced a smile that the blow held firmly in place.

She sucked on the peppermint joint and handed it to me. The minty coolness met the weed's burning flavor and the chemical drip of the coke, blending into one heady sensation that made me fall backward and sink into the couch as if it were a warm snowbank. Clara climbed onto my lap.

"And what do you want for Christmas, little girl?"

"A key," she said immediately. "*De perrico.*"

I hoped she couldn't feel my heart plummet from her perch. "Perrico"—Spanish for "parakeet"—was local slang for coke.

"That's too much parakeet for a pretty little bird like you," I replied.

"No for me, bebe. I cut and sell. Then we have fuuun." She pouted in a way that made me wish I could buy her all of Colombia.

"I dunno, babe."

"For school money. For better job," she attempted.

"Why don't I just give you money for that, then?"

"No. I make it. And more."

I hated how right she was. Flipping a kilo of coke at her club, or between her and Mariana working at the bikini bar... they'd clean up. Even more if they cooked it to crack. Then repeat customers, bigger buys, bigger scores... probably not going to be used as school money at that point, though.

Unless I made sure she stayed on the straight and narrow. Relatively speaking, I mean.

"I'll think about it. You'd have to be a really, really nice girl."

She coyly narrowed her eyes. "I'm a nice girl." My heart rose again. She tugged at the elastic of my boxers. "You wanna go down my chimney, bebe?"

I extinguished the peppermint joint and grabbed her pillowy ass in both hands.

"Did you leave me some cookies?"

*

The next morning, we bundled up and I hailed a cab to take us back downtown. I wasn't up for another arduous train-trek, and anyway I always liked seeing Clara safely to the door of the Pussycat. As we pulled away, I pondered giving the driver the address of my apartment or Trooley's.

I went with the former, just so I could pregame. With Clara now ensconced in her exotic realm for the day, I started noticing my other surroundings again. It started with a "Support The Troops" sticker on the taxi console. Then by default, my eyes did recon on the driver.

I instantly began questioning if I had any reason to be hallucinating.

The back of the driver's head was a crisscross of scars where hair had staunchly refused to grow in. A strap that appeared to lead to an eye-patch ran across the back of his head.

Two fingers were missing from his right hand.

Almost subconsciously, I uttered one of the few Vietnamese phrases I'd ever learned, asking if he was a Degar soldier.

He responded in elegant, perfectly-enunciated English, in a resonant baritone voice.

"Why yes, I am a veteran of Degar descent. How did you know?"

"I thought I killed you on Christmas. 1972."

"Excuse me?" He turned and looked me full in the face. It wasn't an instant realization, but it was a singular one.

"Jiminy Christmas," he breathed. I suppressed a weird laugh.

The light turned green. He didn't notice.

"Change of plans," I stated. "We're going to Trooley's Tourist Tavern, right now. You and me." I couldn't contain my shock, but added in a stunned monotone, "'Tis the season to be jolly."

Several cars behind us honked. The cabbie immediately cut left and continued, now toward the bar.

A few moments of introspective silence passed. Fat snowflakes whirled outside like puzzle pieces fitting perfectly into their picturesque snowbanks.

The driver broke the silence in a surprisingly worried tone. "Please don't make an attempt to kill me. I'm armed and would unfortunately have to reciprocate."

"What?"

The driver spoke evenly, but anxiously. "I didn't give the enemy any intel on you guys. I wasn't a double agent. They were just... there. I had no way of contacting..."

"Stop," I said. "You didn't do anything wrong. Jesus. We were the ones who called in a fucking airstrike. I thought I burned you alive."

"I trained and worked with the Americans long enough, I figured an airstrike would follow," the cabbie noted, his one good eye probing my face via the rearview. "I ran out of there like hell was on my heels. I was worried YOU guys were done for."

"Came close. Not as close as it did you, though. Jesus, you were just a kid. You didn't deserve to lose an eye and half a hand just because we were too ass-backwards to spot an ambush. And on fucking Christmas. Jesus."

Another stop light. He turned, his one eye doubling-down on a meaningful stare. "Forget the eye, forget the hand. You gave me the greatest Christmas present I could have possibly desired: plausible hope, and the realistic expectation of escape from an impossible, terrifying and violent end. Do you know how rare that is?"

"I'm glad things worked out for the best," was all my stunned mind could murmur.

The driver persisted, forceful but friendly. "Do you understand what I'm saying? I'm not sure I could even know *how* to offer that level of ruthlessly effective gratitude to anyone else. You're not exactly going to get picked off by V.C. coming out of the subway tunnels or fall in a pungi pit going down Broadway. There's no way I can ever repay you!

"Sir, you killed seven men to save me, and you didn't even know my name."

The whirling snow outside seemed to give a low, ghostly whistle of appreciation in the wind. I glanced at the faded photograph on the license stuck behind the bulletproof glass of the driver's partition, and sort of hated that despite the gravity of the situation, I still couldn't stifle a snicker.

"Phuc? Your name is *Phuc Tat*?"

Phuc rolled his one good eye hard enough to serve extra for the missing one.

"Yes, you base-humored beast. In my language, it means 'blessings and luck.' Don't hate—appreciate."

The Fourth Day of Christmas.

The next several hours were spent in the kind of clarity-cultivating haze that only a dark bar and a long-lost person of importance can induce.

First, Phuc demanded to learn everything about me. I swooped through what must have seemed like a bland personal history in comparison... I'd served the rest of my war tour mostly uneventfully, had left Vietnam in 1973 and had never been back. I'd gone home to NYC, did the standard wife/job/apartment thing, put it on autopilot for the next thirty years. Initially thought I could have been a jazz or rock drummer at one of the clubs downtown, settled for pounding garbage cans into trucks for a very decent city wage. Still, that wasn't enough to keep an upwardly-mobile New York Wife happy, and an appropriate-feeling divorce followed. I'd retired a few years ago and got by on a fair union pension and the seasonal Santa thing. Phuc got a chuckle out of that.

"And how does it feel to be a person of part-time magical character?" he asked.

I laughed some of my French Hens beer foam into my beard. "One of the Batman villains said that there's no true despair without hope. That's basically true for everyone in real-life Gotham. Maybe the rest of America too, maybe the whole world. I wouldn't know anymore. Magic's the same deal. There's nothing that makes reality hurt as bad as being offered the glimmer of magic."

"I don't know about that," Phuc mused. "What you did for me was damned close to magic. Perhaps myopic magic, but magic nonetheless."

I didn't like talking about this sort of shit now that it was no longer my professional obligation, either as a soldier or as Santa. I switched the subject, genuinely interested in my new friend Phuc. "How's your English so good?"

"My parents were Degar, but we were all influenced by the French missionaries that came to our region when I was young. I grew up with Christmas and all the trimmings, including *Petit Papa Noel*— that's you, Mr. Claus. When the war ended, I took what little cash I had and made my way to France... I might have behaved a little inappropriately, but it paid the bills, and it was Paris... I put myself through hell, but I also put myself through the Sorbonne."

"So why are you driving a taxicab?"

Phuc shrugged. "American Dream, right? 'On The Road'? It just works for me. I'm my own boss, I'm not stuck in an office or a foxhole, and it makes me feel useful. Particularly with my side-gig. And that's where yooooooou..."—he tipped his martini glass at me, then inhaled half of it without missing a conversational beat—"are in for a Christmas miracle."

"I'm done with the holiday cheer," I said, skulling more of my beer. "I'll try my luck again on St. Patrick's Day."

Phuc chuckled. "Oh, I think you're in luck. You see, I too do a bit of superheroic sanitation, as it were."

"How do you mean?"

"I get a lot of interesting clients in my cab. Some of them admire my mobility, my resourcefulness. Some inquire as to my former life, as you did, and are interested to learn that I was an American-trained soldier who'd seen so much battle. Sam, you know the question that follows, what people ask when they learn things like that."

I did. It was a terrible question, one that nobody in their right mind should ever ask a man who's seen the horrors of war.

"I never talk about my kill count," I said sternly. "To anyone."

"I understand that, Sam. And I do indeed understand why. However, the difference between us is, that discussion is one *I* entertain. And one that I have, let's say, extrapolated."

I wasn't sure if the beer was hitting me harder than usual, or the weird events of the last few days were wearing on me harder than I thought. Subtlety was not going to tiptoe through this discussion any further. "Phuc, are you telling me you're a contract killer?"

Phuc's one eye went wide in mock-horror. "Heavens no! Nothing that assiduous. However... I may have, once or twice, used my well-honed skills and spacious car trunk to aid in the... removal of certain societal blights."

"Certain blights that were in human form, I take it?"

"A wife-beating Triad underling and an unscrupulous pedophilic pimp, specifically. I assure you, they are not missed. Doesn't sound like your unsavory Santa successor would be, either."

I probably should have been shocked, but I just muttered, "Amen to that."

We sat in somber but understanding silence for a minute.

"It's all relative," Phuc mused. "That Christmas we underwent that little rumble in the jungle? The Americans were dropping legendary bombs on Hanoi. You and I had it easy, comparatively."

"Operation Linebacker II," I remembered. "Largest heavy bomber strike since the end of World War II. The Prime Minister of Sweden compared it to the Holocaust, we strafed Hanoi so hard."

"And yet we called it a 'success.'"

"A success no one talks about."

"So a push, then, as the blackjack players say. It's all relative. We tried to fight evil, yet our enemies were nothing compared to the horrors that those above us wrought in the name of supposed good. I tried to be useful my whole life, but it just ended me up as another damaged face, haunted every day about how I could have done better. But all that, that was just history. History may be written by the winners, but the future is written by the legends. And you, Mr. Claus, are something straight out of legend." Phuc nodded a bit sassily at me. "I thought I couldn't pay you back, but I can. Let me be of use to you. You saved me, let me save you back. It's the gift of a lifetime."

Giving a life... or taking it? I thought. I pictured Carson Carnahan sitting in my Santa throne. *Gross.* But...

"I just... I know that meeting you has been a great stroke of luck, but I just can't see this ending well," I admitted. "No matter how useful it'd be, for both of us."

"It's the greatest of luck, and the greatest of Christmas presents. Feeling useful."

"It's not useful, Phuc, it's troublesome as hell. It's *murder.*"

Phuc shook his head more hyperbolically than necessary. "You need a mission. I need penance. The world needs less evil. How is that not useful? To EVERYONE?"

I sipped my French Hen.

"You're not wrong."

"Just say it, you know I'm right. People are ill at ease with the idea that there can be such overt predators—like Carnahan, or anyone else coasting on capitalist spoils - in the world. Because it's definitely not just an idea, it's a reality - but it's a reality that one never, ever wants to experience. And ideally, *shouldn't* experience. So, it takes predatory measures of a different sort to combat them. Relatively speaking, this isn't even near the worst of what you or I have done in life. But it might be among some of the best, if it works right..."

"Right and wrong are relative, you just said that."

"They are. But heroic is another level. The glory is yours. I'm just the middleman evening out the push."

"I don't know about this. I'm no superhero. I'm just an average guy now."

Phuc smirked at me. "Really? Sam, look in the mirror. You might look like shit, but dammit, honey, you're Santa Claus. And it's time you started cracking down on the naughty list."

"Oh Jesus," I said.

"Yeah! Do it as a birthday present to him, if you have to."

"No, no. What you said... cracking down on the naughty list. Jesus, Phuc, I've got it."

Phuc gave a demure grin and cocked a dramatic, impeccably-groomed eyebrow. "Santa Claus is goin' to town!"

*

Three phone calls secured my idea. One to Clara, one to Marcos's bikini-bartender girlfriend Mariana, and one to the lovely lady-voiced robot that electronically helmed The

Secret Service, the best drug-delivery operation in town. Fortunately, thanks to my own habits and the frequency of those of my friends, I was in very good standing with The Secret Service "agents." I have no idea who "them" is—the voice on the other end of the phone is the perpetually-pleasant lady-robot, the transactions are done exclusively via a secure online account, and the deliveries of any weight are dead-drops in an impartial secure location. But if it was good enough shit for Clara and her scores of stripper friends, it was good enough for my plans.

I called requesting thirty six ounces of cocaine—two point two pounds, one full kilogram brick—or, as they are popularly known on the streets, a "bird." Though the volume was a bit ridiculous even by The Secret Service's standards, I was told my called-in bird would be ready tomorrow. Half of the money was taken in deposit from an account I kept exclusively to satisfy Clara. The rest would be provided at the pickup.

And just like that, I was dreaming of a White Christmas.

The Fifth Day of Christmas.

Everyone knows that a drug deal isn't really a drug deal if you pay in funds appropriated from elsewhere. It doesn't count. It's like how you're never an addict if you only smoke someone else's cigarettes or snort their coke.

I wasn't about to spend a whole bunch of my actual cash on the sizeable coke score, but getting rid of some excess crap lying around never hurt. The thing is, sometimes people hold onto bad memories just because they're valuable. Not valuable in a learning way, valuable in a greedy way. I had a few I could easily hock to help set things right. Anyway, maybe it'd make some poor slob's Christmas, scoring some bling on the relative cheap.

The Sanitation Department provided me with a healthy pension. My apartment had been rent-controlled for decades now. On paper, I wasn't doing too badly. And I was somehow adept at spreading seasonal joy in ways few others can. This time, I was just going to do it a little differently.

I dug the rings out of the old Macanudo cigar box that I kept a few important documents and things in. I had six rings that I took to the pawn shop. The guy behind the bulletproof-glass didn't even bother scrutinizing the stones with his loupe, at first. He just scratched the rings across a sandpapery pad in front of him, testing quality.

Only one came up fake. My ex had given it to me. No wonder that evil bitch hadn't tried to claw it off of me in the divorce. The rest were not only real, but infused with decent diamonds that I had been assured the quality of, long ago in a war-torn nation where barter could win violent favors and nightly poker games were easy to rack up high pots, when your day-to-day existence was always a gamble.

The total haul got me over half the cash I needed for the bird.

The rest I wrote off from my savings account as my Christmas present to the city of New York, and to all of

235

effort-promoting, forward-thinking, non-hip humanity in general.

Meanwhile, Phuc had been working on some stocking stuffers.

That had been his cheesy code-phrase to me for his work stalking Santastic. "Stalking" stuffers. As dumb as the code was, the results were impeccable. I got a text reading "Got the BEST stocking stuffers, will be great to hang over the fire!" I left immediately to meet Phuc at the bar for more details.

I stopped by the bank and deposited the five rings' worth of money. Then I went straight to Trooley's to drink off my doubts.

The Sixth Day of Christmas.

Trooley's was swinging that night, as the house band was sinking their teeth into a set, and their livers into the usual copious whiskey. Tonight they were blasting out perverse versions of holiday classics, which of course felt like serendipitous sound-tracking.

Onstage, beneath the taxidermied moose-head covered in long-liberated bras, the rocking quartet known as U™ wailed out a different version of their favorite things...

Bongrips and booty and big drug collections
Bright flaming cocktails and armed insurrection
Whiskey so strong that your throat fucking stings
These are a few of my favorite things...

Phuc was sitting in one of the booths near the black-lit pool tables. His wide, blue-white smile shone out like the Cheshire Cat as I approached. Sinking into the leather banquette and plunking my pint of French Hens down on the tabletop (this one bearing a collection of ski mountain trail maps that had been immortalized under half an inch of bar-top epoxy sometime in the 1960s), I simply smiled back, effectively tipping over the veritable Christmas stocking of informational goodies.

"Santastic is even more of a fraud than you think," Phuc gushed. "It's ridiculous. I followed him to some shitty hipster bars after their final 'show' in Times Square yesterday, and I made sure I was the one who he hailed when he left. God-*damn*, Sam."

I hadn't yet known him for more than forty-eight hours, but I could tell Phuc was being more effusive than usual. He was obviously very proud of his intelligence gathering score.

"Alright?"

"I totally had him figured for one of my team, but he gets on the phone, and his whole damn demeanor changes. Seriously, like taking off a coat that doesn't fit. He starts talking in this *deeper voice*"—Phac did the impression of it—"and I could tell it was way more natural. But what killed me is what he was talking *about*."

Sam, none of that money is going to AIDS charities. He's taking all of it. The production of *Santastic* is barely more than some singing and dancing once a week in the

Obscene Caffeine coffeehouse down in St. Mark's. It's not just off-Broadway, it's off-off-off Broadway. And it is *definitely* off the books."

"Awful Broadway," I smirked, sipping my beer.

"So then, he tells me to stop, and this girl gets in the car. Some horrible hipster chick. They start making out, totally grossly, he's got one hand inside her ironic ugly Christmas sweater, but she pulls away and asks if he's holding. He pulls out a folded fifty and half a cocktail straw, and they start hooting it up right there in my backseat. I dropped them off at Obscene Caffeine—he barely tipped, of course—and there was a whole posse of other losers there. Sam, our work is cut out for us."

"Us?" I asked. "I'm just putting up the capital."

"Well," Phuc said. "Your investment is going to pay off bigtime. This kid is a scumbag. You pick your enemies well!"

"I've had enough enemies for this life, Phuc. I shouldn't even care enough to hate him." The moment I openly elucidated this thought, I began feeling curiously bad.

"Well, you care enough to make this city better for the people who can't do it by themselves. And not by some crappy show-and-dance cash-grab or CHEATING CHARITIES. You're having an actual initiative get undertaken. It's inspiring."

"I'm glad. Because you're the one who's got to be inspired here."

The band, behind us, continued fervently.

Anarchy, nihilists, coups in each nation
Watching the world burn to man's decimation
Demons descending from bomber-planes' wings
These are a few of my favorite things...

Phuc took a hearty slug of his martini. "There's more," he enthused. "This should buck you up. Santastic might not be batting for my team, but you'll never guess who is."

"I don't give a fuck about..."

"Carson Carnahan," Phuc cut me off. I struggled not to spit out my beer.

"Carnahan? Isn't he... I mean... don't you guys pride yourselves on being... you know, super-handsome and muscular and all that?"

"Indeed we do, Sam, indeed we do. And he's holding us all back. And the bears of power are NOT happy about it."

"'Bearers.' The word is 'bearers' of power, not 'bears'," I noted.

Phuc raised the eyebrow over his eye-patch. "Honey, you tell me which of the two of us took college-level English classes. I know the word is 'bearers.' The BEARS of power *hate* Carnahan. For several good reasons."

I gave an open-handed shrug. "Enter through the Hate Entrance."

Phuc's eye and teeth gleamed in the blacklight. "Okay. So, there's this club in Chelsea... SUPER exclusive, completely amazing. It's for larger, more hirsute gentlemen with a proclivity for leather, and the means to enjoy only the finest of things. It's called RareBear. Only the most distinguished of Daddies hang out there."

"Okay?"

"Anyway... Carnahan, with his legacy of loot from Percy's, thirsts for the attention of these guys. Like, Sahara-desert thirsts. It's hard to watch."

"I take it you've seen this firsthand?"

Phuc straightened his posture mock-haughtily. "It should go without saying that my exotic appeal and exceptional bearing are more than welcome there. There's lot of Asian twinks in the world, but considerably fewer Panda Bears. *Anyway*. These guys, they're big, but it's muscle-big. Or maybe just too-many-fine-steaks-and-whiskies big. Not slovenly, hate-weight big, like Carnaham."

"So they hate him for being fat?" I said. "Who cares? I hate *me* for being fat. Carnahan fucking sucks, but at least he's sucking in Santa servitude. He's not on the level of real rich guys."

"Exactly." Phuc shook his head, nonplussed. "His outward appearance is just a hint of the mindset that goes along with being an indentured servant of the Percy's empire, working as a damn Santa to look good for mommy because he can't cut it behind the scenes in the business, but still needs to show up at the store to score any of the family loot-cake. He's the living embodiment of entitled sloth, and now he's trying to act like he's important because he has a super-special job."

"I'm not catching your point here."

"Carnahan thinks his little benevolent spin as Santa makes him even MORE entitled to attention, affection, whatever, that he's *already not getting from these guys*. He's just a whiny little weasel who sits at the bar in RareBear and sulks when all the hot leather daddies go off to smoke cigars in the library without him, or to chain someone else up for a flogging on their St. Andrew's cross. He's not important, interesting, *anything*. Just a waste of space."

"So why do they even let him in?"

"To mess with him. Sometimes... on *slooowww* nights... they let him play as a submissive, literally just by throwing a ball-gag in his fat mouth and locking him in a cage while they talk real business and get down to real... manly things. Problem is, he's now getting a rep for approaching certain well-to-do Wall Streeters at business environments in real life, and, well, let's just say he's not much for conversation or usefulness in the real world, even when untied and ungagged."

"So he's trying to claw his way up in the world, and he's going to fail. Good. I'm happy he's going to know how that feels. Let him dig his own double-wide grave."

Phuc's monocular gaze roamed my face. "Sam... are you okay?"

"It's just... it's fucking silly. This is all just silly. I shouldn't care about any of this."

"Are you having reservations about... my usefulness?" Phuc wondered.

"I mean... you just... I know you want to do this to repay me, but it's not like it's a matter of life and death anymore.

I'll survive, regardless of what happens to Santastic, or Carnahan."

"Ha!" Phak laughed. "Simply *surviving* is different from *achievement*. You of all people should know that."

"But what are we achieving?"

Phuc, glowing purple in the blacklight, took on an ethereal sort of presence.

"We're achieving what we've been fighting for all along. What America wanted to bomb my country for, what they indentured us both as soldiers for, what we came to New York and struggled for, and what these little hipster fucks and one-percent heirs want to gobble up and take as their own, but don't realize that buying or cajoling it or taking it from others doesn't give them more of it. Freedom. The ability to make things better for people who can't do it on their own is liberation—to them, from their oppressors, to us, from the guilt of having to be at either end of this sick societal spectrum. We are killing these entitled bastards' golden goose and eating it for Christmas dinner. For everyone who's not naturally crazy-greedy, we're after the pursuit of happiness that only happens when it's still possible to have a fair shot. We're taking that shot, Sam, before it's too late."

My silence served as obvious acceptance. Down the bar, near the entrance, I saw Clara, Marcos, and Mariana walk in. I waved them over.

We began to lay down our plans. Six schemes a'laying.

Onstage, the band crescendo'd to a glorious finale.

When the gods fight
When your pee stings
When you're going maaad
I simply remember my favorite things
Before the whole worrrld goooes baaad...

As we were heading out, I spotted my old Sanitation Department pal Lenny Lampson sitting at the bar. He was still in uniform and caked with snow. He didn't look like a jolly or happy soul.

"Nice Frosty the Snowman outfit, Lenny."

"Hah. Hey, Sam. Careful out there tonight, it's brutal. Visibility's nil. I nearly buried some hipster twat with my snow plow over in Hell's Kitchen. Who the fuck tries to mush a dog sled using an inner tube and six Pomeranians?"

"It's not your fault, Lenny," I reassured him. "The Idiot Iditarod deserves the danger."

"Hey, you still playin' drums?" Lenny asked, perking up. "Richie's got the flu and the band has a gig at the Christmas parade. We could really use ya."

The band Lenny referred to was the Department of Sanitation's Emerald Society Pipe and Drum Corps. I'd played bass drum for them for years when I was working. I missed it. It's hard to find pure opportunities to work hard and create something really good with like-minded people like that.

"Sure, Lenny. Gimme a call tomorrow."

"You got it Sam. Good seein' you."

Reli ambled over to say goodbye. "Out so soon?"

"Busy week coming up," I said.

She smiled enthusiastically. "You got a new job?!"

"Not exactly," I smiled. I didn't want to say too much, but I couldn't resist a question of my favorite, eternally-amenable bartender. "Reli, if I needed to get a whole bunch of strippers coked to the gills to set them loose on Santastic's shit-show and possibly start trouble, would you let us pre-game here?"

Reli smiled.

"Absolutely christfucking not. My first-person chemical warfare tactics here"—she raised a whiskey tumbler out of thin air—"aren't meant for mass murder."

She slammed the shot, spun a martini shaker in one hand, and placed both delicately on the bar rail.

"But I'll totally host the after-party."

The Seventh Day of Christmas.

As ugly ducklings turn into swans, ugly thoughts can turn into beautiful achievements.

You don't have to like it. You don't even have to understand it. Maybe it's better that way.

But like any incomprehensible, good piece of magic, it still works.

Once your mind goes to these kinds of extremes, there's no recalibrating. It's like escalating a Christmas-lights war with your neighbors... once you have full-sized sleighs on the roof, you're never just going back to simple candles in the windows. And neither are they.

However, to properly process the full extent of the duckling-to-swan growth, I had to see for my own eyes what we were up against. Of course, that didn't mean I wanted to internalize every last detail of things. I went into battle-recon mode and kept sharp for only what I needed to process. The rest just hurt too badly.

Phuc and I went to the franchise of fuckery that was the Obscene Caffeine coffeehouse on St. Marks, clearly the epicenter of the *Santastic* operation. Until a few years ago, the spot had been the famous Wursthaus punk rock club, until coffee apparently became more lucrative than chaos.

Opening the door felt like breaching the entrance of a particularly snug spacecraft. The inhabitants would have been just as happy to have seen us float right back outside into the aether and not inhale their rarified air.

That wasn't happening.

We each ordered a small black coffee, of which there were an unnecessary number of names, modifications, and varietals, and Phuc chatted up the apathetic barista who was wearing both a scarf and cap, despite the abundant warmth indoors.

"So, miss, I understand that this is where the show *Santastic* is being staged?"

The barista girl looked up from her smartphone, a look of insufferable dullness radiating out from behind her yellow thick-rimmed glasses. "Uh, I think that was last week."

I gazed around the bland, fake-barn-wood-paneled walls of Obscene Caffeine. Beneath the glow of ubiquitous

Edison lightbulbs, calculatedly scrappy-looking young people tapped screens and devices. No one spoke to each other. A dull drone of what I eventually realized was ambient synth music slouched from hidden speakers.

Phuc became incrementally more cheerful as the conversation went south, his tone a stark contrast to the cultivated boredom that seemed to permeate the room. "Surely not! We donated some money to your dance corps in Times Square just the other day, and their ads said the show would be appearing at this address!"

"I dunno," the barista half-shrugged. "I think it's over."

Phuc took a different tack. "Miss, I'm here from the press, and I was hoping to review the show. Surely there must be some final performance to occur?"

This perked the barista up enough to hold Phuc's gaze for more than five seconds. "Who do you blog for? The Skinflint? Mawkish? RoboHobo? I'm totally in a band. I can answer questions about that."

Phuc glowered. "No, miss. I'm from the paper, not a blog. I just wanted to learn more about *Santastic*, or perhaps your organization's charity work."

Her gaze sank to the life-raft of her smartphone. "Oh. Yeah, I dunno."

"Could I possibly speak to the young man who is in charge of these things?"

"Braendeyn won't be back until tomorrow. He has cat yoga class tonight."

"I see," Phuc pressed on. "And what of the other young men in his cadre? Are they available?"

"Those guys don't, like, work here."

"Does anybody?" I interjected. A few wayward eyeballs flitted angrily up at me, noticed me noticing their clickbait-filled screens, and retreated.

"If they're not in Times Square, you can see if the Santa squad is out in the park," she said. "Union Square or Washington Square, probably. Wherever the tourists are, ha."

I gave Phuc a look that clearly indicated I was done with this. He gave a small nod.

"Thank you for your time, miss," Phuc told the barista. We turned to leave.

"If... Braendeyn... comes back," I said over my shoulder, loud enough for the sullenly, smugly silent room to hear, "Tell him I'm a gallery owner doing a winter retrospective on up-and-coming finger-paint artists. The adult preschool aesthetic is so *necessary*, right now. You know, rethinking all those boring old conventions about the value of effort and risk and all that. I hope he and I can connect."

With that, Phuc and I left.

Not halfway to the corner, a scruffy-bearded kid in ratty, skintight black jeans, half-unlaced boots, plaid earmuffs over a man-bun, and a very high-end shearling coat ran up from behind us and tapped Phuc on the shoulder.

"Excuse me," he said, already out of breath. "Did you say you were from the press and looking for Braendeyn?"

Phuc gazed at him impassively. "If that's who's running the *Santastic* show, then yes, I am."

The hipster kid pulled off his earmuffs and shook both of our hands. "I can tell you all about it. I'm one of the dancers. There's more to the show than you know."

"Oh really?" Phuc said dubiously. "Not just generic gentricidal bullshit?"

"Really," the kid said. "Someone needs to call him out. He's stealing money from charity, he's not paying the dance crew, he's on drugs all the time, and for real, this sleazy Santa thing is just so uncool. He should be impaled on the North Pole, not representing it. Let me help. I'm Hrothgar."

"How do we know you're being straight with us... Hrothgar?" I asked.

The kid giggled and pulled a fake beard from his coat pocket, donning it over his neck-length real one. A thin but effective Santa hat followed.

"So?" Phuc said.

"So?" the kid admonished. "Sweetie, I'm the understudy."

The Eighth Day of Christmas.

"It's better to destroy than create what's unnecessary."
—8 ½

Trooley's decades-deep blend of crazy and cool had always made it my favorite hangout headquarters, but after the bout of blandness that had been the Obscene Caffeine coffeehouse, I appreciated its frenetic, funky fervor even more that afternoon.

Reli was stringing up Christmas lights over the back-bar, weaving them around the collection of odd perpetual-motion machines that twisted and turned and spun above the booze bottles.

"You know that there's different versions of *The Twelve Days of Christmas* song?" she said. "In one, the eighth day is 'hounds a-running.' Another's 'boy's a-singing.' Dunno if that's better than 'ladies dancing', but I like how there's options."

"We're going for all of the above today," I said, sipping my beer. Phuc nipped at his martini. We had twenty minutes to kill before the plan went into effect.

The hipster kid, Hrothgar, had settled into a few craft beers before telling us his story and telling us just to call him "Roth." He had confirmed everything Phuc had told me about Santastic—real name, Braendeyn—stealing the take, plus more dirt about him leading on the "dancers" by promising them part-time jobs at the coffeehouse and not coming through with that (which, Roth was quick to note, was the reason he'd decided to go turncoat on the Santastic scene.) Braendeyn being a literal crackhead with no knowledge of business practice didn't help either, and Roth—who seemed to have a good brain under that goofy man-bun haircut—was tired of filling in for him when he failed as Santa or as Obscene Caffeine's management.

Well, that covered "boys a-singing." Our snitch had sung like a choir of angels.

Lenny and some of the Sanitation guys had been sitting down the bar, and as was custom in Trooley's, jumped in on the conversation they could contribute to.

"Obscene Caffeine can bite it. Those guys suck. They throw out trash bags full of those goddamn five-dollar cupcakes every night, and the rats go nuts eatin' em all up. Gross, chuckin' a garbage bag fulla rats into the truck."

"Next time you show up there," I instructed Roth, "take any of the food they're going to throw away and save it. We'll give it to the homeless over by Port Authority."

"Cool," said Roth. It sounded genuine.

I felt bad I had to send him out on point as our double-agent in Santastic's operation, but it was what today's plan required.

By the time Phuc and I had gotten to Times Square, a streamlined version of the initiative that we had discussed the other night was underway. We sat on the bleachers that looked out into the sea of bright ads and watched as the Santastic ship hopefully sank.

It was Clara and Mariana on the ground, easily the most attractive women in Times Square despite being bundled under their winter coats. Their beauty made it no problem for them to sidle up next to Santastic for a picture. With Roth conveniently using his body to obscure the sleight of hand, Mariana neatly reverse-pickpocketed a sizeable stash of coke, around a quarter of a kilo, individually wrapped into eightballs for maximum appearance of intent to sell, directly into Santastic's xylophone gig-bag. As they giggled and gushed and pretended to fawn over Santastic, the package was perfectly placed.

The original plan had been so good on paper when we were drunk, but the streamlining would save us all a lot of trouble, I figured. I realized after Reli shot down my idea of facilitating a giant coke-fueled stripper onslaught that we didn't need all the bells and whistles. Just the blow. Two minutes after it was planted, the anonymous tip I'd called in to the police paid off: a pair of officers and a shiny black K-9 murder-dog cruised past Santastic.

They were mid-"dance" number when the dog went ballistic and surged on his leash toward the pretentious but pitiable performers.

The dog caught one of the backup boys straight in the ass.

In the commotion that followed, I stood up on the bleachers, trying not to look too obvious. The dog had the kid on the ground and had a lock on not his ass, but one of those fanny-pack pouches that most of us knew had gone out of style in the '80s.

The backup Santa-hipster had been rocking one. Clara later told me it had been full of some really killer-smelling weed.

The dog was now salivating over its contents as tourists and the Santastic crew screamed.

The blow in Santastic's bag went untouched.

On the pavement, Clara and Mariana clambered for a better look. Opposite them, the cheerfully-costumed Marcos observed. Looking up in my direction, even from across half of Times Square I could clearly see him shake his giant furry character head as a "no."

Screams regarding "police brutality" and an "innocent victim" suddenly made a swath of cell phones appear. The last thing I needed was to be a part of Santastic's big crime scene. Phuc and I muttered our goodbyes as we strode off in different directions.

I went to the Pussycat. So did Clara. She had work to do, and now I did too. I had to try harder next time. And I was already out almost a quarter a key of blow—a cut quarter key, but a ridiculous expense nonetheless.

I assuaged my woes at the Pussycat with the classical definition of the day—nine ladies dancing. They were more than happy to show appreciation for the rest of key that, via Clara, they had been buying pieces of at reasonable rates. I tried to watch her do her Mrs. Claws thing, but her mind was obviously elsewhere, and so was mine. I watched as she gave emphatic but not empathetic lap dances to other guys, and I finally left after a quick cheek-kiss goodbye. I was pissed, and she was sad at seeing me pissed, and there's no amount of merry and bright that can come from even the whitest Christmas there. I think she knew— now that she had basically as much of the blow as she wanted—that it was no way to really be happy, either making easy money off of it or even when abusing the stuff. It just abused you worse for offering that goddamn glimpse of magic and then receding to reality. I left to accentuate that fact. This day had been a major low point just all around.

Then when Phuc texted and I deduced what he was up to, I figured I'd be feeling even worse.

The Ninth Day of Christmas.

I thought I'd hate myself when I heard what happened with Carnahan.

Honestly, I just hated how anticlimactic it was.

From what Phuc told me, a lavish orgy had been taking place at a hotel frequented by the members of RareBear. No expense had been spared—fine liquors, exotic drugs, well-tailored leathers and silks and sex toys of all ilk made their appearances.

Carson stuck out like bullshit in a China shop.

The RareBear crowd weren't holding back this time. Carson had begged to be allowed to wear a leather hood and get tied to the bed, but they didn't want his gross sweaty flab all over the Egyptian silk sheets. Carson had proceeded to walk around the party on all fours with a riding crop in his teeth, begging to be beaten. A few bears took him up on it, though with each swat of the crop they told him he'd been an asshole for trying to weasel up next to them at business meetings and nice cafes in real life.

Carson finally had enough of the abuse he'd brought on himself, and got grabby on some particularly handsome studs locked in a threesome. These things were deeply frowned on, and Phuc, ever helpful, was commissioned with removing him from the party.

As going the extra mile was what these types of power brokers were all about, Phuc took it upon himself to make sure Carson's pity-party had ended permanently.

Phuc had only to suggest that they sneak off for a smoke on a private penthouse balcony, one which several of the RareBears had made sure he had exclusive access to. The maid who was the only outsider on the floor was using a breast pump in a closet, trying to make ends meet for her and her child like so many other brutally-bereft strivers on this compassion-deserted island. Carson and Phuc had been on the private balcony for all of two minutes before their smoke session ended in a messy make-out attempt.

Phuc had slapped Carson across the face, which he said made a sound like dropping a pound of loose deli meat on the floor.

Carson Carnahan, heir to the Percy's Department Store fortune, current head of Holiday Operations, and utterly useless paragon of the pathetic, started to cry.

"NOBODY LIKES ME!"

"And that's nobody's responsibility but yours," Phuc said calmly.

"YOU'RE BEING A BULLY!"

"I'm only repeating a truth you yourself just confirmed. Nobody likes you."

"WHY ARE YOU SO MEAN?"

"The truth can be mean. It can also be nice. But seeing as how you've never made an effort to be nice, the truth will reflect that as such."

"I HATE MYSELF."

"So change. No one else is going to do it for you."

"IT'S TOO HARD."

"Life's hard. And you've already got a leg up with your family money. It's not going to get any easier until you start personally doing better."

"I DON'T KNOW HOW!"

"Have some self-awareness. Work harder on maintaining yourself. Learn from those around you instead of abusing your power to give orders. Understand where your emotions come from. Regulate your physical self. All of your handicaps are self-imposed, and all of them can be fixed. But only by yourself."

"I'LL SHOW THEM!"

And thus, at the place where temper tantrum met tough love, Carson Carnahan had made the choice to side with perpetual pity.

Phuc said that it took a full five minutes for Carson to maneuver his body over the railing.

Around three minutes in, he'd wanted to help, but thought better of it.

The impact of Carson's body weight hitting the sidewalk from fifty-one stories up wasn't pleasant. The blood spatter covered various snowbanks across both sides of the entire block.

It wasn't until some of the street's snow was plowed the next morning that they found one detached, bloated foot, still sporting a men's winter boot from the Percy's collection, piled up in the curb-snow around the corner. The coroner said Carnahan's blood was so distinctly fucked he'd have been in a wheelchair from diabetes within the next year, anyway.

So, as the blackjack dealers say, it was a push.

I'd been at the bar going over drum scores with Lenny. As Carson was hitting the pavement, I was thinking about hitting the bass drum. That chance at musical magnificence felt better than any beat down, literal or metaphorical.

But I'm not gonna lie, I was at Percy's the next afternoon, Santa suit in hand, ready to capture Carnahan's spot as lively and quick as the job description stated.

The Tenth Day of Christmas.

The paper's headline didn't include any "lords a-leaping" puns, which was kind of them.

Stretch was happy to see me. He suspected nothing.

Candy was, of course, not present. I was rehired on the spot by the sympathetic management team who knew how good I was.

I didn't have a drink all shift.

My joy at being reinstated in my job—even under these sort of circumstances—baffled me. I was smiling at least as brightly as any kid who hopped onto my lap and started extolling their wish list. Maybe it was because I knew how good at it I was. Maybe it's because I know how brutally rare actual second chances are. There's no replacing one good thing, even if there's millions of similar ones available. It's a mentality we've lost in our overkill consumer culture. But even if I was a cog in that capitalist machine, I was a happy one there. Helping.

I realized that I didn't even have a wishlist of my own. I had everything I wanted.

Of course, that didn't mean a few Christmas surprises weren't in store.

"What's the alternate lyrics for today, Reli?" I asked, later at the bar.

She flipped open an old songbook, one of many in the random bookshelves scattered around Trooley's Tourist Tavern, and scanned a page.

"Hmm... yesterday's was 'Bears A-Beating'... wonder what was going on the day they composed that! Let's see... today is... ha ha. 'Ten asses racing.' Any idea who that'd fit?"

My phone buzzed. It was Phuc. He'd sent a picture of a mangled bike that was so screwed up, it looked like an avant-garde metal sculpture. I looked up at Reli.

"Set up another round and you'll find out."

Phuc arrived several minutes later. Hrothgar the Hipster—human name, Roth—was in tow.

"I swear I had no idea the street would be that icy," he said, sitting and tucking into an Eight Maids A-Milk Stout. "I mean, I knew the entire route of the Obscene Caffeine Xmas Alleycat bike race, and I knew that most of those fuckers at Obscene Caffeine don't keep their brakes in good repair, and that they've been doing a lot of hard drugs during the day, maybe smoking some freebase now because the coke is getting too pricey or they're trying to stretch some lucky stash they found but... well, there was just no way to know for sure what those crazy kids would get up to." Roth shrugged and sipped.

"They could have been a lot more cautious about proper use of one-way streets, and not running red lights," Phuc added. "I know the nature of Alleycat racing is intentionally daring and risky, but my goodness. They should have at least worn helmets and not Santa hats."

"Oh boy," I said. "You know I hate asking this, but..."

"Ten casualties. Five with broken bones, three with broken bikes, two with broken skulls."

"Damn," I muttered.

"There was just no way I could have known their exact route and made sure it was extra icy with a few gallons of water beforehand," Phuc continued, giving Roth a wink and me a knowing nudge. "It was incomprehensible that I could have stopped, after I'd been waiting appropriately, just beyond the streetlight. No way I knew they'd run the red and be at my mercy. Just terrible.

"At least that's what I told the police."

Phuc shrugged and delicately sipped his martini, tilting up the space where his pinky finger would have been. Roth smiled a genuine smile of achievement, not the smug know-it-all hipster smirk that I knew had graced the faces of the other denizens of Obscene Caffeine.

258

"And you probably get to fill in a bunch of shifts there now, huh?" I asked Roth.

"Well it's not like I want to fill in as Santastic", he replied. "Anyway, I don't mind slinging java. I can read scripts for *real* auditions all day, and the full-time wage'll be good Christmas present money," he said. "I didn't know how I was gonna make my rent this month. I'm no Trustafarian. My parents gave me this jacket for Christmas last year to keep warm, and this year now I can do something nice for them."

"That's nice, son," I said, still pretty sure I was feeling genuinely happy about the day's events. But when Roth went outside to smoke, I turned to Phuc and spoke seriously.

"Look, I know we trained you from a young age to kill, and I know I let you repay a blood debt to me that was really important for both of us, and this bike race accident, well, honestly that just needed to happen. But promise me you won't make a habit of vigilante justice."

"As I live and breathe," Phuc gasped. "The Grinch's heart has grown three sizes today!"

"Shut up and drink your martini. There's sober children in Asia."

"Indeed there are, Sam, indeed there are. Just one more bit of business first though...if I'm supposed to cut out the killing, and our plan is already in motion, what the hell do you suppose is going to happen tomorrow?"

I just grinned. "*Our finest gifts we bring, par-rum-pa-pum-pum.*"

259

"Oh boy," said Phuc. "Well, we already cut down this giant trouble-tree and hauled it home, we might as well light it up."

The Eleventh Day of Christmas.

THE NEW YORK POST—12.24.15—MERRY XXXMAS!

Forget Rockefeller Center, today all the coolest Christmas celebrants were enjoying "the most wonderful time of the year"—in Times Square!

In a show of holiday cheer that brought New Yorkers and visitors from all walks of life together, today a dazzling holiday spectacle took over Times Square in a modern miracle on 42nd street.

In a surprise that warmed hearts while doubtlessly chilling a few bared bodies, twenty-four lovely ladies (some of whom are known better in the summertime as the body-painted, bare-breasted beauties, *Las Desnudas*) paraded their pasties in the pedestrian promenade. The women, who appeared in high spirits and completely immune to the cold despite being clad in little more than sparkly garland and twinkling smiles, danced more rowdily than the Rockettes while a crowd of fans of all ages cheered along.

Their soundtrack was provided in a surprise appearance from New York's Strongest: the Department of Sanitation's Emerald Society Pipe and Drum Corps. Who knew that they had managed to work a funky bagpipe version of *Blue Christmas* into their repertoire?

The oft-maligned costumed characters of Times Square got into the action as well, and some even got to act out their alter-egos when trouble was afoot. After an attempted attack on the *desnuda* darlings by a gang of scraggly Santas that have reportedly been terrorizing the town, reports indicate that a bootleg Batman, an imitation Iron Man, and a faux Elmo teamed up to physically subdue the carousing Clauses. The Santa scuffle, however, took a backseat to the dance party that followed as the delightful *desnudas* encouraged the crowd to dance the day away with them, along to the swinging strains of the Pipe and Drum Corps' version of *Jingle Bell Rock*...

The pipes and drums buzzed and thumped joyously outside the tiny construction port-a-potty I was wedged into. Shaking in front of me, an inch away from being skewered on one of my broken drumsticks, Braendeyn the Santastic quivered and quaked.

In the midst of the fight, where he and ten of his cracked-out cronies had tried in vain to battle the costumed Phuc, Roth, Marcos, and scads of homeless vets who we'd bribed to show up via yesterday's trash bags full of formerly—five-dollar Obscene Caffeine cupcakes, I'd quietly stepped away from the band and forced Santastic in here.

The crowd had been more than focused on the handsome, kilt-uniformed Emerald Society Pipe And Drum Corps who'd arrived at my request, plus the twenty-four half-naked strippers and bikini girls whose imperviousness to the actual snow had been facilitated by

Clara and Mariana's dissemination of the nasal-variety snow.

They hadn't seen us leave at all. And now I could cross one final name off this year's naughty list.

"You stole peoples' trust," I lambasted Santastic. "You stole from charities. And you stole earnings from people who are out here EVERY DAY, eking out a living by giving at least half a damn about this scene. How fucking dare you?" I brandished the drumstick as Santastic—I refused to call him "Braendeyn"—cowered, crouched over the toilet seat.

"I had to! The Obscene Caffeine money is all my dad's! I can't make enough money working there to sustain myself!"

"So it's fine to underpay everyone else there, but you deserve special treatment?"

"I need it! I'm a geeeeenius!" he wailed. "I was supporting the scene by bringing people there with my art! My dad would have to respect it then, if I brought in more customers!"

"But you didn't bring in customers. You just took the money, and squandered it trying to look cool. All while showing a distinct"—I jabbed him with the broken drumstick—"LACK of genius."

"You just don't understand my brilliance. You've probably never even heard of me. I am an IMPORTANT, RESPECTED..."

"Stuff it. Your friends like you for your drugs. Your hangout isn't even cool. The majority of the people you know don't have the intellect or attention span to cultivate anything worth a good goddamn, and are going to get bored of everything here, including you, and leave. The rest won't be able to afford anything here on the money they make with their negligible skill-sets, and you leading them on with a few hours at your shitty, overpriced coffee shop just keeps them stunted as humans and gentricidal to the people who actually worked to do something good for their community. Yeah, how hip is that? The people that you kicked out for all your precious coffee shops, they made a community here before it was cool. THEY did. Not you. Your so-called community has already abandoned you. I'd say they were being intelligent in that choice, but they're probably just being as unobservant and easily distracted as always."

I jabbed the stick into his skinny belly. He shrieked. It was pathetic.

I hadn't been this pathetic in a fight when I was his age.

Of course, now, look at where that mentality had gotten me.

"THIS ISN'T FAIR!" he wailed.

"Life's not fair," I said. "The closest thing that we get to it is the chance to make our own fairness." I withdrew the sharp stick a fraction of an inch. "Open the lid."

"What?!"

"Open the lid."

"Oh gawwwwwd," he moaned.

"He can't hear you. He's listening to the bagpipes for his kid's birthday right now."

"I don't wanna die heeeeeeere," Santastic sobbed. "Pleeeeaaaase. I'll work harder. I'll contribute more to the community. I'll be a better artist. I'll put in effort. Please don't kill me."

"You're going to get very into the community," I said. "From the bottom up."

And with that, I hoisted his skinny hipster ass into the air, dropped him into the port-a-potty, and slammed the lid down over his head. He was dazed but still breathing as I discreetly strode back outside and tied the door shut with a length of festive red packing twine from Percy's.

Re-shouldering my bass drum and hitting it harder than my heartbeat, I rejoined the party.

The Twelfth Day of Christmas. Christmas Eve.

Reli held up her end of the bargain. She always threw a hell of an Orphan Christmas party, but this was one that the ghosts of Christmas past, present, and future would all envy. The bar was jammed with everyone from the now-famous *Times Squaredance*, all still shining from the day's spectacle. Best of all, not a hipster in sight. They must have been too cool for our communal Christmas.

At the end of the bar, I held court with Roth and Phuc as endless rounds appeared before us. "You know, people hate on hipsters when they try to pass off their pretentious half-ass bullshit as art," I told Roth, "But YOU must have some serious acting chops to have been able to straight-faced tell Santastic and his crew it was a good idea to get all yacked up and come fight us, gang-turf style. You might actually have what it takes to be a real actor, if you cut off that man-bun."

"Thanks," Roth smiled and raised his arm (still clad in the rented Ironman costume) and clinked his Eight Maids A-Milk Stout pint to mine. "Maybe someday I'll be able to act as happy as you do when you see all those Christmas kids."

"That's not acting, son," I said. "Not anymore. I've achieved an actual ability to share joy. Well, sharing joy and noble fisticuffs. But mostly joy." Phuc, Roth and I clinked glasses all together, then drank deeply.

"You were an excellent double agent," Phuc, still dressed as Batman, congratulated Roth. He eyeballed me and spoke distinctly. "Not that *I'd* know."

Sergeant Franklin sidled over, freshly shaven and wearing an ancient but clean Army cold-weather jacket. Some of the other homeless vets, similarly sharp from having been taken in by a shelter for the evening, were shooting pool with the still-kilted Sanitation guys and enjoying a few of the many pitchers that we'd bought with the "*Times Squaredance*" proceeds from the delighted crowd.

"Just wanted to say thanks from me and the boys for giving us all those baked goodies. It tastes like organic drywall, but it beats having to go hungry. I can't believe those coffeehouse creeps charge five dollars for that stuff! But hey, we'll raid their trash bags every day if it means consistently copious chow since no one's buying. Maybe even weird out some yuppies in the process and take the property values back down. Well done, sir." He saluted me. I returned it.

Marcos, still in his furry red character suit but without the head, strolled over with the still-shirtless Mariana on one oversized arm. Mariana was wrapped in tinsel like a tree, with ornaments hanging from her earlobes and pasties, and a light-up star on her headband.

"Awesome party, bro!" Marcos said. "Yo, some cat hit me up about the video of me and your boys throwin' down on the Santas... we viral stars now, dawg! I might get a streaming video deal!"

"That's great, man. Maybe now you'll get a promotion, you know, to acting someplace INDOORS on Broadway!"

Marcos laughed. Mariana gave me a hug. "And the *desnudas* have got a bigger following than ever now," she added. "Next summer, there'll be no stopping us! *Tetas para todos!*" The crowd of strippers and bikini-bartendresses that had served as the dance squad cheered voluminously.

Marcos and Mariana tango'd over to the dance floor, ebullient. I took a long sip of my beer to cool my burning brain as the completely captivating Clara strode toward me.

She was wearing the same furry snow boots as she had that morning during the dance party/fight in Times Square, and probably the same red booty shorts. I couldn't tell, as she was wearing my furry Santa jacket as apparently her only other garment. It fell to the tops of her taut thighs and fluffed open at the top to expose her exceptional entourage. A single jingle bell hung deeply down from her neck.

She kissed me so hard I tasted peppermint even over the powerful flavors of the evening's constant beer. I looked into her beautiful brown eyes, which were sharply in focus. She stuffed a wad of something into the sporran I wore over my Emerald Society kilt. Not wanting to take my gaze from her, even for a second, I just kept staring at her, reveling in the moment.

"I sold it, bebe. All of it. Is the cash for you?"

"What about school? That money's yours."

"I make more. That..." She grabbed my sporran, and left her hand lingering near my crotch. "... is what you spent, porsooing happiness for me. With me. Thank you for believing in what I got."

"I believe in much more than that," I said. "I believe in what we'll get next too. But no more perrico, okay? Too loco!"

"*Possible,*" she smiled. She kissed me again.

"Hey! Santa Claus!" Onstage, U™ was getting ready to fire up another set. The singer, a rocker girl dressed in all black but wrapped head-to-toe in multicolored Christmas lights, had beckoned me.

"Yeah?"

"I already know I'm getting coal this year, so let's fire it up! Come up here and rock with us!"

Climbing onstage, I donned my bass drum rig and Santa hat. "More carols?" I asked.

"Hell no!" the bassist, wearing a Santa-skull T-shirt that said "NUCLEAR MISSLETOE", declared.

"Know any Zeppelin?" asked the lead guitarist, who was rocking a black leather Santa hat with black fur. "How about something off *Presence*, Santa?" The band laughed.

I nodded at him, then the drummer, who had Sharpie'd a Santa hat on his biceps Misfits skull tattoo. Perched on his head was a pair of reindeer antlers, entangled with a wayward stripper bra.

"You guys kick it off. I'll jump in. Chimney style." I pounded my bass drum and smiled. The crowd cheered wildly.

I felt myself smiling hard. Real hard, like... well, yeah, fuck you... like a kid on Christmas. I grabbed the mic and hollered at the crowd as the band sprang to life. Around the room, the other drummers saddled on their instruments as well.

To the top of the roof, to the top of the wall
Now bash away, bash away, bash away all!

A FAMILY CHRISTMAS TERROR

CHAPTER 9

"New York's got a lot of crazies in it," Grandpa said. "Doesn't sound like it's changed much since I lived there."

"When did you live there, Grandpa?" Nancy asked.

"The 50's. All hustle and bustle. Nobody stayed still. Everyone trying to make it in the 'big time.' I guess it's still the same."

Jack said, "I don't know, Grandpa. I've got some friends from New York. They tell me some weird shit that happens there." He gulped. "I mean, weird stuff. Hey, Mom, this is, like, the best eggnog ever!"

"Smooth, Jack," Nick said.

"Were you all not here listening to that last story?" Judy looked around at them. "One little 's-word' is not going to curl my hair or make me cast disapproving glances at you." Judy smiled and took a gulp of her nog. "But you are right, though, Jack. This is one of the best batches of this shit I've ever made!

"Judy!"

Judy sipped her eggnog, calm and collected. "Oh come on. Those words have been around for centuries—even longer than Grandpa. Speaking of which, Grandpa, why don't you read the next story? We can have a later dinner," Judy said.

Everyone was still staring at her.

"Read, Grandpa."

"Yes, ma'am. It's called, *I'll be Dead For Christmas.*"

Dan stared at his wife over the rim of his mug. "Sounds interesting."

I'LL BE DEAD FOR CHRISTMAS

KRISTI AHLERS

"*I'll be home for Christmas*" warbled from the speakers. Ainsley rolled her eyes and switched off the radio. The first carol of the season seemed to happen earlier and earlier each year. It meant Christmas was close, and Ainsley Bettencourt loathed this holiday above all else.

Sleet pelted the windshield. The wipers struggled to remove the ice. With the exception of the lighthouse in the distance, the island was totally dark. Ainsley's palms, slick with sweat, gripped the steering wheel as she nosed the car off the ferry and onto the road. The wind buffeted the small compact she'd rented. Ainsley white-knuckled her already tightened grip on the steering wheel, as the car bumped along the small blacktop road.

Christmas. Always a time of sadness. Always a time of terror. Her parents were killed on Christmas Eve. Her aunt died when Ainsley was fourteen, on Christmas Day. They found her body, broken and bleeding, at the base of the lighthouse stairs. Ainsley left Bettencourt Island the

271

minute she turned eighteen, promising herself to never return.

But things change.

And she was back on Bettencourt Island.

On the eve of Christmas.

The headlights shone on the drifting snow, barely cutting through the thick sheet of white. Another gust of wind slammed into the car and it fishtailed for a moment, further heightening her unease.

"Screw this Goddamn island! I'm only fucking here to spend it with Nanna in the first place, and now she won't even answer her stupid phone!" Ainsley picked up her cell phone and pushed the call icon. The soft glow illuminated the inside of the car, making the road even that much more difficult to see.

Ring.

"Come on, Nanna."

Straight to voicemail.

Again.

Ainsley tossed the phone on the passenger seat and tried to ignore the sinking feeling in her gut. After months of doctor's visits and tests, her gram had finally gotten the dreaded diagnosis... cancer. The only reason she'd returned to the miserable island was to spend the holiday with her dying grandmother. Ainsley adored her and vowed she wouldn't let this holiday pass without spending it with the elderly woman who raised her and supported her dreams.

Even when Ainsley left Maine for the bright lights of New York, her grandmother encouraged her, knowing it would take Ainsley away from the home she'd grown up in and the traditions of family.

And the family secrets.

Finally, she crested the hill. On the edge of land, jutting out over the stormy Atlantic, stood the clapboard house and lighthouse. Although fully automated years ago, a Bettencourt had stood sentinel over the coast since the seventeen-hundreds. Ainsley had begged her grandmother to come away with her when she'd left. However, Marie was steadfast in her refusal. This was her home. This is where she'd grown up. This was the place she loved. A place she'd vowed she would be safe.

The light from above flashed its warning to any sailor out on those tempestuous waters. Although the light no longer required the same care and physical effort to keep it illuminating the treacherous waters surrounding the island, it still needed maintenance. Her grandmother had a person do all the heavy upkeep once a week. Ainsley was pleased about this, as she didn't want her seventy-year-old grandmother climbing the spiraling iron stairs to the top of the tower.

The moment Ainsley reached the house, she threw the car door open and stood. Her heart kicked in her chest at the sight of the imposing house from her childhood. To an outsider, the building was a charming white clapboard house, with two stories and a wide wrap-around porch. To Ainsley, the house had always seemed... unwelcoming. A heaviness always seemed present—more so during the week before Christmas.

Swallowing the knot of fear forming in her throat, Ainsley shoved her smartphone into her pocket and slammed the car door. The wind cut jagged currents left and right, almost propelling her forward, like hands on her back pushing her toward the house. Ainsley worked the already drenched hood of her jacket over her head and ran for the door.

A large evergreen wreath, festooned with colorful glass bulbs and a large red velvet ribbon, adorned the door. A door that was unlocked. She hesitated for the space of half a heartbeat and pushed it open with trembling hands. The warmth of the interior smacked her in face after the brutal cold and wind of the storm.

Warm gingerbread, mulled apple cider and peppermint filled the old house, scents that for most would be warm and welcoming. For Ainsley, they reminded her of loss and terror.

Christmas meant evil. She'd never celebrated the Yule season once she'd moved to New York. She never understood the joy of the season; why people cheered when they saw the huge Christmas tree go up in Rockefeller Center; the smiles on the faces of ice skaters on the rink holding hands; or the excitement pouring off the little kids about the coming of the Jolly Old Elf.

Christmas meant death and fear.

She flipped the light switch beside the door, looked around. The hallway was empty. The only sound was the rhythmic ticking of the massive grandfather clock against the wall.

Tick, tock, tick, tock.

"Grandma!" she called, tossing her hood back.

No answer.

Ainsley poked her head into the front parlor. A Christmas tree stood in the corner. A large fir, the colorful lights illuminated and cast their cheery glow over the room. Under the tree sat one small present wrapped in scarlet paper and gold ribbon. The fireplace, where her stocking hung beside her grandmothers, was cold. No fire. Her grandma's favorite rocking chair stood still. No brandy snifter or opened book on the end table.

"Grandma, I'm home."

At the silence in reply, panic ran through her bloodstream. Tossing her coat on the nearby rocker, she quickly searched the downstairs. The old wooden floor creaked when Ainsley's weight touched down in strategic places.

The sound of the storm grew louder, as she made her way up the old stairs to the upper landing. The faint scent of lilacs, a fragrance her grandmother couldn't abide, lingered on the air. Ainsley had also learned to hate the smell of lilacs. Their cloyingly sweet aroma heralded the darkness. The heavy and frightening mantel of oppression Ainsley always experienced in this house.

A chill literally wrapped around her and she rubbed her arms, uncertain where the draft came from. The lilac scent, pungent now, overwhelmed Ainsley to the point where she covered her mouth and gagged. She ran the rest of the way up the stairs until she reached the landing. The light from below did nothing to alleviate the darkness up here. Ainsley reached out and flipped the switch on the wall. The bulb overhead flickered and dimmed before settling on illuminating the space with a dim, yet buttery luminosity.

She took a step toward her grandmother's room and stopped promptly. The distant sound of *Silent Night* drifted on the air.

"Grandma?"

The music grew louder the closer she drew to the partially open room.

Ainsley swallowed, her mouth and throat dry as the Sahara, while she walked down the short hallway—which seemed to grow longer and longer as she approached the door.

"Hello?"

She pushed the door open further and stepped into the room. Heart hammering in her rib cage, she held her breath and flipped on the switch.

The room sat in perfect order.

And empty.

And now silent.

The silence after the sound of the Christmas carol unnerved her, and the sensation of being watched crawled over her skin. She looked around out of the corner of her eye, fearful of what she'd see, and more fearful of what she wouldn't.

She was about to back out of the room and she caught a flash of movement out of the corner of her eye. She stopped and walked back into the space.

"Who's there? Grandma?"

The only sound in the room was that of the storm.

No. She shook her head.

The panic she'd barely managed to keep at bay began to bubble and flow through Ainsley's veins like carbonated water under pressure. It threatened to explode from her and she knew she needed to gain control before all was lost.

She took a moment and pulled out her smartphone. Her grip was tight and she swiped the screen, waking it so she could place a call. She knew she was alone—and yet wasn't.

It's happening again.

Fear left a knot in her throat as she retraced her steps back to the hall. The sensation of being watched overwhelmed her. Ainsley stopped. An icy breath tickled the back of her neck. Closing her eyes, she took a deep breath.

"Ainsley."

The whisper of her name a tremble jolted through her entire body, propelling her toward the staircase. Gripping the wooden railing, Ainsley ran down the stairs.

It was happening again. Fear and panic lashed at Ainsley's heels. She had to find her grandmother.

Logically, Ainsley knew her grandmother hadn't been in the house for quite some time. She wouldn't have let the fire burn low. Never on a stormy Atlantic night like tonight. And especially not when she knew to expect Ainsley.

The lighthouse.

Her grandmother couldn't be out there. Not in this storm.

But it was Christmas Eve. When things that went bump in the night came alive. When the sound reverberating through the house wasn't that of Santa and his reindeer on the roof.

"I'm too late," Ainsley whispered.

She stumbled into the kitchen, the last place she hadn't looked.

Empty.

Ainsley sighed and placed her palm on the table. Bowing her head, she gritted her teeth and fought back the forming tears.

Why?

Why this place?

Why this lighthouse.

Why this damned holiday?

The nightmare of finding her parents on Christmas morning, replayed in her mind. That was the day Christmas stopped being a magical time, and instead, became a time of horror.

A horror she couldn't bear to repeat. Not with Nanna.

Blinking, Ainsley sucked in a fortifying breath and looked up.

A gingerbread replica of the lighthouse sat in the center of the table, a tradition her grandmother had each year. Ainsley smiled, feeling her heart tug in her chest. Although they always made the gingerbread house together weeks before the holiday, her grandmother only allowed her to eat the confection on Christmas Eve. Even this game, this one small happiness, was never enough to ease Ainsley's anxiety when it came to the Yule season.

Turning her back on the memory, Ainsley grabbed her coat and then the flashlight Nanna kept on the counter. Switching it on, she turned toward the door leading to the lighthouse. She reached out, curling her fingers around the ancient brass knob, the mechanism stiff from the North Atlantic cold. She stepped into the breezeway connecting the light to the keeper's house. They built the houses this way to help prevent any fire from back in the day when oil was used to operate the light.

The sound of the storm was deafening as she stood at the now closed door. The wind, cold and severe, took her breath away. Ducking her head against the oncoming gale, she secured her hood and walked slowly over the slippery ground toward the cliff.

"Please don't be here. Please don't be here."

Nausea, hot and acidic, pooled in Ainsley's belly when she came to a stop at the old fence. Sand piled up against the weathered boards and the sea grass bent under the onslaught of the unrelenting wind. The sound of the angry ocean crashing against the rocks filled the air, as lightning illuminated the landscape. The sharp and jagged rocks down below glistened under the assault of water and snow.

Memories of the last time she stood at this fence crashed over her, as fierce and violent as the waves below. She'd been seven. The broken and battered bodies of her mama and daddy rested below her. The Atlantic pulling at them with each breaking wave. The excitement of what

Santa had brought her forever eclipsed by the loss of her parents. By the realization something was wrong here.

Very wrong.

Even now, the memory of her parent's death iced her blood. The sense of loss remained to this day.

Ainsley's jaw began to chatter. She panned her flashlight over the rocks.

"Please don't be there. Please don't be there," she chanted, the mantra ridiculous but better than screaming.

She stepped closer to the edge of the cliff. Her foot slipped and she wind milled her arms to prevent falling to the icy ground. She caught her balance, whimpering as she stepped away from the ledge. Fear stilled her movement. The storm continued to pummel her and the coast. Tipping her head back, she looked to the top of the light where the lantern signal flashed and warned mariners off of the rocky jetty. A light two hundred and seven feet tall. A fall from that height would be deadly.

Or a shove.

Closing her eyes, she sent a prayer heavenward and moved once again closer to the edge of the cliff. With deliberate and slow intent, she focused her gaze where the flashlight cut a path through the darkness.

A scream tore from her throat and she dropped to the wet ground. The sea pulled at her beloved grandmother, battered and broken on the wet rocks below.

"NO!"

She collapsed to her knees on the frozen ground, sealing a palm over her mouth to silence her cries.

280

The wind tore her words away, as she sobbed her heartbreak. The sleet pelted her now uncovered head, but she hardly felt the pain and sting of the ice. She knew she needed to move, needed to call the police. But she couldn't tear her gaze away from the body dancing in the water with the ebb and flow of each wave.

A laugh, diabolical and amused, drifted down the beach.

Ainsley scooted back on her backside shaking her head back and forth.

Her stomach dropped to her feet. Her hearing had to be playing tricks on her. She couldn't have just heard a laugh from down below.

"Ainsley."

The singsong calling of her name forced her to her feet. She slipped and fell as she tried to scramble away from the icy ledge... the sound of a ghostly voice.

"Ainsley."

"No! No!" Ainsley spun around, looking through the darkness for the source of the sound. An icy cold fist tightened around her heart. Holding her breath, Ainsley slowly tipped her head back, exhaling relief when she saw the lighthouse railing empty.

"You're next." The words were spoken aloud, crisp and clear in her ear.

Gasping, Ainsley spun, letting loose a scream. Floating in front of her was a woman, grotesquely formed. Her hair long and unkempt, string-like—almost like seaweed, danced on the air. Her face was white and skeletal, yet Ainsley could make out dark, dead eyes, and bruised, colored bags beneath the eyes. Jagged tears in the thing's skin oozed a black gelatinous muck. The clothes were old, a long full skirt of indeterminate color and a shirtwaist served as a top with mutton sleeves.

The thing raised its arm and pointed a bony finger at Ainsley.

"You're next."

Chapter 2

Ainsley slammed the door shut, setting the old deadbolt with shaking fingers. With her back literally against the wall, she tried to calm her racing heart. Her grandmother was dead. Shattered on the rocks below the lighthouse. Like her parents. Like her aunts.

Like you'll be.

Shaking away the thought, Ainsley took in her surroundings.

The house was quiet. The sound of the storm muffled to her own hearing now. On wobbly legs, she moved into the front parlor, near the glowing Christmas tree. Stripping off her scarf and coat, she dropped them on the rocker and collapsed by the fireplace. Tossing in log after log, Ainsley quickly set a fire, hungry for the warmth it would provide. She struck a match, and watched as the flame flared to life before she set it to the paper and kindling. The flames ate greedily at the wood and soon caught, and heat began to thaw her.

The lone present sitting beneath the Christmas tree caught her eye. Ainsley crawled over to the huge fir and sat cross-legged beside its festive boughs. Tears welled in her eyes, as she ran her finger over the velvet ribbon. She wiped the salty drops away with the back of her hand and unwrapped the small box.

Inside was another antique box, polished golden wood and etched with the old family coat of arms.

Grandma's treasure box.

Curiosity took the place of her despair. With care, she raised the lid and saw a small, burgundy, bound journal at the bottom of the box. Beneath that was a note and two small velvet bags.

My darling Ainsley,

There is so much I should've told you, so much sooner. However, I found it impossible to verbalize the truth, and foolish old woman that I am, though perhaps I could change fate.

By the time you read this, clichéd as it is, I'll be dead. There is no help for it. The curse demands it.

I must get to the purpose of this letter. You must end this now, before you fall prey to the same evil.

You must find the portrait of your ancestress Claire and destroy it.

I mean it, Ainsley.

Burn it to a cinder.

Before you set flame to the canvas, you must salt it with rock salt and holy water. I have secured the vial of holy water and the rock salt in the bags along with this note. I have never seen the portrait, but I knew it existed. It is how she remains here to kill and take her vengeance.

I have enclosed the family journal, but to paraphrase: Before her death, also on Christmas Day 1842, Claire's younger sister painted Claire's likeness as a tribute. She mixed Claire's ashes into the paints she used, as a tribute. Never realizing, I'm sure, that she gave her evil sister the means by which to haunt us all. I've looked everywhere for this painting and sadly have left the lighthouse for you. I simply could not climb its steep stairs, but I'm sure that is where she's keeping it. I am sorry I failed. Forgive me, my beautiful granddaughter and be safe. I love you.

Ainsley placed the letter in her lap.

Her eyes fixed on one word.

Curse.

The fear and the sense of being watched had been true.

Ainsley sat back against the sofa, the note from her grandmother crumpled in her hand. Suddenly, the rocking chair by the fireplace began to move slowly.

Back and forth.

Back and forth.

The floor creaked beneath the chair. The lights flickered and suddenly the radio came on. Crackling and static hissed through the house. The dial moved up and down before it settled on a station and filled the air.

"*I'll be home for Christmas, you can count on me ...*" trilled from the old radio.

An antique radio Ainsley knew wasn't plugged in or functional.

Her breathing turned into a pant; her wide eyes were fixed on the rocking chair. The room got cold and the scent of lilacs and decay overpowered the fragrance of the fir tree. The radio tuned again, this time the carol *Silent Night* began as the rocker began to move faster.

The baby Jesus from the nativity scene on the mantel flew at Ainsley. Screaming, she ducked before the object hit her. Ainsley brushed her hair out of her face and turned. The statue was imbedded in the wall. If it had hit her head...

She scrambled to her feet, shaking from head to toe.

"Stop it!"

The horrifying sound of laughter filled the room—not loud laughter, more soft and muffled, and no less eerie for the volume of it.

Ainsley reached into the box her grandmother gifted her with and pulled out the two drawstring bags and clutched them to her chest. They were a treasure beyond measure.

As quickly as the rocking started, it stopped.

The radio fell silent, and the room once again filled with the woodsy scent of the tree and the spicy fragrance of gingerbread.

Without even realizing it, the heavy oppression that snuck up on Ainsley lifted.

The sound of the storm quieted.

She went to the front door and opened it. Thick fluffy flakes of snow drifted into piles. Her heart sank, the storm didn't look as if it would let up anytime soon. The icy wind tore at her long dark hair and sliced through her. The muffled howling of the storm, due to the snow, seemed to make this even more unsettling.

She closed the door and looked around.

What should I do? Should she be the heroine in those movies she always found herself screaming at: the-too-stupid-to-live-running-back-into-the-haunted-house-with-the-axe-wielding-murderer, or be smart and get to her car and wait out the storm then take the first ferry back to the mainland?

The house shuddered at that moment and Ainsley's eyes flew open. The doors opened and closed, slamming rapidly and loudly.

"Stop it!" Ainsley screamed and tightened her hand on her little bags.

She had a job to do and she needed to do it now.

A shadow crawled across the wall.

The icy feel of its touch enveloped her.

Ainsley knew she needed to put an end to this spirit. Even as a child, she'd always known evil lurked here. But somehow, she'd managed to ignore it. After all, the spirit never showed itself to her.

Until tonight.

With this thought in mind, she stuffed the bags her grandmother had left her, along with her flashlight, into her coat pocket.

Her gloves were still soaking wet with snow, melting and dripping onto the rag-braided rug covering the hardwood floor. She shook her coat and put it back on. Then she tracked to the kitchen and dug around in the junk drawer and secured a lighter in the bag as well.

The lights went out, bathing her in the kitchen in utter darkness. She squeezed her eyes and rooted around on the counter for the flashlight she'd placed there.

"*Ainsley.*"

She closed her eyes and clenched her fists.

"*Ainsley.*" The voice taunted in the darkness.

The air grew frigid and her teeth began to chatter. Fear, unlike anything she'd experienced, coiled around her.

"*Ainsley.*"

The whisper came right beside her ear. The warmth of the ghostly breath and the chill in the air forced Ainsley to squeeze her eyes shut and pray.

Her grandmother was dead outside in the elements. Ainsley was alone in the house, cut off from society—thanks to the storm—with a malevolent entity taunting her.

There was no one here to help her; she was going to have to save herself. She shook off the debilitating fear and frantically felt around for the flashlight. The cool metal light resembled a lifeline to her and she grasped it tightly then flicked it on. She panned the rather bright beam of light around the kitchen. The light settled on an oily looking shape dissipating slowly into the darkness of the corner.

Ainsley carefully crossed to the door that led to the lighthouse. A laugh, blood curdling and childish, wrapped around her before she found herself falling forward after a deliberate push to her back. She caught herself on the door jamb. The power of the spirit was unavoidable, and the danger palatable.

Chapter 3

The climb up the two-hundred-and-seven stairs seemed to take forever. The metal of the handrail burned her hands with the cold through her grandmother's gloves that she had donned before heading to the beacon. The snow managed to drift and pile in the short time since she'd been outside. Her heart seized with the knowledge her grandmother was still out there and would remain on the rocks until the ferry could get back after the storm and the police could come out.

Her steps echoed in the empty tower as she ascended higher and higher. Sweat, despite the cold, trickled down her spine. Her breath wheezed in and out of her mouth, her lungs burned. Her thighs screamed as she reached the second landing. And the sound of the storm echoed in the empty tower stairwell. The whistling and thundering of the surf was almost deafening to her senses.

When she reached the floor with the lens mechanism, she rested her head against the wall. She wheezed with the effort to drag air into her constricted lungs.

The haunting laugh of a ghost filled the air.

"Ohhhhh, Ainsssssssleeeeeeyyyyyy."

Ainsley resisted the urge to cover her ears and rush back down the twisting metal stairs.

She panned the flashlight around the room. There was a desk and old file cabinet against the wall beside it. The light now was fully automated, and this part of the room was a throwback to a bygone era. She took a deep breath. Her grandmother believed the painting that held the spirit of a ghost was in this room. Somewhere. But where?

Ainsley had never been up here. It was stark in its furnishing, and nothing adorned the walls. An old oak desk sat under a small window. Ainsley went over, pulled the chair out, and sat. She started to pull drawers out, looking for a secret compartments. Besides it being a portrait, she didn't know how large it was or what the painting would contain. Oh, how she wished her grandmother had talked to her sooner. She'd wished she'd not been so stupid and stubborn and had spoken to her grandmother about what she'd felt.

Thunder rumbled overhead and lightning lit the room.

A thunderstorm during a snowstorm?

The heavy oppressive feeling once again settled over the room.

All at once, she couldn't breathe. Couldn't see. The fragrance of lilac coated her throat. Gagging, she pushed away from the desk, desperate for fresh air.

She stumbled out onto the landing and clung to the black-lacquered railing, gulping the stale, cold air as a wave of dizziness assailed her. Overwhelmed, she slid down to the ground and tried to draw in enough air to settle herself.

A gust of wind, stale and warm, so at odds with the tempest blowing outside, rushed over her. She gained her feet and pushed away from the railing. Her body revolted, weighing her down, as if dipped in cement.

Forcing herself back into the room, a coat of darkness filled her. Not physical, but an evil darkness.

Is this what grandmother experienced?

At the thought, determination fueled her.

It was time to get this done, do what her grandmother asked of her—it was the least she could do after leaving the old woman alone.

Ainsley began tearing through the file cabinet. She yanked on the bottom drawer and the whole thing shook. She managed to scoot out of the way just as the thing toppled over. Had she remained where she'd been, she'd have received serious injury.

As she gasped for breath, she noted a part of the wall that seemed different—discolored from the rest. Even in the dark, with only a flashlight for illumination, it was obvious.

On hands and knees she crawled to the wall. She tapped on it and noticed it was hollow sounding.

A screeching came from down below. Ainsley quickly hit the wall with her Maglite, and was surprised when the wall easily gave away and left a large hole. She leaned in and looked into the wall, shining the flashlight's bright beam into the space.

There in the dust and damp recess was a rolled canvas.

She reached in and pulled it out.

The wind swirled, yanking at her hair. Lilac filled the space and she sat back and unrolled the canvas, hands shaking as the colors were revealed, and so too was the face of a woman. Her sober expression stared back at Ainsley.

A mirror image of herself.

She gasped and dropped the canvas. A swirling gray mass raced around her like a tempest.

She watched, transfixed with horror, as mist formed into a grotesque and misshapen form of a woman. Her hair was long and dark, stringy and dull. Her eyes were sunken, bruised under the eyes, and pure evil emanated from the dark orbs.

Ainsley grabbed the portrait and zipped it into her coat, since it wouldn't fit in her pocket and turned to leave. The door slammed shut. She tried to pull on the door, turn the handle, but it wouldn't budge. The sound of ghostly laughter filled the air.

Before Ainsley could move or think, something threw her across the room. She slid down the wall, the air knocked from her lungs. Pain radiated through her. A hand pulled her up by her hair and Ainsley resisted the urge to cry out in pain. Although she didn't see the ghost, the smell of her perfume filled the lens room.

"*Ah, poor little Ainsley. Thinking she could have a happy ending and destroy me. Tut, tut.*"

"Why?" Ainsley, managed to gasp out. "Why do you do this?"

"Why? Because my happiness was stolen from me, and I vowed before I died that no one, not one single woman, would ever know true happiness."

"But my grandmother, she was old, she..."

"Was happy!"

The scent of decay now started to permeate the room. The specter let Ainsley go. Panting, she crawled on hands and knees to the center of the room while frantically digging out the bag of rock salt. Quickly, Ainsley poured the salt around her in a circle, remaining within the salty circumference. Inside the circle, she knew she was safe.

For the time being.

Ainsley pulled out her smartphone, noting it was after midnight. She considered calling for help, but what would she say? "Help me, I'm trapped in a lighthouse with a vengeful ghost?"

The door slammed open. A blast of frigid air rushed into the tiny room, blowing her hair around her face, sending the maps and papers, long forgotten on the desk, swirling into the air. She looked down, horrified, as the salt ring she'd poured began to part.

"No!"

She watched, helpless, while the ring protecting her disappeared. She ran toward the door.

"You will die now, Ainsley."

Cold hands covered her shoulder blades and pushed. Hard. Ainsley fell forward, toppling like a rag doll down the twisting stairs. She tucked into herself, trying to protect her head.

After what seemed like forever, she came to a stop on one of the landings. Her head ached and her body screamed. She'd underestimated the ghost and her power. Ainsley sat on the landing, her flashlight gone. The cold blew up from the bottom of the lighthouse numbed her fingers.

She couldn't continue to fight this ghost. And she knew she couldn't wait to get the painting down the stairs to the fireplace in order to destroy it.

She needed to do it here.

Now.

Before she could pull the canvas out of her coat, another icy punch slammed into her, pushing her to the edge of the stairs. Her hands, raw and sore from the first fall, tried in vain to still the forward momentum. She tumbled down the next flight of stairs.

Panic seized her.

She couldn't fall down all two hundred.

She'd die.

Screaming all the will and determination she could muster. Ainsley shot her feet out in an arms-out attempt to stop her downward momentum. A wretched crack rent the air and she came to a stop. Her ribs, no doubt broken, made breathing almost impossible. Unbearable agony ripped through her hip all the way down to the leg and she realized she couldn't move. Blood dripped down her face and into her eye.

Pushing up to sit, she collapsed back to the iron landing. Her shoulder, no doubt as broken as her legs, was useless in the task of getting her upright. Ainsley prayed while she tried to push up with her other arm. Succeeding, she backed herself up against the last flight of stairs. Wincing in pain, she forced herself to dig the painting out of her coat, eventually using her teeth and dropping it in her lap.

Panting, exhausted, she used her good hand to spill the rock salt on the canvas. She tossed them aside, then doused the painting with lighter fluid. The stink of the fuel made her eyes water. The cold liquid seeped through the canvas and onto the fabric of her jeans.

It didn't matter.

Ainsley knew she wasn't getting out of this alive. But she could take this bitch with her.

Her body trembled, going into shock, as she felt around for the lighter. Her fumbling fingers took several tries before she was able to get the light to flare. Crying in pain, she used her good arm to scoot away.as the flames consumed the old painting.

A ghostly scream filled the air, and the flames began to consume the canvas.

The woman's ghostly face appeared in front of Ainsley's. Flames licked at her cheeks, smoke billowing out of her nostrils and eyes sockets. Cold hands seized Ainsley's arms, hoisting her above the ground. Broken and bloody, she could do no more than watch as the burning specter tossed her over the edge of the black iron railing.

Everything moved in slow motion for Ainsley. Flames engulfed the ghost, just as the flames consumed the canvas.

Her screams, once full of menace and taunting, now shrill and panicked.

I did it, Grandma, Ainsley thought, closing her eyes.

The air pillowed her body as she plummeted to the ground.

When she looked up again, the darkness was replaced by a blinding, pure, white light. Her grandmother and mother held out their hands.

"*I'll be home for Christmas,*" sang in the night.

"*Where the love light beams, I'll Be Home For Christmas.*" Ainsley smiled and reached for them, knowing in a moment, her life would be over. But she'd be with the people who loved her most.

For once the Christmas carol didn't leave her sad. Instead, it warmed her with love and ended her fear.

A FAMILY CHRISTMAS TERROR

CHAPTER 10

"I always thought lighthouses were creepy," Nancy said. "I wouldn't have gone there."

"Well, you know," Grandpa began, "Lighthouses were pretty helpful to me a few times."

Dan closed his eyes and put his head back.

"Way back when I was your age, I worked on a fishing trawler off Cape Cod. There were a couple of times storms came in, and if it wasn't for that lighthouse, things could have ended badly."

"Cool," Nick said. "I didn't know that. That must have been awesome."

"It had its moments." Grandpa nodded.

"Well, I'm grateful for the lighthouse too," Dan interrupted. "Otherwise, if you'd wrecked your boat, I wouldn't have been born. Now who wants to read the next story?"

Grandpa smiled." Why don't you read the next little gem here? It's called, *Small Price To Pay.*" He handed the book to Dan.

"I might need a little more of your eggnog, my dear." He raised his empty glass to Judy. "Go a little heavier on your 'secret' ingredient."

Judy took his glass, saying, "I see where Dan gets it now."

"Speaking of..." Dan piped up.

"I suppose..." Judy said, taking the glass from him. "I'm glad I made a full pitcher."

"It *is* the best ever," Nick called after her as she walked to the kitchen. "Go ahead, Dad, read the next one."

SMALL PRICE TO PAY

DON BRUNS

The man started earlier every year with those damned holiday lights. Here it was barely October and he was up on the roof, two members of his construction crew helping string row after row of blinking colored lights. Oh, they weren't blinking yet. That would be reserved for the "grand event" as his neighbor called it. They would blink after all the other lighted decorations were in place.

And every year there was something new. Not to replace, but to add to this menagerie, this massive collection of wired chaos. Casting a harsh, garish glow over the neighborhood, Glen Roberts' creation would draw thousands of vehicles that slowly drove by his house, often parking on Kevin Cleary's lawn. He'd mentioned that to Roberts a couple of times.

"Small price to pay for sharing the holiday spirit, Cleary."

And there was always that toothy smile that accompanied the sentiment. Cleary would have liked to put his fist through that smile. Maybe a bullet. But this was

Arborsville, and it was all about civility and brotherhood. Even the *Arborsville Gazette* agreed.

"Another Holiday Miracle at 188 Arbor Lane," the paper announced. They may as well have announced that 185 Arbor Lane was right across the street and people should feel free to park on his lawn and enjoy the show. People should feel free to let their kids pee on his lawn, because several times, when Cleary looked out his window and saw the parade of cars, trucks and vans, there were little kids doing number one in his yard, obviously with the full support of their parents. He'd never seen a parent doing number one but he wouldn't put it past them. And come spring there were always brown spots in the grass by the road.

He'd mentioned the brown spots and the little brats pissing on his property.

"Hey, Cleary, a little fertilizer, a little water, and it will all be green by summer. Small price to pay."

He'd thought about throwing buckets of urine on his across-the-street neighbor's yard, but he refrained. He'd thought about a lot of things he could do to his neighbor, but would always take a deep breath, and over the years he'd kept it in check. He couldn't eat, he couldn't sleep, and his wife finally suggested selling their house. All because of the asshole across the street and his holiday show.

For sixty-some mornings every year, he would stop his car at the end of the driveway, get out of the vehicle and put ten, twenty, thirty pieces of trash into a Glad bag. Drink cups, French fry containers, sandwich wrappers and the occasional diaper. One morning he'd found a used condom. People were utterly amazing. He considered putting spikes in his yard, dispensers of poison, but he took a deep breath and kept it in check.

For five years he'd mentioned the trash and the every-morning pick up that he did, and for five years Roberts had said through his toothy grin, "Small price to pay." He wanted to destroy that grin. He was ready to take Glen Roberts down, and he quietly decided no one was going to stand in his way.

Cleary wasn't the only one who was tired of the annual calamity. Very cautiously, two other neighbors had reached out and expressed their anger over the disruption of their normally quiet suburb. Cautiously, because it was politically incorrect to rag on the number one event of the year. *USA Today* proclaimed the Arborsville affair as one of the top ten private holiday happenings in the country. If you complained about the "light festival," you were almost un-American. There was a rumor that the *Today Show* was coming this year to do a feature on the event. Now he'd have a national TV show giving even more credibility to the jackass across the street, and the traffic would be worse than ever. Something needed to be done.

And there was that God-awful music. Hooked up to a computer system, there was bass-heavy music that triggered all of the lights—the lights that wrapped around trees and bushes, the lights outlining the roof, the flashing lights around each window, the lights that streaked across Roberts' front yard and up his garage door. His brick chimney was ablaze with those irritating, infuriating lights. And there was the light-up Santa with his sleigh and eight not-so-tiny reindeer. As the bass notes hammered the air, enough to rattle Cleary's front door, the lights would change from green to red, orange to blue, yellow to purple, and the assembled crowd, hundreds of them every night, would often break into rowdy applause.

"Enough is enough," Zeke Elliot said. "I mean, we've threatened before but something has to be done, Kevin."

The three men sat around a felt, green-topped card table in Cleary's basement man- cave, sipping beers and smoking cigars.

"I won't sleep; the new baby is going to be crying all night, and it's just not right," said Bobby Gillian. "It's only my second year here, boys, but I'll be damned if that sumbitch is going to destroy my family for two and a half months."

"I understand," Cleary said. "At least you guys are a couple houses down the road. Those lights blind me from 6 p.m. until 2 a.m. I can't watch TV, can't even hear my TV, and *hell*, I can't enjoy an evening meal. Libby almost demands we go out to eat every night, and stay out as late as possible, and as far as hooking-up with her for two months, forget it." He took a long swallow from the tall glass and tapped his cigar, the ash falling into a ceramic ashtray.

"So," Bobby Gillian looked at both of his co-conspirators, "what do we do?"

"Roberts owns a construction company," Kevin said. "His crew sets up about ninety percent of the show."

"And?" Zeke Elliot threw his hands up. "Are we going to kill the construction workers?"

"No," Cleary said. "I own an electronics firm. As you two know, my company designs custom security and surveillance systems for companies all over the country. We solve problems."

"We've *got* a problem," Gillian nodded. "You got the solution?"

"Maybe. Let me finish. He uses his workers; I'll use mine. Here's my plan, boys. I've given this a lot of thought. A company in Michigan came to us last year. They had a problem with break-ins. It was up in Detroit, and in a bad part of town."

"Isn't every part of Detroit a bad part of town?" Zeke asked.

Cleary nodded. "They wanted something to deter vandals. Vandals that were costing them thousands of dollars every year. So we came up with a trigger system."

"Trigger system?" Gillian looked confused.

"After hours, there were four triggers. If someone walked onto the property, they tripped a trigger. A voice would blare through some heavy-duty speakers telling them to back off. The voice warned of guard dogs and armed security guards."

"Wow," Zeke leaned back. "Serious stuff."

"There were no dogs, no security guards. The company couldn't afford anything like that. But if the intruder advanced, we had a second trigger. The vandal would step through an invisible beam and trip another audio device. Dogs would bark and growl, coming from multiple speakers."

"All for effect." Zeke smiled. "I can't imagine they came any closer."

"Oh, some did," Cleary said. "After all, this was a bad neighborhood. Dogs didn't necessarily scare them. So we had a third trigger. You two will appreciate this. It was the light show."

"Not like our esteemed neighbor," Gillian said.

"Not unlike our neighbor. If you, the intruder, ignored the warning voice, if you ignored the yapping mutts, then we had another surprise. Blinding spot lights highlighting every square inch of the property. These lights could blind you. It was enough to scare off almost everyone. And the vandalism stopped."

"But you said there were four triggers," Zeke pointed out. "If the vandalism stopped, why did you need a fourth trigger?"

"Ah, yes. Four. Now understand the owner of this company was beside himself. Broken windows, damaged machinery, stolen computers and the cops didn't want to come near the place. It was just a dangerous situation."

"Should have moved the company," Gillian said.

"Too expensive He basically told us he didn't care what we had to do. He was willing to do anything to stop the problem. And he emphasized the word *anything*." Cleary wore an almost maniacal grin, getting up and refilling his beer from the tap at the bar. "Anybody else?"

They both held their glasses up and he filled them to the brim with the amber liquid.

"Four triggers," Zeke said. "I assume this story is going to lead to our solution?"

"It is. Patience, Zeke."

They all took a sip and Cleary continued. "If someone got through the warning, then the dogs barking, then the piercing lights, there was one more trigger. Another couple of steps past the light beam brought you to within ten feet of the building itself. My team developed a very shallow underground mesh that surrounded the structure. We buried the narrow mesh in a trench that encircled the business."

"Kind of like that invisible fence for dogs?" Gillian asked.

"Very good, Bobby. It was somewhat like the Invisible Fence."

"So it shocked them and they wouldn't go any further." Zeke nodded. "But I still don't see how that works with Roberts across the street."

"Oh, we weren't sure a shock would stop them," Cleary said, "so we increased the shock. The Invisible Fence requires the dogs to wear a collar. We triggered the system with a light beam and there was no need for a collar. If you crossed that beam the shock system activated."

"How many volts of electricity?" Gillian was leaning in, intrigued with the story.

"It's not the volts, Bobby. Without boring you with details, it is the current transferred, the actual amount of electricity transferred. Lethal current is about 20 mill. amperes. So you could have a million volts, but only say a 0.00001 mill. amperes and it wouldn't kill you. On the other hand you might have 20 volts at 1 ampere. *That* would kill you."

"Kill?" Zeke asked, taking another swallow of his beer. "Kill?"

"Kill," Cleary nodded.

"You killed people?"

"Only two. We basically fried them."

"Jesus." Gillian drained his drink.

"It was enough to stop the problem. The owner always came in an hour early. He'd shut off the trigger system, survey the property, and when he found a burned body, a grotesque charred human form, he buried it on the grounds."

"Oh. My. God." Zeke's mouth hung open and he stared into Cleary's eyes. "Why are you telling us this?"

"Sometimes the end justifies the means. These two were a menace to society. They were thugs who only knew how to destroy things. We eliminated them and the world is a better place."

"Kevin, your system killed them."

"There's justification, Zeke. This is not for the squeamish. You can leave right now and pretend you never heard this conversation."

"Again," Gillian swallowed more of his drink, "why are you telling us this?"

"Because I've had enough. I can't take any more. I want an end to his giant extravaganza and the idea I have for our friend at 188 Arbor Lane is pretty severe. If you two don't mind some casualties, I have a plan to rid us of our problem.

*

The debate raged, fueled by more beer, then whiskey.

"Why don't we just firebomb the place?" Zeke asked.

"Where's the fun in that? I want the bastard to pay for five years of torment."

"Burning up his house isn't payment?"

"And if somebody dies," Gillian said, "I mean, damn, Kevin. What happens to us?"

"It will all appear as an accident."

"You're sure that this is foolproof, and that we'll get rid of that sumbitch forever?"

"First of all, when this takes place I think the Fire Marshal, the Chief of Police, the Mayor and every other civic leader will ban anyone who wants to build a holiday extravaganza. The events will be deemed hazardous. Second of all..."

"Kevin, is there a way we can do this and not have dead bodies?"

"No guarantees, Bobby. Let me explain what I have in mind."

*

The explanation took half an hour exactly. The bleary-eyed audience was hypnotized and only asked a couple of questions at the end.

"Genius," Gillian said.

"Oh, almost genius." Cleary smiled. "But thanks for the vote of confidence."

"Your team can make this?" Zeke asked.

"They will have no idea what they're building and I'm dummying up a contract for a place in Illinois. We're telling them that the main piece is going to a holiday display in Danville."

"I still don't know if I can deal with casualties. Dead bodies? It just seems so... okay, how much?" Zeke drummed his fingers on the green felt.

"Well, let's see how serious you two are."

They both anted up. Five thousand dollars apiece and Cleary picked up the rest. It was a strong debate, but in the end the three of them agreed that if there was, possibly, maybe, remotely, an outside chance that someone got killed, they could live with that. After all, the neighborhood, the community, the city and the state would be quietly, eternally grateful. What was one or two deaths when an entire population would be rid of this major nuisance? And beyond stopping the immediate problem, they were stopping dozens of copiers, stopping those interlopers who would be tempted to duplicate the light show, the extravaganza, stopping that self-centered group of folks who would seek the adulation of the locals and hope for the cover of national magazines and to be featured on morning network news. After another three beers, they had agreed.

*

And so it began. KC Industries started working on the main ingredient. A giant sleigh. A sleigh that could hold up to a dozen people, although no one would actually ride in it. Just a giant stuffed Santa in a plush velvet red suit. A Santa with almost Satan eyes, who would stare laser beams through anyone, even through his large goggles. A Santa that looked exactly like Kevin Cleary. He was proud of that addition. If he stared at the face it would look like gazing into a gigantic mirror.

And this was a sleigh that ran on steel tracks, tracks that would bend and rise to rooftop level. And every fifteen minutes the glittering sled would glide across the track, and take off for the sky. Then, slowly it would slide back down and reset at the other end of the house.

"It's our present," Cleary said. "There is no question when I show him this he'll go ballistic. And we're offering it to him as a gift in gratitude for his giving our neighborhood, our town, the notoriety we've received."

"Damn," Zeke said as they walked through the bustling factory. "That thing is impressive. Obviously it will be the hit of his collection."

"That's what we're hoping for. And I've got someone working on the Claus figure." He didn't mention the uncanny resemblance to his face. "It's going to be a night to remember."

"*The Today Show* is coming in four weeks," Gillian said, watching a crew gluing lights on the vehicle. "Can it be ready by then?"

"Plenty of time," Cleary walked up to the sleigh, putting his hand on the shiny red aluminum. "We still have to install the electronics, but over there," he pointed across the concrete floor, "Marty and his team are almost done with the system. We are about to give *The Today Show* and the entire country the performance of a lifetime."

Zeke and Gillian nodded.

"I still think we need to reconsider the casualty issue," Zeke said.

Cleary smiled. "What has to happen will happen, my friend. My customer in Detroit... no more vandalism." He chuckled.

Two weeks later Cleary invited his co-conspirators back to the workshop. The decorated sleigh, minus the large Santa with the Satan eyes, was mounted on the tracks. The steel rails that ran flat for forty feet then bent upwards, the slope rising to a forty-five-degree angle, were temporarily bolted to the concrete.

"Anybody want to ride along on the test drive?" Cleary asked.

There was a shaking of heads.

Cleary pulled a canvas cover off of an item on the floor, and the three of them were looking into the gleaming eyes of the giant Santa Claus.

"That face, damn, it's yours. Hell, it looks exactly like you, Kevin, and that is just plain creepy." Gillian stepped back.

Goggles were strapped over the piercing orbs, but those eyes seemed to stare into each of their souls.

"This is the guy who will ride in the show."

"Scary," Zeke said. "Those eyes, your eyes, they give me the willies."

"Santa Claus," Gillian said, staring at the figure. "He knows all, sees all. Very scary, Kevin."

"Okay, Johnny, put her in gear."

Lights flashed and the sleigh started its journey, gliding smoothly along the ground. It moved slowly, almost as if preening, showing off its curved body, the brass rails that ran along the sides and the candy-apple-coated exterior covered with brilliantly colored lights.

And then, as if by magic, the sleigh started its climb. Twenty-eight feet up. The same height as the peak of the two story home that Glen Roberts owned.

"Wow," Zeke said. "That's amazing."

"It's going to do a lot more than that, Zeke. That sleigh will do more than you can possibly imagine. There are even rockets in the side panels that will shoot off like fireworks. They're just a little stronger than a bottle rocket. I can only demonstrate the tracks and the climb. That will be what attracts people. The rest will have to come later."

*

After reaching the apex, the sleigh started its slow descent back to the ground. The fifteen minute trip was magical as The Beach Boys sang *Little Saint Nick* the story of a hotrod, souped-up sleigh that could take on all the other street rods.

"What you've told us is amazing," Gillian said. "I understand that you can't put her through her paces right now. This is a one-time event."

"We've tested it all, Bob. This baby is going to blow people's minds."

"And we've got the ideal showcase," Zeke laughed.

"Al Roker is doing the segment," Cleary said. "I believe he is going to get the highest ratings in history when this runs."

"If it delivers." Gillian watched the giant vehicle back down the incline and glide into home base.

"Oh, I guarantee delivery," Cleary said. "Don't doubt me, boys. I did the final work on the system myself. This will be the biggest show of the Christmas season. But remember, there may be collateral damage. You've got to be able to accept that. You're on board with that, right?"

They looked at each other, then reluctantly nodded.

*

The days dragged on. Work across the street seemed tedious as countless numbers of workmen dug holes, planted artificial trees, strung thousands of lights along the gutters and designed lighted patterns on the grass. Then they moved in the real stars of the show. They placed a life-size stable and manger, complete with animated mooing cows, baying donkeys, and groaning goats. There were angels seemingly floating in mid-air and a smaller version of Santa and his reindeer, shimmering in the dark, but never moving.

The entire *Peanuts* gang was featured with Snoopy on his doghouse and Schroeder playing his piano, all outlined in blinking lights. Twelve six-feet-tall nutcrackers lined the driveway and there were at least another dozen tin soldiers standing guard around the yard. Cleary started wondering if there would be any room for his track and sleigh. He was sure his neighbor would find room somewhere.

And two weeks before the show was to begin, traffic was lining up every night to see how far along the extravaganza had progressed. And even though Roberts turned the installed lights on, the best was yet to come.

One week before the anticipated opening, before Al Roker and *The Today Show* crew were to arrive, Cleary and company, fortified with copious amounts of alcohol, walked across the street, and knocked on Glen Roberts' door. His lovely wife Gloria answered, looking extremely suspicious of their motives.

"Hey, Glo, we've got something we'd like to run by you and Glen."

She called to her husband, and the two of them stood in the doorway, never inviting the trio into their spacious home.

"I know in the past we haven't always shown a lot of support for your light show," Cleary said, "but this year, I think we've made up for it."

"How is that, bro?" Roberts asked.

"Well, if you'll look outside, you'll see a huge sleigh and a track."

He pointed to the front of their house where two flatbed trucks were parked.

"What the hell is that?"

"That, my friend, is a custom built sleigh that will rival any holiday display in the country. In the world."

Roberts and his wife stood there, their mouths wide open.

"It's beautiful," he finally stated.

"Every fifteen minutes it travels those tracks and climbs up to the top of your roof."

"Oh, my God. But wait," he paused. "Is this because you want recognition on *The Today Show*?"

"Absolutely not," Cleary said. "Am I right, guys?"

Zeke and Bob nodded.

"This has nothing to do with us. We all chipped in to build this, and there's a stuffed Santa in the cab of that truck that will ride in the sleigh. This is all about you and your display. What do you think?"

"Magnificent." Roberts' eyes were sparkling. "Kevin, Bob, Zeke, I don't know what to say."

"Just being able to watch it perform will be thanks enough," Cleary said.

The crew stepped out of the trucks and started the installation. Everything was working like a charm, just as he knew it would. Cleary and his two partners stayed, talking to Glen and Gloria in their yard while the track was assembled.

"Damn big sleigh," Roberts said. "Must have cost a pretty penny."

"Small price to pay, Glen. Small price to pay."

A handful of cars pulled over to watch the crew set up the contraption, three actually parking in Cleary's front yard. When they pulled away he walked over and picked up two fast-food bags and a French fry box, smiling at Roberts the whole time.

And a week before opening night, that very evening, he pushed the switch on the new display and the sleigh slowly glided across the carefully assembled tracks, and climbed twenty-eight feet into the air, as the Beach Boys sang praises to *The Little St. Nick. "He's got to wear his goggles cause the snow really flies, cruisin' every pad with a little surprise."* As it paused at its highest point, Cleary admired the work. Sleek, elegant, the shiny red coating reflecting the array of green, gold and blue lights molded around the body. Then the sled made its graceful pause and started its slide back down, Roberts actually clapping his hands together and screaming like a small child.

"It's marvelous," he squealed. "And the giant Santa is so real." Smiling he said, "He looks like you, Kevin. The eyes behind the goggles. Like he's watching everyone. He sees you when you're sleeping, he knows when you're awake. What a great idea."

As the neighborhood, the town, the entire Northeast corner of the state got ready for *The Today Show*, Roberts added more and more lights. There was talk of power outages across the city due to the current that the house drew. And dozens of Roberts' construction crew climbed over the house, up trees, up a flag pole and into his empty swimming pool until almost every square inch of the man's property was covered in some lighted decoration.

The night before the big event, Cleary went to his basement and pulled out a metal box, about two feet by three feet wide. The apparatus looked like a sound mixer, with dials, levers and slides. He wanted to try it so bad, but of course he couldn't. It was designed to work for one performance only, when the filming started. Tomorrow night, while Al Roker's team was filming for the next morning's show. If all worked well, and it should, he would flip on his box and take control. And all of the levers and dials and slides would do their thing.

His wife had decided to vacate the premises, choosing to spend the evening playing mah jongg with her strange group of friends. He'd invited the boys over to see the finale. By the time it was finished, the sleigh would be destroyed. He would dispose of the remote control box, and there would be no evidence that the destruction hadn't just been a terrible accident. Maybe faulty wiring, maybe a system error. When you custom build systems, things can go wrong. Like a space shot that explodes, killing astronauts, or one of the early electric cars that blew up with no explanation, killing the driver. When you custom designed systems, things didn't always go as planned. Take for instance that mesh grid up in Detroit. Two people died. Burned to death. Two scum bags. Oh well, back to the drawing board... Or not.

The next morning two big trucks with satellite dishes pulled up out front. Since there was no space in Roberts' driveway, and by parking them in front of Roberts' house it would block the camera shots, they of course pulled up in front of Cleary's house, half on and half off of his lawn. News vans converged with their satellite dishes, not just to cover the spectacle itself, but also to cover the coverage of the spectacle. He overheard a newslady out front talking into a microphone saying, "Brad, it's amazing. *The Today Show* will be here to cover the event. Other news programs are here to cover *The Today Show*, and we're here to cover the organizations that are covering... I'm very confused as to why we are here at all."

He wanted to tell them it was going to be one hell of a show, but he didn't say a word. The proof would be in tomorrow night's performance.

The day dragged on, and finally it was six o'clock. The sun was down and it was time for Glen Roberts to pull the switch. He'd been out front almost all day and been interviewed maybe thirty times. Roker himself had talked to him for ten or fifteen minutes, and Glen had walked him around to the various displays.

"Over here is the five piece choir," he'd said, showing off five angels who were in choir robes, outlined in a heavenly aura of white lights. "And of course Alvin and the Chipmunks over here, and..."

Cleary had walked over to watch some of the festivities. After all, he was a major contributor to the event.

Hundreds of cars, pickups, SUVs and vans were parked all over the street and in neighbors' yards. All day long there had been three police squad cars running up and down the avenue. Now, close to launch time he counted six of them. Half the entire police force was here to make sure everyone behaved themselves. They could possibly control the crowd, but controlling this sprawling display might be a little difficult.

A loud speaker, or a bullhorn, blared loud and clear.

"Ladies, gentlemen, we are about to launch the extravaganza. If you are filming this, you might want to start at the large sleigh with Santa. It's an impressive sight. We hope you all tell your friends and enjoy the show."

Gillian, Zeke and Cleary sipped scotch on Cleary's front porch.

"You can't just diddle with that box right here where everyone can see," Zeke said.

"Zeke," Cleary laughed, "do you seriously think one person is watching us? Come on, man. No one is paying any attention, and if they did, it has nothing to do with what's happening across the street. Every eye, my friend, is watching that display."

"If I can have your attention again for a brief second," the voice paused, waiting for the din to quiet. "You all know that *The Today Show* is filming our opening sequence. You see the lights they've set up. If you could all applaud, yell, squeal, and shout when we give the signal, it would be greatly appreciated. We have the opportunity to make Arborsville a celebrity tonight. Let's do our community proud."

And then just seconds later, the voice shouted out, "Ladies and gentlemen, let's welcome *The Today Show* to Arborsville."

There was a swell of voices, applause and cheers and Cleary smiled.

"Affirmation," he said to his two sidekicks. "They love the fact that a national TV show has shown us their support."

"Kevin," Gillian touched his shoulder. "You have the remote control to the Trojan sleigh."

"Right here, Bob. You know I do."

"You can minimize damage."

"What?"

"We've been talking," Zeke said. "We don't want to be responsible for murdering someone."

"Guys," he said. "I don't plan on killing anyone, but this has been a big part of our conversation. There may be collateral damage, and you agreed that you could deal with that."

"We changed our minds."

"Come on, man," Gillian took a swallow of scotch. "We've been going along with this as if it was a game. We can't just kill someone because—"

"Because he ruins our lives for three months every year? Because he's destroyed our small community, destroyed the quiet, idyllic village that we call home?"

"But if someone is killed..."

Cleary glared at them and slammed his drink on the table, the liquid splashing onto his remote control. "You both put up five thousand dollars to build the contraption. You are co-conspirators and I have you both on tape."

"You what?" Zeke almost choked on his scotch.

"I recorded our conversations in the basement. They're not exactly on 'tape' but if you want the digital recordings, come with me."

They all stood up and walked inside, down the stairs to the card table.

"Kevin," Zeke shook his head. "Don't do this, man. We'll say we thought you were kidding."

"I've got it recorded, boys." He stared at them with that maniacal grin. "You both put up five thousand dollars. Here, let me play these for you." He reached into a drawer built into the bar and pulled out a Walther PPK. "Seriously, guys, I thought we had a pact. I've planned this for a year and you are not getting in my way now. Sorry."

He aimed at Zeke and pulled the trigger. At that close distance, the shot was between the eyes. Brains splattered on the wall as the man crumpled to the ground. Startled by the blast, Gillian jerked, turned and sprinted for the stairs.

"Bobby" Cleary shouted his name and Gillian turned, fear in his wide opened eyes. "You agreed, Bobby. You had no problem with somebody dying."

"My God, Kevin," he stared at Zekes body on the floor, "You've lost your mind. Please, don't shoot me. Please." He was crying, hysterical sobs. "My child, my wife..."

"I've planned this for a long time, Bobby. I've lived across the street from this madman for years and I need to finish him off. You can't get in my way."

"Please, Kevin." He was hysterical. "Do what you have to do. Just please, please, please, don't shoot me. I have a family, Kevin. Please?"

Cleary pulled the trigger and Gillian spun around, grabbing his shoulder. He looked at Cleary, panic spread on his face.

Cleary fired again, this time taking out the right side of Gillian's mouth. The man dropped to his knees.

"Pleash, Kevn. Pleash." The words were mushy, uttered through blood, broken teeth and raw tissue.

"I wanted conspirators, Bobby. Just some friendly supporters. Do you *see* what I mean?" Stepping up to the sniveling man he jammed the barrel of the gun into his left eye socket, smiling as he felt the orb pop. He pulled the trigger. "I guess you can't see." He glanced at the two bodies on the floor, blood draining from the wounds. Damn," Cleary said. "I hate it when there's collateral damage."

He walked back up the stairs, the pistol still clutched in his hand. As he reached the porch he saw they had just activated the sleigh. It had moved possibly five feet and was still thirteen minutes from reaching the roof. Thirteen minutes if the speed maintained. But that wasn't the idea.

Sitting down, he picked up his glass. Most of his drink had splashed onto the remote control, so he drained Zeke's scotch, then pulled Gillian's glass to him and studied it. Half full. He'd need that for later.

Flipping a switch, he saw a green light flash on the console. Contact. He pushed a button on the lower left and saw the lights shut down on the sleigh. A laser-sharp headlight flashed on as the sleigh picked up speed.

Cleary laughed out loud. The slides on his metal box were slick with the remains of his drink but he pushed the first one up and the sleigh moved faster and faster, the music playing from the speakers was no longer *Beach Boy* fun but grinding strings and percussion as if from the bowels of Hell. The volume increased and he could hear the large crowd oohing and ahhing. They had no idea what to expect, but Glen Roberts must have been having a heart attack.

Pushing switch number two he watched just over the satellite trucks as two panels slid open on the sides of the sleigh and immediately he pushed the third slide up. There was a loud scream, like the sound of a rotary saw grinding through hard wood, and from the openings there was a flash of fire and four rockets shot out, whistling through the air. Two rockets exploded into trees, sending hundreds of red hot embers into the crowd as those lights went dark. Another rocket powered its way through a news van in front of Cleary's house, and the vehicle burst into flame. People were screaming and running in all directions. Some bodies hit the ground, and he wasn't sure if they'd succumbed to the shrapnel or were taking precautions. Four more rockets flashed through the night, taking out a picture window in Roberts' house, the glass shattering into fragments. Snoopy and gang were blindsided and the display was blown apart, shards of fiberglass shooting off in all directions.

Preparing for the final assault, he pushed the speed lever. Nothing. The sleigh continued its ascent, but the main event wasn't happening. He pushed another slide and again, nothing. What could have gone wrong? And then it hit him. The scotch. The liquid had gotten into the metal box, destroying the electronics. He pushed, pulled, jabbed at levers, buttons and lifts. And as he threw his hands up in despair, sparks leaped from his metal controller. He threw it to the ground, standing up and leaping back.

The throng was screaming at a fever pitch, cars clogging the road in front of him trying to escape, their horns blaring. People scrambled to get as far away as possible. The sound of rocket-fire echoed down the street. And in horror, he saw the track, his steel marvel, break apart as in slow motion. As the metal separated, the candy-apple-red sleigh slid off the rails and, *oh my God*, turned directly toward his house. Firing two more rockets, taking out a family van and the occupants, leaping flames scorched the vehicle and burning them alive. The sleigh moved faster and faster, mowing down brightly lit choir boys, running over fake trees, lights shattering. And that noise: dissonant chords and percussion from some other dimension blasted at ear splitting levels. He was almost blinded by the laser light on the front of the rogue sled and he stared into the eyes of the oversized, overweight Santa. Those frightening demonic eyes that could pierce through a human's soul. Eyes from the devil. *His* eyes. *His* face. The demon getting closer and closer was him. The stuffed hellion could see him. Cleary knew the giant Claus was aware he wasn't sleeping; he knew he was awake. The larger than life object plowed across the street, crushing another news van, flattening a satellite and smashing an SUV, leaving the four bodies inside crushed in their seats in a hideous gruesome tableau.

Louder and louder the grinding sounds filled the air, screeching above the screams from the scrambling crowd. The devil's own music. Satan's laugh. Cleary jumped, trying to leap the porch railing and run from the impending doom. His right foot caught on the top rail and for a second he dangled between the house and the ground, screaming his own hellish sound. The red sleigh crashed into his porch with such force the front of the house buckled. The blaring crazy music stopped abruptly, and except for wailing sirens and people wailing, there was silence. For one, two, three seconds. Then the sleigh exploded. There was a mighty boom and in less than a moment, a massive fireball engulfed his entire home. In the next second, his body was engulfed in flame, his skin blistering and bubbling in the heat. He shrieked, his pathetic voice lost in the roar of the fire. In the fifth second... he was toast.

*

The Today Show got number one ratings the next morning. They reported that two bystanders were seriously injured by shrapnel from the sleigh, a family of three were incinerated in a van, an operator for JVN News was killed when a rocket hit him in the chest, exploding his internal organs. Four bodies were found in the shell of an SUV, crisp reminders of the power of fire. And remains of three people were found in the house across the street. It took forensics several days to find that two of them had been shot to death. The third person, the owner of the home, Kevin Cleary, had been burned almost beyond recognition. A paramedic on the scene said it appeared he might have died from extreme fright. His eyes had been boiled, but the sockets were wide open and his mouth frozen in a horrific grin. The coroner said it was like the Joker from a Batman movie.

After a thorough inspection of the light show, it was shown that everything seemed to be safe. Tourists from surrounding states poured in, intrigued by the ghoulish aftermath. Within days, Glen Roberts and his construction crew had most of the display up and glowing again. It would take years, however, for the insurance claims to be settled.

"Look at the people, Glo," Roberts smiled at his wife as they watched from their new picture window. "Hundreds, maybe thousands every night. We're making a lot of people very happy."

"It's too bad we had that catastrophe," she said, holding his hand.

"Small price to pay, Glo. Small price to pay."

A FAMILY CHRISTMAS TERROR

CHAPTER 11

"Wow! What a crazy story!" Nick said. "High body count."

"Yeah," Nick added. "And it kind of made me hungry."

Nancy looked at him in disbelief. "You just ate like half a dozen doughnuts and four eggnogs, coffee and brandy..."

"But I can *smell* the turkey." Nick stuck his nose up in air and took a long whiff. "Maybe you and Mom should start getting everything—"

"Me?" Nancy said. "Why? Because I'm a girl, I should have to 'stay in the kitchen?' I don't think so. What're you gonna do, you lazy—?"

"Enough," Dan said roughly.

Nick and Nancy glanced at each other.

"I think it would be nice if *everyone* helped me with dinner this year," Judy said, causing raised eyebrows from Grandpa and Jack.

"A new tradition," Judy said. "I'll make you a deal, Nick. I'll let you have one more eggnog and we can have Grandpa read to us while we fix dinner."

"How come he gets to read?" Jack asked. "I could do that."

"Age has its benefits, my boy." Grandpa laughed.

"Listen, Nick," Dan said, rising unsteadily to his feet and stretching. "Let's read one more story and then help your mother with dinner. You can even read this one."

"Alright, I guess so. What's it called?"

"'*Tis the Season To Be Wicked.*"

"Sounds good." Nick took the book from his father.

'TIS THE SEASON TO BE WICKED

ED DEANGELIS

'Twas the day of Christmas, and all through the Marsh house a creature was stirring, one much louder and wickeder than a simple mouse.

"But, Mmooommm!" seven-year-old Ryan cried out in disappointment. It had happened again! Ryan stood next to a small, sparsely decorated, Charlie-Brown-looking Christmas tree. He was a pudgy little boy, stomach sticking out past the waistband of his white underpants, his plump angelic face crimson with anger.

"Please, baby, just calm down, I'm sorry Santa didn't get you what you asked for." His mother, Julie, sat on a large, brown leather sofa within her small home's cozy living room. She was a slender woman, wrapped in an old, comfy pink fleece robe meant to keep out the frigid temperatures that came with the ice-cold winters in Pennsylvania. Blue eyes partly hidden by her brown, unkempt hair were wet from tears shed at her son's behavior. Julie was in her early thirties, though her beautiful face showed signs of stress and age beyond that number, stress that had begun with joy seven years ago, and had not yet ceased.

"I... wanted... a *new* PlayStation 3! You *promised* if I was good, Santa would get me what I wanted this year. This isn't what I wanted!" The little boy's voice rose in pitch as his plump hands hefted the used game system. They shook with anger and effort as he hurled the refurbished PlayStation 3 toward the fireplace, the same place through which his terrible gift had arrived.

"That's enough!" a deep voice called sternly from the kitchen as Ryan's father, Mark, stepped in, eyes locked upon his son. His bushy black eyebrows furrowed. "If you don't like the gifts Santa brought you, we can send them back to him, and you can have *nothing*!"

"It's not fair," Ryan blubbered now, snot running down his small, piggy nose, spittle spraying from his tiny, sodden mouth. "Santa did it again, Dad! Last year he didn't get me anything I asked for. He used to, but now Santa hates me!"

His father's threat fell on uncaring ears, for little Ryan did not want, nor care, about the sorry excuse for gifts that lay scattered about his bare feet.

"Ryan Marsh, I said that was enough. Get your butt up to your room. NOW!"

Ryan let out a little scream of contempt before kicking a small pile of used video games that lay in front of him, scattering them across the thick brown carpet. Some flew far enough that they landed on the small, decorative rug that the coffee table sat on, where Julie was sitting. He stomped past his parents, one angered, the other stunned, his small feet stomping hard upon the wooden stairs before he let out one last act of defiance. "I hate Santa!" The sound of his bedroom door slamming followed his shrill declaration.

Downstairs, Mark sighed. He sat down and reached out to draw Julie close to him for comfort. Mark felt her tremble as she sobbed silently. A few moments passed, her body finally stilled before a soft whisper passed her lips. "He's getting worse, Mark... I don't know what to do? We can't afford toys like we used to since I lost my job, and no matter what we say or do, he doesn't understand or care."

"I know, baby, I know." Mark's words of comfort seemed to have little effect on his distraught wife. "Don't worry, baby, we'll figure something out. Plus, I am positive he'll grow out of it. You know, I was a rather rotten child." Mark chuckled softly at the memories his comment brought unbidden to his mind.

"You were never this bad, and you know it. Your mother told me that you were a brat, but you were nothing like Ryan. This has to get better, baby. I... *we* need him to grow up. I love our little boy, but we did wrong giving him everything that he wanted."

His thoughts soon snapped back to here and now at his wife's response.

"He will, sweetie, trust me. Now why don't we open up our gifts? Maybe we can salvage what's left of the day and have a slightly peaceful Christmas."

As they opened their gifts, their son—the tiny terror—was forgotten. For a few hours, the parents celebrated Christmas with love and joy, and not with sadness and anger.

But for Ryan, there was no joy, only anger and the festering hate of a spoiled child spurned.

Santa is naughty and he must be punished. Ryan fumed while he sat in his massive bed, surrounded by countless toys, many having only seen a few minutes of play before being discarded.

"Next year, Santa is gonna learn what happens to people who get on *my* naughty list."

The Year of Lessons

Tonight Santa will learn his lesson. I got a special trick, just for him, Ryan thought, as he skipped around the tree, delight in his eyes, but delight that was fueled by cruelty and the thought of retribution. He gathered from under the tree small bits of cotton fluff, laid there to resemble snow. He brought the layers of cotton fabric to the fireplace and laid them gingerly upon the brick. His hand went into the small pocket in his pajama bottoms. His fingers gripped tightly around a handful of small white marbles, a crappy gift Santa had brought him two years ago. They had been discarded at the back of his closet. But now, one of the very gifts Santa had brought him would be used to deliver his own punishment. The thought that Santa's lesson for disappointing Ryan would be taught using his own crappy gifts pleased him immensely.

He sprinkled the marbles in the white cotton, making sure they were camouflaged within the fabric. *Boy, is Santa in for a surprise when his fat butt comes down this chimney. This will let him know I mean business. He better leave the shitty gifts in his bag. Used gifts are for poor people, not for little princes like me.* A soft chuckle left his little, red lips. It was not a kind sound; it was filled with the joy of someone who was sure he were going to inflict pain, and he savored the thought.

"Sweetie, what are you doing?"

Ryan jerked, startled from his devilish thoughts.

His mother had watched him lay the cotton faux snow in front of the fireplace from the staircase leading to the second floor. She made her way downstairs, her body once again wrapped in her favorite pink fleece robe. A look of confusion with a hint of concern knitted upon her features.

Ryan turned and smiled brightly. "I'm just getting things ready for Santa, Mommy!"

Julie sighed, sadness creeping into her features. Her head shook, shoulders slumped. The thought and desire about chastising her son fluttered in her mind for a moment before they died. It wouldn't do any good. Her son *acted* sweet, but that's all it really was—an act. She loved her child, but she and her husband, Mark, had spoiled him too much. And in doing so, they had overlooked what their little boy had become—what they had molded him into. Julie shook her head. She had to believe Mark. She had to trust that he had been like this when he was Ryan's age, and soon enough her little boy would grow up like his father had.

"Go upstairs, my little prince. It's late and Santa won't come if you're awake."

"Of course, Mommy. I don't want Santa to skip over me. Not this year." Ryan forced a wide, disingenuous smile onto his face and nodded his head enthusiastically.

He scuttled past his mother, little eyes alight with glee, as thoughts of Santa slipping and falling danced in his head. Ryan joyfully climbed the stairs, his enthusiasm showing as he jumped from one step to another. *Tonight's the night! No more bad gifts for me on Christmas. Santa will slip and fall and understand that he needs to give me what's on my list!*

Julie studied her son as he did what he was told, for once. She looked at his face as he turned at the top of the stairs. He did not even look at her, but instead stood staring at the trap he had set. A manic smile spread across his normally sweet features. That grin, along with her son's baneful stare, sent a chill through her body, despite the warm robe that was wrapped around her. She could not imagine what was going on in her little boy's head, and secretly, deep down, she did not want to know, and was glad she didn't. Ignorance was a blessing.

Once she heard the door to her son's room shut, Julie turned and made her way over to the fireplace. Squatting down, she began to pick through the cotton, finding marble after marble. She had to really search. Ryan had planted dozens of marbles that were well hidden. But they needed to be picked up, otherwise Ryan would probably throw a tantrum, flinging the faux snow and marbles all over the place. Random marbles upon the floor, scattered to places unknown, were dangerous. So focused was she on her task of cleaning up her son's mischievous antics, along with the whirlwind of thoughts in her head, she failed to notice her husband approach her. His calloused hands touched her shoulders gently. She jerked, releasing a soft squeak of surprise.

"Baby, what are you doing?" Mark's bewildered tone matched the scrunched up eyebrows as he tried to process what the heck his wife was doing squatting in front of their fireplace.

"Why is some of the tree basing ripped off and placed around the bottom of the fireplace?" Mark's bewildered tone soon changed, filling with a weariness and a hint of annoyance. He knew who had done it, just not why. "In the name of God, what is he up to now?"

"I think he's trying to trick or punish Santa for not getting him gifts that he wants. He tore off some of the fake snow you bought. He placed it here to hide these." Julie held out her hand, and small white marbles clacked together softly.

"I'm just picking them up before they get scattered and one of us slips." Julie reached down, lifting the faux snow and giving it a shake. Seeing no marbles rolling here or there, she poured the marbles into the pocket of her robe and stood.

"I better throw these away before—"

"No, sweetie, give them to me. I have a better idea. We need to make sure he understands you can't fool Santa, or else he might just keep trying. Hold on just a moment." Mark stepped away, moving to the family room. He returned quickly coming back with an old candy dish they had gotten years ago. It had sat unused, until now.

"We're going to put the marbles in the candy dish along with a little note from Santa himself, letting Ryan know he can't trick Saint Nick."

"Sweetie, I don't know if that's a good idea. You know how Ryan is. That might cause a... *tantrum*." Julie's body visibly cringed as she uttered that last word.

Mark could hear the pensiveness in his wife's voice, but he brushed aside her concern with his own certainty.

"He's going to be upset regardless. And I would rather just deal with his normal Christmas tantrum, with a little added because of his failed trick, than have to deal with whatever booby-traps he plans for next year if he thinks this one was just too simple. It's already exhausting enough dealing with him. I don't want or *need* to tread carefully through my own house."

"OK, baby, if you're sure." Julie pulled out the marbles and dropped them into the old candy dish and set them on the mantle of the fireplace.

It did not take Mark long to come back with some old parchment printer paper he'd stashed away in his home office. Written upon it in flowing script was the simple statement:

You can't trick me.

"I... I don't know, baby, I really think that this is going to cause more harm than good." That pensive look was on Julie's face once more, lips pursed together as she struggled with herself. She wanted to believe her husband, but tomorrow was already going to be a hard day. It always was. But she loved Mark and had to believe him when he said he had been like this when he was a kid. He had to know what to do, because she realized deep down she had long ago given up the idea that she knew how to properly handle her own child. She had tried spanking and whipping, and that didn't work. It just made him resentful. They had tried taking away the few toys he did love, and in response, he stole her jewelry and hid it until his toys were returned. Yelling didn't work; physical punishment didn't work; and taking away his things most certainly didn't work. All she had left was the thought, the hope, that soon it would be better. Soon Ryan, her little prince, would, as Mark had when he was growing up, decide he was tired of getting into trouble and being punished and would start to behave.

Mark placed the bowl of marbles and the note on the mantle above the fireplace. He turned and made his way back to his Julie who had sat down on the sofa. Her distant eyes still flickered with a lingering sadness.

"We need to be strong, and soon enough everything will be fine. I know he will get better." Mark wrapped his muscled arm around her and placed a soft kiss upon her cheek. "Now, it's Christmas, and Santa has asked me to give you a special gift." Mark winked softly as his free hand slipped down to caress Julie's thigh.

Julie shivered, her once distant eyes suddenly snapped upward, locking with her husband's, a mischievous twinkle appearing in them.

"So why don't you run upstairs while I grab the gifts. Then Santa will be upstairs to give you your special *gift*." Mark's tone deepened as he leaned down, his breath caressed the pale flesh of his wife's neck. His warm lips pressed softly. He could feel her pulse quicken before he pulled away.

Julie tensed at the kiss, a soft sultry little purr escaped her lips. "Oh, Santa baby!" She giggled as she made her way up the stairs. The love and evident desire showed by Mark always put her in a better mood.

Mark smirked, watching her hurry up the stairs, his eyes locked on her energetic steps. *Well, at least Christmas is going to start off well,* Mark mused as he headed to the back of the house and down to the basement. They had stored the gifts down here this year only because Ryan never went into the basement. There was no reason for him to. There was nothing he was interested in down in the basement, just the washer and dryer and old dusty boxes. But behind those were three piles of gifts, each pile wrapped in different paper. The largest, of course, was Ryan's. His *always* had to be the largest.

He carried them up the old, wooden basement stairs, which groaned with each carefully placed step. Before reaching the living room and placing them around the tree, he made sure Julie's and his own pile were kept well away from Ryan's pile. If they were too close, Ryan would open them as well as his own.

Mark smiled as he glanced around the dimly lit room filled with the colors of the season: greens, reds, blues, gold, and silver. They covered the brick walls of their living room, giving the appearance of looking through a Christmas kaleidoscope. The tree looked beautiful; it was much better than previous years. They had managed to find a tree lot with some decent stock left the week before and had gotten a wonderful discount.

Mark's smile grew as he beheld the beauty of his small home, and his eyes were drawn to the mantle above the fireplace, where Julie's newest decoration rested: a miniature sleigh and eight tiny reindeer, with a little old driver who looked so lively and quick. *Ah good old St. Nick*, Mark mused as he began to count the reindeer, humming to himself as childhood poems filled his mind. *Now Dasher! now, Dancer! now, Prancer and Vixen! On, Comet! On, Cupid! on, on Donner and Blitzen!* Mark was always surprised and delighted how such simple phrases could make him feel so happy and seem to make the holidays so much brighter.

But all of this—Mark glanced around, sorrow replacing his recent happiness—all of these things, all the memories they could invoke would do nothing if Ryan didn't behave.

Mark's head lowered and his hands cupped together as he prayed.

"Please, God, let him behave tomorrow. Let us finally have a nice Christmas together."

He knew his wife could not take much more. Year after year, she seemed to become more beaten and worn. Their little boy had been a blessing when he was born, but had become a terror as he grew. Mark knew it was partly his fault. He had spoiled him early on, and in doing so, their little boy had come to expect everything to be handed to him. Julie told him he was descended from royalty, and he now thought of himself as a prince—and princes got whatever they wanted— even from Santa. It would be easier if they just told Ryan that there was no Santa.

But Julie didn't want that. She clung to the memories of her childhood, of wonderful nights of being so excited you almost couldn't go to sleep, and mornings filled with the gathering of family to celebrate the birth of Jesus, along with the treasures that Santa had brought.

So far, those Christmases had escaped their family. He wanted to give her that Christmas, and for that reason he had not fought her on ending this childish fantasy for their son. It would end soon enough. Ryan was getting older, and sooner or later he would find out. Mark hoped for sooner— for all their sakes.

"Baaaaaby," a soft voice called to him from the top of the stairs.

Mark's thoughts suddenly derailed, switching to a much more pleasant track. He smiled warmly, his own eyes filled with that mischievous twinkle. Mark hurriedly made his way up the stairs to his waiting wife. "Ho, Ho, Ho, here comes Santa!"

*

The following day was one of confusion for Mark and Julie. Ryan had come bounding down the stairs, his eyes wide with excitement, but they had not even looked at the tree, nor the gifts below it. Instead, they first focused on the fireplace. He had hurriedly made his way over to inspect the note, along with the marbles. They waited for the worst, but he said nothing. Rather, his cute, chubby face had gone blank, eyes locked on the marbles. Slowly, a look of contemplation crept into his features. But no tantrum. The rest of the day had been strange, peaceful, and odd as Ryan opened gift after gift, the look of intense contemplation now permanently etched on his features. It had been pleasant, although disturbing. Christmas finally ended, as Ryan headed for the stairs. His gifts lay strewn around the tree, not a single one taken with him.

Julie spoke out finally. The uneasy peace nagged at her; something was wrong.

"Baby, are you okay?"

Ryan turned, his eyes focused intensely at the fireplace, his voice toneless.

"Oh yes, Mommy, I'm... fine. I underestimated Santa. That was my mistake... mine, and mine alone."

And with that, Ryan turned and made his way slowly into his room, his scattered gifts left untouched upon the living room floor where they had been unwrapped.

Mark's face beamed, a wide grin upon his rough features, his voice jubilant.

"See, baby? I told you he would get better, and that the note would work. No tantrum. No yelling. I know he wasn't happy, but he handled it better than any other years."

He leaned in to kiss her cheek, his arm wrapping around her, pulling her small frame close.

Julie looked down in her lap, unresponsive to Mark's kiss and words. Her features were troubled. Finally with a deep sigh, she gazed up into her husband's eyes.

"If you say so. Just... something seems wrong."

Mark shook his head and he chuckled. "Don't worry, sweetie, I have a feeling things are going to start getting better from here on out." He planted a soft kiss on his wife's cheek as he helped her up. Their fingers interlaced tenderly as they went upstairs. Julie gazed at her husband, a smile once more appearing on her face when she saw his own smile. He was excited and hopeful. If only she could feel like that all the time, but she couldn't. Something was wrong with Ryan. She couldn't prove it, but she felt it. But those cares, at least for the moment, were wiped away as her husband's lips suddenly found hers. And the night truly ended wonderfully.

The Year of Hope

The stockings in the Marsh house were hung by the chimney with care, in hopes that St. Nicholas soon would be there. Most children were nestled all snug in their beds, while visions of sugar-plums danced in their heads. One child was not nestled; instead he paced back and forth, his young mind awhirl with the fear that indeed, St. Nicholas would soon be here.

"I'm not ready, not enough time," Ryan ranted in hushed tones. His eyes constantly glanced to the clock. Time was racing; it was almost midnight now. His parents were in their room watching TV. If he did not think of something quick, Santa would come. And if he was awake, he would get nothing. But if he did not figure out a way to teach Santa the error of his ways, he would get something almost as terrible as nothing. He would get bad gifts, used things, worn things, and old things. The cruel joke that Santa played was bringing new clothes, something he knew Ryan despised.

But he knew from last year that trying to trick Santa did not work. He had found the marbles, had even placed the note for Ryan to find, shaming him in front of his parents. Santa had made him look like a fool, but Ryan should have known better. Now he did. He was a year older now, and he was learning. Santa had magic, and magic was something Ryan could not yet figure out how to counter. He paced for a while longer. Each minute that ticked by made his pulse quicken and his brain work desperately faster. Ryan's frantic pacing halted suddenly, his body rigid as an alien thought leapt into his mind.

If I can't trick Santa, and I can't hurt Santa, perhaps I can do something for him? These thoughts were strange, and it took Ryan a few moments to develop them, but soon enough a smile crept onto his face, and he jumped into action. Leaving his room, he tiptoed downstairs. His parents were still up. He could hear their muffled voices mingling with the TV in their room. To his annoyance and worry, the stairs creaked as he crept over them, each creak making him wince. If they were alerted to his movements, he would be in trouble, and they would foil his brilliant plan, his chance to finally have a good Christmas.

The lights from his Christmas tree suffused the room in a plethora of blues, reds, and greens, all festive, joyful colors, but the beauty of this tranquil scene was lost to Ryan. All he cared about was that Santa had not yet come. He had not yet lost his chance. As he moved to the tree, he stopped. In all his excitement from his new idea, he had not yet thought of *what* he could bribe Santa with. A memory, long since forgotten, entered his mind.

A week or so ago, he had this same strange idea: giving something to Santa to make him happy. It had occurred at the local grocery mart, when he had been dragged away from his video game because his Mom was lazy and wanted help shopping. He had seen rows upon rows of new cookies, with a small hand-written sign by the grocer, reminding him to not forget the cookies for Santa. Perhaps, Santa would want a different kind of cookie. His mother always bought the same brand of cookie, whether it was Christmas or not. They were a brand called Enjoy Life, some crappy off brand. Ryan had known at that moment, that if he could get Santa something different, some mainstream cookie, maybe, just maybe that would help.

But his mother had ruined everything—like she almost always did. He had pointed at some peanut cookies, only to be told, in a very harsh manner, that those cookies made Santa unhappy. This was all her fault. He had made a simple suggestion to her, that could help make him happy, and all she did was get angry and tell him no. He had forgotten about this until now. He could have had a week or so to think of what else to get Santa, but no, now he had mere minutes. His mother was the one who had caused this problem, so she would have to pay to fix it, but what did she have that Santa would want?

"Jewelry!" The thought leapt into Ryan's mind with such intensity that he couldn't help but say it out loud. His excited utterance made him flinch, and he quickly glanced up at the top of the stairs, but to his relief he neither heard nor saw any signs that his parents had heard him. Ryan spoke in faint tones to himself, it always helped him to think outload. "Ok, where is Mom's jewel..." His gaze once more went to the stairs. His little fists clenched and his feet stomped the carpeted floor.

Mom kept her jewelry upstairs, hidden somewhere. She had moved it after he had taken her ruby bracelet and emerald necklace and hidden them. But he had only done that in retaliation. She had taken some of his toys because of an issue with another kid at school. She had soon given his toys back once she realized the errors of her ways and what her mistake was going to cost her. But afterwards, once he had returned her jewelry, she had taken them out of her jewelry box and hidden them elsewhere. Ryan shook his head. He had to focus on the matter at hand. He only had a little while before Santa came. Ryan began to pace again, pondering the subject of what could he get of any value. His eyes searched around the color-filled room until they landed on the perfect solution: His mother's purse sat there on the hutch against the wall.

Ryan tore through the purse after he had retrieved it from the hutch. Finally, after combing through tons of random junk, he found his mother's wallet. Opening it, Ryan frowned, as he found only twenty-three dollars. Exasperation filled Ryan's voice, his eyes downcast. His little hands tightened, crumpling the cash. "It will have to do."

He quickly made his way over to the small plate of cookies and glass of milk. He placed the money down and quickly smoothed the wrinkled bills as best he could, before putting them under the glass of milk. He knew Santa could not miss them there. He then ran into the kitchen, grabbing a marker and sheet of paper left next to the fridge for his parents to leave notes to one another. Quickly, he scribbled:

Money is for you Santa
Please give me good gifts
I am sorry for marbles last year
It was my parents' idea

He slipped the note between the cookies and milk. Ryan rubbed his hands together, a small devilish grin on his face. Little joy-filled skips took him up the stairs, his previous worried thoughts of being silent now replaced with anticipation for what would no doubt be a mountain of wonderful gifts, just for him. His door slammed loudly just as his parents opened theirs.

Mark stuck his head outside of his room, looking around. He had heard the loud footfalls on the stairs and wondered what his son was up to. A soft sigh escaped his dry, cracked lips. He looked back at Julie, who had just finished wrapping the last of the gifts. There were not many this year, but their little boy's behavior this season had not been as bad as previous years, and this gave them hope that he would not be too upset.

"Well, he's in his room now, but I have no idea what he was doing." Mark turned and began to gather the assorted, scattered gifts lying on the bed. Once gathered, he carefully made his way out of the room, stopping only for a moment at the doorway.

"Be right back, babe. Hopefully, there are no surprises this year." With that thought in mind, Mark made his way slowly down the stairs and into their festively lit living room. After a careful and thorough look around, Mark saw nothing out of place. He quickly went about separating the gifts and placing the largest pile in the front so Ryan would see it when he ran down the stairs. They had always done that.

Mark was finally finished setting out the gifts and was about to head upstairs when he remembered his favorite treat.

"Time to get me some cookies and milk." A joyful tone filled his voice. He was a fan of sweets, as was his son, but Julie did not allow many confections in the house. But as he approached the tray to indulge in his sweet tooth, his joy became confusion. His brow furrowed when he saw the crumpled bills placed under the milk, along with a note. He reached out, picking up the note and read the sloppy hand-writing. Then his eyes glanced upward and his mind tried to process this all.

His gaze fell upon Julie's purse, lying on the large oak hutch, its contents disheveled after having been hastily jammed back inside. Her wallet was at the top of that pile, still unzipped. Mark's face reddened, his hand clenched, ripping some of the paper as it crumpled in his massive, calloused hand. Mark spun around, the large vein on his forehead pulsed prominently, both hands now clenched. He had had enough. Not only had Ryan stolen money from his mother, but then he'd tried to bribe Santa with it. This was going to end now!

"I am gonna spank his ass until he..." Rage melted as his anger met a force it could not overcome or ignore. Julie stood on the stairway. She had seen the whole thing and was shedding large tears.

"Just... please put the money back, baby. Please, it's Christmas."

Her voice so soft and sweet, yet so sad, had snuffed out his rage.

Julie had made her way slowly down the stairs as she spoke, and with her final words she reached her husband. Her small hands rested upon his. Her touch washed over him and his muscles relaxed. A deep breath that Mark had not even realized he had been holding was released. His chest ached.

Julie stretched up onto her tiptoes and kissed him ever so gently, her words, a hushed whisper, spread across his skin like a gentle summer breeze. "Please, baby, just put the money back and let it go."

"Babe, I... we can't let this go. He stole this money. He is trying to bribe Santa with it, for God's sake." Anger flared once more, struggling to stay alive inside of him. His wife's mere presence quelled that attempted resurgence of rage. His body slumped slightly, but his face relaxed and a small smile appeared as he gazed into her eyes.

"Ok, I won't say anything... or do anything to him... but Santa will." He gave Julie a quick but loving kiss before he turned and gathered up the money.

"Go upstairs. I'll be up soon. Santa has to leave our little boy a note, one I am sure will make it so he never does this ever again."

Julie reached a hand out to stop him, but at the last moment hesitated and withdrew. She once again felt that gnawing in her gut, warning her that this was not a good idea. But she said nothing. Her husband knew what he was doing. She had to trust in that. He had been right about the note last year, despite her warning. This year, instead of trying to hurt, he had tried to steal and bribe. Stealing and then trying to bribe Santa was an improvement from trying to harm him, wasn't it?

Julie banished her worries and made her way to her room, a small prayer sent heavenward as she lay down to rest. *Please God, let everything go well tomorrow.*

Stealing and bribery are naughty
No toys for you, Ryan
Santa

Little chubby hands gripped the unrolled parchment paper as Ryan read the note, his confusion evident on his face as he had run downstairs, only to freeze upon seeing such a small pile of gifts. The rolled up parchment had been set neatly on the tray with the empty milk glass and cookie crumbs. The note was dropped hastily, and Ryan lunged for his gifts. He did not open them, but shook each one. He had developed the ability years ago to be able to tell just by shaking a box if it had toys or clothes in it. One by one, he shook each box, grabbing more frantically for the next, when the one he held revealed it only had clothes. He *hated* clothes. And when the final box dropped from his little hands, Ryan sat there, a look of numb shock on his face. Santa had given him nothing but clothes. He had come into his home, eaten his cookies, drunk his milk, taken the money—and then punished him. Santa stole from him! He didn't want the money, but he still took it, Santa was a thief—No, Santa was a *Monster.*

Julie and Mark watched as their son sat there amid a pile of unopened gifts. The toys they had bought were hidden in their closet. Mark had taken them back upstairs as punishment. But there was no screaming, no tantrums. Ryan just sat there, eyes blank, as he stared at the fireplace. The entire day had made Julie's feelings from last night worse, her motherly instinct warning her that something was terribly wrong—and getting worse—but she did not know what. Her son was upset, but he had not screamed or thrown things, so that was good. Yet, she felt that gnawing in her gut, in her soul. And she could ignore it no longer once Ryan had stood and walked past her, his little body seeming to shake as if he was cold, while the room was nice and toasty.

"Baby, are you all right? I'm sorry Santa..." She paused to glare at her husband for a moment. "...didn't leave *any* gifts. I am sure he will leave a lot next year to make up for it."

Ryan turned suddenly, body whipping around faster than she would have thought possible. His response chilled her to her very core. She could hear the venom in her little boy's words and saw a strange feverish look in his eyes.

"Santa... will *pay. He* will *learn.*" Ryan turned, and disappeared upstairs and into his room.

Julie and Mark held each other, her eyes locked upon the empty space where her little boy—her one and only child—had for a moment become something that terrified her. Mark's normally confident gaze was shaken, eyes downcast, doubt filled him. Both parents sat silent, wondering the same thing. Was their son getting better with age... or getting much, much worse?

The Year of Joy

Julie walked slowly inside the local GIANT grocery store. With only a few days until Christmas, she needed to buy food for their dinner, before the store ran out of the food she knew Ryan would expect for his Christmas dinner. Most years, Christmas brought only sadness to Julie, thanks in part to the little terror that walked beside her. Her sweet boy Ryan. This year was different though. Julie walked with her back straight, a warm, almost infectious smile across her face. She felt the slightest bit of joy this season, and that joy brought along hope. Her little boy, Ryan, walked next to her, and this year had been the first of what she hoped would be many better years. Yes, her son still asked for things. Yes, he had his little tantrums, but his mind always seemed to be somewhere else, blunting his actions. She secretly hoped that he was finally growing old enough that they could have a good Christmas—like the ones she used to have as a child. Plus, her loving, but sneaky, husband had been in such high spirits the last few weeks. He was up to something, but she could not figure out what. But the fact that he seemed overly happy just added to the joy of the season, the first joy she had felt after many, many years.

New sneakers squeaked on the cold floor of the store while Ryan pondered and plotted. Another year had almost gone by, and soon enough he would have his revenge. He knew Santa had magic, but surely his magic had limits. Ryan planned to test those limits this year. But attempting to do so had been harder than he had expected. He had needed to keep his parents out of the loop. Too many times they had foiled his plans, scolding him on his ideas. How could they not understand his plight? They watched him suffer year after year at the hands of Stingy Claus, and yet they seemed apathetic to him. They were his parents, and they were meant to provide for him, to protect him and take care of him, till he no longer needed them. Most of the year they did a barely passable job, especially the last few years. But he could not really do anything about that. They were his parents and he needed the things they gave him.

Ryan meandered away from his mother, his thoughts turned toward the plastic containers down the next aisle. He always loved the free candy tubs in the store, all different candies he could just reach in and take. He walked up and frowned. There were different tubs now. Some still had candy, but the others had dried fruits and nuts. *Disgusting!* Pure revulsion masked his face, until, unbidden, a memory from a Christmas past slithered into his mind. A wide and devilish smile spread across his face, and he began to stuff his pockets full of the free gifts.

*

Joy had finally come to the tiny brick house during the harsh winter months. It was Christmas Eve and all was well. Young Ryan lay fast asleep, snuggled up in his bed; dreams of vengeance and blood danced in his head. His mother and father almost danced in their room, for news most wonderful had just been revealed.

"When did this happen?!" exclaimed Julie, her tiny body shaking with excitement that could be seen even through her favorite pink robe.

Mark stood tall and proud beside the massive pile of wrapped gifts he had brought up from the basement. "My promotion went through a few weeks ago, just in time for me to get my first check and the company's holiday bonus. No more money worries, baby. No more bad Christmases."

Mark and Julie embraced. Things were finally going to start getting better. Julie kissed her husband hard, lips pressing into his fever of growing desire. But she broke off the kiss with a sly smirk on her pouty lips.

"Why doesn't Santa head downstairs and set up all the gifts. I'll start filling the tub, and get his special gift all ready." She winked as her pink robe slipped from her slender form, exposing her pale body as she swayed enticingly into the bathroom.

The sway of her hips, the smell of her perfume, and finally the sound of the tub turning on spurred Mark into action. Grabbing the gifts, he carried them downstairs. In total, it took him four trips. Each time he stopped at the bottom of the stairs, setting the piles of gifts next to one another before he separated them. Of course, Ryan's pile was massive. The stack of wrapped gifts would tower over their growing son, a literal mountain of presents. Next, was his wife's, her pile small, but the things inside he knew she would love. She had been wanting that diamond heart pendant for years, but he could never afford it. That was all going to change now. Only the best for the love of his life from now on. He frowned as he was placing the gifts, his eyes drawn to a spot on the carpet in front of the fireplace. It was hard to see with only the tree lights on, but he saw the outlines of clear tree ornaments. Mark wandered over, bending down to inspect the carpet and what lay there. There were a few of the clear ornaments from the tree, although the metal tops and hangers had been taken off.

"What the hell are you doing here?" Mark looked to his bare feet and was grateful he had not stepped on them. Suddenly Mark's thoughts flashed back to an hour ago, when Ryan had gone downstairs to get a drink. He had taken a while and Mark had to yell at him to get his butt upstairs or Santa would pass over them.

"Christ, not again." Mark groaned, as he began to pick up the small little traps his son had left. "Oh well, after this year there will be no more of this shit."

Mark spent the next few minutes looking around, and to his horror, and slight amazement, he discovered a plethora of booby-traps. Mark found a string of fishing wire set along the fireplace, meant to trip Santa so he would fall on the ornaments, and small lumps under the false snow surrounding the tree indicated hidden mousetraps. Mark even found a bunch of his son's small toy cars, which he had stopped playing with a long time ago, spread out around for some unknown reason on the carpet. He assumed they were meant to have Santa step on them and slip. He gathered all of these up, after disarming the mousetraps, of course. The loud snaps filled the mostly silent room when he set each one off. He put them all in a large pile in front of Ryan's gifts. All except the ornaments, which he put away, not wanting to risk them getting broken and having shards of glass on the floor. Normally he would be furious. He should be furious. But the relief bestowed upon him by his promotion, and the hope, no, not the hope, the fact that he *knew*, that this would be the last year, calmed his hand. Plus, his wife was waiting for him. He quickly headed to his office, grabbed some parchment paper and scrawled a simple phrase onto it.

You win

Mark placed it on the pile of booby traps. Next, he grabbed his wife's and his own pile. He placed Julie's on the far side of the tree away from Ryan's gifts. His own gifts he placed closer to Ryan's, but he was less concerned if his got opened by his son. Now that this was all taken care of, he had something to take care of himself.

Mark turned and almost leapt to the stairway. But his body lurched to a stop when he passed the cookies. He chuckled warmly and reached down, speaking to the cookies, a villainous accent affecting his speech.

"Ahh, Mr. Cookies, you thought you could escape my notice. How wrong you were!"

And as quick as that, he reached down and gobbled up his favorite treat, leaving only a few uneaten bits lying scattered on the tray before gulping down the accompanying milk. His hunger sated, his mind once more turned to desires that were not yet sated. He stalled once again when he heard a crumbling sound, as part of Ryan's gift-mountain collapsed. His haste to set it up had left it unstable. Mark turned to rebuild the mountain. He would just make it wider and not as tall. Ryan would still love it. As Mark leaned down to the fallen gifts, close to the tree, his eyes began to water. He stood to wipe them, and his throat began to itch. He was overcome by a sudden burst of hard deep coughs, which shook his body. The coughs passed a few seconds later, and Mark straightened himself.

"Whaa tthhhee helllll?" he spoke, his words slurred as his tongue began to swell. His watering eyes widened, and he frantically looked around. He was having an allergic reaction. *How is this happening?!* He needed his EpiPen! Mark stumbled toward the stairs, onto a portion of the floor that was covered by a thin autumn-colored decorative rug his wife had bought for their living room coffee table. That area had been absent of Ryan's small cars for a reason. As Mark slammed his foot down onto the rug, the small thumb tacks that had been carefully hidden underneath pierced his foot, five in total embedded themselves into the sole of his foot, blood began to dribble out.

Mark toppled forward when his injured foot gave out under the sudden assault of small metal spikes. He tried to cry out, but a dull croak was the only thing that escaped. His throat was starting to close, breathing was becoming harder as Mark lay there upon the floor. But he was not a weak man, and his desire to live was stronger than the pain

CHRISTMAS TERRORS

in his foot or his chest. He pushed himself up, the tacks pulling out of his foot as he drew away from the blood-soaked rug. Mark began to limp his way toward the stairs, a trail of bloody foot marks showing his agonizing progress. Then one by one, he hobbled his way up the stairs. His vision was getting narrow. His heart raced rapidly in his chest. He was not even sure if he was breathing anymore. He could feel his tongue swelling up so large it stuck obscenely out from between his lips. But he had to make it to his room—to *Julie.*

Despite the growing darkness and pain, he made it to the top of the stairs, his eyes mere slits on his bloated face. The door to his bedroom seemed like it was at the end of a long dark tunnel. But he knew he could make it. Just one foot in front of the other, that was all he needed to focus on.

So focused on the task at hand, Mark forgot about the damage done to his foot, the bleeding flesh could not handle the weight placed upon it anymore, and with a whispered cry of anguish his foot gave out, slipping on the blood that still poured from the punctures. Mark began to fall backwards. His last thoughts before his vision went dark and his mind shut off, were of his wife, and her beautiful come-hither eyes.

Julie had just finished filling the massive tub with hot steaming water, when from out in the hallway there arose such a clatter. She sprang out of the bathroom to see what was the matter. Away to the stairway she flew like a flash, robe tied around her with a long pink sash. The flicker of

357

red, blue, and green tree lights filled the room below. And what to her horror-filled eyes did appear?

Nothing short of the sprawled body of her husband. His face swollen, eyes almost shut, and his tongue protruding from his mouth. She screamed, a deep soul-wrenching wail of terror and grief. She had seen this before, long ago, when they were first dating: his allergy. She sprinted, not toward him, but toward the small black case he kept in his dresser. Within seconds, she had the Epipen in hand, her mind and body focused on one task: Save Mark. In her crazed state, Julie's rational thought process was ignored. Her husband was in danger and nothing else mattered. She jumped down the last few steps to land next to him. She heard and felt her ankle break, but the pain did not come. She was too focused, and the flood of chemicals in her body kept the pain away. She collapsed next to Mark and slammed the needle into his thigh, injecting the medicine into his system.

Once the needle was empty, she left it in him, and her hands reached up to cup his face, to shake him, to scream at him to fight, to not leave her alone. Only then, once she had given him the medicine that would save his life, did she notice his glossed-over eyes, and the strange angle his head was bent at. The tortured cry that ripped from Julie's throat would have rivaled a banshee's wail. She lay atop Mark, slender arms wrapping around him, clinging to his still-warm body.

"Mommy?"

The words pierced Julie's grief when she heard her son. She looked up, tears pouring from her beautiful eyes. Ryan had wandered from his bed after hearing all the commotion. He looked confused, but excited, as he made his way down the stairs.

"Did I get him? Did I get Santa?" He stopped and frowned, seeing the body of his father laying there. His head tilted in slight confusion. "Why is Daddy down...?"

"Baby, please get to the phone and call 911. Your father and I are hurt. Hurry, baby!"

But Ryan's frown just deepened; that look of confusion on his face, intensified.

"Why are you and Daddy down here? You're not supposed to be down here!" His little voice rose in anger. "The booby traps were meant for Santa!" His shrill voice grew higher as it filled with more rage. "I spent all year planning the traps, placing the thumbtacks, the cars, the ornaments. I even gathered small crumbs of peanuts from the store and hid them in the cookies because you told me peanuts make Santa unhappy!" Ryan stomped his little foot right in a small puddle of his father's blood. His face flushed and little fists balled tight.

Julie was frozen, her mind assaulted by her little boy's words—and actions. She temporarily froze, unable to process the horrors that were being piled into her mind and soul.

"You and Dad always mess things up. You always cheat me..." Ryan's rant trailed off as the gleam of presents caught his eye. The gleaming colors from the tree reflected

NEVER FEAR

off a massive pile of gold and green wrapped gifts: his gifts. Without another word or a thought of his parents, Ryan ran down the steps. His father was in the way, so Ryan stepped on him, his little blood-covered foot leaving a bright red mark upon Mark's white T-shirt. Julie reached up, her mind and senses still numb from the horror of the night. She tried to feebly grab him, one hand reaching up shakily as he passed by her. Ryan smacked it away as one would an annoying bug.

He stared at the gifts, and the way the wrapping paper reflected the light. Then he saw the note. Reaching down, he saw the simple admission of defeat from Santa. A maniacal laugh of triumph erupted from him as he danced wildly around the tree—like a pagan of old. Christmas had become a joyous time for him once again. Ryan began to tear into the gifts, the sound of his mother's weeping eventually brought her a slight glance from Ryan. She always had to ruin things. He had finally beaten Santa, and all she could do was cry. It was times like this he wished he had a better family, one who truly cared about him.

As his gaze turned back to his pile of gifts, some still unopened, he spied the small pile of his father's gifts. Crawling over, he grabbed them, and dragged them over to his pile, whispering cheerfully to himself as he did so, "Merry Christmas to me, and to me a wonderful night."

A FAMILY CHRISTMAS TERROR

"That was just *wrong*. I'm glad Grandpa's up next." Nick said and stood up, wavering a little.

"Little shaky there, Nicky?" Jack laughed.

"Okay," Dan said. "We had an agreement. Go help your mother with dinner. That turkey is kind of making me hungry too."

"What about you, Dad? Jack asked, half-joking.

"What about me?" Dad looked up at him. His eyes were a bit glassy.

Jack shook his head and followed the others to the kitchen.

Judy assigned each of them tasks and turned to Grandpa, who was seated on a barstool at the counter. "Everyone has their duties, Grandpa. Start the next story."

"Except Dad," Nick muttered. Jack gave him an elbow.

"Just waiting for you to give me the green light, Judy. Let's see... this one's called *Esmeralda's Stocking*."

"Esmeralda... like in *The Hunchback of Notre Dame*?" Jack asked, grabbing some fresh asparagus to cut.

"As a matter of fact, the story opens with two quotes from it. Interesting," Grandpa said and started to read.

ESMERALDA'S STOCKING

LISA MANNETTI

> *"That straw pallet is a gift from heaven."* —Victor Hugo
>
> *"So, you have the gift of prophecy?"* —Victor Hugo

West Chester, New York: Summer 1961

An end-of-August day and the wind picked up—
nothing unusual she told herself; nothing she hadn't felt
nearly every late summer she could remember. The
humidity dropped, the sky went from the faded, washed-
out gray of her daughter's favorite shorty pajamas to the
sharp, clear blue of the Mediterranean. Nothing she hadn't
seen before—a routine weather pattern—not unlike the
round of her weekdays these last five years: coffee and a
cigarette, making breakfast and later, lunch for Robin and,
like today, folding clean clothes while she napped in her

room on the second floor. Still, she felt a subtle shift—as small, perhaps, as a rill of soil sliding down the slight mound of an anthill—and the breeze prickled along her skin and she felt the tiny hairs on her arms stand up. But it was nothing. Nothing. Old memories of the anticipatory feelings that came when school was about to start, shopping for # 2 yellow Ticonderoga pencils and new Buster Brown shoes, and crisp September air, and Robin was about to start kindergarten. That was it. She glanced out the sunroom window, and saw the wind toss the dark green leaves of the old maple, heard their whispering interplay; watched the rush of moving shadows on the lawn. It was nothing after all, and surely the dream she'd awakened from that morning—the dream about her father's death on Christmas Eve 1950—meant nothing. Just another long-ago memory from the time before Robin came into the world. All life was change, Paulette knew; she'd been a nurse back before her daughter was born and seen the death angel by her father's bed, by a hundred patients' beds, and a dream or a memory, even a painful one, was no harbinger—the changes ahead, she was sure, did not hold anything ominous, did not cradle another death.

*

With the wind-driven damp sheets flapping against the skin of her arms and legs, clothespins moving steadily from flowered apron pocket to fingers, to her clamped lips and back to hands, to the rope stretched across the back yard, she was pegging laundry and thinking simultaneously that she loved the smell of line-dried linens and that at dinner the night before, Luc had begun to talk about purchasing a gas dryer this coming winter.

Robin was in the wading pool, playing amid an assortment of floating pink plastic cups and saucers, and using the kitchen strainer to make "summer tea" from the grass clippings—enough to make pretend tea for half of China, Paulette smiled to herself—that Robin had managed to import from the lawn.

"You have to ask Mommy."

Paulette looked up. On the other side of the hedge that separated their properties, she could vaguely see Alma Briggs, hands pushed inside the greenery to move it aside, talking to Robin.

"Miss Alma has invited me over for lemonade and cookies," Robin said, turning.

"Well...."

"Pleeease..."

"Rob—"

"Please, oh please? Mrs. Myrtle made ginger snaps—"

"Honestly. It's no trouble at all, Paulette—Myrtle is bringing Mother downstairs and we thought it'd be nicer to sit out here in the shade. You come too, if you'd like."

"Use the towel and dry off, Robin. Then go on upstairs and put on your sandals and sundress..."

"Are you coming, too, Mommy?"

"Not today, honey—maybe another time." She smiled. "Thanks anyhow, Alma—give my best to Myrtle and Mrs. Briggs, and don't let Robin eat more than two cookies."

"Three—"

"Robin—"

"Daddy says the French love to bargain—it's in our blood." Robin ran careening past her onto the driveway leading to the back porch, and Paulette shook her head and smiled. "Don't forget to put on your underwear, young lady, and hang that wet bathing suit on the side of the tub."

*

Paulette liked the Briggs family—and they adored Robin—but somehow today she didn't feel like sitting on the painted white metal glider that left waffle marks on her thighs—even when she wore slacks or a skirt—and making small talk with her elderly neighbors.

Miss Alma—a blue rinse lady—was in her mid to late seventies Paulette guessed, and she was a sharp-as-a-tack former school teacher who hadn't missed a day of classes in something like forty years. Myrtle Briggs was married to Alma's brother Howard and they sported identical shades of white hair—when they sat together, they reminded Paulette of dandelion fluff. She'd never gotten straight whether Howie or Alma was the eldest, but really, all three—brother and sister and sister-in-law—seemed like budding youths compared to the sparse-haired matriarchal Mrs. Hannah Briggs. She was sharp-as-a-tack, too, and she'd been born just over 100 years ago, she always said proudly and, as Robin recited enthusiastically, "Mrs. Briggs had been 'just five years old at the time, and remembered when Abraham Lincoln was shot.'"

*

Some three-quarters of an hour later, Paulette walked around the block to retrieve Robin from the Briggs's yard. She pushed open the wooden privacy gate and saw the three old women sitting on the double glider, gently pushing against the slightly elevated iron "floor" making it rock. Robin was curled up, her head against Mrs. Hannah Briggs's arm and sitting opposite Myrtle and Alma. The remains of the lemonade—glasses, peels, an empty cookie plate, and four crumpled dainty napkins sat on a small white wrought iron table near the fancy glider. Myrtle and Alma were fanning themselves and, as they pumped to rock the seats, Paulette could see they wore their stockings rolled to just below the knee—1920s style—and they both wore dated summer shoes—thin "tie" heels made from soft, perforated, pink leather like the loose weaving Robin used when she made nylon loop potholders at the village's free summer program day camp across the street in the park. Hannah appeared to be reading the newspaper aloud to Robin. Robin could read after a fashion—books like *One Fish, Two Fish, Red Fish, Blue Fish* or *The Cat in the Hat* because she'd memorized them, and here and there she could pick out a word and she was *beginning* to read, but the newspaper was beyond her skills.

"Say thank you, Robbie, and let's be on our way." Paulette smiled broadly—hoping to forestall conversation—and all three heads swiveled in her direction. Even Mrs. Briggs turned her cataract-whited empty eyes toward Paulette.

"But she was just getting to the good part," Robin crumped.

"Now, please, sweetie. Daddy will be home soon and we have to get the picnic basket packed."

"For the beach?" Her eyes went as wide as the sand dollars that occasionally washed up on the shore. The Oakland beach was free after 5 p.m. and you could stay till dusk, but usually she and Luc didn't let Robbie do more than wade—there were no lifeguards on duty in the evening.

"Yep." More smiles.

"Bye, Miss Alma! Bye, Mrs. Myrtle and thank you for the delicious cookies. Bye Mrs. Briggs—" She flew to Paulette and grabbed her hand. "Bye-bye, and thank you again!"

"Such a nice, polite little girl—and so intelligent, too." Paulette heard one of them say, the others assenting. All three of them had wavery voices, but she thought it had been Mrs. Briggs—the blind old woman—who'd spoken in praise of her daughter.

*

Paulette was packing the last of the picnic basket and she sent Robin upstairs to dig through the bottom of the closet and retrieve Luc's beach sneakers (the only place he wore that kind of casual footwear). She lowered the green canvas awnings on the west side of the house, and began to open windows on the north and east side to begin to let the cooling late afternoon air circulate. The wind had died down, it was hot again. She heard Robin drop the sneakers on the floor by Luc's side of the bed, and then heard her clomping down the front stairs. The basket was done and she poured herself a cup of coffee, then sat at the kitchen table. She heard the wooden front door bang open, then closed; Robin came bounding into the kitchen bearing *The Daily Item.*

"Read me the newspaper, Mommy! Read me the paper!"

Paulette folded it in half and read: "Mayor Thomas Iasillo—"

"Who's he?"

"He's the mayor of our town."

"Yeah. Okay, read about something else."

"Village to install parking meters on Main Street—"

"Isn't there anything at all about Indians?" Robin said.

"Indians?"

"When Mrs. Briggs reads me the paper, she reads all about crossing the country in a covered wagon. And cooking over campfires. And the time her sister nearly got scalped by a red Indian in the Nebraska territory. And lots more about homesteading—"

369

"She does?"

"Yes, she does," Robin said seriously. "I thought we got the same newspaper, but the one that the Briggs get is completely different. How can that be, Mom? Theirs says *Daily Item*, too. Are you sure there's nothing—maybe in the back—about Pawnee Indians or Hereford cows on the trail, or the time the Carson baby was gored by a bull?"

Paulette understood at once. Mrs. Briggs was blind of course, and she was telling Robin stories from her youth— but *pretending* to read the paper aloud. Now that Paulette thought about it, Alma had mentioned at some point she'd first taught in a one room school house out west, so maybe the stories were true.

"You know honey, Mrs. Briggs is a lot older than Mommy. You know that don't you?"

"Sure!"

"How do you know?" Paulette wasn't sure Robin— smart as she was—really had any concept of age beyond the fact that all adults seemed grown-up *and* old.

"Her skin when you kiss her cheek is like leather. Yours is much softer. When will your skin be like leather, Mommy?"

"Not for a long time, I hope." Paulette was trying not to laugh, and she went on patiently. "The thing is, Robin, sometimes when people are very old they lose certain faculties—parts of themselves."

"Like what?"

"Well, like Mrs. Briggs. She's lost her sight. She can't see. We call that being blind, Robin. Mrs. Briggs is blind."

Paulette sped on. "Mrs. Briggs is a wonderful woman, and she's entertaining you by telling you stories—but they're stories from *history*—not what's in the daily newspaper. Do you understand?"

Robin shrugged. "Okay, if you say so. But she told me today I was wearing a very pretty yellow sundress...so I guess she's not *too* blind."

"I guess not, honey." Paulette decided that Mrs. Briggs was even sharper than she seemed—the old lady had clearly heard Alma or Myrtle remark on the dress and stored up that nugget of information. Like fortune tellers— like the Provençal gypsies her own mother had told Paulette about—doing cold readings, she thought. *No*, none of it mattered, she told herself. The summer lemonade parties, the homemade candied apples for Halloween, hot cocoa and peppermint sticks for Robin after sledding in the winter. They all doted on her. *All* the Briggs family, she told herself, were good neighbors.

West Chester, New York: Autumn 1961

"Mommy!! What am I going to be this year?" Truth be told, Robin was such a small kid that Paulette guessed she probably hadn't outgrown last year's pumpkin costume. At the most, she thought, she'd have to spring for a new pair of orange tights at Woolworth's.

"Pumpkin? It's a great costume—" Which it was— Paulette's mother, Estelle, had made it and she had a creative gift when it came to sewing.

"Sister Mary Frances says we *have* to be a saint," Robin said in going-on-six fashion: part announcement, part whine.

"Let me talk to Mama Estelle," Paulette said. "She'll think of something." God, she thought, I hope it's not an Infant of Prague outfit, it'll cost a fortune with all that satin and Robin won't want to wear it when she goes trick-or-treating at night—not when the rest of the neighborhood is dressed as witches, skeletons and the ever-popular white-sheeted ghost. There's no bragging rights or scare factor when you're dressed like baby Jesus or the Blessed Mother. She's so tiny she doesn't even need *half* a sheet; I can cut eyes out from a pillowcase, if necessary, Paulette decided, and call it done.

But Paulette's mother surprised them all and even Paulette was excited when she brought home the jingling toy tambourine with the fluttering ribbons and the green flounced skirt and gypsy headscarf for Robin's Halloween.

*

Naturally, Paulette didn't own any necklaces made from coins—gold or otherwise—but she thought Robin would do very nicely with some beads and a two or three bangle bracelets. There were no zippers and the costume's bodice-blouse tied in the back and she was helping Robin get ready for the morning kindergarten session.

"But Mommy, what will Sister say? I'm supposed to be a saint—"

"You tell Sister Mary Frances that you're Saint Sara the Gypsy, who gave alms to the poor in France."

"Was she a real saint?"

"Absolutely. You just have to leave the tambourine at home for now—and, instead, take this basket."

"What's in there?" Robin asked looking under the cloth napkin. "Is that alms?"

"Yes."

"It looks like bread."

"It *is* bread. But for today, it's alms for the poor."

"I don't think Sister will like it—" Robin shook her head.

"Are you kidding? With half the class dressed like the Blessed Mother, and the other half dressed like Saint Joseph, she'll love it." Actually, Paulette thought the other kids' mothers were pretty canny—*their* offspring already had costumes for the Nativity play on tap in December. She went on: "Sister will be thrilled. Variety. It's the spice of life, kiddo."

"If you say so." She shrugged. "But tonight—"

"Tonight, yes, you can carry the tambourine."

*

"Robin, that necklace's only to borrow—not for keeps—and you have to be very careful. I really mean it."

"Mrs. Briggs wanted me to wear it—she said I'd be the *perfect* Esmeralda."

The mistake, Paulette thought, was her own. She'd suggested that on the way home from King Street Elementary School Robin stop and show the Briggs beldames her Saint Sara costume. "For tonight," Robin had chirped, "I have a real tambourine and I get to be a *real* gypsy." Immediately Alma—or maybe it was Myrtle—consulted with Mother Briggs and Paulette heard rummaging upstairs (presumably in a dresser drawer) and then the old lady glided down the straight staircase on her moving chair, carrying the necklace in her crabbed white claw of a hand.

Paulette had no idea if it the gaudy green gem was real or "paste"—as De Maupassant famously called costume jewelry—but that didn't matter. "I'm not kidding. It goes back as soon as you're done trick-or-treating."

Like all kids—and not a few adults—in the metropolitan area, Robin was addicted to Channel 9 WOR-TV's Million Dollar Movie—which opened with Tara's theme and ran one film almost continuously for a week at a time. Robin could recite the come-on: "If you missed any part of this movie or would like to see it again, the next showing begins immediately." Just how much of *The Hunchback of Notre Dame* Robin understood was doubtful—though when Paulette caught her tossing the satin bolsters over the stair railing and made it very clear that Robin was stopping that at once, and furthermore, would also *not* be filling the big soup kettle with water she planned to pretend was molten lead and throwing *that* over the balustrade, and when she continued snatching up and heaving sofa cushions, Paulette threatened to spank her bottom, and Robin yelled "Sanctuary!"—it was obvious she got the whole Quasimodo-Charles Laughton character. And though she'd never been spanked, Robin obeyed more or less: Paulette watched her running up and down the stairs bent-over—a pillow stuffed behind her shoulders inside one of Luc's sweaters—with her fingers simultaneously pushing her nose up and pulling her right eye down...watched as Robin lay back on the landing kicking her legs and feet and shouting, "Guillaume...Gabrielle...Big *Ma-a—Rie!*"

Paulette's concession to the American version of the holiday was to serve a hot dog and sauerkraut and mulled cider dinner—which, Robin in her excitement, scarcely touched; neither did Luc, who was to stay home and hand out goodies to the neighborhood, because he didn't like cabbage or cider—with or without rum—or frankfurters. They were nothing, he swore, like the delicious *saucissons* Provençal. Paulette scraped plates while Robin sped into her costume.

"First stop to see the Misses Briggs," Robin declared. "I want to show them my costume." She banged the tambourine against her palm.

"No. Last stop, Robin, to share some of your treats— *and*, to return the necklace."

*

"Why Howie... Myrtle... look at this: Esmeralda, the gypsy girl, has come trick-or- treating right here in our neighborhood."

"And I'm French too," Robin put in helpfully.

"Adorable. Come in, dear—and you, too Paulette. Mother will want to see this!"

The treat table had been set up in the wide foyer—a plate with huge caramel apples and small orange drawstring bags. Howard and Myrtle helped Robin, as Paulette moved through the tied-back green velvet curtains toward the living room. "Only one of each, Robbie," she called over her shoulder.

The old ladies, Paula saw, had decorated the mantel with bright red and gold, and flaming orange leaves— gathered in the park, no doubt. Small pumpkins sat along the wooden edge; two round black-amethyst vases spilled a profusion of bittersweet and ivy from either end; and tiny glassed-in votive candles twinkled here and there. This was not the sort of house, Paulette thought, where one found store-bought dangling cardboard skeletons or gaudy papier-mâché witches. Very Victorian. More turn-of-the-century than mid-century. But maybe *which* century was the real question, she mused.

"The fireplace looks lovely," Paulette said honestly. "Feels good, too" she added, rubbing her hands. There was a heavy pot—something whitish bubbled and frothed inside—hanging above the grate; it was the first time Paulette had noticed that this fireplace had an iron swing hook—the sort one associated with colonial times, colonial cooking—in this part of the country at least. Paulette had never seen one in any of the World War I era houses in the neighborhood—

"Month has an R in it...care for a bowl of oyster stew?" The old lady, propped in a rocking chair, nodded toward the flames. "'Course in my day, mind you, it was more likely we ate *prairie* oysters—hah!" She laughed. "Still, a body gets used to things, and I was used to an iron swing-arm inside a fireplace—so was 'most every homesteader in my time—and Howard, he rigged up this one for me," Hannah said. "Food tastes better, somehow, when it's cooked over a wood fire."

"Yes, I know."

"You might at that—being French and all," she said. 'Course, the colonials hereabouts didn't have much use for the French, and by the time I was born in 1860, nobody had any use for the Indians—even if those wars helped us Americans eventually throw off the Brits. Freedom is a great thing." She paused. "But they herded all the Indians into territories and onto reservations. Ever tell you about the time I saw my own sister scalped?"

"Yes. Or maybe Alma told me—"

"Hid behind a rock on the trail, but they found me. Know why they didn't take my tresses, Missus?"

Paulette shook her head slowly.

"Can't guess? Your ma told me how after nursing school you wanted to go out west and work with the Indians—said you felt sorry for them. That was very unusual. But she wouldn't let you go." Hannah wiped her lips with the back of her hand. "Well, you met Luc and had Robin, so you're better off, girlie. But, can't you guess why they let me go?"

"No... " Paulette said again.

"Sure, you can—you being part gypsy and all—like your ma told me." The old woman turned her white, blind eyes on Paulette and the younger woman would have sworn she was being stared at with the intensity of a searchlight. "And old squaw-woman—a seeress—stopped 'em," she said. "Told those braves to let me be 'cause I had a gift—"

"A gift? I don't understand?"

"Same as yours." The old woman's hand suddenly shot out and clamped down on Paulette's wrist. She found herself wincing at the woman's surprising strength and thinking crazily that Robin was right—Hannah's skin was like leather—like stiff, tanned *hide*. "Same as your girl's—though sometimes it skips a generation."

"What gift?" Paulette wrenched her arm free

"The gift of seein'" the old woman said, tapping alongside her right eye. "The gift of knowin,' the gift of prophecy."

"*I don't know*. I don't know what you're talking about."

"Sure you do," Hannah Briggs said, nodding, then sitting back and winding her knobby hands over the down-curved arms of the rocker. "Of course you know. You saw the angel of death when your father passed," she said. "And you saw your father beckon that angel—crooked his finger calling her, didn't he? And what did he whisper? 'Come closer...' wasn't that it, Missus?"

"Robin—" she began.

"Robin knows *that* story," said Mrs. Briggs.

"She doesn't—"

The old woman shrugged. "Well maybe she overheard it, and maybe she just *knows* certain things. Like I did. Things other girls her age haven't a notion in the world of. Doesn't matter," she said. "Anyhow, here's a story for you, Missus—though if you let yourself, I wouldn't even have to tell it. You'd know it. Same as that angel by your father's death bed—you'd *see* it." The rocker creaked once, twice, and then the old woman began to speak in a half-whispered, papery voice.

*

Paulette had stood there by the fire, arms folded across her chest, and tried very hard not to listen to what Mrs. Briggs told her; she convinced herself she'd actually been successful at blocking out that avid, nearly feverish voice. When they came in just after 8 p.m., Luc was nodding over a *Life* magazine in the wing chair. She'd let Robin eat one candy bar, untied the gypsy costume and just sent her daughter upstairs to get into her pajamas and brush her teeth, when she discovered the shiny green gem in the bottom of Robin's paper spook-ridden trick-or-treat bag.

She was so angry at the thought that Robin had somehow wheedled Alma or Myrtle into parting with the necklace—or worse, filched it—Paulette was on the verge of dragging her from her low single bed. Instead, she steeled herself and picked up the phone.

*

"Yes, Paulette, this is Alma. What's that you say? Robin still has Mother's necklace? Well, Myrt gave it to her, of course—we both did. No, she didn't whine or plead. Really. Oh, pshaw, let her keep it... What? No! It isn't any heirloom... An emerald?" Alma laughed. "That's no emerald, my dear. No, it's—what Mother? Hang on Paulette. Just one second. Yes, it's shiny all right, but Mother says it's nothing but a semi-precious green sunstone. They mine 'em out Oregon way, she says..."

Paulette could picture Alma—tall and slim and still ramrod straight—standing by the black Bell telephone in the hallway, old Mrs. Briggs in her wooden rocker by the fire, and tiny white-haired Myrtle scurrying back and forth between the ancient woman and her elderly daughter, hovering over both of them. "I couldn't possibly let her keep it, Alma," she said. "It's very kind of you *not* to make a fuss, but Robin knows better than that—"

"Better than what? That chain isn't gold, Paulette—I'm surprised it's not as green as the stone by now. I played with it sometimes when I was a girl after Mother gave it to me one birthday—what did you say Mother?" Pause. "She says it was for Christmas one year, not my birthday. And Myrtle says she wore it for over the holidays when first Howie courted her and—hang on Paulette. What's that

Mother? Yes, all right, I'll tell her. Listen, Paulette, it's not even a genuine antique. Not yet, anyhow. Mother got it when she was nine or ten. Says some old Plains squaw must've had a husband or an uncle or a brother who traded with one of Plateau Indians and the Plains squaw—hang on Paulette... She was what? Oh... Mother says the squaw was Pawnee or maybe Ponca and told her it would clarify her vision. She gave it to Mother in the winter around 1870—or thereabouts. Says none of us have daughters—or any children—for that matter, and to go ahead and let Robin keep it. Like Mother said, it's just a green sunstone—not some emerald—but it's still a nice little memento for Robin, for dressing up like Esmeralda, the gypsy.

"I appreciate that Alma, I really do. But we'll be over in the morning to return it."

*

Just before sunset on Wednesday evening, about four weeks after they returned Hannah Briggs's green sunstone Indian necklace, Paulette was checking her recipe book for a dressing with *marrons*—chestnuts—to give the damn turkey some French flair, and Robin was nattering a series of kindergarten-gleaned facts about Abraham Lincoln and how because of him Thanksgiving was celebrated the fourth Thursday in November, when the phone rang.

"Bouchard residence, this is Robin." Pause. "Mommy, it's for you." Robin held the receiver outstretched, and Paulette took it up.

"Paulette, this is Alma. I hate to disturb you—with the holiday practically on top of us, I know you must be getting things ready...but," she hesitated, then cleared her throat. "But we think Mother died a little while ago in her sleep. And, well, I hate to ask—but, you being a nurse—Paulette, could you come over?"

"Certainly, Alma. I'll be right there."

"Robin?" she began.

"—Luc came home early; she won't be here alone."

Paulette put on her wool coat and a fringed scarf for the short walk around the block, thinking just before she rang the bell that, under duress the three remaining Briggses had reverted to behavior typical of their prior farming life out on the prairies: when illness or death came, you relied on your nearest neighbors for help, you didn't automatically summon a town doctor, who might be—who most likely lived—an hour's long, hard ride away.

*

Upstairs, alone in the old woman's darkened bedroom, she found more signs of last-century-homesteaders' customs and rituals: Evidently Alma and Myrtle had worried that rigor mortis might set Hannah's jaw agape and, in a time and place where there was no embalming, the undertaker might have to break the ancient bones to close up her mouth for the viewing in her casket. The sisters-in law had torn an old white sheet or timeworn pillowcase into strips, knotted the bandages on top of her head to bind the age-shrunken mandible firmly shut.

Paulette understood, but she also knew tying up the old woman's jaw was completely unnecessary; she turned on the bedside lamp and began to unwind the cloth. Then, all at once, beneath her schooled fingers she felt the faint, thready beat of Hannah's pulse. *My god*, she thought, *they were wrong—she's alive.* She unwrapped the bandages quickly, then began rubbing the old woman's hands and patting her cheeks. Her eyes fluttered open and she whispered, "Ah. Thank you, Missus—that's ever so much better..." Paulette fluffed the pillow behind the frail shoulders so Mrs. Briggs could sit higher and breathe a bit more easily, announced she'd be right back, and then went to tell Miss Alma and Howard and Mrs. Myrtle that Hannah was alive and Paulette would stay with her for a while. In turn, they each took Paulette's hands, told her how grateful they were for her help.

"It won't be long," Paulette said, turning to climb the stairs again. "I can nurse her through the end..."

*

"Gif-f-f-t-s-s-s," the old woman hissed softly. Her eyes, white and filmy beneath the half-closed lids, were crescent moons lying sideways, twinned in heavy mist. She nodded slowly. "Gifts," she said again. The sound of that weak voice was, to Paulette's ears, both hideously plump— fulsome—and sibilant. "Legacies... and gifts... all of them traps." Hannah's mouth—the grayish lips now drawn inward and sickle-thin—trembled as she exhaled; Paulette, sitting next to the iron bed, her palms lightly riding Hannah's bony fingers, felt that low cool breath on her own hands and she shivered.

Suddenly she was back in memory on the day of the dismissed premonition last summer. Time folded in on itself ...and then it was Halloween night. Mrs. Briggs, her mouth slippery and wet with milky oyster stew, was telling Paulette hideous things—things Paulette had stubbornly blocked from her conscious thoughts till now:

"Of course you know about this gift—hah! Goddamn curse I call it—you have it, too, and so does Robin. Oh, that knowing," Mrs. Briggs had said. "Terrible.... But what could anyone do? *Anyone*, even an adult—much less a child—living in a sod hut or a weather-beaten cabin on those endlessly empty, sky-crushed plains.... *Nobody in my world could've done a single thing.* Still, I saw it. Six months, maybe a year before it happened. Saw the actor fellow— that Booth—creep into Ford's theater, put the gun to the back of Lincoln's head and pull the trigger," she said. "That sound in my skull—deafening. I never stopped hearing it." She shook her head slowly. "Same thing when I was twenty—already married to my Robert and living back east out Connecticut way. Yes. I was older and closer the second time. But not close enough to the rail station in Washington, D.C. to be able to stop Garfield's assassination....There's no worse feeling than that sense of being completely *helpless*." Hannah turned her head toward the flames and Paulette had seen the firelight glinting here and there on her scalp through her thin white hair. "Ask Alma—she knows what it is to carry the burden of knowing, to heft the worse burden of being powerless. Her time of knowing first came when she was fourteen, maybe fifteen—she felt it black and bristling for five long years. But she couldn't stop it either. Buffalo, New York. The Pan-American exhibit...and McKinley was felled in 1901. You never get over it. *Never.* Time doesn't heal those deaths, Missus."

Paulette said nothing.

"Every gift carries an obligation—to be gracious, kind, grateful. Always a dilemma, Missus, minor though it be." Her hands curved, clenching the arms of the worn rocking chair. "But these dark gifts are traps." The fire gave off a loud, sharp *crack!* and Paulette heard the embers shift and tumble. "You wouldn't think just knowing a thing can wound you—that seeing the future can pierce your mind and crumble your soul....but it's so."

Now, in the old woman's narrow bedroom on this Thanksgiving eve, there were the sudden sounds of three desperate, pained breaths, and Paulette was startled from her unsettling reverie. This time, she did not see the death angel, but the old pioneer woman, Hannah Briggs, born in 1860, age 101, was gone.

West Chester, New York: December 1961
First snowfall of the season: the fat, drifting flakes huge and desultory—and destined to melt quickly in the

southern New York climate. Caroling and the Nativity play. Mama Estelle made Robin's angel costume and tinsel crown. In the rushed weeks preceding Christmas, Paulette—shopping, decorating the house, baking cookies and wrapping gifts—had no time to think about Hannah: a dying woman maundering about visions and portents and death.

It was, she thought, perhaps the last year that Robin might believe in Saint Nicholas—every kindergartener with older siblings was on fire to spread the joyfully desolate tidings: *There is no Santa! Your parents* buy *the gifts!*

Luc was a practical man, and Paulette bought her daughter a sampling of useful presents: a cozy flannel nightgown sprinkled with tiny blue sheep; a red wool beret and matching mittens; *The Cat in the Hat Comes Back; Bartholomew and the Oobleck; Thidwick the Big-Hearted Moose.* On impulse in Macy's, she picked up a pair of beginner's ice skates with leather straps Robin could fasten over her brown rubber boots. Paulette was most excited though, at the thought of seeing her daughter's face when she tore the wrapping paper from a most impractical gift: A blond, pony-tailed Barbie clad in a black and white striped bathing suit, black high heels, minute pearl earrings, and tiny white sunglasses. She splurged on a second outfit; Estelle, as thrifty as Luc, began to seek out material and patterns for doll clothes to expand Barbie's wardrobe beyond pedestrian beach wear—to the cocktail hour and the cruise line. Paulette, oohing and aahing over the teeny red chiffon dinner dress, the pleated tennis outfit, and ski togs Estelle had sewn, could hardly wait.

*

Christmas morning and all cheer had fled. Instead, a brief moment of surprised delight turned almost instantly to harrowing sobs and tears; the Barbie doll still lay untouched in its bright Mattel box, still wrapped in gold ribbon and white paper with stars.

Robin, sitting cross-legged by the fireplace, had gleefully—at first—pulled out nuts, oranges, hard candy and a plastic blow-up bubble kit. She rocked the red felt stocking back and forth, then squeezed, searching for further tell-tale lumps.

"Any coal?" Luc teased.

Robin pushed her small hand all the way inside down to the toe, yanked, and then upended the stocking to shake out the prize. What clattered on to the rug shocked Paulette, but she knew instinctively, Robbie hadn't stolen it and no one had put it there: Gleaming in the tree plights, lay the green sunstone Indian necklace.

"It's Mrs. Briggs' emerald," Robin began to say, catching it up in her hand and closing her fingers around it.

Then all at once she moaned, her eyes rolled up, and she swayed toward the carpet.

"Catch her, Luc!"

"Are you all right? What happened? What happened, Robin? What's wrong?"

Paulette could not console her daughter; she picked Robin up and carried her to bed.

"Tell me, Robbie. Tell me what's wrong—please!"

"*Life* magazine," she cried. "*All the pictures.* There's blood on a pink skirt, and a little boy saluting, and oh, Mommy, they've killed him, they've shot our president. Soon—next year or the year after, a man with a gun is going to shoot that boy's daddy dead." She covered her face with her hands. "Texas. President Kennedy," she wept.

"Ssh, ssh...ssh, now, honey, it will be okay."

But of course, Paulette knew it wouldn't be all right.

No, not any more right than the necklace that held an emerald for the gypsy girl named for a green gem; bright gleam winking in the light when she danced on the worn stone steps of Notre Dame before all of Paris: beggars and poets and nobles. Sad green-gemmed girl touched the hearts of a hunchback, an archbishop, and the king himself. Fell in love with shining Phoebus, captain of the guards, god of the sun—

Sun...

Sunstone. In its brilliant blinding glare, you could see things clearly.

Perhaps, too clearly.

A FAMILY CHRISTMAS TERROR

"I didn't think that was going to happen. Did you, Mom?" Nancy said, rolling out the dough.

"No, I was surprised. Make sure the dough is evenly spread out. I don't want lumps in my slices. Your father will never forgive me." Judy went back to stirring the gravy.

"No lumps in the gravy, either," Dan said, entering the kitchen. He stumbled against the counter and his mug fell to the floor and shattered.

"God damn it!"

"What's wrong? Are you okay, Dan?" Judy rushed over to her husband who was on his knees picking up the broken glass shards.

"I'm fine. I just tripped. Ow! Look what you made me do!"

"Dad, you're bleeding," Jack said.

"I'm fine. Your mother made me cut my finger on the broken glass," Dan said, standing.

389

Judy's face hardened. "Jack, get your father a Band-Aid."

"You got it." Jack left the kitchen. "Don't start the next story without me."

"Nancy, pour me another eggnog," Dan said while holding a paper towel over his wound.

Grandpa touched Nancy on the arm. "Maybe hold off till dinner."

"Really, Dad?" Dan gave his father a scowl. "I'll get it myself."

"Here you go, Dad," Jack handed the Band-Aid to his mother, who put it on her husband's finger, saying, "Okay, disaster averted. Everyone back to their chores. Grandpa, continue."

"Ah, let's see..." He cleared his throat. "*Sleigh Me.*"

SLEIGH ME

ELLE J ROSSI

> *"There are some people who want to throw their arms round you just because it's Christmas. There are other people who want to strangle you just because it is Christmas." —Robert Staughton Lynd*

"Would you put that thing away already?"

I slid my gaze toward my twin, while continuing to rapid text with my thumb. The dark obscured my view, but I didn't need to see Stephen's face to know his expression was the same one of somber annoyance he'd been wearing for the last two weeks. My palm burned with the need to smack him upside the head. "What's your problem? Do you want me to drive?"

Say no.

Say no.

Say no.

"No."

Thank God. I hated this stretch of road. We hadn't passed a streetlight, or another car for that matter, in at least thirty miles. It was as if the rest of the world didn't exist. Stephen and I could go out the way we came in. Together. No one would find us for days. Not if this blizzard kept up. We'd freeze to death.

Oh my God, what if I had to eat my brother to stay alive?

I sucked in a deep breath to stop a full-body shudder, reached over and turned up the heat. Snow had been falling steadily for the last two hours. The creak of the windshield wipers was seriously grating on my nerves. I wanted to crank some music to drown out the piercing whistle of the wind. Stephen wouldn't appreciate the jolt to his concentration. Or so he'd told me the last time I had turned it up.

"But... "

Here he goes. Dude had a "but" for every situation whether you needed one or not.

"You're so attached to that damn phone, it's like the thing is an extension of your fingers. I'm driving through this shit-storm. The least you could do is attempt to be good company?"

I reached over and patted his arm. "Aww... When did you turn sixty-five? If you wanted me to pay more attention to you, all you had to do was ask." Rolling my eyes, I hit send, switched to vibrate, and stuck my phone under my leg. "Do I need to remind you that I wanted to wait until morning, wait the weather out?" *Wait out the dark.*

But *nooooo*, Stephen hadn't cared about the snow or the dark. All he cared about was getting the hell away from Bakersfield, putting some distance between the campus and his broken heart. I got it. I really did, but dealing with his pissy attitude was getting harder by the minute.

He sighed and slumped back in his seat. "I didn't know the weather would get this bad."

Yes, he did. Pointing it out would only cause more tension. "It's Christmas, Stephen. Let's try to be happy. Okay?"

"What are you talking about? I am happy."

I swallowed a groan. "Um, no. You're so far from happy you've crossed over into Scroogeville." And wouldn't Mom get a kick out of that? She thrived on drama and loved to throw around *I-told-you-so* like she was an all-knowing genius and we were the underlings who would never amount to anything. What Stephen needed was a distraction—something to remind him that the world and his happiness didn't revolve around Miss Allison Peters. It wasn't that I hated Allison or anything. But stomping on my brother's heart made her the enemy in my book.

"I know what we should do."

"What?" Stephen asked, the one word dripping with suspicion.

"Come on. Why do you say it like that?"

He grunted. "Because your ideas always lead to trouble."

"Not always." I'd give him usually, but not always. For being twins, we couldn't have been more different. We might look alike, with matching blond hair and bright blue eyes, but that's where the similarities ended. Stephen had always been the brooder, while I grabbed on to positivity like a lifeline, for that's exactly what it was. Except when it came to the dark and long stretches of road. Then I turned from Queen Positive to Queen Someone's-gonna-slice-me-to-pieces. I should probably stop watching horror movies. If I had one addiction, that was it. It wasn't my fault. Most little girls grew up hearing fairy tales about Snow White and Cinderella, Christmas tales of Frosty and Rudolph. Not this girl. My bedtime stories consisted of tales of Jeffrey Dahmer and Ted Bundy, Krampus, Frau Perchta, and Hans Trapp.

"Anyway," I said, trying not to sound bitter. "Do you remember the Christmas village I used to work at?"

He tapped the steering wheel in time with the windshield wipers. "Sleigh Land? Yeah, I remember. Why?"

"I was thinking we could stop there on our way home." I'd kill for some of their famous cider.

"You want to stop and walk around in a blizzard like this?"

I did. Anything to stretch out the time before we got home. Ever since Dad had died, Mom had nixed holiday celebrations. Our mother had never been an exuberant person, but there had been moments when she'd let down the walls and truly enjoyed life. Those days were long gone. The walls were thicker than ever and on the off chance she laughed about something, the sound came out forced and brittle, like slowly cracking glass. Stephen held hope she'd snap out of it, but I knew in my heart that our father's death had been the catalyst for a destiny that had always been headed toward disaster. Secretly, I suspected our mother was slightly, if not wholly, insane. If I had to hear one more time how Dad was killed by evil, when in fact he'd died from a heart attack, I'd probably join her on the crazy train. If I had to guess, I'd say those dark tales she liked to read to me got to her too.

Was it any wonder I was scared of the dark?

And things that go bump in the night?

We were only going home because the campus was deserted this time of year, and more so, because it was expected. We'd managed to skip out last year by lying. We'd told Mom that we both had to work. I still felt guilty about that. But being around her during Christmas sucked. "Yes. I really do," I answered. "It'll probably be our only chance to see some holiday lights."

"Yeah, I guess you're right about that. We'll see, Stella. If this shit keeps up, they might be closed before we get there."

I mussed Stephen's hair. Always the doubter. "It'll be open. I have faith." All I wanted was a little festive happiness before the misery set in. Seriously, was that too much to ask?

We drove in silence for another hour. The longest hour of my life. The weather didn't get better. It got worse. Ice mixed with snow, and the wipers groaned with the effort of keeping up with the storm. I peeked at the speedometer enough times to earn a scowl from my driver. At this rate we'd be lucky to make it home before New Year's.

"Man, this sucks."

I laughed to ease some of the tension. "That it does. Do you have any idea where we are?"

"I don't even know if we're on the road anymore. I can't see anything. "

I said a silent prayer, thankful that boys liked trucks. If we weren't in a four-wheel-drive, we would have been stuck hours ago. "Okay, that's a little scary." A whole lot scary. "Hey, this blizzard is bad, like too bad for a serial killer to be out, right?"

"You really need to lay off the horror flicks, sis."

I chewed on the edge of my thumb. "Yeah, I know. But you didn't answer my question."

He snorted. "I don't even think Santa would come out in this."

That made me feel moderately better.

"But..."

Oh, no. Not another *but*.

"We might have to pull over soon and wait this out. I've got a couple of blankets behind the seat. We'll be fine."

No way. I'd rather walk than sit like a piece of bait, just waiting for something to come along and tear us to shreds. "Not yet, okay?"

"Soon."

I leaned forward, straining to see something, anything but the snow, and the ice, and the dark. I counted the sluggish swish of the wipers.

One...

Two...

Three...

Fifty...

I squealed and punched Stephen's shoulder.

"What the hell?"

"We made it!" I'd never been so relieved in my life.

"Made it where, Stella?"

I scooted to the edge of my seat and tapped the windshield. "Sleigh Land is up ahead, on the right. See it?"

Stephen leaned closer to the windshield, his chin inching over the top of the steering wheel. Strings of lights twinkled in the distance, a beacon of hope.

"Yeah, I see it. I can't believe they're open."

"I can," I said, bouncing in my seat. "You can't really cancel Christmas. Besides..." I glanced at the clock. "It's only eight o'clock."

Chuckling, he said, "I guess you're right. You know it will probably take us an hour to get there."

I shrugged. "Doesn't matter."

"Why don't you call Mom and tell her we're making progress and it shouldn't be too much longer?"

I groaned. "You call her."

"Stop being a baby. I'm driving and I know you're dying to check your messages."

He had a point. My leg had practically gone numb from all the vibrations. "Fine." I pulled the phone out and scrolled through my messages before pulling up my contact list. Blowing out a breath, I hit the call button. Nothing happened. I tried again. Still nothing.

"No service." I shouldn't have been relieved, but I was.

"Maybe we should skip Sleigh Land."

I shook my head. "No." I sighed, evened out my tone. "I promise we don't have to stay for long, but I really need a jolt of 'Merry Merry.' Besides, Mom probably took her pills and crashed already."

If I knew that for sure, I'd agree to skip the Christmas village. But like her moods, her sleeping patterns were unpredictable.

"Maybe. We'll see."

I flipped on the overhead light and batted my eyelashes, stuck out my lower lip. Cheap move, but desperate times and all. "Please? It can be your Christmas present to me."

He reached up and turned the light off. "Really? You, lover of all things sparkly, will accept a trip to Sleigh Land as your present."

That right there showed how much I really didn't want to go home. I pretended to mull it over. "Yes. One trip to Sleigh Land and you're totally off the hook."

Smirking, he said, "Done."

I beamed, and then I swore the angels must have been singing because the snow stopped falling, completely stopped, like someone had shut off the faucet. One moment we were shrouded in darkness, the next we were less than a half-mile from Sleigh Land. Cue the creepy organ music.

"Um..."

Stephen clenched the wheel, his knuckles as white as the snow. "Yeah, I know. I thought we were much farther away."

I glanced around, an uncomfortable feeling settling between my shoulder blades. Definitely time to switch to

Hallmark movies. "The snow must have messed with our perception."

"Probably. You sure you want to stop?"

I stared at the lights, at the illuminated candy cane signs that marked the parking lot. Memories of some of the best times of my life played out like an old movie in my mind. "Yes. Absolutely."

We pulled into the parking lot and I noted only a sprinkling of cars. All covered with inches of snow, as if they had been there for a while. They probably belonged to the employees.

Stephen eased into a parking space and cut the ignition. I heard bells and music, children's laughter and buzzing lights. Those sounds, sounds of happiness, enveloped me and the tightness in my shoulders slid away.

I pulled on my gloves and hat and jumped out of the truck. My feet hit a patch of ice. I went down hard, shrieking like a little girl. I heard Stephen laughing as he rounded the truck to help me up. Then I was the one laughing because he went down too, landing with an audible snarl.

"Oh my God. We are a pair." I grabbed onto the door and pulled myself up.

"A pair of stupids." He brushed off his coat and hit *lock* on his key fob before shoving his keys in his front pocket.

"I hope no one got that on video. We could go viral."

"You wish. I think we're good though. I don't see anyone else out here."

The village looked as deserted as the roads. I tried not to dwell on that; I really did. Yet, prickles of anxiety skated along my spine. "I don't know if it would be safer to hang on to each other or not." I scooted my feet instead of taking a step.

Stephen nudged me along. "I vote for not. "

"Chicken."

He barked out a laugh and we made our way toward the entrance. I hadn't heard him laugh in way too long. Despite his protest, I linked my arm through his as we passed under the crisscrossed candy canes held by giant toy soldiers. On our right sat a small cabin, more the size of an outhouse than anything. I'd been sixteen the last time I'd sat in that little gingerbread house, collecting payment and handing out maps.

Stephen pulled out his wallet, but when we got to the window, no one was there. Lights flickered inside.

"Maybe they're closed for the night."

A breath of frigid air seared my lungs. I rubbed my gloved hands together. "No way. The music is on." I knew the routine. Thirty minutes before closing time, they'd shut off the music and start dimming the lights. Still, I looked around and didn't see another soul. Where was the laughter coming from? I shoved my hands in my coat pockets to hide that fact that I was shaking.

Stephen shrugged. "Guess we're getting in free. You're a cheap date."

I shook my head. "I don't know. Maybe we should just go. Mom is probably worried."

That earned me a wry look.

"Now you're worried about Mom? Not buying it. You're just scared."

I shoved him. "So what?"

"This was your idea." He grabbed my hand and tugged me along. "Come on. Let's see if we can find anyone else and then we'll hit it."

He was right. This was my idea, and he did seem to be having fun. The least I could do was go along for the ride. I'd just have to keep my eyes peeled for serial killers lurking in the shadows. And murderous elves. And mutant reindeer. Suddenly, dealing with Mom seemed a whole lot safer.

We walked along the winding path. Bing Crosby crooned from the overhead speakers. Every building we came across was empty. The lights really were pretty, but I couldn't ditch the nagging feeling that something bad was going to happen. I wondered if female intuition ran parallel to paranoia. I wondered if that's what my mother had thought at first.

I shrieked when an elf dashed into our path before running away, disappearing behind another gingerbread house, the biggest house in the village. Santa's house.

Stephen laughed, tugged on my hair. "Chill, Stella. It's all part of the fun."

"Really?" I asked, my gaze darting around. "Because he looked like he was seriously running for his life." I willed my heart to calm and worried the pounding organ would blast a hole through my chest. "You're probably right, though. Fun. At least we're not alone anymore." Surely the elf was part of the staff. But what if he wasn't?

I stared at the house, the twinkling lights that flashed red rather than the traditional white they'd used for as long as I could remember. Cold seeped into my bones. "Stephen?"

"Yeah?"

"Do you see that?"

"See what?"

I pointed toward the house. I should have gone with my gut when we first got here. I should have grabbed his hand and raced back to the truck. But I didn't. Instead, I crept toward the house, toward the body that lay prone just outside the open door.

The woman wore red shoes, the tips sinking into the fresh snow. Green and white striped tights covered her legs. Her long jacket was green with red cuffs and collar. I recognized the standard Sleigh Land uniform. I still had mine.

"What the hell?" Stephen crouched next to the body.

I shook my head. Back and forth. Back and forth. "Don't touch her. Something's wrong."

He looked up at me, his brows creased. "Obviously. Check your phone. See if you have any signal. We have to get her some help."

Something told me she was beyond help. Still, I pulled my phone from my pocket and checked for bars. Not a single one appeared on the screen.

Stephen inched closer.

"Don't touch her!"

He whipped around. "Jesus, Stella. I have to check for a pulse."

"She doesn't have one."

"How do you know?" He turned back and moved her dark hair away from her neck. He flipped the body over and shook her as if he could jar her back to life.

"I just—" The words lodged in my throat. I fought to remain standing, dizziness swamping me. "Stop it. She's dead. Please, Stephen. Stop touching her."

"You're right. You're right." Stephen said, easing the dead woman back to the ground.

I stared at the gaping wound on her chest, swore I could see exposed organs beneath broken ribs. Blood slipped from her body and leached into the snow. So much blood.

What happened to her? Her eyes were wide open, staring at nothing yet reflecting the horror she must have felt when the animal struck. Surely it was an animal. One with claws and teeth. Nothing else could have done this to her. I spotted two more bodies huddled in the corner of the room. Both wore elf costumes just like the woman. They didn't move. Blood pooled around their legs.

Stephen stood, wiping frantically at the blood soaking through his jeans.

I backed away from the massacre. My feet struggled to keep up with the pounding of my heart. "Let's go. We have to get out of here." Children's laughter echoed in the distance, taunting me.

I barely heard my brother's warning over my own panicked breathing. I stumbled backward. Someone grabbed me from behind and I screamed. Stephen's eyes mimicked the dead woman's, wide and full of horror. He raced toward me. I couldn't move, other than to flick my gaze down. Strong hands, tipped with black claws gripped my forearms. Tighter, tighter they squeezed. I whimpered in pain. My thoughts were frantic even as everything seemed to slow down around me. *Think, think, think.*

"Move!" Stephen picked up speed.

I twisted my body as he pulled a linebacker move and drilled his shoulder into my captor's gut. The momentum sent us all into a tailspin. I landed on top of Stephen, who landed on top of . . .

I swallowed another scream, grabbed Stephen's coat and pulled with every ounce of strength I had. Our feet tangled and we fell again.

The creature pushed Stephen away and we went flying across the path. I landed on my back. All air left my chest in one *whoosh*. Frozen, I bit back a cry as the monster walked toward us. He was dressed like Santa, had a long beard like Santa and a large bag strapped to his back, but his legs were all animal, with cloven hooves like a goat or a deer. His skin was tinged green, his teeth long and sharp—rows and rows of teeth. He had a hooked nose and elf-like ears with multiple piercings. Two red horns jutted from his forehead. He laughed, the sound sharp and sinister as if he'd emerged from the depths of Hell. We struggled to get to our feet. His fetid breath washed over me and I gagged.

This wasn't Santa Claus.

This was Krampus.

Krampus didn't exist. He didn't. Like Santa, he was a myth told to children to get them to behave. But he looked just as my mother had described him.

"I am no myth."

The cadence of his voice nearly shredded my skin.

I shoved off the ground as he flicked his long, black tongue toward me like a frog catching a fly. His tongue scraped along my cheek. Stephen grabbed my arm and pulled me away. We ran toward the entrance, the sound of hooves clacking on the cement just behind us.

Clack.

Clack.

Clack.

Stephen slipped and went down on all fours. Krampus snagged Stephen's ankle and pulled him backward. Stephen clawed at the ground but couldn't manage to gain any purchase. I reached for his hand. Desperation clogged my throat.

"Go, Stella!" His voice quivered.

I shook my head. "I can't. I'm not leaving you."

Krampus sank his claws into Stephen's leg. Blood spurted like a geyser, nailing Krampus in the face. My twin wailed and I felt the pain as if it was my own. That tongue—that grotesque tongue—lapped at Stephen's blood.

I launched myself at the beast, wishing I had a weapon. I slammed into Krampus, my bones jarring at the impact. His hand clamped around my neck and he lifted me off the ground. I kicked and punched, fought with everything I had, trying to buy Stephen some time. Krampus gave me a brutal shake and threw me like a ragdoll. I landed in a heap, tears streaming down my face.

He latched on to Stephen again. He tore at him with claws and teeth, beating him with a bundle of branches, shredding his skin to the bone. I watched, horrified, paralyzed, as Krampus destroyed the other half of me. The sky was raining blood, a deluge of claret gore.

I squeezed my eyes shut, but I couldn't erase the images. The screams, the screams, the screams were too loud. I pushed my palms tight to my ears, but nothing could drown out the sound of my brother's agony.

Silence.

Too much silence.

This wasn't real.

An organ rendition of *Silent Night* filled the air.

The music swelled and still, I kept my eyes clamped shut.

Maybe I was just as insane as Mom. A genetic defect that made me see things that didn't really exist. I took a deep breath and opened my eyes. Krampus stood about twenty feet away, stuffing Stephen's mangled body into his bag. I gagged as Stephen's blood, along with who knew how many others, soaked through the bag, staining the snow bright red.

I couldn't save my brother, but he would want me to save myself. Grief swamped me, but fear and self-preservation won out. I stood, my feet unsteady beneath me.

One step.

Two.

Hot breaths feathered across my neck, branches cracked against my back nearly knocking me down. I didn't hesitate. I took off, headed for the truck until I remembered Stephen had the keys. I looked over my shoulder, certain Krampus followed me, but I didn't see him. I needed a place to hide. Somewhere to hole up until help came.

I dove beneath a crop of evergreens, slithered back as far as I could. He would find me. I knew he would. He would see my footprints in the snow. I should keep moving. Keep running. But I knew it wouldn't matter. The end result would be the same. He would come. And he would kill me.

Why was Krampus here? He was the anti-Santa, the evil monster that punished children who misbehaved. What had any of us done to deserve such punishment? I thought about the horrible thoughts I'd had about my mother, about how we'd skipped out on Christmas last year. But what about the others Krampus had killed? Maybe this was the ultimate retribution for secrets and lies. The reasons didn't matter. He was coming to get me.

My nerves huddled together beneath my skin, a panicked bundle seeking comfort that would never come. I ripped off my gloves and scratched, scoring my nails across my cold skin, leaving trails of blood like a map, a confession of my ensuing insanity.

I raised my hands over my head, praying, begging for someone to take away this pain and terror. Hooves clacked just beyond the trees, a mocking answer to my futile prayers.

Clack.

Clack.

Clack.

Thick, black claws parted the branches.

He reached in, snapped his fingers together like a lobster claw. I pressed my back against the trunk of the tree, but his sharp claws scraped my neck. He pulled his arm back, blood—my blood, dripped from his fingers.

Clutching my throat, I scrambled to crawl out the backside of the trees. He latched on and wrapped a chain around my ankle, dragging me just like he had dragged Stephen.

Cold. So cold.

Mom was right. Evil existed.

The trees disappeared and I was face down in the snow, my tears freezing on my cheeks. He flipped me over. A pair of horrific green eyes peered at me, and I knew, I knew, I knew...

A slash of his claws. Once. Twice.

No one could help me now.

A FAMILY CHRISTMAS TERROR

CHAPTER 14

"Krampus is as bad as that Gryla hag from the Iceland story," Nick said.

"I told you that in Europe there were many Christmas stories that were told to make children behave," Judy said. "And if you make lumps in those potatoes, you are going to find out what real punishment is, mister."

"I can't help it. This is hard," Nick whined.

"Oh please." Nancy grabbed the bowl of potatoes from him. "Let me do it."

Nick pulled her close and gave Nancy a fat wet kiss on the cheek.

"Oh Christ, Nick." Nancy wiped her cheek. "Stop being such a jerk."

"And how weird is it that those two people in *Sleigh Me* were twin brother and sister?" Nick said.

"Yeah, it's like the book knew," Jack said.

Everyone stopped what they were doing for a moment. Thinking.

Jack broke the silence. "Where do you want me to put the vegetables, Mom?"

"On the table." Judy walked over to the oven. "Nick come get the turkey out. Why don't we let Jack carve this year, since your *father* sliced his finger."

"I'm fine," Dan insisted. "But I wouldn't mind a break. I'll read the next story while you all serve me." He went to Grandpa and took the book.

"My voice could use the rest. I'll just enjoy this wonderful meal, prepared by my wonderful family." Grandpa took a swig and finished off his eggnog. "On this most wonderful time of the year."

Judy noticed him finish his drink and go to refill it. "That was very sweet, Grandpa." She leaned over and kissed him on the forehead.

Dan scowled at them, then took his seat at the head of the table and began to read, *"A Crimson Christmas..."*

A CRIMSON CHRISTMAS

DEBBY GRAHL

Outside the large picture window, snow fell gently blanketing the quaint New England town in pristine white. A fire burned low in the brick fireplace while Christmas carols played softly from the stereo. A freshly cut Frasier fir stood in the corner, decorated with twinkling lights, colored glass balls, and an array of ornaments his children had collected throughout the years.

Nicholas Klaus, an nondescript man of average height, stared at the boxes containing the Christmas village his wife had purchased from an estate sale. He scowled. That was just what they needed, more Christmas crap. There wasn't an inch in the house that didn't already hold some kind of snowman or Santa figurine. He despised Christmas and everything associated with it.

For his children's sake, he'd tried to put the past out of his mind, but how was he to enjoy a time of year that brought back nothing but horrific memories? At the age of ten he had awakened Christmas morning to find his parents' mutilated bodies lying near the glowing tree, their blood dripping from its branches and coating the packages below. The investigation had gone on for months, but the killer had never been caught. It was as if he'd disappeared into thin air. Nightmare images of bloody bodies still haunted Nicholas' dreams. He squeezed his eyes shut and willed the memory from his mind, but each year it seemed to sear deeper and deeper into his soul.

He took a deep breath and tried to focus on the here and now. He glanced at the Santa clock's digital display. It was getting late, and he'd promised to set up the village under the tree. His children had been sent off to bed, and his wife was upstairs wrapping gifts. His mouth formed a thin grim line. It seemed that each year she was spending more and more on presents. As the old cliché says, did she think he was made of money?

Nicholas moved to where a large Cherrywood box sat upon a table. With reverence he opened the lid. Inside, lying on a bed of velvet, were whimsical carved figures, each depicting a member of his family painted in their holiday finest. Woodworking had been a skill passed down through the generations on his father's side. Each figure had been crafted from the wood of a blackthorn tree. Nicholas couldn't help but admire his own craftsmanship as he unwrapped the lifelike figure of his daughter and son building a snowman. Setting the figure on the table, he turned to the boxes containing the village.

Soon he had fluffy fake snow spread out beneath the tree. He arranged the tacky Christmas houses, the old-fashioned lamp posts, and the plastic magnetic ice-skating pond. He laid the track for the train, assembled the Santa Claus Express with the flatcar loaded with little Christmas trees, then carefully placed the carved figures along with the ceramic characters his wife had chosen. It looked perfect. And he hated it.

He connected the extension cords, plugged them into the surge protector, hit the switch, and watched as the tiny village seemed to come to life. The lamps blinked on, skaters bumped around in a circle, and the train chugged by.

"Nicholas, it looks wonderful. The children will love it," Candace Klaus said coming into the living room. She bent down to get a closer look. "I knew as soon as I saw those little village houses, they'd be perfect under the tree. And all the different people, aren't they cute? The ice-skaters going around the pond remind me so much of the children. Oh, and here comes the train. Nicholas, they're going to be so excited."

Nicholas's reply was a grunt.

Candace stood and clapped her hands. "How I love Christmas. Tomorrow we'll go cut down a tree for my parents. The children are really looking forward to it. Then later there's the parade. I told Mayor Balsam you'd be willing to be one of the elves and hand out presents to the children. They're just small items, mostly candy. We wouldn't want to outdo Santa, would we?" she concluded with a laugh.

413

Nicholas gritted his teeth. Was the silly woman so totally oblivious of his internal torment? Be an elf? Not likely. He stared at her Santa night cap, matching sleep shirt, and candy cane-striped socks. A sneer of distaste crossed his face. "Aren't you a little old to dress like that?"

Confusion and hurt filled her eyes, then she smiled. "Everyone's a kid at Christmas." She turned back to the village and reached for one of the carved figures. "Each time I see these I'm amazed at how lifelike they are. I don't understand why no one in your family ever went into business selling them."

"They're not meant to be sold," Nicholas replied, taking the figure representing himself cutting down a tree from Candace's hand. "This was given to me as a small child." Remembering the strange bonding sensation he'd felt the first time he'd held the figure, Nicholas shook his head. *It's only a piece of wood*, he thought, as he replaced it in the bed of fake snow.

Suddenly the lights of the village brightened, then there was a popping noise, and a spark, and all went dark.

"The hell with Christmas and all that goes with it!" Nicholas shouted. He angrily tossed the last log on the fire and grabbed his axe.

"Nicholas, where are you going?" Candace called.

"To cut down that damn tree."

"But it's eleven o'clock at night."

The slamming of the door was his only response.

Chapter 2

CHRISTMAS TERRORS

A flash of light streaked across the dark sky. Nicholas, startled, his axe raised, paused and quickly looked around. There wasn't a sound. The only illumination came from the newly fallen snow. In front of him stood an evergreen. Nicholas gripped the handle of the axe and with a few quick strikes the tree fell. He lashed it to the sled and winding his way through the pines, headed toward home.

The next morning, Nicholas awoke to the sound of his wife and children singing along with Burl Ives, and the smell of cookies baking. Scowling, he threw off the blanket, quickly dressed, and headed for the kitchen.

"Good morning, dear," Candace said with a bright smile. "Coffee's ready."

"Mom's making pancakes shaped like gingerbread men," his daughter Holly added excitedly.

"And there's hot chocolate," his son Chris announced, a wet brown mustache surrounding his mouth.

Snowball, a fluffy white mutt of no discernible heritage, barked gleefully while chasing his squeaky green elf toy.

Nicholas took in his cheerful family, the counters full of cookies, candy and fruitcake, and frowned in disgust. How he wished they'd all go away and leave him alone.

"Did you cut down the tree for us to take to my parents?" Candace asked as she filled his plate.

Nicholas nodded.

"I can't wait to get to Grandma and Grandpa's house," Holly said. "We get to help decorate their tree."

"And afterward Grandpa's taking us to the ice-skating pond," Chris said. "Dad, will you come too?"

Nicholas shook his head. "Not this time."

"I plan on staying with Mom to help her with the baking," Candace said. "Nicholas, why don't you go and at least watch the children skate?"

Nicholas wiped his mouth and tossed down his napkin. "We'll see."

"We have a big day ahead of us," Candace said. "Don't forget tonight is the Christmas parade. And we're all supposed to be in it. I think it's wonderful they want everyone in the town to participate."

"Even Snowball!" Holly and Chris shouted in unison.

Nicholas, unable to listen to any more of their joyful chatter, rose from his chair. "I'm going for a walk."

"Don't be long," Candace called. "We need to leave soon."

When Nicholas stepped outside, Fred the mailman was just pulling up in his truck.

"Good morning to you, Nicholas," he said with a smile as he handed Nicholas a stack of mail. "More Christmas cards I'm guessing. Tell Holly and Chris I made sure their letters to Santa were placed directly into the North Pole express mailbox."

Nicholas nodded as he shoved the envelopes through the mail slot in his front door.

Fred waved and drove off. Nicholas shook his head. Even the damn mail truck was decorated for the holidays. Entering the small town, Nicholas passed the sweet shop. Miss Cringle, a short plump woman with rosy pink cheeks, stuck her head out of the store window. "Nicholas, please tell Candace the candy canes she ordered for the tree are ready."

Again Nicholas nodded. He hurried past the bank, post office, and police station picking up speed as his most hated shop in the town, Always Christmas, came into view. Just as he was even with the door, it opened and the proprietor, Miss Garland, stepped out.

"Good morning, Nicholas. What perfect timing. I was about to go to your house and bring you the star Candace ordered for the top of the tree. If it's all right with you, I'll let you take it home and save me the trip."

Nicholas took in her red elf hat, blinking Rudolf sweater, and jingle bell skirt with total revulsion. "You look absolutely ridiculous," he snarled before turning and walking away.

He passed a family loaded down with packages coming out of Winters General Store. Realizing he hadn't bought any presents, he hesitated, then shrugged. *Oh, the hell with it, Candace probably has more than enough.*

Ahead, The Nutcracker Tavern, with its wide porch, stone fireplace, and long oak bar, was one of Nicholas's favorite places. He thought about stopping in for an eggnog or two until he saw the sign advertising live carol singing every day until Christmas.

Frowning in disgust, he headed toward the ice-skating pond. Seated on a bench, he gazed across the frozen water toward the church. It too was resplendent with candles and wreaths. Adjacent to the church stood a nativity scene complete with a wooden manger above which hung a

417

golden angel whose eyes Nicholas could have sworn were staring into his. It had to be his imagination. The angel was too far away. But a sudden unease chilled him.

Nicholas glanced around at the scattering of colorfully decorated houses, a warm glow emanating from their windows, and a fierce anger began to burn inside him. He hated everything about this place. Why did he have to grow up here? Why couldn't he have been born somewhere normal? Christmas Town. What a silly name. Where did they think they were, the North Pole? He laughed derisively. Day after day he had to look at all these people with their stupid happy faces and jolly Christmas spirits. Bah humbug is right. There had been so many times he'd thought about getting on the train and never coming back.

The sound of laughing children reminded Nicholas that he needed to get home, but still he hesitated. Why should they all be so joyous when he was so miserable? The noisy children came into view wearing their red and green stocking caps, carrying their skates, and pulling a sled. Nicholas quickly rose and hurried away.

In the middle of town stood a ten-foot tree covered with lights, red crystal balls, and shiny tinsel. At its base, plastic elves carried packages to place in a life-size sleigh complete with Santa and his reindeer. As Nicholas took in the scene, he realized how much he abhorred the color red. It was everywhere, from the bows on the street lights to the ribboned garland strung across the shops. When he looked back at the elves, Nicholas blinked in surprise. Their sneering faces seemed to mock him. He could have sworn he heard one of them laughingly ask, "Do you think anyone really cares how you feel?"

His pulse quickened and he felt every pounding beat of his heart. He glanced around. The street was empty. With a snarl, he kicked over each elf, knocked down the reindeer and punched a hole in Santa's bulbous nose. Feeling better than he had all day, he continued toward home.

In his front yard, a snowman stood wearing his old hat and scarf. Lights intertwined with garland spread across the porch roof and over the eves. A wreath hung on the door, and red Christmas bells danced in the wind. His breath began to come in short gasps. He opened and closed his hands. For a minute he just stood there, then an uncontrollable rage blossomed inside him. Everything around him seemed to turn red. With a bellow, he toppled the snowman. He jerked down the bells and threw them into the yard, then snatched the wreath from the door and stomped it beneath his feet. In the corner of the porch stood his axe.

Chapter 3

"There you are Nicholas," Candace said as he entered the kitchen. "Where in the world have you been? The children were getting antsy so they've already left for my parents, and I'm ready to go."

Tins of cookies lined the counter, and a gingerbread house covered in gumdrops sat in the middle of the table.

Candace cocked her head. "Nicholas, are you all right? You have a strange look on your face."

Teeth bared, Nicholas swept the tins of cookies onto the floor and with his fist smashed the gingerbread house. When he turned to his wife, satisfaction at the shock on her face fueled him.

"Nicholas, what's the matter with you?" Candace gasped as she backed away.

"You stupid woman, you never understood. Year after year you bring out all these repugnant decorations insisting I help you put them up." He shoved his face within inches of hers. "You taunt me with memories I'm trying to forget. Well, my dear, this is how I remember Christmas."

Nicholas grinned with satisfaction at the sheer terror that filled Candace's face as he reared back with the axe held high. Her mouth open ready to scream, he sank the axe in her neck.

Adrenalin pumped through him at the sight of her blood as it splattered the walls, dripped down the cabinets, and pooled onto the floor. He narrowed his eyes in anger when he saw her head wasn't quite severed, still attached by thin tendons. As her lifeless body crumpled to the floor, Nicholas brought the axe down one more time, until his wife's head, her mouth still open in a silent scream, slid, in her own blood, across the kitchen floor.

Nicholas chortled with glee, as with one swift kick, he lofted her head into the air, to land in a bowl of poinsettias. "Now you can be your own decoration."

With utter joy, Nicholas walked through the house, destroying everything in his path that had to do with Christmas. When he stepped onto his porch, twilight was setting in. The sled carrying the tree for his in-laws sat waiting. A smile spread across his face. Why not? Year after year he's had to put up with the people of this town and all their holiday happiness. Well, no more. If they love the color red so much, he'd give them what they wanted. He'd show them what a red Christmas was really like. Eyes glowing with anticipation, Nicholas picked up the rope handle to the sled.

Candace's parents, Carol and Jack Card, lived on the other side of a thick stand of evergreens. As Nicholas maneuvered the sled through the trees, the swish of the runners as it slid over the snow the only sound, a bird suddenly flew past to land on a branch directly in front of him. The snow-white dove's eyes bored into Nicholas's, rendering him incapable of movement. An internal battle of wills roiled inside him, until his lips parted in an ominous grin and the axe flew through the air. Disappointment wiped the grin from Nicholas's face as the dove easily rose to a higher branch.

Muttering under his breath, Nicholas proceeded on his way, but knew the dove followed closely behind.

As he exited the trees, a horse-drawn sleigh approached carrying a couple cuddled close together and waving cheerfully as they drew near. "Hello. Merry Christmas to you, good sir. We're heading for the parade. Would you like a ride?"

Nicholas's grip tightened on his axe as the sleigh came to a halt.

The man leaned forward. "Sir, is that blood on you? Have you been injured? May we be of assistance?"

Nicholas glanced down and saw his wife's blood covering his hands, coat and pants. His head began to pound as cold sweat trickled down his back. He swallowed the saliva that pooled in his mouth. He flexed his hand on the axe.

"Thank you for the kind offer," he said with a smile. "I'm fine, but I can't say the same for you. I'm afraid you're going to miss the parade." With a mighty swing, he buried the axe blade deep in the man's chest, cutting through his jacket and sweater. Blood spewing, his eyes bulging, gasping for breath, the man's hands twitched as he feebly tried to remove the axe. Nicholas wrenched it free, leaving a gaping wound, exposing cracked ribs and beneath them his pulsating heart, beating its last. Sobbing, the woman, visibly shaking, her teeth chattering, tried to scramble from the sleigh. Nicholas chuckled low. "And where do you think you're going?"

"Please, please, don't hurt me," she cried.

Nicholas' nostrils flared as the smell of fresh blood permeated the air. "Oh, I'm not going to hurt you," he said with a smirk. "I'm going to kill you."

When she screamed, he split her skull open. As her head lolled, with another swift strike he sent her head flying. Blood soaked their jackets, ran down the side of the sleigh and lay crimson upon the crisp snow. As the horses whinnied and began to run, Nicholas tossed the severed head back into the sleigh. When her head landed in her lap, Nicholas couldn't help but chuckle. "Good catch."

Nicholas walked to where the snow wasn't streaked with blood and used it to scrub the gore from his hands and face, thankful his jacket was black and would hide the stains.

By the time he'd reached his in-laws, it was full dark. Candles burned in the windows of the two-story gabled house, while the outside was lit with thousands of tiny colored lights. As he approached the porch, Carol opened the door. She wore a red sweater with sparkles that read Merry Christmas, a matching red skirt, and shiny white boots. "There you are, Nicholas. I was becoming concerned. Jack has taken the children to the parade, and I said I'd stay and wait for you." She peered around him. "Where's Candace? Do you have the tree?"

At the sight of her, Nicholas clenched his teeth. How he loathed this woman. Always cheerful. Acting as if she was Mother Christmas herself. "Candace couldn't make it, but I have your tree."

Carol knitted her brows. "That's strange. The children told me she was just waiting for you to return, then she'd be here."

"She's doing some last minute decorating." Nicholas hoped she couldn't hear the tension in his voice. He wanted to be done here and complete his night's work. "Now tell me where you want this tree. You don't want to be late for the parade, do you?"

Carol hesitated before opening the door wide. "The stand is in the corner. If you could just place the tree there, we'll straighten it later."

Nicholas, keeping the tree in front of him to hide his coat, did as she asked. As he turned, he spotted the boxes of decorations waiting to be placed on the tree. Suddenly in his mind he was transported back in time, envisioning his parents' bloody bodies. The room came in and out of focus. He shook his head trying to clear away the images.

"Nicholas, are you all right?" Carol asked.

Next to him lay a big red bow with a silver bell, and he reached for it.

As Nicholas walked away from the house, he couldn't help but glance back. There, the big red bow encircling her neck, Carol hung from a hook on the porch, swaying slightly in the wind, her eyes bulging and her tongue protruding from the corner of her mouth, the silver bell dinging with the breeze.

Whistling a holiday tune, he picked up his axe and headed for town.

When he neared the ice-skating pond, he paused. Candace had told him that after the parade there was to be a big skating party with roasted chestnuts and hot chocolate. An idea formed in his mind, and he cautiously made his way onto the smooth surface of the pond. He began to chop holes into the ice, small enough not to be readily seen, but weakening it for an unsuspecting skater.

Suddenly the dark water was suffused with a golden glow. Nicholas looked up to see the angel from the nativity, her body pulsating with light, which, as Nicholas watched, became brighter and brighter. Once again her eyes seemed to lock with his. She was nothing more than plastic and plaster, he told himself as he slowly backed away, but a frisson of fear still coiled in his stomach. With his concentration on the angel, he didn't notice the lone lost ice skate until his foot bumped against it. Without a second thought, he reached down and picked it up. Taking a few steps forward, and with all his strength, he hurled the skate across the pond. Satisfaction spread through him as he watched the serrated tip imbed itself in the angel's chest. A loud popping noise filled the night as the angel blew apart, a spear of light knocking Nicholas down, its force hurling the axe from his hand.

Shaken, Nicholas rose to his feet and walked to where his axe lay, its blade impaled in the ice. Jerking it free, Nicholas snarled an expletive under his breath, as he continued into town.

As he rounded the corner and passed Miss Cozy's quilt shop, Miss Cozy herself was in her display window arranging an intricately stitched quilt representing children sledding down a hill. Spotting Nicholas, she franticly waved him in.

Smiling to himself and thinking, *This one is going to be easy*, Nicholas opened the shop's front door.

"Nicholas, thank goodness I saw you," Miss Cozy said excitedly. "I don't know if you have Candace's present yet, but she was in the other day and fell in love with my holly berry quilt. If you'd like to see it, I have it right here on a rack."

Nicholas nodded and followed her to where the quilt was hanging. Pretending to admire Miss Cozy's design of deep green leaves covered with plump cranberries, Nicholas spotted an object lying on the counter that he recognized. As the thought took shape in his mind, he reached for the basting gun.

"Be careful," Miss Cozy exclaimed. "I have very sharp tacks in that."

"I was counting on that," Nicholas said as he shot the tiny barbed tacks into her eyes. She screamed and tried to cover her face, but Nicholas emptied the gun into her head, hands and arms.

Nicholas knocked her to the floor and grabbed a pair of scissors. He stabbed them into her throat until bloody bubbles foamed out and ran down her chin. As a low gurgling noise came from her mouth, and her arms and feet twitched, Nicholas quickly wrapped her in the quilt, expeditiously suffocating her.

When he stood, he noticed a sign which read, 'Have a Holly Jolly Christmas'. Nicholas, using a staple gun, attached it to the rolled-up quilt. Then, singing a Christmas tune, he picked up his axe and headed for the door.

Out on the sidewalk he passed the barber shop, its striped pole bright red and green. Sounds of the parade preparation could be heard. He was almost finished making his rounds. He had just crossed the street when police officer Yule came into view.

"Good evening, Nicholas," he said with a nod. "You had better hurry. They're lining up for the parade."

What a perfect trophy you would make, Nicholas thought as he contemplated the best way to exterminate Officer Yule. A mental image of his head spiked on top of the town Christmas tree made Nicholas smile. But before he could make a move, Miss Plum stepped from her doorway and called Officer Yule's name. To Nicholas's disappointment, he tipped his hat to Nicholas and walked away.

Nicholas, smiling to himself, moved away in the opposite direction. He was more cunning than the people of this town. He placed the axe over his shoulder and headed toward his next unsuspecting victim.

Chapter 4

There wasn't a sound in the house as Nicholas made his way down the stairs. How he loved the peace and quiet. Those thoughts had no sooner entered his mind when a low whistling sound interrupted the silence. The soft early sunlight streamed through the window as Nicholas entered his living room.

"What in the world?" Nicholas murmured in puzzlement as he saw the brightly lit Christmas tree and the train as it toot-tooted its way around the village. Frowning, Nicholas moved closer. The damned thing must have come back on by itself.

It wasn't until he knelt next to the village that he noticed something was wrong. Confusion filled his face as he took in the scene of devastation. The porcelain figures lay broken, their tiny heads scattered throughout the village. A hole had been punched in the ice rink, the skaters no longer to be seen. The snow, once pristine white, was now covered with tiny droplets of red.

"What the hell?" Anger shot through Nicholas. Who could have done such a thing? The carved figures his family had made, where were they? He peered closer. Tears filled his eyes as he reached for the miniature sleigh, its passengers mutilated beyond repair. A low chuckle began to fill the room. Nicholas glanced around, but saw no one. The chuckle got louder. Nicholas looked back at the village in shocked disbelief. The carved figure of himself cutting down a pine tree was looking back at him, a slow malevolent grin spreading across its face.

"It's been a while, Nicholas, but here I am again."

Frozen in horror, Nicholas watched as the figure, axe in hand, began to grow taller and taller until he stood towering over Nicholas.

Immobilized with fear, Nicholas could do nothing but stare into a face so like his own, but the face of a murderer. The dark place in Nicholas's mind opened, and suppressed memories came rushing back. Bile churned in his stomach and filled his throat as he stumbled to his feet. "It was you," he cried. "You killed my parents and all those townspeople."

The figure snorted. "Now you're getting a conscience? I only did what you didn't have the guts to do yourself. He gently began to swing the axe back and forth. "You're the one who despises Christmas. Isn't it you who hated your parents for forcing you to dress like an elf and walk in the Christmas parade, spend hours helping to bake cookies and string popcorn for the tree, crawl on the snowy roof stringing lights and hanging wreaths?"

"You're pure evil. I never wanted you to kill anyone," Nicholas cried. "I just wanted Christmas to go away."

"You should have thought of that before you once again wished for me to come."

Nicholas's entire body went cold. With a barely audible voice, he said, "I never wished for you."

The figure shrugged. "Believe what you want, we both know the truth. I have done your bidding. What's done is done."

Sudden panic beyond anything he'd ever felt coursed through Nicholas. The house was still too quiet. Where were Candace and his children? They should have been up by now. He had to swallow twice before his words would come. "Where are my wife and children?"

The figure only smiled.

For the first time since he'd entered the living room, Nicholas took in the rest of his surroundings. Like an automaton, he slowly walked through the destruction heading toward the kitchen, dreading with every step what he might find. His scream echoed throughout the house as he fell to his knees next to Candace's headless body.

"Candace, no." he sobbed. As he knelt on the floor, a fierce hatred burned in his eyes. "My children. What have you done with my children?"

Again the figure shrugged. "I believe they were going skating."

A bellow of anguish and rage filled the air as Nicholas tore the bloody axe from the figure's grasp.

A loud pounding began at the front door. "Police, let us in."

The axe dropped from Nicholas's hand. "I will not pay for what you did."

The figure laughed. "Nicholas, you know who I am."

Before Nicholas could take a step, the front door burst open and, with his gun drawn, Officer Yule, followed by Candace's father charged in, more police right behind them.

"There's the murdering monster," Candace's father exclaimed. He charged at Nicholas, but was restrained by two police officers.

"Nicholas Klaus, I'm arresting you on suspicion of multiple murders," Officer Yule stated as he brought out his handcuffs.

Nicholas began to back away. "I'm innocent. You have to believe me. He's the one you want." Nicholas pointed behind him. "Not me."

Officer Yule narrowed his eyes. "Playing games isn't going to help. Now come with me."

"I'm not playing games," Nicholas shouted. "Arrest *him*." Again Nicholas pointed to where the figure had been standing.

"Arrest who?" Officer Yule asked.

"Him." Nicholas turned to see nothing but a little carved figure of a man cutting down a tree laying on the floor at his feet.

A FAMILY CHRISTMAS TERROR

"I'm glad you read that story during the appetizers, Daddy," Nancy said. "That was a little too gory for me. Can you read another one? This is fun, even if the stories are pretty awful. I'm glad I'm not reading them at night alone in my bed."

"Really," Nick said, dipping his remaining shrimp into his sister's cocktail sauce. "From what I hear you're never alone in bed."

"Oh shit," Jack said under his breath.

Nancy turned on Nick. "At least I'm not failing all my classes! You're such an *asshole*."

"*Enough!*" Judy yelled and held up a hand at Dan who was about to interject. "We'll discuss this tomorrow. You two are not going to ruin my Christmas dinner with your bickering."

Jack popped a roll into his mouth and started to speak.

"And *you*..." Judy pointed her finger at him. "...*don't* talk with your mouth full."

Jack swallowed hard. "Sorry, Mom."

Nancy turned to her father. "Daddy, can I read the next story?"

"Maybe we should eat first," Grandpa said.

"I *have* to know what the next story is," Nancy said, a little too vehemently.

Dan nodded at his daughter. "Yeah. Me too. We've broken every other tradition today... Why not? Any objections?"

The family didn't say a word. Even Judy begrudgingly gave in. "What's next, Nancy?" she asked.

Nancy took the book from Dan. "*A Cabin In The Woods.*"

A CABIN IN THE WOODS

LIAH PENN

Well, there it was, not quite as I remembered it; smaller, really, with faded blue paint on the paneled front door, the screen door coming off the hinges. I circled to the side and looked up at the closed shutters of the high loft window, one of them hanging precariously, like a small boy might hang from an apple tree. The house still had the massive trellis which held beach plumbs in the summer months, now only tendrils of dead and brittle vine, weaving through the slats. The snow dusted everything in crystalline splendor. It was December. It was my first Christmas back since my brother's death.

I stood in front of the cabin, its façade still smiling, though gap toothed, now, with a broken pane in the upper storm window, and paint peeling from the front baluster. There were hatch marks by the front door, tiny slits cut into the frame with initials carved next to them. I found mine, still two inches beneath my chin. The painted deck was marbled by the countless wheels of match box cars, racing down the slope to the other side, the occasional traffic accident, and sometime pedestrian mishap along the way. The faded door, although still in need of work, seemed to wink at me as the screen door flapped in the breeze. It needed so much work. I hoped my family could see past the decay to what remained.

Tommy Harris, Pinky McGraw and Izzy Thomas ran these steps, hung from the railings and sulked, at times, in the dark corner of the front porch swing. Specters, now, swirling through my memory like winged insects we had collected on the beach and in the woods, captured momentarily in mason jars, then set free. I ran my fingers along the porch swing, now dry rotted, the paint chipped and peeling. It was here a first kiss was given, many years later, with Izzy Thomas, running my fingers through her salty hair, our mouths tasting of the brackish lake and beach plumbs plucked from the vine. It was here that they laid my brother's body, dripping wet, across the planks.

"Phillip?" My wife came up the pathway, an overnight bag trailing behind her in the snow. "Oh my goodness. It looks so..."

"I know. It needs work." I came to her on the pathway and planted a kiss on her lips, tasting a bit of the past, sweet and salty. She pulled away.

"We need help," she said. Her voice cut like a finely honed knife.

I took the overnight bag from her hand and plodded up the path to the front door. The lock on the door was old and rusting and it took several tries before I could pry it open.

The wood, swollen and abandoned, scraped across the hardwood floor. From behind me, my wife groaned, as if anticipating the damage I had just caused.

"Maybe in the spring..." I said, but she cut me off.

"Just help the boys, would you?"

I deposited the bag a few steps into the cabin and left her there to sort out the light switches and heat. Trudging back down the path to the car, I saw my boys, Alex and Freddy, running up the driveway toward me.

"We met a friend!" They nearly tackled me as they grabbed my arms and tried to pull me down to the roadway.

"Good for you," I said. "But first we have to unpack." I shook them from me like squid tentacles and pulled out the key fob. With a click, I opened the trunk and gestured to the piles of luggage, games and sporting equipment the boys had packed. "Start bringing it up to the cabin. Just follow the path."

Alex and Freddy grabbed the nearest armload of stuff and headed toward the cabin. I poked around the trunk and pulled out the heaviest items. The boys could bring their skates and footballs; I would bring the luggage.

My wife had put the heat on and opened up the dusty curtains to let in light. The whole cabin was layered in a decade's worth of dust. My parents had been the last to stay here, spending the last summer of my father's life by the lake. I had stayed away, then, newly married and expecting our first child, Alex. By the time Freddy was born, three years later, both of my parents were gone and the lake house sat empty and unused, mired in probate as my parents' wealth was allocated among their surviving four children.

They voted to give me the cabin. My siblings, that is.

"You need to spend some time out there. Healing time," my sister said.

"I don't need a cabin in the woods," I replied. But she pushed the ancient keys into my hand and turned away. It was settled. I had the cabin, like it or not.

"I wish you'd told me how dirty it was going to be," my wife said, her fingers trailing on the table, a wad of dust building on her fingertip.

"I didn't think." I turned to leave, to get another load from the car.

"That's the problem," she said. "You never think."

I let the comment hang in the air, unsuspended by any response. This was how she was going to be, I thought. I wondered if coming here had been a good idea after all. From the front porch, looking out across woods and down the hill, I could see where the tree line ended and the lake began. The bitter cold had done its work and the lake appeared frozen solid, like all of those Christmases of my childhood. A vast expanse of ice to play hockey on. Just us boys.

I shook the thought from my mind. It had been a long time since I had skated.

The boys flew past me, their open jackets billowing out behind them like super-hero capes. No hats. No gloves. Their spirit and joy keeping them warm and alive.

"C'mon, Dad!" Alex called over his shoulder. I heard the door slam shut behind me. I followed after them, shuffling like an old man, down the pathway and toward the car.

I pulled my ice skates from the trunk. I'd brought them along because they had asked me to. I had no intention of skating. Not now.

"We should sell this place," my wife said, throwing another sheet onto a pile on the floor. "We could get a place on the beach with what we get for this."

I rolled the suitcase into the master bedroom downstairs, ignoring her comment.

"Phillip, did you hear me?" Her voice, now a little shrill, was getting on my nerves.

"We're not selling." How could I? I wanted to create new memories here and somehow push past the specters of my past. I dropped the handle of the suitcase on the floor with a thud. The mattress was covered in a giant plastic sheet. It was a double bed. Not even a queen. We would be sleeping on top of one another. I heard her come through the doorway behind me.

"Shit," she said. "What size is that?"

My parents had slept on a double bed their entire lives. Not like the giant king-bed that my wife and I shared, practically sleeping in different time zones.

"It's a double," I said. I turned toward her, the scowl on her face deepening as she looked at me. "I'll sleep on the couch."

She shrugged. "Whatever suits your fancy." She turned on her heel and left me, staring at the barren mattress.

Loud thuds from upstairs startled me from my reverie. The boys were choosing bunk beds from the upstairs loft. I heard the sound of doors opening and closing. Exploring. Doing what boys do.

"Come get your luggage!" my wife shrieked and the noises stopped momentarily, followed by the patter of their stockinged feet on the stairs.

I went into the kitchen. The refrigerator was not on, so I found the dusty old plug and stuck it in the socket, waiting for the whir of the motor. Nothing. I hadn't thought of that, either.

"It's not working?" she asked.

"Nope." I fiddled with the switches inside. Maybe it was turned off. But nothing seemed to work.

Alex was trying to peer over my shoulder.

"Did you plug it in, Dad?"

"Yes, I plugged it in."

"Did you turn it on, Dad?"

"Yes, I turned it on."

Freddy was dumping the groceries onto the counter and separating the snacks from the fruit and meat.

"Why don't we use the outside? It's cold enough, isn't it?" he asked.

I looked over at my wife. Her face seemed to melt when she looked at the kids, not the hard edges and sarcasm that I got treated to.

"What a smart boy, Freddy." She looked up at me. "We can manage a few days with an outdoor refrigerator."

I heaved sigh of relief. But she wasn't about to let me go for my stupidity.

"Daddy should have checked on the cabin before we made these plans. But Daddy doesn't think."

I let the comment roll off my shoulders. Disengage, I told myself.

The boys took an armload of "outside groceries" and put them on the old cedar bench on the front porch, lining everything neatly up on the flat surface.

"Now what?" Freddy asked.

"Unpack and then you can go exploring. But not far. You don't know your way around here yet."

They flew back up the stairs and I could hear them opening drawers and shoving suitcases under beds. I looked over at my wife.

"I'll clean upstairs. And make the beds if you want to do the downstairs."

She grunted her consent. I grabbed a dust cloth and some cleaner and headed upstairs to the room that I had shared with my siblings so long ago.

It took about two hours to put the little cabin to right, dusting, cleaning sinks, flushing the blue winterizer down the toilets. I tried the refrigerator again but it still failed to turn on. We would have to leave the food on the porch for this weekend. I could get a new refrigerator brought up in the spring.

The front door crashed open and the boys flew back in, their cheeks rosy, their noses dripping.

"We saw our friend," Alex said. My wife peeled his jacket off and swiped a tissue under his nose.

"Where?"

"By the lake. He was going skating. Can we go too?"

I shook my head. I pictured my brother, his fair hair trapped under a hat, pushing out from the lake edge. I wasn't ready. "It's late. It'll be dark in half an hour. Maybe tomorrow. But I'll have to check the ice first."

Freddy was vibrating with excitement. "Tomorrow? Yay!"

My wife had collapsed onto the old plaid couch, a paper cup of red wine in her hand.

"Did you check to see if the stove worked?"

I shook my head. "No, not yet."

"Well, could you? Or we'll be eating out tonight."

She tossed the wine back in a single gulp and crossed her arms over her chest. She had been a beautiful girl at one time, and she was probably a beautiful woman. But her hard edges and sarcasm destroyed any beauty that I could see. Her long dark hair was held back with a clip and she shook it loose. Maybe this trip would relax her. Maybe the woman I once knew would come back to me.

"Can you?" She crumbled the paper cup in her hand. Her hard edges softened only slightly. "Check the stove, that is?"

Of course the stove didn't work. The pilot was probably out, but I couldn't figure out how to start it. We bundled back up into our coats and boots and trudged back down the pathway to the car, the boys leading the way with flashlights. There was one place in town that remained open during the winter months. We piled into the car, shaking snow off our boots, and headed down the road, past the lake, toward town.

"There he is," Alex said. From the rear view mirror, I could see him pointing.

"Where who is?" I asked.

"Our friend. He said he was going skating."

I glanced out the window, past my wife's stiff visage. "Where? I don't see anyone."

We passed through a grove of pines and when I looked again, there was no one there.

"Can't see him anymore," Alex said. "He's too far *that* way."

I looked over my shoulder at Alex's gesture.

"For God's sake, Phillip, watch the road," my wife shrieked. I jerked the wheel to the right. I had drifted into the oncoming lane. Luckily there was no traffic, but the roads were slick and I ran up onto the snow pile on the right side of the road as I overcorrected.

"Sorry," I said. The boys thought it was funny the way the snow flew up over the car and they laughed all the way into town.

McRay's was a diner built in the 50's with deep burgundy booths of slick vinyl and Formica tabletops. It was a little worse for wear but clean and the food was good. They had old fashioned meatloaf topped by Ketchup, tuna casserole and burgers from the grill. Breakfast was served all day long. I order eggs and bacon and the boys chose burgers. My wife picked at the plastic cover to the menu and tried in vain to find something healthy.

"Do you have salad?" she asked the counter man who had come from behind to wait on us.

"No ma'am. Not this time of year. We got stick to your ribs kind of food. How about the special? Corn and crab soup with a side of fresh French bread. Or our world famous meatloaf and mashed potatoes?"

She wrinkled her nose. I squirmed uncomfortably in my seat. "This isn't exactly Manhattan," I said.

"I know," she replied, her voice like ice. "How about a turkey sandwich? Can you make that?"

"Yes ma'am. What kind of bread would you like?"

My wife tapped her manicured fingertip on the menu. Tap. Tap. Tap. I wanted to pull the menu from her grasp. I didn't.

"Do you have a ciabatta bread?"

The counterman visibly rolled his eyes. "No, ma'am. We have white toast, whole wheat toast or a hamburger bun."

I resisted the impulse to laugh and squeezed the top of my thigh with my hand.

"I'll take the whole wheat." She tossed the menu toward him. He scooped it, and the remaining menus, from the table top. "I forgot how pedestrian this place is," she said.

The boys were unwrapping and re-wrapping their silverware, handed to them rolled up in a napkin with a paper band sealed around the middle.

"This place is cool." Alex wrapped his silverware again and placed it propped up between his water glass and Freddy's, creating a little bridge.

"Don't." Freddy knocked the silverware off his glass and lifted the tumbler to his mouth. He took a fake sip and put the glass back down.

"Daddy, Freddy just destroyed my bridge!"

My wife fumbled for her purse. "Let me out, Phillip. I need a cigarette." I slid out of the booth and let her pass by before sitting back down. Alex was arranging the salt and pepper shakers like bridge supports, undeterred by Freddy's destructive power.

"C'mon guys, there's an old-fashioned juke box at the back." I dug into my pockets for some quarters. I found three.

"What's a juke box?" Freddy held out his hand for a quarter. I placed it in the middle of his palm and closed the fingers over it, the tiny warm fingers, soft and baby-like still. I wanted to kiss the little guy but I refrained. He was shying away from public displays of affection lately and I didn't want to embarrass him. Instead, I gave his hand a little squeeze and we emptied the booth and headed to the rear of the diner.

The juke box still used old .45 records that popped out of a slot and fell onto a turntable before the needle dropped onto the appropriate track. We used our quarters to select

Elvis, Little Richard and Chuck Berry. The boys slid around the linoleum floor, shaking their hips and twirling until they grew dizzy. I watched them from a counter stool until I felt the cold presence of my wife at my elbow.

"You're getting them all wound up. They'll never go to bed now." She walked off, sliding her butt along the booth until she was up against the wall. As if trying to stay as far away from me as possible.

The counter man had returned with plates of hot food traveling up to his elbows.

"C'mon, boys. Time to eat." I herded them back to their side of the booth as the man put the steaming hot burgers down in front of them. Each of them had a burger, chips and a dill pickle speared by a tiny sword.

"*En garde*," Alex said, challenging his little brother to a sword fight of miniature proportions. Freddy met his challenge and they parried until my wife's frigid fingers plucked the tiny weapons from their hands.

"Aw, Mom," Freddy said, but he stopped, shrinking in fear when he saw the look on her face.

"Get you folks anything else?" the counter man asked.

"Ketchup," Alex said.

"On the table," the counter man and I replied simultaneously. He laughed.

"Where you folks from? Celebrating the holidays here or just passing through?"

"I wish," my wife said, sarcasm dripping like dew from her lips.

"We're here," I said, ignoring her comment. "Staying at my folks' place." I hesitated. Would this man know them? Or our history? "The Ellis place."

"Oh." He looked me over. "You Phillip Ellis, by chance?"

"Yes, sir." I unraveled my silverware and smoothed a napkin on my lap, waiting for the other shoe to drop.

"I remember you," he said.

I could see it in his eyes. He knew the whole story.

The boys were not ones to let a conversation take place without their input. Alex swished his burger in the ketchup on his plate as if it were a French *au jus*.

"We're going skating tomorrow," he said.

"Really? Now that sounds like fun. Just you two?"

"Nope. Me and Freddy and my dad. And our friend."

The counter man squinted at Alex. "Friend?"

My wife purse her lips. "They met a little boy from town. He was skating on the pond as we left."

So, my wife had seen the boy.

"Do you think it's frozen enough?" I smoothed my napkin again and let the ends curl up over my pinky finger.

"Oh, sure. It's been cold enough. If someone was skating this evening, you'll be fine." He turned to me, his eyes meeting mine. "It's been colder than that winter—when you were here last."

The chill that ran over me started at the tips of my ears and travelled all the way to my toes. I could feel myself shiver. Maybe it wasn't a good idea to go skating. I'd have to check the ice in the morning. The counterman shoved his sleeves up his forearms and smiled.

"Well, you just call, you need anything else."

I pushed my plate of food away. I wasn't hungry anymore.

In the morning, I awoke on the couch with a crick in my neck and my toes sticking out of the end of an ancient sleeping bag. My wife had taken the bed and since I had already volunteered, banished me to the living room. I cranked up the heat and headed to the kitchen to make coffee. There was no coffee pot to be found. Damn, I'd forgotten something else. I dug around the cupboard and found an ancient tin of loose tea. At least I could heat up water, maybe have something hot to drink.

There was no tea kettle but I found a small pot and put the water on to boil. I traipsed out to the porch to get the milk for my tea, shaking in the cold. It didn't feel quite as cold this morning but the sky was gray, threatening snow with low clouds and a taste of ice in the air. I grabbed the milk and the orange juice which was half frozen in its plastic jug.

There were footprints from the side of the porch to the railing, fresh prints actually. Small shoes. The box of Pop Tarts was missing. One of the boys must've gotten up early and sneaked past me in the living room.

I let the door slam behind me as I entered the cabin.

"Guys, get up." I put the milk and juice on the counter to thaw. From our grocery sack, I pulled out two different cereals and placed them on the table. I plundered the cupboards and found bowls and spoons and placed one at each place setting. As the water started to boil, I dug around the drawers until I found a tea strainer into which I placed a small portion of loose tea. I hoped it still had flavor.

My wife shuffled from the bedroom, her hair wild, her cheeks flushed with a good night's sleep. My toes were still cold from my night on the couch.

"What're you yelling for?"

"Trying to get the boys up."

She looked at the counter, her eyes narrowing as she searched for something.

"Really? No coffee maker?" She turned and walked away.

"I looked for one. Maybe we could run into town and buy one. For tomorrow."

She rolled her eyes. "We won't be coming back up here, Phillip. This place is dreary. It needs too much work. It's not the place of your childhood, anymore." She plopped into an arm chair.

"No, it's not." I poured the boiling water into the cup and watched as the tea stems swelled and colored the water. "Not by a long shot."

The boys were excited about the snow. Pristine, crunchy-on-top snow that lay in deep drifts by the lake and came up to their knees. They ran up and down each virgin area, marveling at the deer and bird tracks which left tiny divots in the snow.

"Watch the branches," I said, as I ducked under yet another low-lying limb. They moved like ninjas through the snow. By the time we reached the lake, I was exhausted and sat on a fallen log as they scampered along the beach.

"Can we skate?" Alex asked, tossing a pebble across the ice.

"Maybe this afternoon. I'm a little tired."

Freddy came and stood before me. "You always tired Daddy."

I nodded. "I know, little man. I'm sorry. Maybe after Daddy finds a coffee maker we can skate."

The edge of the shoreline amused them nonetheless. They threw rocks onto the lake and tried to break up the thin ice at the beach edge by pounding it with a branch. It crackled and broke free like pieces of lace candy, fragile and clear. The lake ice appeared pristine—not a skater's track in sight. After giving them free rein for a while, I herded them back up the pathway toward the house.

"Can we play outside?" Alex asked.

"As long as you keep your hats and gloves on, yes. And stay right by the house."

They cheered and slammed me with mini-hugs. I left my boots on the porch and entered the house in stockinged feet, tossing my jacket and gloves onto the kitchen table. My wife had turned on the gas fireplace and curled up with a book and a cup of tea. Her face was relaxed.

"They're staying outside a bit longer."

"You told them to stay by the house?" she asked, tenting her paperback.

"Of course. They promised to stay nearby. They'll be fine. Do you want me to run into town and get a coffee maker?"

She fingered her book. "Do they have a Walmart?"

"No."

She picked up her book and began reading again. "Do whatever you want. Just don't spend a lot of money."

And just like that, I was dismissed.

I drove along the road to town, the music blaring, my palm keeping beat on the steering wheel. I knew my marriage was a mess but I had no idea how to fix it. And I didn't want the boys to be the product of a broken home. Right now, they noticed none of the tension. They were happy-go-lucky kids and I wanted them to stay that way.

There was no Walmart, but there was a small general store that specialized in carrying the types of things that lakeside owners would need. And while there wasn't a selection of coffee makers, they had an adequate one for now. I picked up a packet of filters and a bag of French roast to go along with it. I walked through the store with my armful of possessions and looked at the touristy items: flags, snow globes, bottle openers and T-shirts. I selected a photo frame that looked halfway decent and brought my selections to the counter.

"Up for the holidays?" The cashier smiled at me as she scanned and bagged each item. "You look familiar. You own a place up here?"

"Well, my parents' place. I just inherited it."

"Oh, which one is that?" She wrapped the frame in brown paper and slid it into the paper sack on the counter.

"The Ellis place."

Her mouth opened just a little as if she was going to say something, but she stopped herself. She looked down at the cash register and told me the total. "I'd have thought you'd want to sell it. You know, after. . ."

"Nope," I interrupted her. "Still in the family." I looked around the store with exaggerated cheer. "Have any popcorn? I'm thinking the kids would love that."

She pointed out the aisle and I ambled that way. My God, I thought as I grabbed two pans of Jiffy Pop from the shelf. Would history never die?

Coming over the rise from town, I saw a figure skating on the ice. A child, probably about nine or ten years old, the same age as my kids. He was by himself. He raced up and down the ice in dark jacket, a red cap on his head, playing phantom hockey by himself. My brother and I had done that as children. I lost him through the trees as I neared the cabin. I wondered if the little boy was a visitor or lived here year round. Maybe it was the boy my sons had met.

They scrambled down to the car while I unloaded my packages.

"Alex, carry this one, would you?"

He peeked in and saw the aluminum pan of Jiffy Pop. "What's this, Dad?"

"Popcorn. We'll make it tonight."

They ran up the pathway to the house, their boots churning up twigs and leaves as they ran. I closed the trunk and walked over to the edge of the woods, looking down toward the lake. The boy was no longer in sight.

My wife was holding the Jiffy Pop in her hands when I entered the cabin.

"I didn't think they even made this anymore."

I shrugged. "Seemed like a good idea. Since we have no TV, I thought it might be a fun thing to do tonight."

She didn't respond and put the packages on the counter. I handed her the coffee maker.

"Did you get filters?" Her tone was like ice. She clearly hadn't expected me to remember.

"Filters and coffee," I said, and pulled the items from the bag with a flourish. She pursed her lips, and with a slight roll of the eyes, turned and walked away. There was no pleasing her.

"We're going back out," Freddy said. I looked down at his feet and realized they had left their boots on and the snow was falling off in clumps, leaving patches of mud and water in the living room.

"Out, out," I replied. "Stay close. Lunch in an hour." I grabbed some paper towels and mopped up the mess. My wife had returned to the chair and sat engrossed in her book. She hadn't even noticed the mess.

At noon, I made grilled cheese sandwiches and tomato soup for everyone. The boys came in pink and glowing, excited about the fox they had seen in the woods and the pinecones they had collected in abundance. Freddy showed me a crooked branch that was completely dried out but had retained the shape of a cane, including the handle part on top. He left it by the front door, bark peeling off in wet, loamy sheets.

"Our friend wants us to go skating. Can we go?" Alex asked.

I shook my head. "Not today, guys. I still haven't unpacked. And you know what tomorrow is, don't you?"

They nodded eagerly. "Christmas Eve!" they shouted with delight. My wife ignored the fuss and read her book at the table, dipping her sandwich into the soup and eating in silence.

"Put your skates by the door and we'll go first thing in the morning."

Christmas Eve dawned overcast and gray, the clouds still threatening snow, but now with a wind that scoured the snow from the lake and whipped the tree branches free of snow.

"Half an hour," I told the boys. "It's very cold outside. I don't want you getting frost bite."

They raced to the door bundled in their winter gear and threw open the door.

"Ew, Daddy, it really *is* cold!" Freddy shrieked. But he laughed as he took off down the hill toward the lake followed by his brother. He was waving the crooked stick/cane and screaming with total abandonment. Alex gave me a look and followed after him. He was my reserved child. Curious, but careful. Not one to take a dare. Like his namesake.

My wife was picking up the breakfast dishes, her hair piled on top of her head, no makeup, looking like the girl I had fallen in love with. She caught me looking at her and turned away.

I took my phone from the charger. I wanted to get a picture of the boys to put in the frame I had purchased in town. My wife may make me miserable, but the boys brought me total joy. They were the only happiness that I had experienced in so many years. They reminded me of my childhood, when things were innocent and carefree. Until my brother died.

I shook the thought away.

I bundled up and headed down toward the lake. In the distance, I could see the boys running along the beach with another child in a dark jacket and red hat. The same boy as yesterday. I was thrilled that they had found a friend. He was about their size, but other than that, they were all too far away to see clearly. I tried to take a photo with the phone but they were mere pinpricks on the screen.

I brought the phone back inside, fearful that the cold weather might ruin it. My wife was ensconced in her chair, the same paperback spread over her knees. I dropped the phone on the table.

"I took a picture of the boys," I said.

She ignored me.

I went back outside.

In the distance, I could see the clouds gathering on the horizon. It looked very dark, more like rain than snow, but I wasn't very used to the weather up here anymore. It might simply be the tree line that made it look dark. I looked for the boys and saw a flash of red in the woods. The other boy's hat.

From around the back of the house, Alex and Freddy came running at full speed.

"I lost my glove," Freddy said, holding up his hand, waxy and white.

"Inside." I grabbed his hand and blew warm air on it. "C'mon. We'll find the glove later."

We stumbled in together and I held his little hand between my own to warm it. He was fine after a few minutes.

"It's prickly," he said. My wife removed the boys' outerwear and hung it on the chair backs to dry.

"The sensation is just coming back to your fingers," she said. She swept a blond curl from Freddy's forehead and kissed him. My heart ached. What had happened to us? I looked down to the floor and closed my eyes.

We wrapped the boys' Christmas gifts late that night after hanging real stockings on the fireplace screen. The Jiffy Pop had been a hit and we sat on the sofa eating popcorn and telling Christmas stories until the boys nodded off to sleep. I carried each of them upstairs to the bunk room and tucked them in, kissing their warm noses and cheeks as they slept. By the time I came back down, my wife had spread the wrapping paper on the kitchen table along with scissors and tape. They were still of the age for baseballs and board games, and we seemed to have a ridiculous amount of things to wrap. By one o'clock, everything was done and arranged around the fireplace screen.

"I didn't get you anything," my wife said. "You said you wanted that thing for your bike."

"That's fine. I'll get it when we get back. I need to order it off the internet anyway." I didn't tell her that I had gotten her something: a pendant with two diamonds to represent the boys. I would surprise her in the morning. Maybe I could thaw that heart of hers a little.

I slept on the couch for the third night in a row. By morning, the fire had been reduce to gray coals and my feet were cold again. I stoked up the fire then tapped on the bedroom door.

"Come in," my wife said. I opened the door to find her holding my phone in her hand. She held it to me. "Who's this?" she asked.

She had the photo from the day before on the screen.

"I don't know. Someone they were playing with. You know, their friend."

She put the phone on the nightstand. "It looks kind of like... oh, nevermind." She threw the covers off. "Too bad you were so far away. It would have made a great picture."

We ate a hot breakfast of frozen waffles with syrup before letting the boys tear into their pile of gifts. The wrapping paper was tossed into the fireplace where it erupted in a rainbow of colors much to their delight. They had been given new ice skates and warm wool socks.

"They are very sharp," I explained, showing them the snap-on blade protector. "And don't walk on the floor with blades unless these are on. You'll see when we get home. They pop on and off really easily."

"Can we play hockey?" Alex had one skate on and one off.

"Anything you want to do."

"Did you play hockey when you were little?"

My wife looked at me over their heads and gave the tiniest little shake of her head.

"No. I never played. But it will be fun for all of us to learn together."

We had brought a cold ham and pre-made stuffing and potatoes with us. My wife opened the front door to bring in the Christmas dinner.

"It's actually a lot warmer," she said. "I don't think Freddy has to worry about frostbite."

I followed her to the porch to help her, but once outside, I took her by the shoulders.

"I have something for you," I said. I pulled the small box from my pocket.

"Phillip, I thought we were past this."

"Please open it." I put it in her hand and closed her fingers over the top. I wanted to kiss her but I knew she would resist.

She gave me a look before opening the box. When she saw the pendant I thought she would smile. "What is this?"

"It represents our children. A diamond for each of them."

She threw the box at me. "You're just like your mother," she said. "Full of Catholic guilt." She marched

457

past me with an armload of food. I plucked the box up from the porch floor and put it back into my pocket. I just couldn't win.

We ate Christmas dinner late in the afternoon, silence yawning over us like a canyon. Even the boys seemed to notice. They peered from one of us to another. Finally, Alex picked up his skates.

"Can we go down to the lake?"

As much as I didn't want to, I had put them off for too long. "Sure. I'll get my skates and we can go for a little bit."

I helped clear the table but my wife shooed me off. "Go with them." It was the only thing she had said to me in hours. I gladly donned my jacket and slung my old skates over my shoulder. Freddy threw his one glove onto the porch.

"I don't need it anymore. Look, our friend is on the ice!" he yelled. He and Alex ran the rest of the way down the hill. I trudged on behind them. By the time I got to the foot of the path, they had their skates on.

"Can we go?" Freddy asked. In the distance, I could see the other boy skating clear across the middle of the lake.

"Go ahead. I'll catch up." I sat down on an overturned tree and began to unlace my boots. I had one boot off and was getting my foot into the skate when I heard the crack. It sounded like a pistol. My head snapped up and I looked around, but I didn't know what that sound could be.

Boom. It went off again. I fumbled with my laces. I didn't like the sound of that, whatever it was. I tore my other boot off, then stood, one-legged, to look for the boys.

The lake was separating. A crack the width of a shoelace was spreading across the ice at the speed of sound. I had one skate on and one off. I hobbled to the edge of the lake. The three boys were skating toward me, racing one another. They hadn't heard it. They didn't know about the lake.

"Get off the ice!" I yelled at them and began waving furiously. Their heads were down and they pumped their arms, trying to outdo one another. The boy with the red hat was gaining on them. He appeared at the front of the pack and with a sudden burst of speed, he was coming right at me, right to the edge.

The boys disappeared. First Freddy. Then Alex. Through the ice and into the lake without a sound.

I screamed their names as the boy turned to look at them, then back at me.

I hobbled to the edge and my skate plunged through the ice. I brought it up and tried to take another step but the ice broke off in pieces as the lake water flooded into my skate. I dove onto the ice, but the lake cracked under me, and there I was, waist deep in the black water, my feet sinking into the lake mud. I lunged, grasping at the sheets of ice which broke off in my hands.

The boy turned back to me. He was still skating. I didn't understand how he hadn't fallen through the ice. He skated up to me, his feet seemingly suspended above the ice.

"Hey, Phillip." He reached out his hand to me as if to pull me from the lake. Beneath the red hat I saw the face of my older brother, Alex. My dead brother. Forever eleven.

459

"What are you doing here?" I screamed. I couldn't feel my legs; the water was so cold. I fumbled for my phone, but it was underwater, in my front pants pocket. This couldn't be happening. Where were my boys?

"I was tired of skating alone," he said, his voice cold and detached. "So I brought along some friends."

He turned around and skated toward the hole in the ice. And in the cold Christmas evening, he disappeared. Just as he had, thirty years ago. When I had dared him to go out onto the ice, alone, and skate.

Here I was, once again, standing in the cold lake. Helpless. I flailed my arms, but there was no use. I couldn't move. Just like then. Thirty years. To the day.

How could I tell my wife that it had happened again?

A FAMILY CHRISTMAS TERROR

"That was a family I'd never want to be a part of," Jack said. "Imagine being married to a woman like that."

"I can't imagine *you* being married to a woman." Nick grinned into his turkey.

"What do you mean by that?" Jack demanded.

"Oh I think you know, twinkle toes," Nancy added, winking at Jack.

"Uhh—well, this was about the best Christmas dinner I can remember—including the ones with your grandma," Grandpa said and patted his stomach. "Why don't we put the book away and we can all help clean up."

"How about one more story?" Nick said. "I'll read it."

"How about we let our food settle for a bit, then have some coffee and dessert?" Dan said.

Duly chastened, Nick nodded. "Or that."

Grandpa motioned with his hand to Dan. "How about we have a glass of that twenty-five-year-old port that I got you for Christmas?"

461

"Well, I don't know..." Dan said uncertainly. "Is there more eggnog?"

"Dan, don't be selfish," Judy said.

"Could—"

Dan cut Nick off, knowing what the question would be. "Yes, you can all have some port if you want." He moved unsteadily to the liquor cabinet and returned with a beautifully designed cut-glass bottle. "Let's go into the family room and be comfortable."

When the family was all situated with their drinks, Dan said, "Now remember, port is meant to be sipped. You read, Nick, so that you won't be so tempted to gulp."

"Here you are, brother dear." Nancy snarled and handed him the book. She whispered in his ear, "This *isn't* over."

Before Jack sat, he cuffed the back of Nick's head a little too roughly. "And don't spill any port on the book."

Nick rubbed the back of his head. "I won't. Dick. This one's called, *Silent Fright.*"

SILENT FRIGHT

CRYSTAL PERKINS

The First Noel

I've lived without sound my whole life. I don't usually feel like I'm missing out on anything. Except for this time of year. Christmas. My parents love Christmas carols, and they take every chance they can to listen to them, and see them performed. They smile indulgently as I just stand next to them mouthing the words, but I know they wish I could sing with them. I see the sorrow in their eyes, the disappointment they feel because I can't join in on their Christmas "fun."

I don't feel their happiness, or sense of "fun" when it comes to those songs. I can sense the vibrations of the songs, read the words on the pages of sheets that invariably get handed out when groups are singing together, and I see the happiness on the faces of everyone around me as their mouths move, singing along. It's not enough to make *me* happy. At these times, I wish for the gift of hearing. I want to experience the sounds and the camaraderie that comes with singing along.

I'm here at my school's dress rehearsal for tonight's Christmas pageant. I'll stand where they tell me, and read lips so I know what everyone else is doing, but once again, I'll feel left out. Sure, the other kids and the teacher will smile at me, and we'll all pretend that I'm just like them, but I know they're wishing I wasn't there to make things harder. Just another day in the life of a deaf twelve-year-old girl.

There's a new little girl already in the room when I walk in. She has on a tattered, red velvet Christmas dress, and she looks like she hasn't had a shower in days, if not weeks. The white bow around her waist is falling off, and I want to tell her, but I also don't want to embarrass her. She already looks uncomfortable being here in the room with us. It's hard to be new, and different, so I let her be.

Strangely, everyone else ignores her. I expected at least one of the other kids to point her out, or say something mean. It's the nature of the pack. Those who want to lead seek out the weak and exploit their weakness to make themselves look strong. Yet the ones I would expect to ridicule the girl for her dirty dress seem to not realize she is there. That's another thing that happens sometimes. Objects—and people—of no importance get ignored. Ignorance is often better than attention, so I'm strangely happy for her.

The teacher has us take our places, and the little girl covers her ears and starts to scream. I see her mouth open and know that sound has to be coming out. Still, no one pays attention. I get in place, and feel the vibrations of the music as it starts. Mouths are open all around me, and I do my expected part, standing there with a smile on my face.

I keep glancing to the girl, watching as she rocks back and forth with her hands still over her ears. Do the other kids sound that bad? They'd have to, for her to be reacting this way. For once, maybe it's a good thing that I'm deaf.

*

I'm still thinking about the girl when I arrive back at the school with my parents that night. Will she be here? Will her dress be fixed? Will she have taken a shower? I suddenly realize that even though she looked so unclean, I didn't smell her. Without hearing, my other senses are pretty heightened, so I would've noticed. Just another strange thing to ponder as I stand on the stage, my fake smile firmly in place.

Right before we start, I see the girl again. She steps out in front of the first row, in the middle of the stage. She is crying and shaking. Honestly, she looks terrified, and I wonder again why no one seems to care. I care, but I remained glued to my spot as I feel the music begin. And then it happens.

I see her open her mouth again, but this time it's not in a scream. This time, she's singing the words to the song that's being played. *The First Noel*. She starts to glow, looking like an angel, and people start to die.

I can't hear the screams of terror, but I can see it. I can see the adults in the audience start to stand before they fall.

They writhe on the ground as blood pours from their ears, their noses, theirs mouths. I can't move, and I can tell that none of the other children here can either. As the blood gushing from the adults around me flows across the floor, I can't look away. It travels around the chairs, over the feet of the children, stopping only when it encounters an adult struggling on the floor.

It doesn't seep into their clothing, like you'd think. Oh no, the blood seems to become solid, banding around the people on the floor, like it's trying to help them on their way to the end. It wraps them like a web, taking the last of the life from those people, like it's alive and committing murder.

There is no one who can help as my parents, my teachers, and every other adult in the room succumbs to the bloody "monsters." I finally pull my eyes from the scene in front of me, and look around to see the kids next to me staring in horror as everyone we know and love is left in a puddle of blood. The blood once again goes back to liquid form, once life has been taken.

When I look to the girl again, she is still singing. Not the same song, but one I can't decipher. I can read lips like nobody's business, but I can't understand what she's saying. I know without a doubt that she caused this massacre to happen. She killed every adult in this room. I just don't know why.

What I *do* know is that for once, I'm thankful I couldn't hear the words, and I never again want to be anywhere where Christmas carols are. Because as sure as I know that

that little girl killed them, I also know the carols had a part in it too.

"On the second day of Christmas"

I've been in my current foster home for six months. This one's a little better than the last, but none of them are great. They all know how to sign—I wouldn't be placed with them if they didn't—but once my case worker is gone, they pretend that they don't. I would probably have a better chance at a good home if my reputation didn't precede me, but it always does.

After what happened at the Christmas pageant two years ago, I tried to tell everyone about the girl. No one believed me, because no one else saw her. The thought of a little girl in a tattered dress causing a massacre was not something anyone was willing to believe. They also didn't believe that the blood seemed to come alive. Never mind the fact that two years later no one still has a clue what happened. Well, no one except for me—the crazy girl.

Theories have abounded, from some kind of chemical warfare to a gas leak. Not one thing these so called "experts" come up with has been able to give a reason for all of us children still living and breathing. There is no question that we were there, and yet we lived, while they all died.

My former classmates are all spread out around the country now. I've gone to the library and seen stories on the internet about how some have capitalized on the horror we saw that day. They have book deals, movie deals, and even record deals. Then there are the others. The ones who couldn't get past what we saw, who took their own lives. Those are the ones I can relate to.

Many nights I have fought sleep, because when I sleep, I sometimes dream. I dream of a girl who glows and sings words I can't hear or read on her lips. I dream of my parents and their friends on the ground, with blood coming out of every orifice as they tear at their own skin, and then have the life squeezed out of them by their own blood. I dream, and I wait. I know that *that* Christmas was not a one-time thing. I know it with all my heart. The only thing I don't know is when it will happen again.

Last year, I went to church with the foster family I had then, and sobbed as the Christmas songs were played. I could feel the joy of the people around me, and I prayed harder than I ever have, asking God to please not let the people around me die. He must've heard my prayer, because everyone walked out unscathed that night. Everyone but me. The terror I felt throughout the service was palpable. I could feel it in every fiber of my being, and at one time, it even felt like I could see it. I didn't see *her*, but I was afraid I might. Afraid that my fear would bring her back.

She didn't come, but after that family saw how distressed I was, they said I ruined Christmas for them. They claimed the other kids—their biological kids—had a horrible time, and were inconsolable after seeing me fall apart. That's a lie. The only reason those spoiled brats had a bad time is because they didn't think their pile of presents was enough. Even when I was forced to give my gifts to them as well, as penance for what I "did," it wasn't enough. I was the easy one to blame, and it was even easier for them to send me away.

My current foster mother comes into the attic room I've been given and tells me I need to get dressed for the town tree lighting. I shake my head, and she takes that to mean that I couldn't read her lips. I see her mouth form the words again, and once again, I shake my head. I can tell that she's angry when she signs the same thing to me, and she's even madder when I sign back that I'm not going. She gets right up in my face and tells me that if I want to stay in this home, then yes, I am going. I start to move my hands to tell her I'd rather leave, but then where would I go. I'm pretty sure they're running out of people who can sign that are willing to take me. I sigh and nod my head. I'll go.

*

The town square is already filled with people when we arrive. It looks like the entire town has come out for this event. We border the big city I used to live in, and while we're not nearly as large, the population here is not small either. Seeing everyone at once is a little overwhelming.

My family pushes their way to the front, pulling me along with them. I see a choir on the big stage, and I start to shake. I turn to push my way back out of here, but my foster father clamps a hand on my arm. I see his mouth move and can tell that he's demanding I stay and behave. I try to shake free, not caring about the consequences right now. I just know I need to leave before the choir starts. I *need* to.

It's too late. I can feel the music start. I turn back to see the choir in their fancy clothes—and notice a boy in a torn, dirty suit. He looks to be around five, and I know. *I know.* There's going to be another massacre. I try to yell, but my throat is dry, and underused. I can feel a sound come out as my throat vibrates, but I know it's not enough. I pull on the family's arms, but they just turn and laugh at me.

Until the birds come, and then I can see *their* screams. The crows swoop so close to me that I can feel the tips of their wings on my cheeks. They don't attack me as I stand still, watching the horror around me. But they're close. Very close. *Too* close. It's like they want me, but they can't have me. I don't know why, but I do know I'm responsible for what's happening. Again.

It's not the same this time, but it's just as deadly. The birds seem to be multiplying, and slowly pecking and tearing the adults to death. Once again, the children aren't moving. I want to move, but I can't look away. I shouldn't be watching the silent screams of the victims as they are torn to death, but I must. I have to see what I somehow caused to happen.

The birds peck and swallow. Over and over. Unlike the blood, these deaths aren't quick. It's slow, terrifying. A few adults try to run, but there are just too many birds. I watch a face being slowly torn off, revealing the bones beneath, but I focus on something else as the bird goes for the meaty eye.

I rub my arms, even though I know I'm not being taken apart. I still feel something on me. Like when you brush a bug off your shoulder, but still think it could be there, and for hours you feel *something*. That's how I feel as I watch thousands of blackbirds slowly tear apart the adults. I feel like something is on me, touching me, even though I can't see it.

When I can tear my eyes away, I see the boy. I knew he'd still be singing, and he is. Like the girl, I can't tell what words are coming out of his mouth, and I can't understand why no one notices him. All I know is that that girl and this boy are angry, and from the looks of them, it's no wonder. I just don't know how they're doing what they're doing. Or why I'm the only one who seems to be able to see them. I *do* know that they didn't come to me last year in the church, and that tells me they are truly on the side of evil. Just another reason to be scared.

The other children and I must stand there for hours; although time passes so quickly, it only feels like minutes. I'm disgusted by the carcasses that have been mostly cleaned of their flesh, but I find that I don't feel much more than that. I'm sorry this happened to these people, because I know that somehow I'm connected, but I don't really care that they're dead. I guess that makes me a bad person, but I can't change how I feel. And apparently, I can't change the fates of adults who come in contact with me when Christmas carols are being sung. I tried to stay home, but I was forced to go. That woman and her husband died because of it, but I can't say I didn't try, because I really did.

We Three

Three years. It's been three years since the last ones died. I'm seventeen and emancipated now. The system had to wait until I was sixteen to let me out of it, but I wasn't placed with a family for the two years after the boy appeared and the birds attacked. I lived in group homes where no one cared if it was Christmas, and they definitely didn't sing any carols.

At sixteen, I was offered the chance to live on my own and get a small amount of money from the state. I jumped at the chance. Just because I can't hear doesn't mean I don't know how to take care of myself. I've been cooking and cleaning for years, as well as communicating with notes and hand signals when people couldn't sign. I'm told there are apps on phones now that can help with communication, but that's not something I can afford. I live a simple life and I can wait for small luxuries like a fancy cell phone.

My biological parents had large life insurance policies that I'll have access to when I turn eighteen. I don't know what I want to do yet, maybe college, maybe not. I can decide once the money is in my bank account—there's really no use in counting on it yet anyway. So for now, it's ramen some days, and pork chops when I can afford them. I could have it so much worse, and I'm truly thankful that

I'm still alive, haven't gone crazy, and have something to eat every night.

The only problem with the whole emancipation thing is that I still have to go to school. A social worker checks in with me every week, and makes sure I'm caring for myself. The one I have is actually pretty good. She's even brought me a bag of groceries to help tide over my meager offerings for a little longer. Even so, she still looks at me like most people do.

I may have escaped the state I grew up in, but I can't escape the ghosts of my past. The people who died while I was around. There is absolutely no other common denominator. The people in the city I grew up in had nothing in common with the small town that suffered such a similar fate. Nothing except me, that is.

I'm well-known now—the girl who sees children who aren't really there and thinks her Christmases are cursed. Well, I think they're cursed. Since no one else believes that I've really seen the children, or that the carols are what is causing the mass deaths, I must be crazy. Obviously.

I'm not crazy, but I *am* scared. Very scared. Three years may seem like a short time to most people, and the Christmas season is even shorter, but to me it seems to last forever. I have learned to stock up on as many things as I can afford, so that I can avoid stores. Their carols are piped in but I still don't feel safe if I know they're playing. Those birds came way too close to me and I'm not looking for a repeat performance of carols, downtrodden children who cause blood to gush from people, or birds. I'm not ashamed to say I hide. I'll admit it freely if someone asks. They never do. They just cross the street if they see me coming, or scoot their desks away from me in class. I'm all alone, and most days, I'm really okay with that.

*

My sociology teacher is requiring us to attend one school sporting event in order to observe how people act at these things. I've been putting it off, but I finally used my free ticket tonight. I watch the people walk in from my perch at the top of the stands and try to determine why they're here. All of them are in red or green, which I find odd. This game is in December, but from what I've witnessed at school, the people here care more for football than following the traditions of Christ. No one is charitable toward me, or even slightly welcoming. I moved here because research said it was a good town, and I thought it would be small enough for me to escape to. That hasn't been the case, and so yeah, I'm stymied by the Christmas colors.

Everyone stands up and looks to the middle of the field. I don't know what's going on but I stand too. What I see turns my blood to ice. No...no...NO! They cannot have a choir on the field. I don't want to watch people die again. I can handle it but I don't *want* to. I know I'm powerless to stop it when I see the three children walking to stand in front of the choir.

Like the other two I've seen, these children have torn and soiled clothing on. Their faces and other exposed skin are covered with dirt and their hair appears unwashed. The three of them look straight at me as the choir opens their mouths. I know they're singing... and I know death is coming. Even if I could yell, these people wouldn't believe me. No one believes me and I fear no one ever will.

As I watch with more than a little morbid fascination taking over me, I see the adults in the crowd transform. There are no birds, and there isn't blood dripping from them, but something's happening. I don't know what, until they all turn to me. Every single adult turns their attention on me, and I see it. Things I've only read about in books or seen on TV. They've turned into ghouls, complete with red eyes and sharp teeth.

I press my back against the wall behind me and prepare to be eaten alive. There's no other outcome. I don't have water, fire, or any other weapon at my disposal to ward them off. I don't fear death, but I must admit that the thought of being eaten alive terrifies me just a little. Or a lot.

My fears are unwarranted as they turn from me and run for the football field where all of the students have fled. Ignoring small children, the adults go for the teenagers. Those kids try to fight, but it's no use. I see death once again and this time it's the most gruesome yet.

Parents, teachers, coaches—the ones who are supposed to protect us—begin to feed in earnest. They bite and tear at the flesh of their victims with those sharp teeth. They're eating those teenagers like they'd eat a steak. I see them savor each bite and my stomach turns. I haven't eaten enough to throw up but I dry heave a few times. The other deaths were bad, but this...this is something on a whole new level.

I watch those things...ghouls...bite the flesh off my classmates, and yet again, I feel no sadness. Disgust at what I'm seeing, yes, but that's it. No sadness, or even remorse, that I somehow caused this. If anything, I feel relief. When they all turned to me, I thought I'd die tonight, but I'm safe for the moment. Not forever. I know that without a doubt. But for now, I'll live to see another day. And face more scrutiny as the only teenage survivor of the ghoul attack of 2015.

"Fall on Your Knees"

I'm eighteen now, an adult. A *very* wealthy adult. I live in a mansion, have servants who know sign language, and eat three hearty meals per day. My past is not forgotten but people tend to ignore it now that I'm rich. It's funny how all sins can be forgiven when money is involved. Not that I think I committed a sin that was responsible for the deaths of hundreds of people. I never purposely did anything to cause those massacres.

Besides knowing sign language, I required that the people working for me don't celebrate Christmas. It may be discriminatory but I don't care. There's no one to force me to sing in a choir or go to a tree lighting ceremony, and since I got my GED online, there's no class that requires me to attend a sporting event. I've become a recluse, and with no chance of Christmas carols, I'm safe now. Completely and totally safe from whatever forces chose me as their catalyst along with those damn songs. Songs I could never hear, yet am terrified of.

Money can't buy me happiness but it *can* allow me to do what I want, when I want. And what I want is to live out my life with a full stomach and no mention of Christmas or carols ever again. December is just another month to me now. Snow may fall and lights may twinkle in the distance, but no one crossing through my front door will do so in the name of holidays—happy or otherwise.

*

It's December 24th, and nothing is different here at my home. At least nothing *should* be different. I sense that something is wrong as I enter the grand foyer. My butler is gesturing wildly with his hands and I rush over to see what the problem is. And then it happens.

A small group of children are gathered outside my front door. I don't know who let them in the gates but I know what's about to happen; and I'm too late to stop it. These are not ordinary children. Oh no, these are the ones who've haunted my dreams for years. The little girl in the tattered dress, the boy in the torn suit, and the three who look like they need a bath and a meal.

What's odd to me is that my butler sees them, too. Did all of the adults in my past see them before they died? If they were visible to the adults, why not the other children besides me? And why did no one realize that I was telling the truth before they died? Or did they? Did those ghouls realize that I was telling the truth and look to me in that moment, not to attack me, but to let me know they were sorry for ever doubting me? I'll never know the answers to those questions, but I do know my money can't save me now.

I sign to my butler, telling him to run. He gives me a sad look and then does as I ask. I wasn't sure he'd even be able to, but they let him go. It's me they want. I always thought that, but once he's gone, I know it's true. I hear their words in my head. They are the first words I have ever heard and they terrify me. The fact that I hear them at all terrifies me. This is not a happy thing, this "gift" of hearing. It's another part of my curse. They aren't exactly singing; it's more like chanting and it doesn't really sound right. It sounds like children trying to rhyme, which I guess, in fact, it is.

Here we are to claim you,
Join us, you know you want to.
Every year, we were forced to sing these songs,
Songs of hope, but for us they're wrong.
We suffered at the hands of fate,
And we were killed when we ran away.
You are us, and we are you,
All children from the same womb.
One for all, but not you for us,
You survived when we turned to dust.
Hearing lost saved you then,

But now we come to do you in.
Adults we kill to right our wrongs,
Now come with us and sing our songs

Before I can even process all of what I've heard, my nose starts to bleed. I wipe it and see the bright red blood staining my hand. I want to beg for my life, and tell them I haven't had it easy either, but I don't get the chance.

I feel the wings before the beak and I know the birds have come. For real this time. Not just a shadow feeling—the birds are really here for me. I fall to my knees as blood starts pouring out of other parts of me and the birds begin to peck in earnest at my flesh. Moments later, I sense a larger presence and turn to see my butler behind me. He didn't escape. I've failed us both. Those are my last thoughts as he takes his first bite.

I can't hear my scream as blood comes for me, squeezing the life out of me as the birds try and get some of my flesh before my ghoul butler takes it all. I didn't feel sadness for those adults who died, and right now, I don't feel sadness for myself. Ironically, it's the children I'm sorry for.

They suffered for the beloved songs so many people love and I have a strange sense that they're telling the truth. I *am* one of them. I don't understand how my lack of hearing saved me until now, but I know in my bones that it did. I will not become one of them, though. They can kill me but I won't be an instrument of death. I just won't.

The children smile at me as I succumb to the horrors they've sent for me. I don't want to be one of them and I'm no longer a child. Neither of those things matter to them as I slowly, painfully die.

At least... there will be no more carols, only utter, true silence.

A FAMILY CHRISTMAS TERROR

"I guess it would be pretty terrible to be deaf," Nancy said. "But at least I wouldn't have to listen to Nick."

"You're right there." Grandpa finished off his port. "Okay, what about those apple slices I can smell?"

"Oh, they're cooling now," Judy said. "I also have a lemon meringue pie Aunt Gloria baked, pumpkin pie from Aunt Dolly, and mincemeat from... I don't remember. They were all delivered at once."

"Maybe the person who gave us the mincemeat—*yick*—also gave us the book?" Nick said.

Jack added, "Yeah mincemeat is a Christmas *terror* all its own."

"I like it," Dan said. "I'll have vanilla ice cream *and* whipped cream on mine."

Judy raised an eyebrow. "Both? I thought you were trying to lose weight?"

"Jesus, Judy, it's *fucking* Christmas," Dan said through gritted teeth.

481

"Double that order," Jack quickly added.

"Triple," from Nick.

"Quadruple," Grandpa called.

"Enough," Judy said. "Come help me, Nicky."

"But—"

"Give the book to Jack or your father and come help me," she snapped.

"*Nick, help your mother!*" Dan said and belched.

"Jeez, all right, Dad."

"That's a good boy." She patted him on the head.

"I'm not a dog, Mom."

"Then stop acting like a little bitch," Jack said.

"Good one, Jack." Nancy said.

"What?" Jack said, looking at everyone. He picked up the book from the chair where Nick had left it. "Let's see... *A Time for Reflections.* Intriguing title."

A TIME FOR REFLECTIONS

G. R. LINDEN

December 22, 1881

While he would never admit it to himself, Lewis was frightened. He was about to enter a brand-new world and he had no idea what to expect. Already he felt things changing: the white snow on the banks giving way to brown drudge, the crisp, chill air becoming a warm, wet blanket that seemed to engulf you no matter where you were. It was December, and if the weather here was so decidedly odd, what would the rest of his new home be like? Not for the first time Lewis wished his pa was there with him.

But Pa was dead, and Mother didn't want him around anymore. So here he was, shipped off to stay with his mother's brother, a man he had never met before.

The breath left him as he caught his first sight of the strange cityscape he would be calling home. It was dirtier than St. Louis had been, busier too. But for all its grime, there was a beauty to it, an unquantifiable mystique that made him forget the apprehensions that had gripped him only moments ago. Not for the first time he wondered what his new life in New Orleans would entail.

The sharp shriek of the steamboat whistle shocked him, nearly causing him to jump out of his shoes. He fought to regain his composure as his cheeks turned red under the condescending looks of the nearby adult passengers. Lewis gathered his luggage and joined his fellow travelers in preparing to disembark.

As the steamboat sidled into the dock, Lewis tried to get a better look at his new habitat, but his vision was blocked at every turn. One man even knocked over his luggage before yelling at Lewis to stay out of the way of his betters and muttering something about pathetic orphans and being underfoot. That man would find his pocket watch gone the next time he went to look for it.

Pickpocketing wasn't something they taught good lads at school. Lewis had learned it from some kids he'd met after Pa died, what his mother had called a "bad crowd." It was part of the reason she'd sent him away.

It wasn't that Lewis didn't know stealing was wrong. He was simply of the opinion that being mean was wrong-er.

When the boat was finally moored, Lewis had to fight tooth and nail just to remain upright against the throng of disembarking humanity. His knuckles turned white from his efforts to hold on to his luggage. He managed to fight himself free and get to a quiet place on the docks.

His eyes darted through the crowd, looking for someone who was looking for him

The problem was that Lewis had no idea who he was supposed to be looking for. He'd never met his uncle and had only an old photograph his mother had given him to identify the man from. Standing on his tiptoes did little to help matters. Why did adults have to be so tall?

"Lewis! Lewis Everhart!" The sound came roaring out of the crowd like an orchestral overture. It took Lewis a second to locate the source of the booming bass that called his name, but only a second.

The voice belonged to a man of mixed origin who stood a hand above the rest of the multitude. The top hat he wore accentuated his height in the same way his too-tight sky-blue vest highlighted his portliness. His suit was blood-red, and where his tie should have been hung a loose collection of what looked to Lewis a lot like bones. Lewis dismissed this thought as merely a trick of the distance. No civilized man wore bones around his neck.

Like Moses parting the Red Sea, the crowd gave way before him. Lewis had never seen white men give way to a mulatto before. He thought it was rather grand. Lewis also thought that Mother wouldn't approve at all, which made the whole thing doubly grand.

The man locked eyes on him as if he had known where Lewis was all along. When Lewis said the man was big, he didn't just mean that he was tall or wide; he meant that this man was big in a way that people felt in their souls. There was a presence about him.

A young couple shyly held up their baby to the man as he passed. He stopped, said a few words, and traced something on the baby's head. The child's parents seemed overcome and began kissing his hands, but he gently waived them on their way and he continued toward Lewis.

Now that the behemoth of a man was standing in front of him, Lewis could see clearly that he was indeed wearing a necklace made of bones.

Lewis gulped as the man opened his mouth to speak.

"Ah, young Master Everhart, you've got de same energy as your uncle about you. I'd recognize it anywhere. Allow me te introduce me self. I am Doctor Antoine Laveau at your service." Doctor Laveau removed his top hat and made a deep, formal bow.

"It's a pleasure to meet you, Doctor Laveau." Lewis tried to match the bow and almost fell over.

"Please call me Antoine." The burly man picked up Lewis' luggage. "Come now. I will take you te your uncle. He wanted ta collect you himself, but he has much work still te do if he is ta succeed dis night."

"Succeed?" Lewis had absolutely no idea what Antoine was talking about and the man's strange accent wasn't helping.

"You have arrived on an evening dat is most auspicious. Tonight your uncle means ta see beyond de veil and in ta de realms beyond."

"Oh." Not really knowing what to say to that Lewis simply fell silent. His new home made less and less sense to him by the moment.

As their carriage made its way through the crowded cobblestone streets, Lewis struggled to pay attention to the history lesson that Antoine was offering him. Rather, his focus lay with the marvelous and strange architecture that surrounded them.

They passed a beautiful cathedral that looked like nothing Lewis had seen before, and the streets were lined with balconies where he could see a wide array of peoples relaxing and looking out on the people below.

Perhaps what struck Lewis the most were the Christmas wreaths he saw on every gas lamp. To him it was the most incredible oddity to see a city covered in holly and wreaths with no snow on the ground.

As they moved out of what Antoine had called the French Quarter, the wrought iron facades and colorful two-story buildings gave way to larger, more American-looking buildings. Antoine had stopped his history lesson and gone back to talking about Lewis' uncle.

"Gideon is a brilliant man, but he is misunderstood by many. Dey laugh at his theories and ask for proof. When he brings dem proof, dey decry it as a fabrication. Dey mock what dey do not understand. But dough dey may ridicule his theories, dey respect your uncle. Some of dem even fear him. You know how I know dis?"

Lewis did not. He indicated this by staring blankly back at Doctor Laveau, who by the speed with which he carried on, apparently meant the question to be a rhetorical one anyway.

"Because when dey speak of your uncle, when dey speak of de foolish Professor Gideon Giles and his far-fetched experiments, dey do so in a whisper." Antione's words were laced with menace but were not as off-putting as the laughter that followed them.

Lewis wasn't sure what Antoine meant by telling him all this. He knew that his mother was not overly fond of her brother and considered him an embarrassment. In Lewis' mind that was a point in his uncle's favor. The truth was he knew very little about his Uncle Gideon, other than he had fought in the war and was now a professor of some kind.

Their mud-spattered carriage pulled up to a mansion that would have been described as palatial if not for the general sense of foreboding it exuded. Where the other estates they had passed looked bright and classical in their design, his uncle's was more Gothic in nature. It would have been far more at home in medieval Europe than modern America.

Antoine walked him to the door as the footman collected Lewis' baggage. The knocker looked comically small in his gargantuan hand as he banged it three times.

The door opened and a small, matronly looking woman appeared. She gave a quick glance at Antoine before taking a long look at Lewis.

"Ah, Doctor Laveau, you have delivered our weary traveler. The professor will be most grateful to you. You'll find him in the laboratory. He was anxious that you attend to him immediately upon your return." The woman's words were sharp and clear, enunciating each word with clipped precision.

"Den I leave you in Mrs. Dunham's capable care, young Lewis." Antoine gave Lewis' back a pat and made his way into the house.

"Right this way, Master Everheart. Your uncle had me fix up one of the upstairs rooms for you." Lewis followed Mrs. Dunham closely, certain that he did not want to become lost in this place. Myriad stuffed animal heads were mounted on the walls. Some he recognized easy enough: bears, lions, alligators, and the like. But some were decidedly strange: the impossibly large head of a spider, the impossibly small head of a bull, and a just plain impossible head that looked to be an elephant with antlers and an extra eye. Lewis thought the shadows must be playing tricks on him because he would have sworn that the heads were watching him as he climbed the stairs.

"Here we are. Prepared especially for you. You'll find your luggage in the corner. I'll let you get settled. Dinner is at six." Lewis simply nodded as Mrs. Dunham went through her checklist. His attention was engaged by the small firearm that was resting on his pillow, a firearm that Mrs. Dunham seemed to be taking no notice of at all.

The housekeeper left him, and Lewis walked slowly toward the bed. He was certain that if he moved too quickly, the pistol would disappear, proving to be a figment of his overactive imagination. When he finally reached it, Lewis took it carefully in his hands. He could tell by the weight that it wasn't loaded.

He examined it carefully. It was a beautiful piece, silver-plated and balanced perfectly. Lewis hadn't held a gun since before his pa had died.

"My father gave me that gun when I was your age."

Lewis turned with a start. Standing in the doorway was his uncle. The man was older than he had looked in the photo Lewis' mother had given him, but he was still possessed of a wiry frame and a certain air of youthful sophistication. It was the eyes that gave him away, dark brown eyes that somehow managed to be hard and curious at the same time.

"Truth be told, I almost killed your mother with that a few times. Fortunately for you, I was a rather awful shot back then." Lewis couldn't tell whether or not his uncle was joking. "Consider it an early Christmas present. I assume you know how to shoot?"

"Pa taught me a little, but Mother forbade it once she found out." And Lewis hated her for it.

"That sounds like my sister dear. Very well. I'll take you out for target practice starting tomorrow. No sense you losing an appendage out of ignorance." His uncle pulled a whistle out of his pocket and put it to his mouth. "I have one more present for you."

Gideon blew the whistle twice and looked expectantly down the hallway. A few seconds later a rather large Border collie came bounding into Gideon's arms. Lewis' uncle dropped to one knee and petted the exuberant dog for a few seconds before commanding him to sit.

"Lewis, I'd like you to meet your newest companion. I'm afraid I've never been particularly good at naming things, so it's up to you to decide what to call him." Lewis needed less than a moment to answer.

"I'd like to call him Will, if that's all right. After my father."

"I think Will is a fine name for a dog." His uncle smiled then gave a sharp cough. "There, that's done then. I've always said there are three things a boy your age needs: a gun, a dog, and an education. I've taken care of the first two, and tonight we'll get to work on the third. Dinner is at six sharp and Mrs. Dunham abhors tardiness. I'll leave you to get acquainted with your new friend."

Dinner came too quickly for Lewis, but not wanting to make a bad impression on his first night in his new home, he pulled himself away from Will and managed to get dressed and downstairs in time.

Dinner consisted of pork chops smothered in some kind of gravy, a new species of pepper Lewis had never seen, stuffed with cheese and beef, and a serving of what Antoine had called jambalaya. It was all delicious and a vast improvement on the disappointingly small portions of soup Lewis had been eating on the way down the river. It was safe to say that the food on Lewis' plate had his undivided attention.

Which was good because he had only a fleeting comprehension of what Gideon and Antoine were discussing.

"I accept that there are things beyond the current understanding of science, but I will not accept that this will always be the case. To the first cave dwellers fire seemed to be a gift from the gods. The sun, the moon, and the stars were all worshiped before we came to understand them for what they really are. Gravity itself baffled the scientific community and was held to be merely an extension of God's will until a man of intellect proved otherwise. What you call mysticism is merely a state of natural laws that we have yet to unravel."

"Science is a powerful ding, Professor. 'Dis is true, but it does not solve all de mysteries of God's creation. De spirits are here te guide us, but dey will not be chained by man's laws."

Gideon guffawed at Antoine's assertions. "God is a myth. These spirits of yours are no more than apparitions. Imprints of consciousness left behind. No more than energy trapped between our reality and another." His uncle said in rebuttal.

"God is all around you, Professor. You simply choose not te believe. Tonight you will have de proof you need." Antoine spoke with supreme confidence.

"Yes, I very much believe I will."

The conversation continued but became increasingly more technical and centered on the specifics of this great experiment that was to occur after supper. And thus it was increasingly beyond Lewis' ability to comprehend.

Lewis let his thoughts dwell on his uncle's statement that God was a myth. He had never heard anyone speak such a thought out loud. While it was true that his mother had been more interested in church activities than his pa, his father had been able to quote his Scripture by chapter and verse and had insisted that Lewis be able to do the same.

But with his father dead and his mother run off to San Francisco in search of a rich husband, he wondered if there really was a God after all. And if there was, why was everyone so certain he was benevolent?

After dinner Lewis, with Will now at his side, was ushered down to what he presumed to be his uncle's laboratory. He could only presume because, while it seemed unlikely to be anything else, it also looked nothing like what Lewis thought a scientific laboratory should look like.

Incense burned throughout the room, combining with the odd bits of steam that various gadgets and doodads were popping out, to make the lab's atmosphere heavy and difficult to breathe. Where Lewis would have expected to find the shelves lined with beakers and sundries, instead they were lined with hollowed-out skulls and other, more unfamiliar oddities. The far wall was perhaps the most surprising as it served as a rack for a variety of heavily modified firearms.

Lewis highly doubted that this room was typical for a university professor.

"Stand by the door. If you see fire, ghosts, or any unnatural atmospheric occurrences, run and get Mrs. Dunham. Understood?" The oddness of his uncle's command was overshadowed by the severity of its delivery.

"Yes sir," Lewis responded fairly bewildered.

Gideon double-checked his equipment while Antoine drew a circle and some other markings on the floor. From his spot in the doorway it was difficult for Lewis to see what they might be. When he was done, he positioned himself in the center of the circle, sat down cross-legged, and began mixing various herbs and liquids. Gideon paced impatiently and looked over the equipment twice more before Antoine spoke.

"I am ready te begin, Professor. May de spirits smile upon us." Antoine produced a flask from his pocket and took a swig before handing it to Gideon.

"Here's to not blowing ourselves up." His uncle took his own long tug on the flask and threw the switch attached to a large piece of machinery. Cords ran from the machine to two separate brackets that stood on opposite sides of the room.

The machine and Antione began to hum in unison as the lights flickered and dimmed.

"Come on, work, damn you, work," came his uncle's quiet imploring. Antoine ceased his humming and began chanting in a powerful voice and blowing some sort of white powder into the air.

The laboratory crackled with energy. Sparks flew from various pieces of equipment. Will whined and barked from behind Lewis' legs, the poor creature frightened out of his mind. Gideon cackled as Antoine continued his chanting, calling to unknown spirits. Madness had taken hold of the room and only Lewis seemed to notice or care.

Colors began to swirl as the energy coalesced at the center of his uncle's contraption. A horizontal funnel of electricity and fire appeared out of thin air, boring a hole through reality itself. Wind rushed around the room, sending papers flying all around.

A maddening cacophony of unholy shrieks attacked his ears. Lewis tried to cover them, but to no avail. The screams reached him no matter what he tried, drilling through his every defense and straight into his soul.

The cyclone expanded until its edges were touching Gideon's machines. Suddenly the funnel snapped back and locked into place, creating a wall of electricity and fire at the center of the lab.

Distorted images began to appear in the brackets, flickering fragments of creatures and people that should have been impossible for them to view.

The images came into focus and the room calmed. Before them, bracketed by his uncle's invention and humming with the power of Antoine's spirits, was a vision of an unearthly wasteland.

"It worked," was Gideon's breathless reply to the successful culmination of his maniacal endeavor.

Lewis left the safety of the doorway and a still whimpering Will and stepped toward his uncle's experiment. In a voice of awe and wonder he spoke his first words since this lunacy had begun.

"What is it?"

"That is another dimension." Smug satisfaction filled his uncle's words.

"You uncle has built a window into de mind of God."

"Nonsense. It's not a window. It's a mirror. A mirror that shows us the reflections of all our might-have-beens. Observe." Gideon walked over to one of the brackets and began adjusting dials. As he did, the image changed.

A group of children were playing a game of baseball in a park. The children were from all different backgrounds: black, white, mixed, even a few Chinese boys among them. Standing by the foul line, watching over everyone, was grey-haired Antoine smiling from ear to ear.

"Not a bad find for de first attempt," said Antoine, wearing the same exact smile his mirrored self wore.

"You don't even like baseball," was Gideon's teasingly gruff reply.

"No, but I do enjoy seeing de little ones enjoying demselves," Antoine pointed out with a hearty laugh.

"If I wanted to watch a baseball game, I'd go to the park. Let's see if we can't find something a bit more worthy of our genius, shall we?" Gideon turned the dials and a new moving portrait came into focus.

A man walked across a field of corpses, dressed in grey and blue. He moved frantically, searching the faces of the bodies. When he found the one he was looking for, he fell to his knees and began to weep uncontrollably. Lewis realized the man they saw was Gideon, only much younger. Younger even than the picture his mother had given him.

Gideon shifted the dials and the picture changed again.

Lewis gasped. The new image showed Lewis sitting in front of a Christmas tree, digging through his stocking. His mother was there, laughing and handing Lewis more presents to open. In the corner of the room, sitting in a rocking chair as if he didn't have a care in the world, was his father.

He felt Antoine's firm grip on his shoulder. He couldn't tell if it was meant to be reassuring, or if it was there to keep him from running headlong into his favorite dream.

"It's not real, Lewis. It's nothing but a mirage." His uncle's words rang hollow in is ears. It wasn't a mirage. His father was right there. Close enough to touch.

He didn't realize his hand had been reaching out to do just that until Antoine knocked it away. Gideon quickly reset the dials on his machine and the image became a wall of red and blue energy.

"I think that's enough for tonight. Antoine, why don't you take Lewis up to bed while I clean up down here."

Numbly, Lewis allowed himself to be led away from the life he had always wanted.

*

Just before midnight, after everyone else had gone to bed, Lewis snuck back down to his uncle's laboratory. The blue-red wall still hummed, its glow lighting the otherwise darkened room. Carefully he moved the dials the way his uncle had until he had again found the image of his family. He sat there for hours, watching them open presents, play with his new toys, eat Christmas dinner. Smiling and laughing. Being a family.

Sometime after he had run out of tears, but before dawn, Lewis heard a noise coming from down the hall. Not wanting to be caught playing with his uncle's experiment, he rushed out of the laboratory and back to his room, completely forgetting to reset the dials on the mirror.

December 23, 1881

Lewis didn't see his reflection reach for the mirror's edge. He didn't smell the skin burning as his doppelganger's hand crossed the portal's threshold and entered our world. He didn't know that the happy life he had seen for himself had been a lie, a fabrication concocted by a creature so desperate to escape Hell that it would endure the flesh melting off its bones to be liberated from its torments. Nor did he know that after the demon had suffered through such an ordeal, it would hunger. No, Lewis was ignorant of all these things and one more. Lewis also didn't know that Mrs. Dunham always awoke in the early hours of the morning to bake fresh bread for the day.

*

After a night of unsettling dreams, Lewis opened his eyes at Will's insistent nuzzling. The Border collie was whimpering with some urgency. Lewis dressed quickly and followed his new pup down the stairs.

The first thing to hit him was the smell, a layer of stench that coated the entire first floor of the house. Vile, putrid air filled his nostrils and roiled his insides. Lewis blocked out the smell as best he could and continued down the stairs. If Will could manage it with his canine sense of smell, then so could Lewis.

Further and further into the house they went, finding more and more signs of distress. Bookcases and end tables were strewn about, haphazardly knocked over by some unknown force. Fingernail scratches laced the walls, marring the beautiful woodwork Lewis had been introduced to only the day before.

Finally they came upon his uncle. Gideon stood like a statue in the doorway, oblivious to their approach. Still whimpering, Will stayed in the hallway as Lewis moved past his uncle and into the kitchen, a decision that he immediately regretted.

Horrifying could not begin to describe the tableau of gore that lay before him. Mrs. Dunham's body lay in front of the stove. She had been ripped open and unburdened of her internal organs. The few ribs that had not been broken were now protruding from her hollowed-out corpse at an angle of ninety degrees. Her head lay a few feet away. It was only missing its tongue. Mrs. Dunham's eyes remained open, forever imprinted with the terror of her final moments. Lewis' stomach heaved. He managed to swallow down the vomit, but the taste of bile lingered in his mouth. He stepped out of the room, fearing that he would be unable to keep control of another such outburst.

There was a heavy knocking at the door and unseen chimes began ringing throughout the house. Will barked at the noise, and Lewis was sure that his pup shared his master's fear and discomfort.

The noise jolted Gideon from his dire contemplations, and finally he too stepped away from the terrible scene.

"That will be the police. Perhaps it's best if you took Will to the library, keep him out of the way while they're here. I'll join you shortly."

Lewis knew that the task was meant to keep them both out of the way and he would normally bristle at being condescended to, but in this particular instance he was grateful to his uncle for the opportunity to get as far away from this horrid scene as possible.

Lewis only took three wrong turns on his way to the library. The further from the smell they got, the more Will seemed to perk up, though his new pup was still quite rattled from the experience.

They sat in silence in the library as the police did their work. Nearly an hour had gone by when his uncle stepped through the door, with Antoine trailing in his wake.

"Yours were not de only ill words ta reach me doorstep dis morning. Der were two other poor souls ta share Mrs. Dunham's fate last night."

"Tell me," was Gideon's cold response to the disturbing news.

"Remi St. Croix was found in de basement of Touro, ripped te shreds, and pieces of Walter Jackson were found in tree different rooms of de iron works on Tchoupitoulas. Der be no coincidence about dis Professor. Dis be the work of Loa. We have unleashed de evil spirits on our home. Dis blood be on our hands." Antoine trembled as he spoke the last words.

"What exactly we've unleashed is yet to be assessed. But I do agree with you that this is no coincidence and the burden of guilt is ours to bear."

Lewis felt a sinking feeling in his gut. If these murders were a result of his uncle's mirror, then they were Lewis' fault. He'd been the one to sneak back down and play with the dials. Lewis wanted to say something but held his tongue. Gideon was his uncle, but he'd only met the man last night. What did one say at a time like this? How could he tell his uncle that he was responsible for these people's horrible deaths?

"Three murders in three different wards. Even if we lucked upon a group of honest officers, they won't know what they're truly up against. How could they if we don't even know? Without our involvement there is no chance that this does not become a bloodbath of Biblical scale. Besides which is the matter of a debt to be repaid." Gideon paused for moment. "Lewis, grab your pistol. We're going out."

"Out" by Gideon's definition was the crime scene closest to his residence, a hospital called Touro Infirmary. Lewis' first full day in New Orleans was not going as he had expected. It was shocking to him that his uncle could be so untouched by the gruesome murder of his housekeeper, but if the man felt any emotion at all, he was keeping it buried deep inside.

The approach to the hospital was clogged by a crowd of gawkers and hysterical citizens. A line of stalwart officers had their batons out and were quite literally beating the mob back with a stick. With a mix of contempt and frustration, Gideon instructed their driver to keep moving.

"Maybe we have more luck at de Ironworks?" said Antoine.

"We'd better," was his uncle's terse reply.

The additional half-mile ride was more than a frustrating annoyance for Lewis, as it left him with time to dwell on the horrible deaths multiple people had suffered because of his own weakness. The thought ate away at him as they arrived at their secondary destination.

Gideon was a striking sight as he climbed out of the carriage. His hat was slightly askew, and he had removed his jacket and rolled up his white shirtsleeves. His maroon vest was accentuated by a purple cravat that was the color of royalty. The silver-plated pistols that hung naturally on each of his uncle's hips and the dark glasses that covered his eyes gave his cultivated aura of refined casualness a lethal seriousness.

Gideon handed Lewis his black medical bag and started giving orders.

"Lewis, stay here and out of trouble. Antione, work some of that voodoo doctor charm and get us in to see that body." Lewis' stomach revolted at merely the thought of seeing another sight like Mrs. Dunham, and for once he was glad to be left holding the bag.

From where they exited the carriage, they could see the police carrying three different black bags from the building. The sight of three body bags sent Lewis into panic spiral. Antoine had said that there had been only one death here. His heart ached and his breath shortened as the weight of two more deaths crushed down upon his soul.

Lewis was not the only one shaken by the thought of two more bodies. Antoine's voice cracked as he spoke to the officer impeding their path.

"Excuse me, constable, but I was told der had been only de one man killed."

"That's right," the constable replied coarsely.

"Why den tree bags?"

"He was killed in a very nasty way." The constable paused to let the words sink in.

"If you'll allow me, my name is Professor Gideon Giles. I'm with the university, and I'm doing some research. I was hoping I might get a look at the room where the unfortunate man was found." Gideon started to walk past the officer, but he was stopped with a firm hand.

"I don't care who you're with. No one's getting in here without a badge. Now get moving before I haul you down for irritating an officer." The officer stared them down until, reluctantly, Gideon walked away.

"Damn. I need to know what happened in there. I wouldn't even need to see the scene. Just a look at the detective's notebook would be enough," his uncle complained once they were out of earshot.

Lewis could see the head detective giving orders to various officers and had an idea.

He dropped his uncle's medical bag and ducked away from Gideon and Antoine. Making sure his path would take him right by the detective, he took off at full speed toward the body bags, screaming "Daddy" at the top of his lungs.

"Whoa, lad, slow down. What's the matter?" Sure enough the detective stepped in front of him to block his way.

On command, Lewis began to bawl his eyes out.

"That's my daddy." Lewis called upon all the anguish he had felt at his father's death to sell it.

"What's your daddy's name?" The detective was dour, but there was genuine concern there. Lewis' plan would work.

"Joe. Joe King." Sometimes Lewis was too clever for his own good.

"Then that's not your daddy. Now why would you think it was?"

"He works here. I haven't been able to find him all morning."

"Well, if I was your daddy, I'd need a drink after seeing a sight like this. He's likely at the saloon and will be home later. Best if you go home and wait for him there."

"Okay. I'm sorry, sir. I was just scarred it might be him." Lewis reduced the waterworks to a light sob and let his teary, eye contact work its magic.

Feeling awkward and unsure of what to do, the detective bent down and gave Lewis a hug to reassure him.

Lewis took the opportunity to carefully slip his hands into the man's breast pocket and remove his notebook. When the detective broke the hug, he was none the wiser. Lewis rubbed his eyes dry and thanked the man for both his knowing and unknowing assistance.

"Thank you, sir, I feel better now."

"I'm glad to hear it. Run along then, lad. This is no place for a boy your age."

Lewis did as he was told. He was well away from the crowd of gawkers by the time Gideon and Antoine caught up with him.

"What the devil was that all about?"

"You wanted a look at the detective's notebook." Lewis produced the notebook from his pocket and handed it to his uncle.

"Impressive," said Antoine.

"Most," said Gideon with a nod of approval. "Now let's see what we have here. The victim is Walter Jackson. He comes in early to get the smelter heated up for the day. He was found when the first shift came in. Or rather, his devoured, mostly to the bone, legs were found in the front office, then his arm by the changing station, and finally the rest of him by the smelter. Ripped open like the others. Missing most his internal organs along with his eyes and his tongue. The detective's current working theory is animal attack."

"He was a good man," Antoine bowed his head and said a silent prayer. "Der is nah'ting der we didn't know already."

"No there isn't." Gideon must have seen the disappointment on Lewis' face because he quickly added, "Not right now at least, but every bit of information helps. This was a good get, Lewis. Well done."

"What do we do now?" he asked bypassing his uncle's patronizing remark.

"Now we search all of Uptown and pray we get lucky," was Gideon's uninspired response.

And so they hunted. They spent hours walking the streets, checking every building and alley, canvasing the neighborhood, looking for any sign of the foul, murdering beast they had set loose upon the world.

They were still patrolling well after sunset when a Creole woman came running down the street in a fit of hysteria.

"A demon! A demon from hell! It killed him! Ripped him apart. Loa! Loa!!" The words came rushing out of the woman in a jumble, barely audible between sobs.

"Calm, sweet sister. It will be alright. Where did ya see de beast?" Antoine spoke in a melodic, soothing voice, but the woman refused to be slowed by their questions. She continued to scream and flee, leaving her direction of origin as their only clue.

They hurried toward the source of the woman's fright. Will must have sensed his fear. The Border collie was never more than a foot away, constantly searching the shadows for threats to his master. Maybe that was why the pup was the first to find the demon's latest meal.

Lewis was horrified to find yet another mangled corpse, but was more than a little relieved to find the creature already gone. From the looks of it, the victim had been a lamplighter in the middle of his evening rounds. The man's equipment and the lack of light on half the street made that much obvious. Faced with his imminent doom, he had run back toward the light, perhaps hoping it might provide some discouragement to his attacker. Or maybe he was just following that primal instinct that made human beings identify darkness as danger and light as safety. Whatever his motivation, he did not make it far.

The man had been slashed open just like the others. His throat was torn out, and of his limbs, only the left arm remained attached to the body. Bits of flesh and bone were scattered about like debris from a sunken ship. Blood pooled beneath the body, the dark red looking black underneath the moonlight. This man's death had not been a humane one. Indeed it had been about as horrible a death as Lewis could imagine anyone ever having.

Gideon cautiously stepped around the various pieces of corpse and bent down low to examine what remained of the man's upper torso.

"The teeth marks are different here than on the other three bodies. Those were definitely human or at least a close approximation. These are more canine in nature," was his uncle's assessment.

"Dogs, or maybe der be more den one creature?" Antoine put forth as an explanation. The thought of more than one of these horrible monsters roaming the streets sent shivers down Lewis' spine.

"No, the attack patterns are too similar, and if more than one of these things was loose, I think we'd have seen more signs of it at the house. There were no attacks during the day, but then the sun goes down and another body shows up." Gideon paced as he considered the problem. He stopped when he reached a conclusion. "It's hibernating during the day, using its victims as food to fuel some sort of metamorphosis."

"Dat is a long leap, Professor." The incredulity in Antoine's tone was light, but it was there.

"Perhaps, but it fits the evidence. There's nothing else we're going to learn here." Gideon nodded to the police officers who were beginning to arrive on the scene. "Let's leave the police to their work while we tend to ours."

Casually they moved away from the body and melted back into the gathering crowd of onlookers. When they were clear of the crowd, they found themselves standing on the edge between the lighted streets behind them and the darkened path before them. If Lewis hadn't been so completely terrified, he might have found the setting rather literary.

"No lamplighter ta finish de rounds." From the tone in Antoine's voice Lewis could tell he wasn't the only one who was ill at ease, not that a little bit of nighttime would faze his uncle.

"That's unfortunate. You'd think there would be redundancies for things like this. Lewis, hand me my bag."

Lewis did as he was told. His uncle pulled out three lengths of cloth and a thermos. Carefully he soaked each piece of cloth with whatever liquid the thermos contained. Gideon then broke off three lengths of wood from a nearby tree and wrapped the ends with the soaked cloth. He handed one to each of them and used his lighter to light each one in turn. At the end of two minutes' time they each held a brightly burning torch. "I'll take point, Antoine guard our rear, Lewis stay between us and stay close."

As they moved into the unlit section of the city, Lewis could feel the darkness increase around them despite the fire they held in their hands. The blackness weighed on him, an outward sign of the shadows that now marred his own soul. Envy was one the deadly sins, and his envy of a mirage had cost four people their lives already. Maybe his mother had been right to get as far away as possible from him. Maybe he really was good for nothing.

A woman's high pitched scream cut through the night, freezing the party in its tracks.

"Whe..." Lewis started to ask where the scream had come from, but held his tongue at Gideon's raised hand.

Another scream came, cut off abruptly by some unknown horror.

"This way," was all his uncle said as they rushed toward the cry for help, knowing they would not get there in time.

A few minutes of sprinting through a maze of side streets brought them to two partially consumed corpses. To Lewis they had the look of a young couple, or at least the remnants of one. The man lay face down in the street. His spine had been removed, and most of his right side had been eaten away. His gnawed-upon legs had been haphazardly discarded a few feet away.

The woman looked to be lying face-down as well until Lewis got closer and saw that she was in fact right-side up. It was simply her head that had been twisted all the way round. Her rib cage had been ripped open in the same fashion as Mrs. Dunham's, though her insides were not entirely missing but rather lay next to her, half eaten.

Lewis looked at the scene and made a mental inventory of the items surrounding the bodies. He tried to stay cold and detached like his uncle, pushing down his guilt and focusing on the problem at hand. He could deal with the additional blemishes on his soul later, after they'd stopped this demon. Somewhere inside him he registered the fact that he no longer wretched automatically at a sight such as this, and that worried him immensely.

"It appears we interrupted the beast. On your guard. It may still be lurking about." Gideon emphasized his point by drawing his pistol. Lewis imitated his uncle, though he doubted he'd be much good with his in this light.

A shadow moved in the corner of his eye. Lewis turned, raising his pistol, but saw nothing there.

"Top hat, bonnet, cigarette case, lighter, and a walking cane. That's it. Nothing that tells us why these people. Damn it all to hell I'm missing something." Gideon's voice was tight and full of rage. Lewis wanted to tell his uncle that this was his fault, but shame stopped him from confessing his role in all of this.

Again something stirred at the edge of his vision. Again Lewis turned with his pistol raised only to find nothing waiting for him. He took a few steps forward to be certain, but his torch revealed nothing but an empty sidewalk. His guilty conscience had him jumping at shadows.

"Lewis, what de ya see?" Antoine asked.

"Nothing. Just a figment of my imagination." He started to walk back toward his companions when Will began barking in earnest. The collie's warnings were soon joined by a deep, guttural growling noise.

"Down boy!" screamed Antoine as something leaped out of the darkness at Lewis. The shape was intercepted in midair by Will. The pair fell back into the night. A few seconds of barking and growling and the collie burst back into the light with a shadowy figure hot on his tail. Gunshots rang out as Gideon unloaded into the figure with his pistol.

The shots did nothing to slow the creature down. Indeed, the only evidence that it had been hit at all were the bits of blood that flew from it as Gideon's bullets struck flesh.

It was only a few paces from Lewis now.

The beast snarled with its wolfish snout, its beady, scarlet eyes burning with hate.

Lewis raised his pistol to fire, but his finger froze on the trigger. Fear and guilt gripped him. He didn't want to die, but maybe it was the fate he deserved for unleashing this demon on the world.

At the last possible moment Antoine stepped between Lewis and the beast. The creature's teeth sunk into the large man's arm, causing him to drop his torch. Lewis cowered as Antoine brought his own pistol to bear, firing multiple rounds into the creature's belly.

The beast released its grip on Antoine as it howled in rage and pain. Antoine's dropped torch flickered on the ground next to the beast, alternatingly draping their foe in darkness and light.

The beast stood upright like a man, just short of six feet in height. The demon's skin was a patchwork of oozing blood-red bits and charred, cracked pieces as black as coal. Its hands were closer to claws in description and it possessed long, spindly talons for feet. Blood dripped from its teeth and ran down its naked form. Lewis didn't know if this was the Devil, but if it wasn't, it was certainly one of his spawn.

Gideon had reloaded his pistol and wasted no time in unleashing another torrent of gunfire. The beast let out an unearthly scream and took off into the night.

"Report!" barked Gideon.

"Alive," came Antoine's rueful call.

"Lewis?" His uncle's voice had a note of worry to it. Lewis was still too stunned by the events of the last few minutes to find his voice.

"Lewis! Lewis!" The second shout finally snapped Lewis out of his stupor.

"I'm all right." Lewis felt like he was the farthest thing from all right he could be.

"Antoine, you're injured." His uncle spoke the words as cold assessment rather than caring inquiry.

"It be no ding." The blood soaking the voodoo doctor's sleeve suggested otherwise.

"We have to go after it." That what not what Lewis wanted to do, but he felt that he had a responsibility stop the creature before it could kill again. Whatever the cost.

"Nonsense. Between us we put a dozen bullets in the monster and we hardly slowed it down. If we give chase, we'll end up like those two there." Gideon pointed to the disemboweled couple, and Lewis needed only a quick glance to lose his will to continue the hunt. "Come on. Back to the house. With any luck the demon will be dormant again until tomorrow night. We need to regroup and come up with a plan, one a little bit more advanced than our previous shoot-and-pray strategy. Chin up, everyone. We had a bad night, but tomorrow will be different."

"Why is that?" Lewis didn't understand why his uncle didn't share his own despondency at the beast's escape.

"Because now we know what we're up against. And once you understand your enemy, you can beat your enemy."

December 24, 1881

By the time Lewis awoke, it was already approaching midday. Will lay next to him on the bed, looking worriedly at his master. After he dressed, he found his uncle and Antoine in the dining room, poring over maps and books and the policeman's notebook he had stolen an eternity ago. They looked haggard. Lewis doubted they had gotten much sleep, if they had gotten any at all. Another thing to feel guilty about. At least Antoine's wounds had been dressed.

"There's something I'm missing. Something that connects the attacks that I'm not seeing." Gideon's voice was strained and his frustration was visibly boiling over.

"You said last night that you knew what we were up against." Doubt filled Lewis.

"I do. The problem is that I don't know what I know yet. All the information is here. I just have to piece it together." His uncle spoke with what Lewis considered to be an unearned confidence. "We have to go over the other murders again. What connects them?"

"De tree before dawn yesterday. None during de day. Den tree more last night," Antoine recapped for them all.

"Then none again today. It hibernates during the day. We'd already sussed that out. No, I mean the individual victims. That thing covered a lot of ground the last two nights in what could hardly be called a straight line. Why that route? Why those people?"

"It was looking for the easiest kills?" Lewis posited.

"Hardly. It completely bypassed the orphanage, and why go to the basement of the infirmary then leave when there you have plenty of tasty, immobile human snacks above you? List every victim in order for me, telling me where and how they were found."

"Mrs. Dunham was in de kitchen baking de morning bread. Remi was in de basement at Touro Infirmary working on de building boiler. Walter Jackson was getting ready for de day at de ironworks. Dey found him by de—"

"By the smelter! That's it! The missing piece! Right in front of me the whole time. How could I be so stupid as to miss it? It's so obvious. Can't you see it?" Lewis looked to see if Antoine understood what his uncle was going on about. It was a comfort to him that the large man looked as lost as he was. "The heat! It's drawn to heat! Mrs. Dunham had the oven going. St. Croix was stoking the boiler at Touro. Jackson was working a smelter—"

"—De Gaslamp lighter had a torch wid him..." came Antoine's wide eyed comprehension.

"There was a cigarette case and a lighter by the couple." Lewis excitedly chimed in.

"Now put it all together. Everything we know about this monstrosity. It's nocturnal, it's drawn to sources of heat, it's hiding somewhere in City Park, and bullets merely seem to annoy it." Lewis could see the gears turning in his uncle's head now.

"Dat seems te be de long and de short of it," Antoine affirmed.

"So if we can't kill it, we'll have to send it back to where it came from."

"Ain't no easy ding to trick de Devil back to Hell Professor."

515

"We'll need some sort of heat source, something large enough to lure the beast to us. We won't be able to get it to the lab. We'll need some place wide open in or near the park." His uncle was pacing again.

"Den it's a good ding Papa Noel rides tonight." The words stopped Gideon mid-stride. A smile broke out all over his face.

"Antoine, you're a genius. Can you make the arrangements in time?"

"It shouldn't be a problem. Can you say de same?"

"Are you asking if I can build a portable generator capable of powering an extradimensional portal between now and sundown? Antoine, please, I'll be done with an hour to spare."

"Best be to it den." Without further discussion Antoine headed out the door.

Gideon was about to do the same when the need to confess suddenly overwhelmed Lewis.

"Uncle..." The words stuck in his throat. "Uncle, there's something I have to tell you."

"Lewis, I need to get to my laboratory." His uncle looked at him and his facial expression went from stern to concern in an instant. "Lewis, what is it?"

"It's just that..." Lewis forced himself to tell his uncle his shameful secret. "The truth is that this is all my fault. I snuck back down to your laboratory after everyone had gone to bed. I know I shouldn't have, but I couldn't help it. I just wanted to see him again. I turned the dials back to where you had them before. I swear all I did was watch them. I didn't touch anything other than the dials, honest. They're all dead because of me." Tears filled his eyes and he began to sob uncontrollably.

"Is that what's been eating at you this whole time? Lewis, I'm going to say something now, and I want you to listen very closely because it's important that you believe me. None of this is your fault. It can't be because the fault lies with me. I tampered with the natural order of things. More than that, I did so in the most cavalier way possible. There should have been nothing for you to find when you snuck back down. It was the height of arrogance and idiocy to leave that connection open and unmonitored. I have no idea what possessed me to do so, especially in light of the obvious temptation it offered you. Everything that has happened has been a result of my hubris and not your innocent desire to see your father alive and happy again. You are a good lad, Lewis, as good as I've seen."

"But mother said—"

"My sister is a ghastly woman completely unable to look beyond her own petty needs. What your father saw in her I'll never know. How she could send you down here alone to stay with a stranger, at Christmas of all times, absolutely boggles my mind, but I'm damn glad she did. Now, there'll be time for feeling feelings later, but right now we need to get to work. We have a beast to slay and honor to regain. Are you with me?"

"Yes sir," Lewis said. Will barked his affirmation as well.

The work took most of the afternoon, but Gideon was good to his word. They finished loading the equipment onto the wagon while the sun was still two fingers over the horizon. Gideon, Lewis, and Will rode to the park in silence. Lewis assumed that his uncle was too preoccupied with going over the plan in his head to speak, and Will was too preoccupied with sticking his head out the window and barking at passing streetcars to pay much attention to his master.

Their destination was well into the park, a clearing somewhere along the bank of the Mississippi. They found Antoine waiting for them when they arrived. Lewis was still completely in the dark about what the plan was. If he had to guess, he would say the giant, twelve-foot-high stack of wood they were setting up next to them was going to be involved in some manner or another. But something about the demeanor of the two adults made him think it was best not to ask questions at the moment. He simply got to work unloading the wagon.

Gideon had not just brought with him a stack of lab equipment. He'd also loaded the wagon with a small armory. Lewis pulled out a gun with a single long barrel and some kind of pumping mechanism attached to the bottom. He had never seen anything like it before although, given the frequency at which he had been making that observation lately, he supposed his uncle's custom firearm was apropos. While he was admiring it, his uncle came up behind him and snatched it out of his grasp.

"What is that?"

"It's a shotgun."

"It doesn't look like any shotgun I've ever seen."

"That's because it's a repeating shotgun, one of the many tricks I have hidden up my sleeve and years ahead of anything that bastard Browning's come up with. Any other questions?" His uncle meant it as a dismissal.

"Who's Papa Noel?" Lewis asked immediately

"Cajun Santa Claus. Every year on Christmas Eve people light huge bonfires to guide him in. Now back to work." Suddenly their plan made much more sense to Lewis.

By the time they had set up the equipment to Gideon's satisfaction, the sun had sunk long past the horizon and given way to the black of night. The general apprehension Lewis had felt all day was now completely gone, replaced by a more palpable sense of doom.

"The generator has limited power. Once you turn it on, we'll have less than five minutes to drive the demon back to whatever hell it came from. Stay out of sight, and don't throw the switch until you hear me shout for it. Understand?"

Lewis nodded at his uncle's instructions.

Across the river, giant pillars of fire came roaring to life as families began to light their bonfires in celebration of Christmas.

"Dey light the way for Papa Noel," came a jubilant shout from Antoine.

"Then we'd best do the same," was the gruffer response from his uncle as he lit the pyre next to him. Antoine had long since chased off any other revelers on their side of the river, so when Gideon started their specially chosen bonfire, it stood out like a fiery beacon against the dark. If they were right about the demon's attraction to heat, it would be impossible for the creature to resist the bonfire's lure.

"What now?" Lewis asked

"Now we wait for the Devil to show himself," was his uncle's intense reply.

They did not have to wait long.

The ground trembled under their feet, alerting them to the demon's approach. The beast let loose with a horrible cry as it stepped out into the moonlight. This was not the same creature they had faced the previous evening. In its day of hibernation it had grown almost six feet and now stood over twelve feet high. Massive leathery wings had sprouted from its back, each one as wide as the beast was tall. Its skin was the deep black of the void, making the demon almost impossible to see.

"Bigger than I remember. And with wings. That's certainly an unfortunate development." His uncle spoke the words casually, showing defiance through his nonchalance.

Gideon opened fire with both pistols, unloading shot after shot into the demon's chest. A roar of anger escaped its throat.

"I tink you got its attention," Antoine called out, staff in one hand, pistol in the other.

"Yes, I think you might be right," Gideon responded as the beast increased its speed from a lumbering stride to a quick gallop.

The demon closed the distance between itself and Gideon in mere moments. Lewis cringed as the boom of gunfire turned into the hollow clicks of an empty chamber.

His uncle let his now useless weapons fall from his hands, diving toward his right to escape the beast's slashing claws. Lewis watched his uncle repeat the tactic twice more, each escape narrower than the last, the creature allowing Gideon no time to do anything but dodge.

Eventually Gideon's luck gave out and the demon's claws found flesh. His uncle cried out, instinctively reaching out for the newly formed gash in his thigh.

The creature raised its hand back to strike, ready to deliver the deathblow.

"Gideon! Roll!" Antoine bellowed while unleashing his own barrage of pistol fire. The bullets did minimal damage, succeeding only in puncturing a few holes in the creature's leathery wings, but they did manage to distract the beast long enough for Gideon to roll clear.

The creature swept its wing back at its attacker. The wing struck Antoine with incredible force and sent the large man flying through the air. He landed in a heap, clearly dazed by the blow.

The demon turned its attention back to Gideon, who was struggling to get upright.

Lewis pulled his pistol from its holster.

His uncle had told him to remain hidden, but if Lewis didn't act now, the monstrosity was sure to devour both Antoine and Gideon. Lewis was old enough to know that sometimes doing what is right means not doing what you're told.

He inhaled deeply, aimed, and pulled the trigger as he exhaled. The shot exploded from his gun with a thunderclap, the recoil nearly ripping his arm out of its socket. The bullet struck home, burying itself in the creature's shoulder.

Its howl cut through the night. The beast turned, its fiery red eyes locking in on Lewis.

"Lewis, run!" He did not need to hear his uncle's advice to heed it.

The ground rumbled underneath the demon's lengthy stride. Lewis' legs pumped up and down with the fury of a railroad piston, but he was quickly losing his lead. A loose branch sent him tumbling to the ground, and Lewis knew he was about to die.

Or at least he would have if not for his faithful pup. Will came sprinting out of the shadows, letting out a howl as the collie launched itself into the creature's knees. The demon bellowed and toppled over, mirroring Lewis' fall of only moments before.

The monstrosity's flailing hands caught Will with a glancing blow that sent the dog flying through the air.

Lewis scrambled to his feet, and it was then that he realized his mistake.

CHRISTMAS TERRORS

In fleeing from the demon he'd led the creature too far away from Gideon's invention. Now, as the beast righted itself, it stood between Lewis and his companions and was headed toward him and further away from his uncle's trap.

Antoine and Gideon were running toward them, but both were injured and moving slowly. Lewis was on his own, and somehow he had to force the beast back in the right direction.

He could figure out only one way to do that. He just prayed that he was fast enough and small enough not to die.

The demon was fully recovered now, gaining momentum with every step. Lewis had seconds to act or be eaten.

Lewis did the only thing he could do to avoid being gruesomely devoured. He sprinted headlong toward the creature that wanted him for supper.

There was a moment of confusion in the beast's eyes, then a soul wrenching noise erupted from its throat. Lewis thought it must be laughter. Lewis responded with a war cry of his own, screaming manically as he rushed forward to impending doom.

When the beast was only steps away Lewis, raised his pistol and fired.

The demon pulled up, covering its face as Lewis ran between its enormous legs.

Lewis didn't dare slow down or look back. He made a beeline for the generator, hoping he had bought himself enough distance to make it in time.

The trembling earth beneath him told him that his time was quickly running out. He pushed his young legs harder than he ever had in his life.

Lewis could clearly see his companions now.

Gideon stood ready with a shotgun as Antoine retook his position in his chalk circle.

Strange, ethereal shapes began to form around Antoine as he pointed his staff to the heavens and mumbled incantations to the wind.

Lewis rushed past Antoine and Gideon, feeling the demon's hot breath on his neck as he pushed to cover the last few yards between himself and his uncle's generator before the beast could consume him.

The explosion of a shotgun blast was followed by another howl of rage from the demon. Lewis was almost to the generator now. He went into a baseball slide, gliding across the dewy grass and coming to a stop with the generator's switch in his hand.

"Now!" his uncle screamed.

Blue sparks of electricity started flying out of Gideon's machines, supercharging the air while simultaneously blackening any bit of earth they touched. Reality began to twist as colors became fluid and comingled. The same horizontal funnel of electricity and fire that had appeared in his uncle's lab two nights ago began to form, tearing a hole in the fabric of the universe. A chorus of infernal shrieks poured forth from the opening, cutting through Lewis' defenses like a dagger to his soul.

The wind howled and thunder bellowed as lighting rained down all around them.

Antoine slammed his staff into the ground and shouted something indecipherable. The phantoms that had been gathering around him went flying toward the creature, harrying it in a way that Lewis did not understand.

The demon staggered backwards as Gideon unloaded shotgun blast after shotgun blast into its chest, delivering on the deadly promises of its maker.

Lassos of light and fire emerged from the portal, wrapping themselves around the demon's limbs. It howled in pain as it was pulled unwillingly toward the red-blue wall that had spawned it.

With one last swipe of its massive claw, the beast seized Gideon by the ankle and yanked him to the ground, trying to pull him with it into the awaiting abyss. Lewis could only watch as his uncle's specialized shotgun went flying out of his grasp and out of his reach.

Lewis knew he was too far away to reach his uncle before he was pulled through the gateway. He looked to Antoine but saw that he too would be unable to close the distance in time. Gideon had only moments before the hell beast dragged him through the gateway.

With a flick of his wrist Gideon produced a pistol from his coat sleeve. Taking no time to aim he fired off a shot at the generator.

There was a blinding flash of light, and a deafening blast ripped through the air as the generator exploded and the portal collapsed upon itself.

Scorched equipment and spent shotgun shells littered the earth. It was quiet. Not a sound to be heard except for crackling of the bonfire's flame.

And at the center of it all sat the severed right hand of the demon.

December 25, 1881

His uncle stood up, dusted himself off, carefully replaced his hat on his head, and said in a uniquely unflappable voice, "Well, I think it's safe to say we missed Midnight Mass. I'm not sure about the rest of you, but I think could do with a spot of breakfast. Doctor Laveau, I believe your wife is hosting Reveillon this year?"

Antoine let out a hearty laugh and Lewis joined him. Will came running into his arms, covering his face in kisses. Lewis decided that Christmas with his uncle was vastly preferable to spending the holidays with his mother.

A FAMILY CHRISTMAS TERROR

Grandpa said, "The time period reminded me of some old Jules Verne novels—one of my favorites."

"Yeah, it was kind of Steampunk too," Jack said.

"It went great with the apple slices, Judy," Dan said, looking a bit uncomfortable.

Jack added. "Yeah, Mom, they were your best ever."

Nancy screamed. "DAD!"

There was a splattering sound as Dan turned his head and threw up apple slices, mincemeat pie, and the rest of Christmas dinner.

"You threw up on my phone!" Nancy shrieked, and—gagging—tried to retrieve it from the warm pile of steaming vomit.

"You shouldn't have left it on the couch." Nick grinned.

"*Fuck you*, Nicky." And she stormed up the stairs with her dripping phone held out in front of her. "I *hate* this family!"

Grandpa spoke first and clapped his hands. "Well... what's the next story?"

Dan wiped his mouth and said, "Go ahead, Jack. You've got the book. What is it?"

Jack glanced at his mother, who was oddly fixated on something in the fireplace. He scanned the title. "This is called *Black Friday.*"

BLACK FRIDAY

CONNIE CORCORAN WILSON

December 19, 2014, Friday

"If your mother could see you now!" Ricky's dad wiped the red gore dripping from the six-year-old's bloody nose. "Look at you!" Mr. Towlerton's voice was more anguished than angry. "You're gonna' have a shiner under your left eye. And you've got a bloody nose—AGAIN! This is the third time you've been in trouble at school in the last three weeks. When is this going to stop, Ricky? Who were you fighting with *this* time? What were you fighting about?"

Tom Towlerton sounded more pained than angry. He was distressed and disturbed.

Ricky sniffled. He wiped his runny nose across the sleeve of his holiday-themed reindeer sweater. His hassled father walked across the room to the kitchen sink. Tom grabbed a dish towel hanging from the handle of the oven door, ran warm water over it in the kitchen sink, then twisted it to wring out the excess moisture. She walked back to where Ricky sat, disconsolate, at the kitchen table.

Tom used the dish towel like a cold compress, wiping away much of the grit from his son's face.

The chair Ricky was occupying was dubbed "the hot seat." Ricky only sat there when he was being punished. He served his Time Outs in this particular chair. His usual spot at the Towlerton dinner table was directly across from "the hot seat." His mom, Marion, would normally be seated between Tom and Ricky. She would pass the food to her family during meals. Jump up to get them all second helpings from the stove. Ask the two about their day. Tell them about her own day. Inquire about Ricky's homework. At least, Marion did all that until November 27th, 2014.

Marion Towlerton hadn't been in her usual dinner table seat since November 28th, Black Friday, the day after Thanksgiving.

Tom Towlerton shook his head slowly back and forth, looking at his disheveled son, Ricky's appearance now slightly improved. Tom scowled, a sign of parental disapproval. He bent down on one knee to wipe clean his young son's tear-streaked face with the dampened cloth. The grime and blood from Ricky's altercation with classmate Johnny Dodge was transferred from Ricky's face to the dish towel. This was no Shroud of Turin moment. Tom flung the grungy dishtowel toward the sink. It fell short and hit the floor with a wet thud.

"Mom always said you shouldn't use a dish towel like that," Ricky said, implying shy disapproval, trying to change the subject. "She'd say, 'Dish towels are for dishes; hand towels are for hands.'" Ricky looked up at his hassled father, big brown eyes large and wet with unshed tears. Ricky's slight childish lisp on the letter "s" was like an arrow to his father's already-broken heart.

"Mom's not here," his dad responded. Tom cleared his throat to regain his composure and remain calm. "She's looking down from heaven. She's wondering why you keep getting in all these fights at school."

"I wasn't *at* school, Dad. I was on my way home from school. It was our last day before Christmas—the start of Christmas vacation."

"Well..." Tom Towlerton almost smiled. *(Maybe the kid will grow up to be a lawyer someday, the way he argues with me.)* "Really, Ricky. You've got to try harder to get along with everybody, whether you're at school or on the bus or walking home. Whatever. Wherever. Whenever." Tom paused, and then asked, "Exactly where were you when this fight with Johnny Dodge happened?"

"Twelfth Street. Just past the Nativity scene in front of St. John's Church. Standing in front of Anderson's Department Store with the life-sized Santa cut-out, where Santa is sitting in the fake sleigh in the window."

"So, what was the fight about *this* time?"

"Same thing," said Ricky, sniffling and looking down at the floor.

November 27, 2014

The guests had all enjoyed the annual Thanksgiving meal at the Towlertons. Twenty-five aunts, uncles,

531

cousins, in-laws and, of course, Tom, Marion and Ricky Towlerton. It was Marion's crowning achievement each year to put on the biggest and best Thanksgiving dinner for all the Towlerton relatives, who came from far and near for the feed. The traditional turkey. Dressing. Mashed potatoes. Gravy. Green bean casserole. Scalloped corn. Salads. Rolls. Pies. The whole shebang, preceded by plenty of hors d'oeuvres and libations. Marion always began cooking three days in advance. The entire family looked forward to eating her great food—(*even if some of the relatives were not normally on good terms throughout the rest of the year*). For one day annually, peace reigned. As the meal ended, Marion's sister-in-law, Trudy, asked her, "Are you going out tomorrow to take advantage of all the big sales?" Trudy was a bargain hunter. She would spare no effort to be first in line for the $100 big-screen plasma TV on sale at Best Buy. In fact, once Trudy had slept outside Target in a tent after their Thanksgiving feast, intent upon getting the bargain of the morning. She was Tom's younger sister and a lot of fun, but Marion didn't share Trudy's love of shopping. Nor did Marion approve of Trudy's smoking inside her house. Tom was supposed to tell Trudy not to smoke in the house, but Tom generally avoided confrontation of any kind and wouldn't reprimand his younger sister, even though Tom and Marion had had many private conversations about what a nasty habit smoking was and how it was also a health hazard for young children. Tom's continued silence about Trudy's smoking when they were around Trudy was a bone of contention.

"I don't know, Trudy," Marion said. "The mall will be a mad house..."

"Yes it will be, silly," said Trudy with a laugh. "That's part of the fun. And—-too—all the Christmas decorations will be up at the Galleria. They've got a humongous Santa's house near the skating rink this year, instead of in that children's area. Ricky will love it. You can take him there and get pictures."

"I don't know. Ricky's almost seven," said Marion. "He's getting kind of old for Santa Claus, don't you think? Do you think he still really believes in that stuff?"

"Sure he does," said Trudy. "I heard him telling his cousin Michael that Santa was *real*. Michael wasn't so sure—but, then, Michael is almost ten. Ricky's at that age where kids still believe." Trudy took a drag on her after-dinner cigarette, irritating Marion who was too polite to ask her to put it out. "You've got maybe one good year left. You ought to take Ricky out to see Santa. Get a picture of him sitting on Santa's lap. Enjoy the innocence of childhood one last time. He'll grow like a weed and be too big next year."

And with that, Trudy stubbed out her cigarette in the empty pie plate, got up, and disappeared, heading for the bathroom. Marion waved her hands ineffectually in the air trying to dispel the smoke. Then she hustled the dead cancer-stick to the nearest waste receptacle, muttering under her breath.

Trudy, when urging the Galleria visit, said all this to Marion as though she were an authority. "Besides," Trudy had added, "the madhouse aspect is part of the fun. You should see the lengths some people will go to just to get a bargain!" Trudy laughed cheerfully, failing to recognize the irony of her remark.

Marion sighed, indecisive.

After all the guests left, the words "the innocence of childhood" kept reverberating in Marion's head. Ricky *did* believe in Santa Claus—right now. Would Ricky still believe in him next year, when he was almost eight? *How many more years will Ricky be an innocent child who believes in all the childhood myths?*

She walked into the bedroom, turning off the lights after cleaning up from the evening's festivities, and asked Tom, "Do you think I should take Ricky to the mall tomorrow—Black Friday—to get a picture of him with Santa?"

"I dunno'," said Tom. "Do you *want* to?" Tom was peeling off his socks. Next, he would throw them toward the hamper—and probably miss, as usual.

"Part of me wants to. And part of me doesn't want to fight the crowds out in force bargain hunting the day after Thanksgiving." Marion sighed.

"Well, decide which part of you is strongest and go with that." Tom smiled and walked over to hug his wife, who was removing her jeans. "The Galleria is pretty upscale. All those fancy jewelry stores. Shops like that luggage place that we can't afford. Nordstrom's. Neiman Marcus." Always pragmatic, he added, "If you go, stick with Santa and avoid the stores."

"Oh, Tom. You know that one of the biggest stores is right near where Santa has set up shop this year. I don't have to go *in* the stores, but I'm definitely going to be exposed to all the shoppers who *are* going in all those expensive stores. Ricky will probably come home wanting some horrifically priced monstrosity from Neiman Marcus' window—like a life-sized giraffe or something." They both laughed.

"Well, just keep ye olde budget in mind, hon. Meeting Santa ought to be a big enough thrill for a short visit to the glorious Galleria. Then you can come home and make meatloaf for the three us. We'll be absorbing the cost of this year's Thanksgiving Mega-Feed for a month or so. And, by the way, your usual wonderful job, Dear. Food was *great!*" He pecked his wife of a decade on the cheek.

"Why, thank you, kind sir," said Marion, pretending to curtsey. "I'm glad you enjoyed it. There was absolutely no turkey left over—and that bird originally weighed over twenty pounds. And all the scalloped corn is gone too."

"Well, we'll deal with that tragedy tomorrow. We can buy one of those small turkey breasts and start all over, can't we? We still have the dressing and mashed potatoes and gravy—right?"

"Yes, dear," Marion said, with mock obeisance, sinking down next to him on the bed and enfolding him in her arms in a loving embrace.

Friday, November 28, 2014

Bright and early on Black Friday, Marion and Ricky hopped in the tan Hyundai Tucson van and started driving toward the Galleria Mall at 5085 Westheimer Road, near Post Oak Boulevard. The Galleria in Dallas was not new, although it had been remodeled in 2006. It was the 7th largest mall in America. It got its name from the Galleria Vittorio Emanuele, a shopping arcade in Milan, Italy.

Walking into the mall, Marion never failed to be impressed by the barrel vaulted glass ceiling, interlaced with iron, identical to the treatment above the huge ice skating rink. Although *her* family was not wealthy enough to spend $200,000 at stores like Hermes, Saks and Chanel, Marion still felt the Dallas Galleria was the best true "mall" in the United States, given its scale, size, and mix of luxury and upscale shopping, plus offerings for mid-range buyers like the Towlertons.

This year, rather than having Santa set up in the Little Galleria children's play area, the man-in-red's opulent throne was situated quite near exactly those high-end stores that Tom had warned Marion to avoid. Still, if Santa was receiving his subjects there, that was where Marion and Ricky needed to be. And that was where they were headed.

Marion and Ricky made their way through the throng of holiday shoppers. Marion felt almost claustrophobic in the crush of people. True, the economy was doing better, but this was ridiculous! She was just about to pull Ricky from the throng and exit the mall entirely, when he spied the top of Santa's house and began excitedly pulling his mother toward it through the massive crowd.

"Look, Mom! It's Santa's house. Santa is here!" His face lit up like the sun rising in the east.

Marion knew this, of course, but she had remained mum about the day's plans, hoping to surprise her young son with their planned appointment with the Merry Man in Red. Nothing would do, now, but that they move as quickly as possible to join the other Christmas shoppers in line, waiting for Santa's elves to guide them through the roped-off area until it was Ricky's turn to sit on Santa's lap and tell Santa what he wanted for Christmas.

As they listened to a small cherubic-faced blond boy of about two scream bloody murder in the cordoned off area— a child who definitely needed a nap—Ricky became more and more excited at the prospect of telling Santa about the video games he'd like. The games for his iPad. The skates he had his eye on.

The noise level in the mall was deafening. It was always a bit noisy on weekends, as the sound would travel up to the extremely high vaulted glass ceilings, necessary to provide light in the huge mall, but today the babble was particularly loud. Marion heard what she thought was the sound of firecrackers. *How can they let someone set off firecrackers in the Galleria?*

Ricky had just reached the head of the line. He was being ushered toward Santa by two green-suited elves in pointy-toed boots, elf caps, and red-and-white striped vests paired with green leggings. Ricky climbed onto

Santa's lap. The kindly old gentleman (*and he was a really GOOD Santa*, Marion thought) was just beginning the first of his "Ho! Ho! Ho's!" when Ricky turned to his mother (*standing nearby to offer moral support*) and said, "What's that noise, Mom?"

And then they both saw them: three armed men, faces covered with ski masks, smashing the windows of the expensive jewelry store nearby. Smashing and grabbing. Scooping up the jewelry displayed in the cases. Dumping the loot into black soft-sided bags that were slung across their shoulders. Moving quickly toward them.

A middle-aged mall security guard came running from the Main Galleria, the rink/Nordstrom side, but before the rent-a-cop could reach the center of the storm, he was cut down by gunfire. The shots immediately set off complete crowd chaos. People were running. Falling. Screaming. The guard dragged himself behind a planter, leg and left torso bleeding profusely. A second shot rang out. The guard lay still.

A little girl, standing with her mother, next in line behind Ricky, age four, was so frightened that she began shrieking at the top of her lungs and promptly wet her pants. The smell of urine wafted toward Marion and Ricky.

Santa appeared to be an elderly gentleman with a real white beard (no wig or fake beard.) He looked baffled by the sudden disturbance swelling around his opulent house. Slow to comprehend, perhaps his hearing wasn't as keen as that of younger folk. Santa didn't seem to realize what was happening—until it was too late.

Having ransacked the chi chi stores nearby (Saks. Chanel. Hermes. Neiman Marcus.), three masked gunmen were demanding of everyone that they "hit the ground." Marion, standing next to Ricky and Santa, was too stunned to move at all. Even if she had understood what was being asked of her, she would not have left her child there, vulnerable and alone. She remained standing erect after the gunman's edict. The shortest of the masked and vested trio shot Marion. The bullets entered her abdomen, right shoulder, hip and the right side of her head. She fell to the ground, hitting the terrazzo floor with as much force as though she'd jumped from the balcony above. She lay there, mortally wounded, covered in blood.

When the gunman yelled "Throw over your purse, lady!" at her, it was as though Marion were in a trance. Marion did not comply. She wasn't defying the masked man. She had not fully comprehended what was occurring, initially—too petrified to move. The consequence was death. Nor had the elderly Santa Claus quite figured out what was happening.

"Mama! Mama!" The cries of children echoed throughout the area, a cacophony of terror. One of those shouting was Ricky, who watched in horror as his mother was shot a second and a third time. He remembered nothing but Santa clutching him one moment and his mother bleeding on the floor the next. Although he cried out once, he couldn't hear himself screaming above the din. He was petrified into silence by what happened next.

The gunman turned toward the very life-like Santa and said, "I always hated you, you son-of-a-bitch. You never brought me one damn thing I asked for!" The smash-and-grab thief pulled the trigger. He shot Santa in the head from nearly point-blank range. The mall Santa, bleeding profusely from a ragged hole in the middle of what was left of his forehead, slumped onto the terrified child still seated on his lap. Because Santa died nearly immediately—(*in a horrible and grisly fashion*)—his considerable girth collapsed onto the stunned child (*whose scream was cut short by the impact of the portly adult man*). The costumed figure's body shielded the six-year-old as Santa collapsed onto him, Santa's red suit appearing unstained by the blood dripping from his face to his chest, a liquid which matched the outfit, now giving it a sodden look.

At this point, still silent, Ricky wriggled free of the dead man atop him. He ran to his mother. She gurgled twice. Death throes. Ricky threw himself onto her body. He clutched his mother around the waist, screaming, "Get up, Mommy! Get up!" His arms were red with her blood. And then Ricky fell silent. He didn't utter another sound or make another move for ninety minutes.

That is how and where the authorities found him, an hour later, after the S.W.A.T. team entered the mall and gunned down the trio of would-be robbers. One of the shooters was still exchanging gunfire with officers sixty minutes after Ricky's turn on Santa's lap. The killer had barricaded himself inside the Chanel store.

Ricky lay atop his mother's body, bloodied, unmoving. Shaken. In shock. The police and emergency personnel who emerged from the gunfight victorious went from victim to victim lying on the Galleria floor, searching desperately and frantically for signs of life. When they reached Marion and Ricky, they found the small boy curled in the fetal position, perfectly motionless. Silent. Apparently catatonic. He was unharmed.

At least physically.

Marion Towlerton's funeral was held on Saturday, December 6th.

Ricky's Aunt Trudy came to Dallas from San Antonio (where she and her husband and her ten-year-old son Michael lived) and stayed for a week, taking care of Ricky and her brother Tom. Eventually, Trudy returned to her own family in San Antonio.

School was still in session. Tom Towlerton knew that Marion would not have wanted her only child to miss weeks and weeks of classroom instruction under any circumstances. Tom vowed to try to make Ricky's life as normal as possible for a child who had just witnessed his mother murdered in cold blood. As normal as possible for a child who had felt the clutches of the Grim Reaper while visiting the mall for a happy outing with his mom. As normal as possible for someone who has experienced abject terror and utter hysteria and remained catatonic throughout ninety minutes of chaos—a lack of movement which probably saved Ricky's life from the savagery of the gunmen. The armed assailants opened fire on any unarmed shopper who moved. Twenty-six people were killed, six of them under the age of ten.

No one was spared. If a woman didn't hand over her purse quickly enough, she was shot. If a male shopper refused to throw his wallet to one of the trio when commanded to do so, he too, was shot. In some cases, the individual would be shot whether he complied with the orders of the armed trio or not. The bloody scene was horrific.

"One of the worst mall massacres in history," trumpeted CNN.

Of course, CNN meant one of the worst mall massacres in *United States* history. There had been a far worse mall shooting in Nairobi, Kenya just one year past. On September 21st, 2013, four unidentified gunmen attacked the upscale Westgate Shopping Mall in an attack that lasted three days. Sixty-seven people died, including the four attackers. More than one hundred-seventy-five people were wounded. All four of the gunmen, Islamic zealots from the group al-Shabaab, were killed.

The deadliest United States mall killing, prior to the Dallas Galleria attack that killed Marion Towlerton, was on December 5, 2007, in Omaha, Nebraska. Eight people were shot and killed by nineteen-year-old Robert Hawkins, who then committed suicide.

Virginia Tech. Sandy Hook. Columbine. So many mass shootings in so many other public places, but the deadliest United States mall shooting now was the shooting at the

Dallas Galleria Mall that claimed Marion Towlerton's life and that of fourteen other unsuspecting victims (not including the three attackers.)

On December 8th, 2014, just 11 days after watching his mother die at the Galleria Mall in Dallas, Ricky returned to his first-grade classroom at Ronald E. McNair Elementary School.

At first, everyone treated Ricky as though he were made of glass. They acted as though he might break at any moment. They gave him a wide berth. Special counseling sessions were set up for many of the school's students. There were eight sections of first grade. In those eight sections, at least five children knew of someone who had died at the mall. However, none of them except Ricky had actually been *at* the mall during the attack. And none of them except Ricky had lost a parent to such senseless violence.

All affected youngsters of whatever age at Ronald E. McNair Elementary School were told they could talk about their feelings with a counselor. Many of them, including Ricky, took advantage of this special service.

But some of the less-sensitive young boys in Ricky's class, when the children were alone or playing on the playground, would ask him: "How did it happen? What was it like? Weren't you scared?"

At first, Ricky would just shake his head. He wouldn't respond. He refused to talk about it. Later, however, after two or three days of repeated interrogation by classmates, he began to speak to his friends in first grade about his visit to Santa Claus.

When Ricky told Jimmy Baker about Santa's death, Jimmy was sympathetic and said to Ricky, "How awful that must have been for you! I would have been *so* frightened!"

But there were far more Johnny Dodges in Ricky's large first-grade class than there were sensitive Jimmy Bakers, plus there were the students in older elementary grades. After three days, one of them, Max Black, said, "You're stupid. Santa isn't real." Ricky had just recounted (*for what was beginning to feel like the one millionth time*) how Santa was shot. How Santa Claus had slumped forward, crushing him, right after Marion was shot and killed.

Max Black was held back in first grade. He still did not know how to read in third grade, despite being almost ten. He was a sullen boy of Serbian descent who seemed to always have a knack of bringing down any happy gathering. It was not surprising that he was the one who interrupted Ricky. At the time, Ricky was on the playground talking with a trio of first-graders, two from his class and one slightly older boy he did not know well.

"Santa saved my life," Ricky said solemnly. "After the bad man with the mask shot him—right here—-(*Ricky pointed to his own forehead*)—Santa kind of slumped forward onto me. My mom was already on the floor. She was bleeding real bad." Ricky sniffled at this point, unable to go on.

"What happened next?" asked Max. Max had all the sensitivity of a charging rhino.

"Santa. Santa happened next. He got shot. But he saved me when he fell on me."

"You know that Santa Claus isn't real, don't you, Ricky?" repeated Max Black, his voice a verbal sneer.

Ricky looked at Max and said, defiantly, "Yes he is."

Max laughed. A short unpleasant staccato outburst. "No he isn't, retard. Only babies think Santa Claus is real."

Ricky hit Max in the shoulder. Max hit Ricky back in the face. Black eye and bloody nose number one.

When Ricky returned home from school the weekend of December 13th, after a disagreement with a different classmate, he wasn't sporting a bloody nose or a black eye. But his shirt was torn.

"What happened to your shirt, Ricky?" his father asked.

"This big kid who's in Miss Simpson's first grade section—- he tore it," Ricky said.

Tom gave Ricky the standard lecture about getting along with others and taking care of one's belongings. He didn't know the extent of the pushing and shoving that had occurred on the playground during recess (*which Ricky started*). The incident was forgotten.

On Monday, December 15th

Ricky was involved in another incident with a different boy during gym class. Principal Soames called Tom Towlerton and asked him to come into his office for a conference.

"Mr. Towlerton, I know things have been rough for you and Ricky since—well, since what happened—but he seems to be acting out. We wondered if you'd thought of getting him some private psychiatric counseling. He's been through a terrible ordeal. In fact, he's lucky to be alive. It has to have affected him. We'd like to help him get over it."

"Get over it!" Tom said. Sarcastic. Incredulous. "HE WATCHED HIS MOTHER DIE! How do you 'get over' that?" Tom stormed from the office, angry, without responding further, other than to say he'd think about the psychiatric sessions the school principal suggested.

Tom did arrange for a few private sessions with a psychiatrist, Dr. Rothstein, when he learned it would be covered by his employee insurance at Exxon-Mobile. The sessions were privileged, which meant that the shrink didn't really share every single confidence Ricky told him with Tom Towlerton, but Dr. Rothstein did say to Tom, "You know—it's nice to see a little kid like Ricky after working with so many jaded teenagers. Did you know Ricky still believes in Santa Claus?" Dr. Rothstein smiled as he told Tom this small detail.

"Yes—I know," replied Tom. "It's the main reason Marion took him to the Galleria that day. She wanted to get a picture of Ricky on Santa's lap." Tom thought, *If only Marion hadn't taken Ricky to the Mall to get that picture, she might still be alive today...*

As though reading his mind, Dr. Rothstein said, "Well, don't blame Marion for taking Ricky to see Santa. And don't think it's a bad thing that Ricky still believes in him. It's actually kind of refreshing to meet a little kid who still has that kind of childish innocence. So many kids lose the wonder so young."

With those closing remarks, the two men shook hands and Tom exited Dr. Rothstein's office, where he had stopped for an update on Ricky's progress.

December 19, 2014

Tom Towlerton sat down in his wife's seat, next to his shaken son—a little boy still covered in cuts and scratches and dirt that Tom's efforts had not quite successfully removed. Tom asked, "What happened with Johnny Dodge today, outside Anderson's Department Store? What do you mean by 'the usual?'"

Ricky sat there for a moment, stubbornly bullheaded. Quiet in a sullen way. He didn't know if he wanted to respond. Then he began to speak.

"Dad—every single one of the fights I've been in since...since Mom died....they've all been about the same thing. Kids ask me about the shooting. At first, I try not to talk about it, try not to tell them anything. But they won't leave me alone. At recess, on the bus, walking home, in class: they all want to know the same things. What was it like? Were you scared? How did you survive? What did you do?

At first—like I said—I didn't say anything. But then I started to answer them. (*Tom's heart broke a little bit when Ricky lisped the word 'started' in his six-year-old's voice.*) And

547

tonight, when Johnny Dodge and I were standing in front of that Christmas display in Anderson's Department Store window, I told Johnny, 'That's not the *REAL* Santa Claus. That's just a cardboard cutout of him in a fake sleigh.' Johnny laughed at me and said, 'Dummy—there *is* no *REAL* Santa Claus!'"

"And what did you say, Ricky?" his weary father asked, inwardly fearing the answer.

"I told Johnny Dodge, 'Santa Claus is *too* real! I watched him *die*.'"

A FAMILY CHRISTMAS TERROR

CHAPTER 19

"That was pleasant," Judy said.

"I think I'm getting sober," Nick added.

Grandpa said, "Judy, another round of port for whoever wants—or needs—one after that story— except Dan, of course."

"Mind your own business, old man." Dan shakily raised his glass.

"I've already got the decanter, Dan," Judy said, rolling her eyes in disgust. She filled his glass.

"More!" Dan roared, pushing his glass at her, dark red liquid sloshing over the sides.

Judy looked at the pile of vomit on the couch. "Are you going to clean that up?"

Dan looked at it, then back at her. He shrugged. He picked up a cushion and dropped it over the smelly mess. "There. Happy?"

Judy stared steely-eyed at him, turned and set the bottle on the mantel. She walked to the foot of the stairs and turned back to the men. "Thank you for ruining the day, *Dan!* Merry *FUCKING CHRISTMAS!*" And she stomped up the stairs.

"What's her problem?" Dan muttered into his drink.

Nick silently walked to the mantel and grabbed the bottle. He sat back down and took a swig.

Jack looked at the others. "*Secret Satan: A Christmas Story.*"

SECRET SATAN:
A CHRISTMAS TALE

JEFF DEPEW

Pitch wiped the honey off his hands with a dirty rag and gazed around Hell. He sighed. Was his shift over yet? He stood beside an immense, circular abyss, miles across. When he looked up through the swirling, smoky air, he could sometimes catch a glimmer of light. Up Top. The surface world. Home of the humans. And above that? Heaven.

If he walked down and around the winding paths along the edge of the Abyss, he would eventually find himself at another level, complete with its own type of sinner and specific torment. And if he followed the paths even further, walking down and down and down, he would get to the bottom. The Pit. Lakes of fire. Immense palaces made of human bones. Cauldrons of boiling human fat. Constant screaming. And the Big Guy himself. Satan. But nope. Pitch was up here, in a place that was barely part of Hell.

Fifteen hundred years of loyal servitude to his Infernal Lord and Master, and he made one little mistake. It wasn't even his fault. Eons ago, he had been the assistant manager of the premier banquet hall on Level Nine. Not a prestigious job, but not bad. Pitch had been preparing for the Feast of Empusa, who, at the time, was one of Satan's concubines. It was a grand affair, and her retinue of imps had painstakingly planned the menu. Pitch was given a menu that called for "Twenty-One Year Olds." So Pitch (with much difficulty, thank you very much) had found a dozen twenty-one-year-old virgins and served them up, lightly broiled. How was he supposed to know the menu should have read "Twenty One-Year Olds"? Apparently, Empusa favored infants. The fatter the better.

Well, it hadn't been a pretty scene, and Empusa was not forgiving. Even though she didn't complain until after she'd devoured the twenty-one-year-olds. And had asked if there were any more. But, a mistake had been made. She had been dishonored. And Pitch was in charge. So he had been demoted up several Levels. All because of a misplaced hyphen.

The rules of punctuation were a lost art, Pitch mused. So now he was stuck here, working in one of the outer levels of Hell, beside the black waters of the River Acheron. The Uncommitted, souls who had never made any real decisions in life, spent eternity here. The weak, the complacent, the yes-men, three-year community college students and the like. There were some angels here, those who had not taken sides in the Great Battle. But they pretty much kept to themselves. The human Shades wandered about aimlessly over rocky terrain covered with writhing, biting worms and beetles. Stinging wasps, hornets, and mosquitoes filled the air, darting and swooping at the exposed flesh of the Damned.

A ragged crimson banner zigzagged through the air, several feet off the ground, fruitlessly pursued by dozens of desperate souls. Others struggled to stand on rocks or sought shelter in narrow crevices, seeking a brief respite from the constantly biting insects. Good luck with that.

Pitch sighed again. Back to work. He began wheeling his battered, wooden pushcart over the rocky, worm-covered ground. Fat, obscene worms burst as the wheels crushed them. Shrill shrieks followed in his wake, along with the stench of their bright green ichor. They wouldn't stay dead for long though. Nothing died down here. Except my dreams, Pitch waxed poetically.

There were walkways and paths carved into the sides of the cavern by centuries of use, but they were not well maintained by any means, and the pushcart rattled and bounced as he pushed it along. Ancient torches were set into the walls, although they didn't really provide any light. Just added to the smoky air.

Pitch scowled, swatting a particularly determined wasp. The stinging insects didn't bother Pitch. Their stingers couldn't penetrate his thick, pebbly skin, so they basically left him alone. When one was foolish enough to try to sting him, more often than not Pitch grabbed it, squeezed its head, and ate it. A minor perquisite of his current job. Speaking of jobs, it was show time.

"Hey, losers! I got your insect repellent! Get your insect repellant! Guaranteed relief!" Ragged heads turned. Hollowed eyes widened in anticipation and hope. Tattered, emaciated forms shuffled toward him, crowded around him, skeletal hands open and grasping.

"Hold on, take your turn. There's plenty for everyone!" Pitch said, rapidly handing out tubes labeled "Insect Repellent-Extra Strength." In less than five minutes, he had given away his entire supply.

"Sorry, all out. Get me next time." The shades drifted off, clumsily smearing the amber fluid on their exposed bodies. Others, further back, returned empty-handed to their spots along the rock walls. A scuffle broke out as three or four Shades fought over one bottle.

Moans began to pick up. Swarms of insects were aggressively besieging the Shades who had taken the tubes. The ragged souls weakly swung their arms and swatted vainly at the insects, but it made no difference. One of them, completely covered with hornets and wasps stumbled into the side of a cliff and fell over. Biting insects swarmed over it, and within seconds, there was nothing left but glistening bone.

Pitch stood, arms akimbo, watching his handiwork. He had spent the better part of the morning squeezing out the actual insect repellant and refilling the tubes with honey.

He felt no pleasure in this. Not like he used to. It was too easy. And they fell for it every time. He did it three times a day, every day. Not that there were "days" and "nights" down here. However, there was the time clock, and that was what mattered. The work cycle determined when they worked, when they ate, when they slept. And speaking of the time clock, he was almost off. In fact, Vlad, his replacement, was slowly making his way up the circular path. Pitch wheeled the cart back to the plastic bear-shaped honey bottles, which were magically refilling, as they did three times a day, and took off his leather apron.

Pitch was short by human standards, about four feet tall and just as wide. He had no neck to speak of, had to turn his entire torso to look from side to side. His skin was dark orange and very pebbly and tough. His eyes were large, with vertical slits like a cat's. His nose was broad over a large mouth full of short, sharp teeth. His arms were long and muscular and hung down past his knees, although his legs were short and bowlegged. He wore a soiled breechcloth made of some type of skin; lizard, or human, he wasn't sure. And he served his master faithfully.

He finished wiping down the cart. He kicked a skull over the edge of the Circle. He watched it bounce off the rock walls and disappear into the darkness below. Below. That's where all the action was. Not up here with these losers. Pitch ducked as the banner flew close to his head, followed by dozens of emaciated, insect-bitten poor souls chasing it in vain.

"Watch it, you morons," he growled, shoving one of the stragglers. The Shade was an old woman, and she weighed almost nothing. She staggered toward the edge of the rocky path that led around the edge of the Pit. She stood on the edge, her arms pin-wheeling for balance, mouth open in a silent scream. A heavy arm reached out, planted a meaty hand on her bony chest, and shoved. She went over the edge, tumbled in the swirling air, caught by the wind, and slammed into the side of the pit. Her battered, broken body fluttered downward.

Vlad, a heavyset Level Three demon, guffawed. He was wearing his usual outfit of mismatched chainmail and armor. Today he had on a metal Viking helmet with a ram's horn on either side of it. It was much too small, and Vlad had fashioned a chinstrap out of a length of tendon, which was tightly knotted beneath his protruding lower jaw.

"That was a good one, eh, Pitch?" he said, gazing happily into the pit. "She spun at least three times before she hit the side. Normally the best I can get is two, maybe two and a half."

Pitch nodded beside him. "Yeah. Barnaby said he got a seven spinner once, but you know Barnaby."

"Full of shit," agreed Vlad. "The secret is to aim for the middle of the Abyss. Avoid the sides as much as possible. Anyways, how was it today?"

"How is it every day?" Pitch shrugged. "You know nothing ever changes."

"Is that so bad?" Vlad asked pulling two time cards from an uneven slot on the rock wall. He glanced at them and handed one to Pitch. Pitch slid his card in the time clock until there was an audible click. A puff of black smoke came from the top of the time clock. Pitch put his card back in the slot in the wall as Vlad clocked in.

"I guess," Pitch lied. Like many of the Legions in Hell, Vlad was content. He had a place and a purpose. He was a demon, a tormentor of lost souls. And that was enough for him. But Pitch felt something was missing. He was so close to Hell and could even see the flames at times, but was unable to get any closer. He was so far from the action down in the Pit. Barnaby, of course, said that he had met Satan twice, but as everyone knew, Barnaby was a liar. He wasn't called Barnaby the Deceitful for nothing.

Vlad sat on a wooden stool, emptying a bottle of insect repellant into a wide pool filled with murky water. Beside the pool was a handwritten, wooden sign stating "Drinking Water." Several skeletons lay nearby. Vlad nodded out over the Abyss.

"I know you'd rather be down there, but I like it up here. No pressure. They tell me when to get up, when to work, when to quit. It's easy. And I get to mess with these jokers—oh no you don't!" A shade was reaching for one of the bottles. Vlad picked him up by the scruff of his neck, shook him, and slammed him into a huge boulder. His skull collapsed with a loud crunch. Bits of bone and brain splattered the rock. Vlad turned and flung him headlong into the Abyss. They watched him fall.

"Two spinner," Vlad remarked disappointedly, getting back to work.

"You'd better be careful," warned Pitch. "You've lost two already." Loss Prevention allowed them to "... misplace, reallocate, destroy, or devour..." seven souls per shift. Pitch had never lost more than one. But did anyone recognize that? Of course not.

Vlad shrugged. "What am I going to do? I'm a passionate guy. And it's not like they're losing anything." He nodded, gesturing toward the unfortunate soul he had just thrown over the cliff. "That joker'll be back by my next shift."

Pitch couldn't think of a response to that. "Well, see you tomorrow." He nodded as he headed down the path to his cave.

"You too, buddy." Vlad nodded. "And Pitch—"

Pitch paused, turned back.

"Relax, man. You're too stressed out. Have some fun." He showed his enormous teeth in an encouraging smile. A Shade had been sneaking towards him saw that smile and slowly backed away. Vlad scowled at him. "You'd better keep moving."

As Pitch slowly made his way around the circular, stone path, occasionally kicking a skull out of his way, he wondered why he couldn't relax. Things weren't so bad. He had a good job, a comfortable sleeping mat, and a few acquaintances and friends. It could be worse, he thought, watching as another shade fell through the air. Pitch shook his head. Vlad loved his work.

A dark shape flew up and snatched the unfortunate soul out of midair. A harpy. Her leathery bat wings flapped rapidly, holding her suspended in space as she tore at the shade. Clawed hands pulled and twisted, and with a wet popping sound, she tore off an arm. She let go of the body, which continued its descent.

"Hey, Pitch." She nodded, her mouth full of blood and rotten meat. Her yellow eyes glinted in the misty light.

"Oh hi, Sybal." Pitch waved. "What's up?"

She landed beside him, still tearing at the arm. "I'm passing the word. He's doing Christmas again."

Sybal wiped her mouth with a feathered forearm and held out the bloodied limb out to Pitch.

He shook his head at the offered arm. He had outgrown a taste for human flesh years ago.

"Christmas already?" It was so hard to measure time down here. Most Demonkind were not even aware of the concept of time. Eternity was just... eternity. But ages ago Pitch had found a soiled copy of a 1952 Greenway Auto Parts calendar. It was full of scantily-clad human females engaging in various recreational activities. He kept it in his hovel, beside his sleeping mat. He didn't understand how months worked, but he liked to keep track of the seasons and holidays. When he got home, he would change the month to December.

"I still don't understand why, out of all the Surface holidays, he chose Christmas." Pitch shook his head in bewilderment.

"The way I hear it, the Big Guy likes to throw a bone to the unfortunate ones every once in a while. I guess that just because we're in Hell, it doesn't have to be "hell," if you know what I'm saying."

"I guess." Pitch shrugged. "But Christmas?"

"It's also a big 'fuck you' to Him." She nodded upwards.

He glanced up, then met her gaze. "So I suppose they're doing the Secret Santa again?"

"Yeah." She sucked the flesh off the pinkie finger, looked over the arm one more time, grunted, and flung it over the edge. "I just signed up." She glanced around, motioned at a female Shade struggling to fill a battered colander from a muddied water hole. "Hey, you! Come here!"

The Shade bowed its shoulder and approached. Sybal reached out and grabbed her shroud, pulling her close. She used it to wipe her mouth and shoved the Shade away. "Get back to work!" The Shade put its head down and returned to its endless task. Sybal turned back to Pitch. "I gotta go. I'll see you later."

Pitch held up a claw and watched her leap over the abyss, catch an updraft, and rocket up and away.

*

The commissary was unusually loud and boisterous. The Christmas decorations and the excitement and uncertainty of the upcoming Secret Santa gift exchange had buoyed the spirits of the Demonkind. Garlands made of intestines stretched across the length of one wall. The upside-down crosses were turned right-side up. Volunteer imps wearing crimson Santa caps had been nailed to each one.

Laughter and chatter rang throughout the cavern as Pitch approached the food line. He took a battered metal tray from the stack and slid it along the counter. A heavyset Shade wearing a loincloth and a stained chef's hat spooned some type of brown sludge onto his tray. Pitch peered at it. He wasn't sure what it was, but there was something wriggling in it, so it couldn't be too bad. He looked over at the other choices of side dishes on the steam table.

"What's that?" he asked, indicating a red, mucus-like liquid in which an eyeball floated. The Shade looked at him vacantly. Pitch shook his head. "Forget it. Just give me some. With extra eyeballs."

Pitch glanced around for a familiar face. A burst of laughter caught his attention and he glanced over to the right. Of course. The SCS table. They always sat together, with their matching jackets: black with white sleeves along with the fiery-red badge emblazoned with "SCS." The Soul Collection Squad.

Occasionally Satan would leave the confines of Hell and travel Up Top. Often, while there, he would come to some type of "arrangement" with a human. Some wanted ultimate power; others asked for fortune, fame, knowledge. Always with the knowledge, Pitch thought. When would they learn? Too much knowledge is a curse.

The Soul Collection Squad was a group of specially trained and selected demons who would travel up and arrive just as a human whose soul had been claimed by Satan was about to die. As it turned out, many humans who entered into contracts with Satan were not always willing to "come quietly" when it was their time. So Satan had assembled a group of enforcers whose job it was to make sure, when the humans' contracts were up, they wound up in Hell.

When a contract was due, the Collection Squad would travel up and surround the body, protecting it from Death, and yank out the soul. They never came willingly. Always kicking and screaming, pleading: "I didn't mean it" "I'm sorry!" "Christ, please forgive me!" As if that ever helped. Soul in tow, the Squad would return to Hell and leave Death behind with his empty vessel. "Bastards!" he would reportedly shout, shaking a bony fist. But he wasn't really mad. It was business. It was the way things were.

In the Long Ago, Pitch had dreamed of being part of the Soul Collection Squad. That was before things went north and he was demoted. All he wanted to do now was maintain a low profile, do his job, and eventually try for a promotion. Another shout, followed by raucous laughter from the SCS table. Pitch sighed and found a seat across the room.

Pitch was joined by Ogilvie, an enormous, flaming ifrit whom he had worked with before in Level Six. There were some other demons he recognized, but he didn't know their names or duties. All anyone could talk about was the Secret Santa.

In the past, Satan always participated. And he liked everyone else to as well. It was considered bad form not to. The actual gift exchange ceremony would take place in the main hall in Pandemonium, the greatest of Satan's palaces. Satan towered over all on his immense throne, attended by his imps and concubines, as hundreds of demons and members of his inner circle watched and exchanged gifts. Satan commented and praised, or, in most cases, openly mocked and derided those whose gifts he considered less than worthy.

And he always saved himself for last. The grand finale. If Satan picked your name, the gifts could be phenomenal. There was talk that he had once given a two-year pass Up Top, and another time he had presented Hitler, wearing nothing but a spiked collar, as a personal valet. If Satan drew your name, it could be existence changing.

On the other hand, you definitely did not want to PICK Satan's name. He was extremely critical of his gifts and often punitive if he did not like them. And he liked very few gifts. How could he? He had everything. There were stories about how he had tortured and even imprisoned givers of less-than-worthy gifts. Many demons swore away from the Secret Santa gift exchange just so they wouldn't be the one to pull Satan's name.

Another downside to the whole gift exchange was that whoever picked your name would give you a terrible gift. Last Secret Santa, Vlad's gift was supposed to be the thigh bone of Pope St. Fabian. At least that's what the card had said. Instead, it had been the leg bone of a goat. A goat. It just wasn't worth the aggravation.

And then there was the choosing a gift for some demon you didn't even know. What were you supposed to get? True, this was one of the few occasions when demons were allowed to go Up Top to obtain a gift if they wished, but most just scrounged around or rummaged through their belongings or the trash piles and came up with something they didn't want anymore. As far as Pitch was concerned, the only reason to enter the gift exchange was for the slight chance that Satan pulled your name. And what were the odds of that? So why bother?

During lunch, a crowd had been growing just outside the entrance to the canteen. After eating, Pitch walked over and saw demons surrounding a Shade on his hands and knees, supporting a carved wooden crate labeled "Secret Santa." A line of demons had formed, and he watched as they each approached the box, one at a time, wrote their name down (or made their mark, in the case of the Cyclopes) on a scrap of paper, fold it, and stick it in the slot at the top of the crate. Two enormous Djinn stood on either side of the crate, arms folded across massive chests, their burning eyes scanning the crowd.

The crowd hushed. Pitch followed their gaze. A trio of striking Succubi strolled over, and the demons parted to let them pass. They wore sheer gowns, which, like their hair, flowed around them, even though there was no breeze. They seemed to move in slow motion as they approached the front of the line. Even the Djinn were eyeing them. The Succubi spoke quietly, heads together, and then each put a slip of paper in the slot. They glanced haughtily around at the staring throng. One of them caught Pitch's gaze. She whispered to the other two, who looked him up and down with their beautiful, pitiless eyes, and laughed quietly as they strode away, hips swaying. A few of the others turned to look at Pitch curiously. One of the SCS guys, a huge Minotaur, elbowed another and stifled his laughter.

Pitch scowled. Who the Heaven were they to laugh at him? He wasn't good enough to enter the Secret Santa? Fine. He strode up to the crate, snatched a piece of paper, scrawled his name, folded it, and shoved it in the slot. Done. He took three steps away and paused. *What have I done?*

*

A pop! woke Pitch up. A small scroll hung suspended in the air beside him. He mumbled something and rolled over. The scroll floated over him. Pitch tried to go back to sleep. Something nudged his cheek. He brushed it away. Nudge. Nudge. He opened his eyes and batted the scroll away. It zipped out of reach and then came back to rest in front of him. Pitch sighed, sat up, and snatched the scroll. He untied the rough twine and unrolled it. A small, shiny paper square fell out and he picked it up. A twelve-hour Surface Pass. For getting a gift.

He tore open the scroll and scanned it up and down.

"Congratulations, you have decided to participate in the Secret Santa Gift Exchange. You will be giving a gift to..."

Pitch closed his eyes. He opened them again and looked at the scroll. Nope. Still there.

You will be buying a gift for SATAN.

Pitch stared at the scroll. He put it down, stood up, and walked to the opening of his hovel. He was having trouble breathing. He went back to his pallet and sat down and picked up the scroll.

How did this happen? Exactly what he DIDN'T want. Out of all the things he wanted, this was the last. He crumpled up the scroll and put his head in his claws.

*

"So I hear you decided to do Secret Santa." Vlad leaned against the time clock.

Pitch looked up from the bottle of insect repellant he was emptying. "Yeah. Yeah"

"So who'd you get?"

"I dunno. Some minor demon. I forget his name." He looked away.

"Huh." Vlad sounded doubtful. "I got some joker named Drizzle. Down on Level Four."

"What are you going to get him?" Pitch asked hopefully. He needed an idea. Any idea.

"I took a dagger off a newly arrived Shade. Supposed to have been one of the daggers that stabbed Caesar." It was common practice for many Demonkind to await the arrival of Charon's ferryboat, which brought the newly dead to the shores of the Underworld. The Shades' first experience with the hospitality of Hell was often when they were beaten, robbed, torn limb from limb, and occasionally partially devoured. They couldn't be killed, as they were already dead, but reconstituting themselves from the bits and pieces left behind was a difficult, agonizing procedure.

"That's a good idea." Pitch nodded. He paused. "So... have you heard who got Satan's name?

"Nope." Vlad shook his heavy head. "Nobody's said nothing. At least to me."

Pitch pretended to think about this. "I wonder who it could be. What do you think they'll get him?"

"Hold on." Vlad growled and grabbed a nearby Shade that had been sneaking toward the insect repellant. "How many times do I have to tell you?" He lifted the Shade up, holding him by the shoulder and leg. He grunted and pulled and tore the Shade in half, showering himself and Pitch with gore. Blood and internal organs slid out of the body, splattering wetly on the ground. Vlad laughed at the still struggling Shade and threw the pieces over his shoulder. Maggots and worms burrowed up from the ground to get at the blood and torn flesh.

"Hey!" Pitch said, wiping his face.

"Sorry, buddy," Vlad replied, licking blood off his hands. "But anyway, who knows what to get Satan? I'm sure as Heaven glad I didn't pick his name. Remember a couple times back when that satyr gave him a portrait painted with the blood of innocents? Satan had him drawn and quartered right there in the main hall and had the pieces nailed up on the walls?" Vlad chuckled. "I think they're still there."

Pitch stared at him, silent.

At dinner that night all anybody talked about was Secret Santa—who picked whose name, and what gift they were planning on giving and/or getting. Pitch was unusually silent, just listening, not eating. The Demonkind jabbered on about legendary swords with jeweled hilts, skulls with eyes of flame, enchanted rings, magical haunches of never-ending meat. But none of these gifts spoke to him. Satan would already have all of these things—and then some. No, Pitch had to find him something unusual, something special... but what?

Doubt and uncertainty ringing in his head, he got up from the table, deposited his tray, and headed home.

Pitch had never been Up Top before, but had heard all about it. Few of the Demonkind had, until the advent of the Secret Santa. Sure, there was a possession here and there, or some fool summoned up a demon once in a while, but these were rare, and more often than not, Satan was involved.

When Pitch went Up Top, he wouldn't be alone. Thousands of Demonkind would be invading the Earth, in various guises, over the next few work cycles. They couldn't just go Up Top in their usual forms. That would cause panic and, more importantly, remove doubt. The Big Guy (God) was very particular about faith. "Anyone can perform a miracle and people will believe," He'd once said. "But how many can NOT perform a miracle and still get people to believe? Hmm? That's the trick. I haven't done anything in thousands of years and they still believe." He could so smug sometimes.

*

He sat in his hovel, leaning against the wall. He couldn't sleep.

Satan. What do you get Satan for Christmas? He had everything. And if he didn't have it, he didn't want it. Precious gems, gold, silver, the Daggers of Megiddo in a display case—Satan had it. A pool filled with unholy water. A pillar of salt. A jar containing an unbaptized infant. Marble statues, gold statues, statues made of shit, living (or unliving) statues forbidden to move. There was nothing new in Hell. That's why they went to Earth to get gifts.

No one but Satan ever got a "new" gift in Hell. Everything had to found or stolen. They called it "regifting," and Satan had sent a cadre of demons Up Top to spread the concept of regifting in order to infect and spoil the "true meaning of Christmas." Surprisingly, the humans had taken to regifting like flies to offal. When the demons had returned telling tales of the vast amount of loot in the Human marketplaces, Satan had decided to allow them to travel there to get gifts. The only catch was they weren't allowed to pay for anything. Apparently that was another way for Satan to soil/ruin Christmas.

The only approved way Up Top was through one of the portals. There were two located on each level, and they were closely monitored and heavily guarded. Unauthorized travel Up Top was strictly monitored. No one was allowed Up without a pass, and the passes were only good for a few Earth hours. Occasionally a demon was allowed out for longer, for a more involved job like a possession. Pitch's pass was only good for the next work cycle, so he would have to work fast.

At this time, most of the Earth marketplaces were crammed with shoppers, so a little extra chaos would go unnoticed. Some of the Demons loved taking the forms of children and heading to the toy aisles to wreak havoc: opening boxes, tearing apart toys, screaming. Pitch had heard of a place called "Walm-Aht" where the demons especially loved to go during Christmas time. Chaotic. Noisy. Almost like Hell.

The portals were built into the rock walls. They were fairly wide, so several demons could travel at a time, which helped the line move quickly. From a distance, the portals resembled caves. But as one got closer, you could see a faint blue light undulating at the far end, deep inside. Pitch waited in line, listening to the excited talk around him. He wished he could share their enthusiasm. Once he was at the front, he showed his card to one of the Minotaurs standing guard and was nodded through. He stepped into the portal.

"Remember to close the door behind you," the Minotaur growled.

Pitch turned back as he entered the portal. "What—" he had time to ask before he was seized.

A sudden burst of bright white light and it felt as though his body had being grabbed by a giant fist and crumpled up into a ball. He was pulled, twisted, and turned inside out. Everything went black. He smacked hard into a cold, wet surface, and all was still.

Pitch groaned and opened his eyes. There had to be a better way to travel Up Top than this. He had heard rumors of an ebony staircase that moved, and all you had to do was stand on it and you would be taken up. It was only accessible through a room in Satan's palace. Barnaby insisted he had been on it twice, but... you know. Barnaby.

He got to his feet and looked around. He was in a small cubicle with walls that did not quite reach all the way to the floor or ceiling. Was this a prison cell of some type? There was a white porcelain seat with a hole in the middle. But why would—? Pitch looked in the hole. Ah. Human feces. Then he remembered. A toilet. He never understood the human desire to eliminate their waste. Why not leave it out to fester and bloom? How else do you keep others away from your sleeping mat? He fumbled with the latch on the door for a moment and stepped out into a larger, shiny room. Mirrors were set above a long counter that ran the length of the wall. There were more circular, white porcelain openings in the counter. Ah, were these toilets as well? Before he could find out, he remembered the Minotaur's warning and turned and closed the stall door. There was a sign on it that read "Out of Order." So this would be his way back as well.

Pitch approached the counter and looked in the openings. No feces. He caught his reflection in the mirror and he jerked back. He'd seen humans, of course, but only in their undead state. He'd never really paid much attention to them. Was this what living humans looked like? Pitch moved closer. A round, pink human face gazed back at him.

Short brown hair. He held up his hands. Pink. With five (five?) round-tipped fingers. They would be worthless for ripping out an enemy's throat. The eyes were small and round and the teeth were laughable. So few and so flat. What did they eat up here—paste? He was wearing a black, short-sleeved shirt with "HERE COMES TROUBLE!" stenciled in garish green neon across the front. Pitch felt around behind him. No tail. Interesting. He pulled the front of his shorts out and looked down. He was male.

The door burst open and two humans entered. Pitch backed away, thought about racing back to the stall, and then remembered. I look just like them. As far as they know, I'm human too. He watched them closely.

"...and when I see Santa I'm going to give him a big hug!" the smaller human proclaimed excitedly.

The larger one, most likely a guard or keeper of some sort, smiled and nodded. "I'm sure he'll love that. Everyone loves a hug." He helped the small one unfasten his pants and approach yet another porcelain receptacle, but this one was built vertically into the wall. Pitch watched, curious. Ahh. That's what it was for. The adult human glanced at Pitch. "Are you going to see Santa, too?"

"Uhh. Umm. Yes?" Pitch started at the sound of his voice. Clear and high pitched. Almost like a female's. And the way his voice resonated in this tiled chamber! He began hooting and shouting, listening with delight as his voice reverberated around the room. The larger human bent down beside the smaller one and whispered something in his ear. His eyes never left Pitch. As they made their way out of the bathroom, they stayed as far away from Pitch as possible. The smaller one turned and waved his hand and called out, "Bye! See you in line!" as the door closed.

Line? What line? Remembering that he had only a limited amount of time to find a gift, Pitch yanked the door and ventured out.

Sparkles. Noise. Humans. Glitter. White. Green. Red. Everywhere. He spun around, trying to find some sense of direction. He wasn't sure where he was, but it seemed to be some type of indoor trading post or marketplace. He saw the word "MACY'S" plastered on walls and pillars, surrounded by tinsel and streamers. Green, pointed trees decorated with small shiny objects were placed seemingly everywhere. Signs pointed him in different directions: Housewares, For Him, For Her, Home Furnishings, and on and on.

He walked through the crowded marketplace, eyes darting all around. Would Satan like a necklace? He had so many. Pitch approached a table and picked up a black cylinder with a clear top. He wasn't sure what that was, but it was black and shiny. It appeared to be a container of some kind. He glanced at the sign: Coffee Grinder. What's coffee? Did Satan like coffee? He sighed and put the cylinder back. This was hopeless. He had no idea what to get.

He spotted several Demonkind in various guises throughout the store. One, wearing the form of a tall human male, was at a glass case, asking to try on a diamond bracelet. As the worker turned away to retrieve it, the demon quickly reached out and snatched a ring off of the counter. Another was surreptitiously tearing the price tags off of clothing items. Pitch wished he had time to enjoy himself, but he needed to get moving.

A group of humans, two adults—male and female—and three smaller ones, hurried past. He heard one of the young ones point to a sign and squeal.

"Santa! Santa's this way!"

Pitch turned. He'd heard of Santa. He lived Up Top. He was some kind of minor god. He accepted offerings of sweetened breads and bovine mammary liquid, and in exchange, gave gifts to human children every Christmas. Surely Santa would know what to give Satan.

Pitch followed the human family group (which was what he assumed they were) to the end of a long queue. It consisted of similar family groups, with tense, harried, overstimulated young ones. Two demons were in line. One wore the form of an infant in a wheeled carriage of some sort. He was gleefully screaming his heart out, but to the humans, he appeared to be crying. The other demon, posing as a maternal figure, paid no attention and placidly tapped on some sort of glowing device in her hands. Pitch noticed many of the parents were doing the same, ignoring their children for these strange small glowing devices. What were they? He sidled up and glanced over the shoulder of an adult woman to sneak a peek at her device. A kitten? They were looking at pictures of kittens? But why? Sure, kittens were delicious, but humans didn't eat them. They kept them as household servants. At least that's what he'd been told. The line moved forward and Pitch went with it.

Near the end of the line he passed beneath a red-and-white arch that read "Welcome to the North Pole." White, sparkly powder was spread the floor on either side of the queue. Pitch wondered if it was edible. Large, colorfully decorated boxes sat in piles here and there. A small fence made of large, red-and-white canes lined a red-and-white brick path. Pitch scoffed. That fence wouldn't keep anyone out.

More humans wearing colorful green-and-red outfits with pointed hats were taking the children by the hand away from their adults. The children were led toward a red-garbed figure sitting on a large throne. The parents stood to the side and watched their offspring. Pitch pushed forward for a better look. Were they being sacrificed? An old white-bearded human, wearing a suit of red, sat atop a golden throne. Pitch had seen his likeness on posters throughout the store. This was Santa. He squeezed between a large human woman and her husband. A tiny child of indeterminate sex stood between them, idly exploring a nostril with a dirty finger.

"Hey! Watch it!" The woman grabbed his shoulder. "Come on, kid, you have to wait your turn." Pitch glared at her, but backed off. The first rule of going Up Top was "Blend in." The woman looked down at him smugly. She yanked her child's hand out of his/her nose and held it tightly. The child took his/her other hand, pointed a finger, and got back to work.

Finally it was Pitch's turn. A smiling female human approached him, holding out her hand. She was wearing a green dress and a red pointed hat. Her ears were also pointed, but Pitch saw with disappointment that they were false ears. False ears?

"Come on with me, sweetheart." Pitch took her hand and she led him along the fake-brick walkway.

"Are you excited to see Santa?"

Pitch looked up at her big red smile and blinked.

"Don't be scared, sweetheart." She knelt beside him and whispered conspiratorially in his ear. "What are you going to ask Santa for?"

"I'm not sure," Pitch replied. Which was the truth. What did one ask Santa for? He remembered the small human in the bathroom. "Should I hug him?"

"Of course! Santa loves hugs from little boys and girls! It's his favorite thing, next to milk and cookies!" She giggled unconvincingly. She glanced around at the adult humans.

"Where are your mommy and daddy?"

"Oh, they're in Hell," Pitch replied, looking past her. Santa was speaking earnestly to a young human female whose face was flush with excitement. She was leaving, but turned and reached up and put her arms around him. Santa laughed good-naturedly and put his arms around her. That was a hug. Pitch knew that much. The girl released Santa and clambered down the steps with the help of yet another Santa's helper. Two adult humans were there to greet her at the bottom. They held up their kitten viewers at her and then they hugged her. So much hugging.

"It's your turn," said the female Santa's helper, shoving Pitch forward. There was no inflection in her voice. She avoided looking at him.

Santa's throne was not as grand as Satan's, but it was still something. He could see right away that the gold wasn't real. And where were the human skulls?

Pitch walked up the steps. Santa was beaming broadly. Another of Santa's helpers stood beside him, this one a scrawny male with a spotty face. As Pitch stepped on the top level, he reached down and lifted Pitch up. Pitch was too startled to resist and before he knew it, he was planted on Santa's lap. He looked up at the twinkling eyes, the ruddy cheeks, remembered himself, and reached around Santa as far as his stubby human arms could go. Santa laughed and put an arm around his shoulder. Pitch held on. A hug. His first hug. It was odd, being this close to someone and not inflicting pain on them. Pitch didn't know if he liked it or not. Santa continued to laugh, but when he removed his arm from Pitch's shoulder and the laughter became forced, Pitch let go.

"So what's your name, buddy?" asked Santa.

"Umm... Pitch, sir."

"Pitch, hmm. That's a wonderful name! So what would you like me to bring you for Christmas?"

"Umm... well it's not for me, exactly."

Santa looked puzzled. But then his familiar smile returned. "Ho ho ho! What a good little boy! So who would like me to bring a present for?"

Thirty seconds later, two burly Santa's helpers were half dragging, half carrying Pitch past the line of waiting humans. He had time to note that several pointed their kitten viewing devices at him as he passed. There were audible clicks.

"Wait! He didn't even tell me what to—" They ignored his protests, releasing him just inside what appeared to be the main doors. Pitch squinted against the bright light shining through the transparent doors. The two Santa's helpers strode away without looking back.

Pitch sighed. What now? He had no gift and time was running out. He tried to imagine a best-case scenario if he had no gift to give Satan. The best-case scenario was the same as the worst-case scenario. Dismal. Humiliation, torment, demotion. If he was lucky.

He looked around in a last ditch effort to find a gift. A comfy chair? Clothing? Quality footwear? No. No. No! He wanted to scream in frustration. Why couldn't he have picked Vlad's name? A bloody bone. A broken spoon. Vlad would be overjoyed at either gift.

He strode back into the bowels of Macy's, his head lowered in defeat. That's when he heard it. A beautiful tinkling sound. Music. But not like the muddy music that blared through the hidden speakers in the ceiling. No—this was more delicate... more elegant. This music spoke to him.

He followed the sound past a large plastic tree covered with white clumps of powdered plastic. Beside the tree was a table on which sat several small boxes. One of them was open, and a tiny figure spun slowly as the music played.

Pitch was enthralled. He moved closer. The delicate figure slowed and stopped and the music died. Before he could react, an older human woman stepped up and picked up the box. She held it in one hand and twisted some type of key in the back of it. Pitch could clearly hear the gears turning. She smiled down at him. Her hair was white, but she didn't have a beard. At least not one that he could see.

"Do you like it?"

Pitch nodded. The less he spoke, the better, it seemed.

"It's a music box. Do you recognize that song?"

Pitch shook his head.

"It's called 'I'm a Little Teapot.' She held it out to him. "Just open it and it plays."

Pitch held his hands out and gazed at the music box reverently. It was white and had two small drawers. The inside was a deep red cloth of some kind, and when opened, the lid had a mirror that reflected the tiny dancing figure. The woman picked up another one.

"Now this one plays 'Jingle Bells' and has a little snowman inside. Is this for your mommy or your sister?"

Pitch shook his head, his eyes never leaving the delicate twirling figure. Just slowly turning. So small. So beautiful. He snapped it shut and opened it again.

"Do, uh, you have any other ones?" He gestured to the boxes on the table. "Besides these?" He looked up hopefully.

"Oh yes, we have several more right over here." She turned and began walking toward a wall display. When she turned back to Pitch, he was gone.

*

Pitch made it back to the portal without any problems. There was a wait as several other demons stood outside the stall. One of them was holding a large grandfather clock and looking nervously at the door. Another was wearing a fluffy fur coat that dragged on the floor. A large demon in the guise of an elderly human female sat in one of the sinks, happily relieving herself.

When it was Pitch's turn, he cradled the music box to his chest, took a deep breath, and stepped into the stall. Once again the familiar feeling of being crushed into a tiny ball, the dizziness, and he slammed to the ground in the portal cavern. He looked down at the the music box and turned it around. He opened it and the music began playing. Perfect.

Pitch hurried back to his hovel, carefully keeping the music box hidden.

*

For the next few work cycles, Pitch kept a low profile. He showed up for his shift, worked diligently, ate in the canteen, and returned to his hovel. The gift exchange was fast approaching, and Pitch wasn't sure how he felt. The music box, he was sure, was the only one of its kind in Hell. But was it enough?

*

The Secret Santa gift exchange had arrived. Pitch joined the legions of demons outside the gates of Satan's primary palace. Pandemonium was greater than he ever could have imagined: tall ebony walls that seemed to go on forever. It was more of a city than a palace. There were guard towers that overlooked the main entrance. Harpies flew high above the battlements. The main gate was massive, and the demons could easily walk through the main entrance twenty abreast. Pitch glanced up at the heavy portcullis, which had been raised for this special occasion. Several rotted bodies were stuck to the spikes at the bottom. Nice touch.

The great hall was immense. It seemed to go on as far as he could see, immense black columns holding up a ceiling which he could barely see. At the end of the long hall was the throne. He saw Vlad in the crowd, holding a gift wrapped in human flesh. But Pitch didn't wave to him. He was so nervous he didn't think he could talk without screaming. The other demons were in a jubilant mood, laughing and chattering. Pitch seemed to be the only one not talking.

Satan, as usual, was surrounded by his retinue. Imps, demons, other fallen angels surrounded his throne, vying for his attention and approval, laughing at his jokes, looking properly solemn, and nodding their heads sagely at his opinions. He was talking animatedly to a gorgon who rested a scaly hand intimately on his forearm.

The gift exchange went on for hours. Satan would call out a name and a demon would approach. Then the one who had selected that demon's name would come forward and present the gift. Over and over and over. Many of the Demonkind grew restless, and Pitch heard muttering, sensed their impatience but knew none would dare leave early. He wished some would. Then he could sneak out with them and forget about this whole horrible experience. But there was no way. If Satan didn't get his gift, he would turn Hell upside down until he found out who had let him down.

Pitch was too nervous to pay close attention. He was terrified out of his mind, his heart pounding so loudly in his chest he was surprised that the demons around him didn't hear. He vaguely heard shrill screams at one point, followed by a burst of fire and an explosion of laughter and applause. All in all, though, it seemed to be a relatively mundane gift exchange. But then the mood changed. The whispers became more excited, urgent.

"And who picked my name?" his Infernal Majesty's voice boomed through the immense chamber. Necks swiveled, heads turned (some completely around) as all looked to see who would step forward.

Pitch gulped and squeezed his way forward and stepped out onto the crimson carpet that led up to the throne. He heard some giggles, which were quickly hushed. All eyes and eye stalks were on him. He walked toward the throne. It seemed to take forever. He got to the base of the throne and paused before the steps that led up. Satan leaned forward, regarding him curiously, arching a well-manicured eyebrow. A large, officious spider holding a clipboard and wearing eight-lensed reading glasses whispered into his ear.

"Ah. You are... Pitch? You serve me in the Outer Regions?"

"Yes, my Lord." Pitch knelt, bowed his head.

"Rise, my faithful servant, and present your Lord and Master with his gift." Pitch didn't have to look around to see that the crowd was inching forward.

He was taking his first step up the stairs to the throne when he heard the first whisper.

"He doesn't have a present."

"Where's his gift?"

Pitch didn't stop. He walked up the steps. The silence was deafening. The only sound was the pad of his feet on the steps. One step. Then another. The steps were higher than he was accustomed to, and he had to use his arms to pull himself up the last one. He could hear the muffled giggles. Pitch didn't stop when he got to the top step. He was resolute and would see this through, whatever the consequences. He pulled himself up onto Satan's knee, reached around him, and gave him a big hug.

The watching demons gasped as one. He heard several weapons clatter to the floor from numb, stunned hands. Pitch felt Satan stiffen and he kept his eyes tightly closed. Whatever was going to happen, he didn't want to see it. It was too late now.

He decided he had held on long enough and was getting ready to let go and subject himself to whatever humiliation and punishment was heading his way when he felt a powerful arm lay across his back. The arm radiated heat, and there was no mistaking whose it was.

*

The demons tumbled out of the portal in a raucous heap of arms, legs, tails, and wings. The shift leader, Agamoth, tall, broad-shouldered, his face creased with scars, stood up first and reached down to pull Pitch to his feet.

"You did good, kid! Congratulations on your first successful Soul Collection. Welcome aboard!"

Pitch beamed. Like all the others, he was wearing a black vest with a red badge emblazoned with the initials S.C.S. over his left breast.

The rest of the squad, having disentangled themselves from each other, circled Pitch, congratulating him, playfully shoving his head, slapping him on the back, shaking his claw.

Behind them, a male Shade, the newest occupant of Hell, sat on the ground, dazed from his trip through a portal.

"Where am I? This is all a mistake, I can assure you," he whimpered most unassuredly. Pitch walked over and grabbed him by the collar of his and yanked him to his feet.

"Welcome to Hell! Get used to it!" The other members of the SCS hooted and screeched their approval.

*

It had been very tense after he had hugged Satan, and the crowd was expecting (and hoping for) blood. Satan had pulled back and looked down at Pitch. A single tear glistened in one eye. A tear! And he mouthed the words, "Thank you," so that only Pitch could see.

After that, events had taken a turn for the surreal. Pitch had been shuffled out of the main chamber and into a small anteroom. The only light came from a fire blazing in the hearth. Pitch was too afraid to touch anything, so he stood in the center of the room. Paintings of warring angels hung from the walls, and he tried to see if could recognize Satan in any of them. He heard muffled screams and chanting from the main hall and began looking for an exit when the spider sidled up beside him. Pitch nearly jumped up out of his loincloth.

"My master expresses his regrets that he is not able to speak with you himself, but..." he made an elaborate gesture with several of his legs. "...duty calls. He has asked me to offer his gratitude for your... uh, gift, and wishes to offer you a boon. What is it you most desire?"

Pitch stared at him. He swiveled his torso, looked around. Was this guy talking to him? Nobody else here.

"Umm, what I most desire?"

"What you most desire. Anything." He tapped his clipboard impatiently.

"Me?"

"Yes. You." The spider sighed, rolling seven of his eyes.

*

When Pitch got home, he hung his SCS vest on a root that stuck out from the wall. He smoothed it out and rubbed a bit of blood off the badge. It was hard to believe he was now in the Soul Collection Squad. Him! Pitch had never really thought about what he most desired because he never dreamed he would get it. He did live in Hell, after all. He knelt down beside his sleeping mat and pulled a rock to one side, exposing a hollow. He reached in and lifted out an object wrapped in rags. He replaced the rock.

Life was good, Pitch thought, lying back on his mat. He reverently peeled back the rags and uncovered the music box. He wound it, opened it, and watched the ballerina twirl. Yes indeed, life was good.

A FAMILY CHRISTMAS
TERROR

CHAPTER 20

"That was a 'Hell' of story," Dan said and started laughing a little too much at his joke.

"Nick, the fire's getting low, "Grandpa said, rubbing his arms. "I'm getting cold. Put on another log. Just don't breathe on it or the whole place'll go up."

Nick staggered to the fireplace. He reached down and picked up a couple of logs from the bin, nearly falling over.

"God, are you trashed," Jack observed, shaking his head.

"Fuck off. I'm not that drunk," Nick said belligerently. He bent down to grab some discarded wrapping paper and tossed it into the fire. He stumbled back to the couch.

"You asshole, Nick. Now it's getting smoky in here from the paper." Jack waved his hands in the air.

"It's not that bad. Quit being a drama queen. You're worse than Nancy. No wonder you can't get a boyfriend." He took long pull from the bottle.

Jack stood and threw the book at Nick. It struck the bottle, ripping it from his mouth and shattering on the floor. Port and glass flew everywhere, spattering the floor and furniture with deep crimson drops.

Nick put his hand to his mouth. His fingers came away bloody. "What the fuck?"

"You're a fucking spoiled brat!" Jack shouted. "Nancy might be whore, but at least she's going to do something with her life. You're the biggest loser in this whole family!"

"At least I'm not a *fag* hiding in the closet!"

"God damn it, Jack! Do you know how much that stuff cost?" slurred Dan.

Jack stared at his dad. "You're unbelievable." He stormed out of the room.

"Guess I'll read, since I've got the book," Nick said and retrieved it from the floor. "Huh. It's not even wet."

"Are you sure you can see the words?" Grandpa said.

"Yes, I can see the words," he said, mockingly. "*The Perfect Present.*"

THE PERFECT PRESENT

MATHEW KAUFMAN

It was a frigid morning in Detroit. Jesus Christ... Seven months a fucking year, it was a frigid morning in Detroit. Darren Childs woke up. The snow outside reflected and intensified the winter sun. This was not where he thought he would be at thirty-eight years old. Living in his bitch-of-a-mother's spare room.

Another day for a pathetic, worthless fuck... He wiped the sleep from his eyes and yawned. His foul morning breath filled his nostrils as he exhaled. Darren stretched his arm out, searching for his glasses on his heavily worn side table.

He knocked several McDonald's cups over. The foul stagnant fluid spilled onto the nightstand.

"Fuck!" he yelled as he slammed his fist onto the table. More plastic drink cups jumped into the air. The sticky fluid splashed on his bed. Darren flicked the liquid off his hand and dried it on his bed sheet.

He stood and stretched before picking up a piss-stained pair of underwear off the pile of trash at the foot of his bed. He pulled them on and walked out of his room. His feet crunched across an open bag of Cheetos in the hallway. Darren lifted a leg and blasted a foul cloud of gas.

"Ha!" he laughed aloud.

Darren descended the stairs toward the sound of pans banging in the kitchen. He rounded the corner, scratching his chest. His mother, Cyndi, was bent down reaching for a rusted frying pan in the lower cupboard.

She was dressed in her whore outfit again. Cheap, overly tight, torn-crotch, blue jeans. She wore an open-top, low-cut shirt and, of course—like a true whore—no bra. It might have been fine if she was twenty, but she wasn't. She was fifty-six years old.

"Jesus Christ, Ma... Put a fuckin' bra on. Your tits are hangin' like oranges in tube socks. You ain't turnin' nobody on with them things!" he ridiculed.

She turned her head and looked back at him, a look of disgust emblazoned on her face.

"Look who's talkin'. Looks like you rubbed a stick-o-butter on them undies," she fired back. "Ain't you gotta work?"

He did have to work. But it wasn't his normal job. It was Christmas Eve. He had his *other* job.

"Yeah. Not 'til late though," he confirmed.

"Good. So you have time?" she asked.

Without waiting for a reply, she moved toward Darren. She kneeled in front of him and gently tugged his underwear down. She took him into her mouth—

Why...? I don't like this... I don't like this... I don't like this... Fuck! Why am I getting hard? This is so fucked! I never should have let this happen. I was so young though. Is this MY fault? I know she has been lonely since Dad left her, but come on.

Sucking and fucking and doing this shit with your son is so—FUCKED! Why did he have to leave? He was an asshole, but at least he never did this! Why is this exciting me? I shouldn't be so turned on.

Fuck. Why am I letting this feel good? Why did it feel so good when I was fourteen? Why did she have to ruin Christmas? A blowjob is not a gift for your son... If I could have just told her no then... Maybe she wouldn't have kept doing this. Maybe... Oh...

Maybe if I hadn't let her do THIS, then I wouldn't have a fucking kid with my mother! Oh... Oh... Fuck...

"I'm g-gonna—" he stuttered and took hold of her hair. He pulled her in tightly.

WHAT THE FUCK IS WRONG WITH ME?

*

Cyndi pulled up his underwear and stood. She returned to her duties as though nothing disturbing had taken place at all. Disgusted, Darren walked out of the kitchen and hurried to his room. Tears rolled down his face and dripped across his crooked smile.

Looks like it's gonna be another fucked-up Christmas. Walking back to his room, he picked up the bag of Cheetos. Grabbing a fistful, he opened his mouth and tossed them in. A cockroach crawled out from inside the bag onto his wrist. Darren flicked it away and continued eating.

He dressed, no shower, and returned to the downstairs.

"I'll be back later," he said to his mother before closing the door.

There, in the driveway, sat his 1970-something Ford Econoline van. It was a putrid, light pea-green color. Well, the parts that weren't rusted were anyway. He kicked through the December snow and shuffled his way to the driver's door.

It opened with a loud creaking noise. Darren entered and started the engine. *Time to go see what the day brings.* He fastened his seatbelt, put the van in drive, and pressed down on the accelerator.

The van lurched into the street and he drove off toward the local Walmart. Walmart had been a favorite place of his to go "looking" for his special projects. *The beautiful thing about Walmart is the goddamn place never closes. So where else would I go to look for some shit-ass parent that waits until the last minute to go out and buy presents?*

Yeah, yeah. I know. They are doing their best to provide for their children. Maybe they can't afford to buy presents or food or whatever. I'm not Barack mother-fuckin' Obama. And I sure ain't that saggy-titted bitch Hillary Clinton. A parent's got a responsibility to take care of their child. They have to put them first. Not sometimes. Not once in a while. All the fucking time! I am so sick of shitty parents taking advantage of their kids.

"No, Jimmy, you can't have that Transformer. No, Bobby, you can't have that Butterfinger. Come on, Darren, just relax. It will feel good, just relax for Mommy."

NO! Never again! Not this year. I'm gonna find her and I will teach that bitch a lesson!

Darren mashed the gas pedal to the floor. The van coughed out a cloud of black smoke and sped faster down the street. In no time he found himself arriving at Walmart. As he pulled in, he looked for a parking space that would be sufficient, one that had a good view of people arriving and one that would allow him to not stick out like a sore thumb in his rust bucket of a van.

That was not going to be easy. The parking lot was packed with herds of cars. Nearly every make and model was represented in the lot.

Darren circled the rows like cowboys wrangling cattle. He inspected each vehicle and looked for signs that the owner was—*Holy Shit!*

There it was, just sitting there! A piece-of-shit fuckin' beater van. It's fucked-up paint fit right in at the parking lot in Walmart. The afternoon sun was setting, so Darren drove the van around to the front. The van sat parked in a clearly marked handicapped spot. No handicap plates, no handicap placard.

Even from his own vehicle, he could see that there, in the third row seat, was an unfastened child seat. Just sitting there. He backed his van into a parking space that bordered the lot's edge and turned off the engine. Darren reached under the seat and retrieved a small, black CaseLogic cassette case from under the seat. He fumbled with the zipper.

Once open, he selected a cassette labeled "Christmas" and slid it into the in-dash cassette player. Bing Crosby's voice broke the silence as he sang, "*It's Beginning to Look a*

Lot Like Christmas." Darren leaned back in the van's bucket seat and began to bob his head along with the music. He faded into thought, remembering the first time—

*

"She had been such a foul cunt, the way she glared at her kid. She was supposed to love her child. Like a mother should. Instead, she looked at her with disdain. She walked out of Walmart, practically dragging her youngest by the arm. The small girl couldn't have been more than seven.

The news announced later that her name was Suzy Stephens and her mom's was Hollie Winters. The fucking bitch couldn't even keep her legs closed long enough to land a husband. Hollie jerked little Suzy's arm a few more times, dragging her to the car. She puffed on a slim cigarette and blew the smoke right at Suzy. What a bitch.

She pissed me off so much... I got out of the vehicle when I couldn't take it anymore. I wanted her dead right there, and I didn't give a shit who saw. I stormed right at them as they walked to the car. I reached into the back of my pants, grabbing hold of the K-Bar knife that I had tucked in there earlier. I was on them in no time.

I went to draw the knife. This was it. I was going to help this poor child. I made one last step toward Hollie. She didn't even see me. I could have stabbed her ten times before she knew what hit her. That is, if it wasn't for the ice.

During that last step, I slipped on a sheet of slick, black ice. My shoulder collided with Hollie's. I shoved the knife back into the sheath just before I smacked the asphalt, hard! I was embarrassed, but what pissed me off more was what that bitch said.

"Watch where the fuck you are going, dipshit," she balked. "Dumb-ass."

Right there, I knew: this bitch had to die! I watched from my back as she jerked Suzy's arm and drug her to her van. I had been too distracted by rage to notice that Hollie was dressed very nicely, and poor Suzy was wearing clothes that were much too small for her. She looked so cold. Hollie really didn't give a shit about her.

This year *had* to be Suzy's best Christmas. It HAD to be!

I picked myself up off the ground and carefully walked back to my van. Hollie drove past me and added insult to the ordeal by flipping me off. I was gonna make that whore eat those fingers. I brushed the snow and gravel off my backside and got in the van.

I turned the key, it roared to life, and I slammed it into gear. I couldn't risk losing her. I tailed her from a distance so she wouldn't see me. I felt like MacGyver or some shit. My heart pounded in my chest. It was exhilarating. I trailed her for a few miles until she made a left turn into Rosebloom Trailer Park. What a dump.

I could see that the complex was very small. Bags of trash were scattered across "lawns" like ornaments. I didn't want her to see me, so I parked at an apartment complex across the street and watched to make sure she didn't leave. I waited until the sun went down. Then, it was time.

I had worn the brown Carhartt overalls and matching jacket I bought with the money I stole from Ma's purse. Snow had started to fall again. This was exactly the white Christmas I had hoped for. It took ten or so minutes to find the vehicle that Hollie had drove off in. It was parked in front of a dilapidated trailer.

Blackish-gray shutters hung loosely from the un-curtained front window. They occasionally slapped against the trailer's aluminum siding. As I peered through the window, I could see clearly that the noise didn't even draw attention. I was sure that would work in my favor.

I took refuge in a row of bushes and spent some time watching the goings-on inside. Hollie could be seen shuffling through the house wearing only her bra and panties. What a slut. She walked to the refrigerator and removed a box of Franzia wine.

She poured herself a plastic NASCAR cup full of it. The box was obviously reaching empty, as Hollie tipped it, draining all of the remaining contents into the Jeff Gordon cup. She took a long drink from the glass and retrieved a candle from the drawer next to her. As she lit the candle, she twisted the holder. Two wings of four candles came into view. A menorah? She was using a menorah for candlelight? Jesus Christ...

I felt sick watching that bitch. She reached over to the shelf next to her and picked up a book. I strained to look at it. It was obviously one of them dirty chick books. *Golden*

Surrender. It had that Fabio guy on the cover right under the name Heather Graham. That guy really needed a shirt! Nipple man! Ha! Yeah, I was a bit terrified that I knew who Fabio was but, fuck off. I was more surprised that she could fuckin' read than of what happened next.

She leaned back in her chair and unsnapped her bra. Uh... What the fuck was going on? The bra slid loosely down her arms as her breasts popped into sight. The worst thing came next, though. That filthy slut took a Jew candle from the middle of the menorah and shoved it right inside her pussy. The damn windows were open! Anyone could have seen!

That was it. It was my time to move. I sprang to my feet and ran across the street until I reached the bottom of the steps. I removed a paint scraper from my back pocket and quickly shoved it into the door jam. With one stiff smack of my hand on its butt, I was in.

I moved rapidly across the room. Funniest thing I ever saw. When I got to her, I punched her in the face as hard as I could, but she was still fuckin' herself with that Jew candle. HA! It popped out of her crotch like a cork from a pop gun. I almost pissed myself.

Anyways, she slumped right away and I put her in a headlock and drug that bitch out of the trailer. Little Suzy never even knew I was there. I got her outside. That was the hard part, until I realized that I'd parked the van across the street and forgot to move it here. FUCK!

What do I do? What do I do? I freaked the fuck out. I had this naked bitch in a choke hold, standing in the dark outside. There was a small snow bank next to her steps, so I punched her a few more times to make sure she was out. If she woke up, I could still bail, I supposed. And I ran for the van.

My heart raced as I jumped in the driver's seat. I turned the key and the engine came to life. I hoped that she didn't do the same! I drove as inconspicuously as possible to the trailer. When I got close, I saw she was still in the snow. Part of me wanted her to be gone 'cuz that would be a great news story. "Someone broke in my house—while I was fuckin' myself—with a big 'ol Jew candle—" Ha! That would have been so awesome.

Oh well. I jumped out of the van and slugged her in the face for good measure and drug her into the back of the van. Shit, I was scared, but it was exhilarating! I "quietly" slammed the back doors and hopped in the front. I didn't even remember to tie her up! I was such a dumb-ass. Luckily for me she didn't wake up.

I drove to Uncle Sam's storage. Uncle Sam was a used-up, fat, fuckin' Vet that couldn't let go of the four years he served. I'm sure he repaired staplers or some shit while he was in. He was curious why I rented such a big storage. I got one just big enough to get the van in, but I told him it was for a boat. I had to listen to his dumb-ass talk about all the fishin' he and his Army buds used to do. Whatever, fuck off already.

When I got there, I hopped out and opened the door and drove the van inside. I closed the door and locked it from the inside. *Holy shit, I actually did it!* Now it was time for the good stuff. I grabbed the chest I had previously stored and drug it to the rear of the van. I retrieved the rope from inside it and opened the van doors. I had stashed a few construction lights, the kind that are on stands too. I plugged them in and aimed them in the back of the van.

I selected a few tools from the toy chest and hopped in the van with them. I quickly used the rope and tied up the *parent of the year*. I started to relax finally. I slapped her a few times to wake her up. It didn't work. I grabbed the ammonia inhalants I bought on Amazon and cracked one open. I didn't know how to use it so I shoved it right up her nose.

It worked!

That bitch screamed! LOUD! I wrapped some rope around her mouth as a makeshift gag. I started to calm her down. I realized that she still had the ammonia in her nose. I bet that shit burned. I left it in—fuck it!

I grabbed my Mountain Dew from the cupholder up front and sat down next to her. We talked. Well, I talked. She freaked the fuck out! I told her all about how great of a mom she was. Oh, I forgot to mention that I was also cutting off her toes one at a time with a pair of rusty, old tin snips while I recited the merits of her parenting.

Blood spurted across the back of the van. After I snipped each, carefully painted I might add, toe off, I looked her right in the eyes while I poured rubbing alcohol onto each wound. Ha! Wouldn't want her to get an infection. Her face turned pale, from the shock I guessed.

The ammonia seemed to keep her awake pretty good though.

"So, I couldn't help but notice back there in your trailer... You were fuckin' yourself. You know that your daughter is in that house right? Do you get off on knowing that she is that close to you while you are doing that? Well, since you like to shove shit in your cunt..." I unzipped my pants.

I wasn't gonna fuck her. She was a filthy bitch, but it sure freaked her out. Her eyes got all big and shit. That was when I knew I had all the power, and it felt good to use it. I was getting a little freaked out though. Beginner's nerves I guess. So I set aside shoving shit in her and moved to her fingers.

"Remember when you flipped me off bitch? Do it again." She shook her head no, obviously terrified, so I pulled out my K-bar and touched it to her left titty, right at the nipple. I yelled at the top of my lungs for her to flip me off. All she did was cry and shake her head no. So I made good on my threat. I sliced off her nipple like a piece of pepperoni. Ha! She screamed loud again. Well, as loud as one could scream with a mouth full of rope, no toes, and a missing nipple.

This time when I told her to flip me off—surprise, she did, I hacked off the other nipple. Why not? I was in charge. I laid the pair of nips on the wheel well behind me. I wasn't sure what I was gonna do with them, but I had time to figure it out.

Now, back to the fingers. I grabbed her right middle finger, the one she flipped me off with. I toyed with it for a minute. I bent it forward and backward through its range of motion until she relaxed just enough. Then I grabbed it as hard as I could and bent it backwards until it snapped at the base. Have you ever heard a finger bone crack? It's loud!

I moved her hand right in front of her face and wiggled the shit out of that busted finger. Man, that bitch sure did cry. Ha! Over the course of ten minutes or so I snapped each finger's bone, and then one at a time I cut through the flesh with my K-bar. Each finger plopped to the floor of the van, still wrigglin'! It was pretty funny.

I had an idea for them fingers though, so I rounded 'em up and put 'em in a small box. This bein' the first time I killed anyone. I got a little worried and decided it was time to get movin' with the rest of the plan. I set the finger box aside and leaned in toward her face. She looked at me—eye to fuckin' eye. You know what that whore did?

Nothin' 'cuz I punched her in the face and broke her pretty little jaw! HA!

She was out cold again. I was pretty much done with her any who, so I grabbed the sheet of plastic I had in the storage and opened it up behind the van and spread it out on the floor. I grabbed the hacksaw and set it in the back of the van while I drug her out by her legs. Once her legs were out of the van, I started with her right leg.

I pressed the saw against her leg and began pushing and pulling it against her skin. Like a hot knife through butter, her skin flayed open. I thought it was gonna be easy the whole time. But I couldn't get that damn saw to bite into her kneecap. That shit was tough. Until I smashed the fuck out of it with a ball-peen hammer anyways.

After that, the lower half of her leg came right off. It was the same way for the other side. Smack, smack, saw, saw. I did the same at her thigh joint but used a crowbar to separate the ball of her femur from the socket.

Oh, after the first lower leg was off, I think she died 'cuz the bitch didn't move. Even when I punched her right in the pussy.

I flipped her around after that and hacked off her arms, first at the elbow, then at the shoulder. As the parts came off, I stacked them in a pile like you would stack logs. Once that was done, I carefully removed her head the same way and set it next to the stack.

This was where I learned a VERY important lesson. I decided that I wanted to cut her torso in half. Why? Why the fuck not? Fuck that whore... So anyways, I tried to think of the best way to do it and settled on the hack saw.

I made the first cut just below the ribs. What's the worst thing you ever smelled? Well, you ain't never smelled nothin' 'til you cut into a sack of shit! I don't know what this bitch ate, but it smelled like she ate nothin' but hot fuckin' garbage. That shit was ripe.

But I was committed at this point, so I hacked my way through, retching a few times. The strange part was the smell was gross, but I learned the guts didn't bother me. I actually felt accomplished when I got her all taken apart. I felt something, like pride maybe. Whatever. Now here is where shit gets good.

So, I grabbed the paper towels and boxes from the front of the storage. I laid out and separated each body part and gave it a wipe down. I assembled boxes of all sizes. Two of each size actually. I carefully lined each one with plastic. I matched the right size box with the right size limb and sealed a part in each one.

I assembled a perfect head-sized box, re-assembled, and sealed the head inside. Get this... Then I wrapped all the boxes in Christmas paper: Santa paper, Rudolph paper, My Little Pony paper. But the box with the head... I wrapped that in One Direction paper. The perfect paper for the perfect present.

It was almost 3:00 a.m. at that point and I needed to get a move on. I pulled the blood-covered plastic up and bagged it in Hefty bags. I did the same with the plastic from inside the van and the paper towels too. I bagged the tools. I bagged everything.

I threw all the bags into the van. I grabbed the nipples I had left in the back of the van and tossed them in the finger box. I loaded all the presents into the van. I took special care to load the present with the head in it up front so I could make sure it didn't roll around. It needed to be the perfect present.

I grabbed the last box, marked "Suit," from the front of the storage. I ripped open the top and pulled out its contents. I placed everything in its correct place.

Everything had to be right. I was determined to give Suzy the best Christmas ever.

I stripped off all of my clothes right down to my underwear. I scratched my ass as I walked over to the box. I made sure it was empty before I gathered and tossed in all of my bloody clothes. I turned around; a smile filled my face. There, spread in perfect order, was my Santa Suit.

I put each piece on carefully and ensured that I tied every tie and knotted every knot. Everything was going to be great for Suzy. I was sure of it. I tossed the box of old clothes in the van with the hefty bags. The back doors closed with a thud that echoed in the storage. I turned off all of the lights and opened the door.

I backed out and drove straight to Suzy's house, singing Christmas carols the entire way. I was a new man! I sang about packages, boxes, and bags. I sang about everything.

When I pulled into the trailer park I drove the long way around so I could see if the cops were there. To my relief, the lights were still off and a lone candle in the menorah was still burning. I shut off the van's lights and drove to the front of the trailer. I put the van in park and shut off the engine.

This part was going to be tricky. I tiptoed to the front door and, as quietly as I could, propped it open. I slunk down the steps and opened the van doors. I grabbed the boxes full of arms and legs, trunks and torsos, but I saved the best two boxes for last.

I grabbed the box that had the head in it and the finger box. I prominently displayed the head box so it would be the first present Suzy saw. It was the perfect place. I scrawled the perfect note on it:

Suzy,

Open me first!

Merry Christmas,

Santa

What I did next, though, that was just for me. I walked to the still flickering candle, blew it out, and tossed it aside. I removed all the candles. Do you know what I did next? I jammed the fingers in the fucking menorah! It was perfect. Menorah fingers! Seriously—that shit was genius. Fucking menorah fingers!

Can you imagine being the person who finds that? Classic! Anyways, I left that shit up on the counter so Suzy couldn't really see it. No sense traumatizing her on such a joyous day! I also picked up the pussy candle and jammed it in the center holder. I took a minute to look around. Everything looked perfect.

Merry Christmas, kiddo," I said quietly as I walked out the door and closed it behind me.

*

Funny feelin' ya get after hackin' up a whore. I remember the next morning—TV programs all over reported this poor kid getting up and un-wrapping her mom's body I took apart. Truth is, that is *kinda* what happened. I imagined it more like this...

The trailer was just startin' to brighten up with the sun rising. Little Suzy opened up her little peepers and immediately filled with Christmas joy! Then poor Suzy remembered that she had to share Christmas with that fuckin' cunt of a mother. The joy quickly left her young heart. But she got up anyway.

Little Suzy searched the house for dear old candle-fuckin' Mommy, but lo and behold! that bitch was nowhere to be found. Suzy stumbled all sleepy-eyed into the living room and bellered something like, "Holy fuck, Santy Clause sure does love me! Look at all these goddamn presents," or whatever kids say these days. HA!

Kids is so sweet and innocent. I imagined that she run over to them presents and hopefully read Santy's note. I'm sure she grabbed the boxes and ripped the Christmas paper off 'em like a tornado ripping through the Midwest.

I can just see her bright little eyes when she opened up that perfect little present—the one with Mom's head in it. She musta smiled from ear to ear when she saw that stupid slut was dead. I can almost see her kickin' dear old Mom's head around like a soccer ball. Running from one room to the next kickin' goals.

I assume the cops came when little Suzy got hungry and there wasn't no one to feed her. I shoulda left her a sandwich or something.

Them news people just don't get what a neat thing I did for Suzy. I figured that what I had done was so good, and I wanted to keep doin' it, that I would do it every year for Christmas. Boy, it sure took a while for them news folk to calm down about it. Poor Suzy lost her mommy. Fuck that shit! Suzy gained her motha-fuckin' independence. Never again will Mom blow random faggots in her living room.

HA! Ding, dong the bitch is dead! HA! HA!

*

The next year was more of the same. I fucked up a lot less though. No trying to kill bitches in the parking lots. No falling on the ice. No being a fuckin' pussy. I felt like Jesus come back to make folk pay for their misdeeds.

There wasn't nothing special about that year's stupid bitch. I started watching folk earlier, and I had seen this blonde bimbo going in and out of Walmart with different guys every fifteen or twenty minutes.

In between trips I snuck over to her van and popped open the back doors. The damn thing wasn't even locked. I slid in under the seat and waited for her to return. I didn't have to wait long. Two or three minutes before she came back, some nigger got in the front seat. I smelled skunk right after and knew he was smokin' weed.

I can't stand that shit. Soon enough, the van was filled with krunk... That's what them colored folk called it I think. She hopped in and I heard them shuffle around, and soon enough his pants were on the floor. I know, 'cuz the belt hit me in the fuckin' face.

I shimmied back a row and listened.

"Baby, you want this big black dick?" he said.

She replied something in her whore language and agreed to fuck him with no rubber. Anyway, they started buckin' and fuckin' and then my worst nightmare came true. A small little voice broke through the moans.

Mommy, when do I get to be a big girl like you? You said it feels so good and it helps pay the rent. I want to help too Mommy, the little girl said.

"Shit," the darkie said. "I wreck that little pussy. I'll even slip you an extra hundo if I can fill it up with cum." That bitch said YES!

Soon enough, the poor little girl's clothes were on the floor. That was it. There was no fuckin' way I was gonna let this happen. When good 'ol Donnie Darko hopped back a seat, I grabbed my K-bar and shoved it right in his neck.

Sure, there was some screaming when he sprayed the back seat with his fuckin' blood. Did you know they bleed the same color blood as the rest of us? I learned something new... Ha!

Anyways, I sprung over the seat and wacked that poor little girl's face on the console and she went out like a light. I hope I didn't hurt her too bad.

Then, there were two!

I grabbed the queen-of-the-blowjobs by the hair as she tried to grab for the driver's door. I yanked her back and immediately began delivering a barrage of closed-fist blows to her dick-suckin' lips. I heard some bones cracking as I punched her. I had to get her out before I broke her all up. So, there was always something I wanted to try.

I put that bitch in Sergeant Slaughter's Camel Clutch. I choked the shit out of her WWF style! I couldn't help myself. I started quoting Sergeant Slaughter.

When I'm through, scuzzbucket, they're gonna scrape you off the walls with a squeegee!

I even quoted his lines from the *GI Joe* movie.

This is for Falcon! I punched her in the face.

This is for me! I punched her in the face.

This is for Duke! I punched her in the face.

And this is for the U.S. of A! I punched that unconscious bitch right in the mother fuckin' tits!

Then I started to feel like a goddamn retard, so I threw her on the floor and hopped in the back to finish off the baby-raper. I yanked the K-bar out of his neck and gave him a little stabby-stab to the back of his neck. He was mostly gone before I got back there, but it was a good time anyways. Another sicko pedophile off the street!

I spit on the floor as I looked at my handiwork. That sure when to shit quick. Now I had to un-fuck the mess. Did I mention that I was covered in fuckin' bright-ass red blood? I was soaked. Jesus Christ I was so wet. I used my hand and squeegeed the red liquid off my arms. I wiped the remainder on the second-row seatback.

Ok, the plan was—

First: Get the keys from the whore purse

Second: Drive the fuck-wagon to the storage

Third: Impart some holiday spirit on the slut

Scratch that.

Third: Tie up and gag the poor kid. Can't let her see the surprise early.

Fourth: Impart some holiday spirit on the slut

Fifth: Sedate the kid and deliver the presents

Sixth: Merry Fucking Christmas!

It pretty much went exactly like that. I neglected to mention a few things that wiggled into the plan as well. So I have always wondered what it would be like to curb-stomp someone *American History X* style. The problem was that it looked like that guy got off too easy. This child-whoring-cunt deserved worse. And I had an idea.

After I fed the poor little kiddo a fistful of Benadryl and she was racked the hell out, I drug Mom's still unconscious body out of the van. It just so happened that there was a nice curb near the door to my storage door.

It was nice and dark and I was so pissed it didn't matter. Anyways, I drug her outside. She was bound and gagged, but I needed her awake for what was about to happen. It'd worked so well the first time that, again, I snapped an ammonia inhalant and jammed it up her nose.

Holy fuck, did she wake up fast! HA!

I could hear her mumbling away through her gag. Whatever. *Enjoy the ability to talk while you can.* I knelt and whispered into her ear. I told her that if she is absolutely silent during what was about to happen, I would let her go.

OBVIOUSLY, I was full of shit! I ain't letting no baby-pimpin, gutter-slut live. She nodded yes and I untied her gag.

Bite the curb, I told her. She looked at me dumbfounded, like I said it in goddamn French. I leaned in again. "Put your cock-suckin' teeth on the curb—NOW!"

Stupidly, she did. I immediately grabbed her by her hair and placed my knee on the back of her head. I wanted to be close so I could hear this. I moved my hands to either side of her face and pushed my weight slowly onto her head.

Now, I gotta ask, do you know what breaking teeth sound like?

Happy! That's what!

As I pushed down I could actually feel the bone teeth grind down the porous cement curb. Every once in a while, a nice loud crack shot through the air as a tooth broke. She howled like a bitch as blood poured from her mouth and pooled on the curb.

Great, somethin' else to clean up. Today was just full of inconvenience.

Anyway, I had to hurry up 'cuz I had a lot left to do. So I stood up and put a bit more of my wrestling knowledge to work and gave that bitch a Hogan-Leg-Drop. Unfortunately, I missed and slammed my ass cheek right on the back of her head.

Oops—HA!

Her jaw popped right off her face. It sounded like a tree branch snapped. It was awesome! I figured fun time was over and drug her back inside the storage unit.

From there I just did what I did before and hacked her up and put her in presents. With all the crazy shit that happened in the van, I never even got the little girl's name. Oh well.

I delivered the presents dressed as Santa again, just like before. This time, I just left a simple note on the Justin Bieber wrapping paper.

Kiddo,
Merry Christmas!
Santa

Oh—yeah—back to today.

I guess the real rookie move was when I lit the van on fire under the bridge. I didn't see that bitch joggin' 'til it was too late. By the time I saw her face lit up by the fire, you stupid motherfuckers were already surrounding me.

By the way, I'm not crazy. I would have complied with anything you told me to do. I don't like cops, but my issue isn't with you. It's really about—

You know the real shit thing about this entire deal? I did what I did because I give a shit about them poor kids. I really didn't give a fuck about them Moms. I made them suffer because they deserved to fuckin' suffer. Not them kids.

I don't give a fuck what you or any other motherfucker thinks about me. I gave those kids the perfect presents!

So, ho, ho, fuckin' ho...

*

Darren leaned back in his chair, rocking it onto two legs. His wrists were bound together by a shiny pair of

Peerless handcuffs. He still wore the now badly stained Santa Claus suit. What a mess.

The detective whispered something into his radio and stood.

"Darren, you have a visitor. She says she's your lawyer," the detective said as he moved to the door. "I'll be right outside."

The detective walked through the door and nodded at the attorney as she stepped into the room and closed the door. As soon as she turned toward Darren, he could see she was carrying a large, black leather purse. He gasped.

"Mom?" he asked. "How did you—"

"Shh, we don't have much time," she said as she raised a finger to her lips.

"Time for what? I'm in jail," Darren said.

"Oh, you know what I mean, young man," she said with a glimmer in her eye.

Hollie walked to Darren's chair and in seconds had his now stiff rod out. Without missing a beat she climbed onto it and forced its length into her.

"I wanted you to have the perfect present, baby boy," she said as she rode him.

What Darren didn't see was that his mother had grabbed a large-caliber handgun out of her bag. She held it behind his head out of sight as she prepared for the inevitable climax.

Darren's face contorted as he finished inside her.

"I wanted you to have the perfect present. I love you," she said.

A loud *bang* broke the silence of their embrace as the gun fired. Blood splashed on the wall to Darren's right. His body went limp. The door burst open and uniformed police officers flooded the room and took her into custody.

The detective entered right behind them. He surveyed the room. A Santa-suit-clad Darren lay dead on the floor. His cock hung limp outside of the suit bottom and his brains were splashed across the wall.

"What a fucked up Christmas," he said, shaking his head. Looks like I'll be late tonight. Good thing I got my baby the perfect present.

A FAMILY CHRISTMAS TERROR

CHAPTER 21

"That was fucking disgusting!" Dan said.

"Sounds like *that* author spent some time in a loony bin," Grandpa added.

"Yeah. That was twisted. Uh oh. I think I'm gonna be sick." Nick tried twice to get up from the couch.

"From the book or the booze?" Grandpa asked.

"Both." Nick finally stood. He fumbled with the book and tossed it to Dan. "Yeah, I'm *definitely* gonna hurl. Like father like son." He laughed and staggered off.

The men listened to Nick make the familiar sounds of his stomach emptying into the upstairs toilet.

"Well, you gonna read that thing or just stare at it? We've got to finish it."

"All right. Don't have a stroke! I was looking where we left off." He thumbed the pages. "Here. *Santa Jack.* Maybe our Jack left too soon. I wonder—"

"Just read, Dan!"

SANTA JACK

F. PAUL WILSON

Friday

"Thank God you're here!" Raymond said as Alicia walked through the Center's employee entrance. "I've been beeping you since eight o'clock. Why didn't...?" His voice trailed off as he looked at her. "Christ, Alicia, you look like absolute, total shit."

That was a somewhat generous assessment of how she felt, but she didn't want to talk about it.

"Thank you, Raymond. You don't know the half of it."

She didn't head for her office, but toward the front reception area instead. Raymond paced her.

"Where are you going?"

"Just give me a minute, will you, Raymond?" she snapped. "I'll be right back."

She regretted being so short with him, but she felt stretched to the breaking point. One more tug in the wrong direction...

She was vaguely aware of Tiffany saying hello as she hurried past the reception desk on her way to the front door. Stepping aside to allow a middle-aged woman and her two grandchildren to enter, Alicia peered through the glass at the street outside, looking for the gray car.

She was sure it had followed her from home. Or maybe not so sure. A gray car—what would you call it? A sedan? She didn't know a damn thing about cars. Couldn't tell a Ford from a Chevy. But whatever it was, she'd kept catching sight of this gray car passing her as she walked. It would turn a block or two ahead of her, disappear for a few minutes, then cruise by again. Never too close. Never too slow. Never a definite sign of interest. But always *there*.

She scanned Seventh Avenue outside, half expecting to see it roll by. Across the street and slightly downtown, she checked the curb in front of the O'Toole Building, squatting at the corner of Twelfth. Its white-tiled, windowless, monolithic facade did not fit here in Greenwich Village. It looked as if a clumsy giant had accidentally dropped the modernistic monstrosity on his way to someplace like Minneapolis.

No gray car, though. But with all the gray cars in Manhattan, how could she be sure?

Her nerves were getting to her. She was becoming paranoid.

But who could blame her after what had been happening?

She headed back to her office. Raymond picked her up in the hall.

"*Now* can we talk?"

"Sorry I snapped at you."

"Don't be silly, honey. Nobody snaps at me. Nobody *dares*."

Alicia managed a smile.

Raymond—never "Ray," always "Raymond"—Denson, NP, had been one of the original caregivers at the Center for Children with AIDS. The Center had MD's who were called "director" and "assistant director," but it was this particular nurse practitioner who ran the place. Alicia doubted the Center would survive if he left. Raymond knew all the ins and outs of the day-to-day functions, all the soft touches for requisitions, knew where all the bodies were buried, so to speak. He clocked in at around fifty, she was sure—God help you if you asked his age—but he kept himself young looking: close-cropped hair, neat mustache, trim, athletic body.

"And about my beeper," she said, "I turned it off. Doctor Collings was covering for me. You knew that."

He paced her down the narrow hallway to her office. All the walls in the Center had been hurriedly erected, and the haste showed. Slapdash taping and spackling, and a quick coat of bright yellow paint that was already wearing though in places. Well, the decor was the least important thing here.

"I know, but this wasn't medical. This wasn't even administrative. This was fucking criminal."

Something in Raymond's voice... his eyes. He was furious. But not at her. But then what?

A premonition chilled her. Were her personal troubles going to spill over into the Center now?

As she continued walking she noted knots of staff—nurses, secretaries, volunteers—all with their heads together, all talking animatedly.

All furious.

An icy gale blew through her.

"All right, Raymond. Lay it on me."

"The toys. Some rat bastard motherfucker stole the toys."

Astonished, disbelieving, Alicia stopped and stared at him. No way. This had to be some cruel, nasty joke. But Raymond was anything but cruel.

And were those tears in the corners of his eyes?

"The donations? Don't tell me–"

But he was nodding and biting his upper lip.

"Aw, no."

"Every last one."

Alicia felt her throat tighten. The toys... she and Raymond—especially Raymond—had been collecting them for months, sending staff and volunteers to forage all through the city for donors—companies, stores, individuals, anybody. The response had been slow at first—who was thinking about Christmas gifts in October? But once Thanksgiving was past, the giving had picked up. Last night they'd had a storeroom full of dolls, trucks, rockets, coloring books, action figures... the works.

"How?"

"Pried open the outer door and took them away through the alley. Must have had some sort of truck to hold everything."

The ground floor of this building had been a business supply store before being converted to the Center for Children with AIDS. The former owners probably had loaded their delivery trucks the same way the thieves had stolen the gifts.

"Isn't that door alarmed? Aren't *all* the doors alarmed?"

Raymond nodded. "Supposed to be. But the alarm didn't go off."

Poor Raymond. He'd put his whole heart into this effort.

Alicia reached her office, tossed her bag onto her desk, and dropped into her chair. Her feet were killing her. She closed her eyes. The day had hardly begun and she felt exhausted. She looked up at Raymond.

"Did anything like this ever happen to Doctor Landis?"

He shook his head. "Never."

"Great. They wait until she's gone, *then* they strike."

"I think that's all for the best, don't you think? I mean, considering her condition."

Alicia had to agree. "Yeah, I guess you're right."

Dr. Rebecca Landis was the director of the Center—at least she had the title. But she was in her third trimester and developing pre-eclamptic symptoms. Her OB had ordered her to stay home in bed.

This only a week after the assistant director had left to take a position at Beth Israel, leaving the place to be "directed" by Alicia and the other pediatric infectious disease specialist, Ted Collings. Ted had begged off any directing duties, claiming a wife and a new baby. And so the burden of administrative duties had fallen on the Center's newbie: Alicia Clayton, MD.

"Any chance it was an inside job?"

"The police are looking into it."

"The police?"

"Yes. Been here and gone. I made out the report."

"Thank you, Raymond." Good old Raymond. She couldn't imagine how he could be more efficient. "What do they think about our chances of getting those toys back?"

"They're going to 'work on it.' But just to make sure they do, I want to call the papers. You okay with that?"

"Yeah, good idea. Make this a high-profile crime. Maybe that'll put extra pressure on the cops."

"Great. I've already spoken to the *Post*. The *News* and the *Times* will have people here later this morning."

"Oh. Well... good. You'll see them, okay?"

"If you wish."

"I wish. Tell them it's not just stealing, and it's not just stealing from little kids—it's stealing from kids who've already got less than nothing, who're carrying a death sentence in their bloodstreams and may not even *be* here next Christmas."

"That's beautiful. Maybe you should–"

"No, please, Raymond. I can't."

Feeling utterly miserable, she tuned out for a moment.

"What else can happen today?" she muttered. "Bad news always comes in threes, doesn't it?

Raymond still hovered beyond her desk. "Something with that 'family matter' you've been dealing with?" he said, then added—pointedly: "All by yourself?"

He knew she'd been seeing lawyers and been preoccupied lately, and he seemed to take it personally that she wouldn't discuss it with him. She felt sorry for him. He freely discussed his personal life with her—more than a few times she'd wanted to block her ears and say "Too much information!"—but she couldn't reciprocate. Her own personal life was pretty much a void, and the disaster area that posed as her family was not something Alicia wanted to share, even with someone as sympathetic and non-judgmental as Raymond.

"Yes. That 'family matter.' But that's not as important as getting those toys back. We had a super Christmas set up for these kids and I don't want it going down the tubes. I want those toys back, Raymond, and dammit—get me the Police Commissioner's number. I'm going to call him myself. I'm going to call him every day until those toys are back."

"I'll look it up right now," he said, and was gone, closing the door behind him.

Alicia folded her arms on the scarred top of her beat-up old desk and dropped her forehead onto them. Everything seemed to be spinning out of control. She felt so helpless, so damn *impotent.* Systems...always these huge, complex, lumbering systems to deal with.

The Center's toys were gone. She'd have to depend on the police to get them back. But they had their own agenda, their own higher priorities, and so she'd have to wait until they got around to hers, if they ever did. She could call the Commissioner until she wore out the buttons on her phone, but he'd probably never take the call.

She pounded her fist on the desk. *Damn* it!

"Excuse me."

Alicia looked up. One of the volunteers, a pretty blonde in her early thirties, stood halfway through the doorway, looking at her.

"I knocked but I guess you didn't hear me."

Alicia straightened and shook back her hair. She put on her professional face.

"Sorry. I was a million miles away, dreaming about chasing down the rats who stole those presents."

The woman slipped her svelte body the rest of the way through and shut the door behind her. Alicia wished she had a body like that.

She'd seen her around a lot. Sometimes she brought her daughter with her—cute little girl, maybe seven or eight. What were their names?

"You won't have to go a million miles to find them," the woman said. "One or two should cover it."

"You're probably right," Alicia said.

Her name... her name... what was her name?

Got it. "Gia, isn't it?"

She smiled. "Gia DiLauro."

A dazzling smile. Alicia wished she had a smile like that. And *Gia*... what a great name. Alicia wished—

Enough.

"Yes, you and your daughter..."

"Vicky."

"Right. Vicky. You donate a lot of time here."

Gia shrugged. "Can't think of a place that needs it more."

"You've got that right."

The Center was a black hole of need.

"Can I talk to you a minute?"

She looked at Gia more closely and saw that her eyes were red. Had she been crying?

"Sure." She had no time, but this woman donated so much of hers to the Center, the least Alicia could do was give her a few minutes. "Sit down. Are you okay?"

"No," she said, gliding into the chair. Her eyes got redder. "I'm so angry I could...I don't like thinking about what I'd like to do to the scum that stole those toys."

"It's okay. The police are working on it."

"But you're not holding your breath, right?"

Alicia shrugged and sighed. "No. I guess not. But they're all we've got."

"Not necessarily."

Alicia looked at her. "What do you mean?"

She leaned forward and lowered her voice. "I know someone..."

Chapter 2

As Jack scrolled through the messages left on the Repairman Jack website, he kept an eye on the TV screen, looking for Dwight Frye.

He was celebrating his discovery of the 1931 version of the *Maltese Falcon* with a Dwight Frye film festival. He had the film running in the front room of his apartment now. Frye played the role of Wilmer Cook in this one, and for Jack's money, he out-psychoed Elisha Cook's portrayal in the later John Huston version. But Ricardo Cortez was onscreen now, and he wasn't such a hot Sam Spade.

Back to the internet.

Most of the questions on Jack's home page were about refrigerators and microwaves, which he didn't mind. Surfers who stumbled onto his page thought he was some sort of appliance answerman. Fine. After no replies to their questions, they'd delete his URL from their bookmarks.

But this one...from a guy named "Jorge."

I BEEN RIPPED OFF. CAN'T GET MONEY OWED TO ME FOR WORK I DO. CAN'T GO ANYWHERE ELSE. CAN YOU FIX?

Yeah. That sounded like business.

Jack typed in a reply to Jorge's email address:

Send me your phone #. I'll be in touch—RJ

He'd call the guy and see what this was about. If he was having trouble with his bookie, tough. But he'd said it was money he'd "earned." So maybe Jorge was a potential customer.

The phone rang but Jack let the machine pick up. He heard his outgoing message... *"Pinocchio Productions—I'm out at the moment. Leave a message after the beep"*... then:

"Jack, this is Dad. Are you there?"

A pause as he waited for Jack to pick up. Jack closed his eyes and didn't move. He felt bad about leaving his father hanging, but he wasn't up to another conversation with him right now.

"All right...when you get in, give me a call. I came across another great opportunity for you down here."

Jack exhaled when he heard the click of the connection breaking.

"Dad," he said softly, "you're making me crazy."

His father had moved down to Florida a few months ago and Jack had thought it was a good idea at the time. Better to be a retired widower down there than in Burlington County, New Jersey.

But as soon as Dad had settled in, he began seeing all sorts of opportunities for Jack. His older brother and sister were both professionals, pillars of their respective communities. They were set. But Jack... Dad still saw his younger son as unfinished business.

His brother and sister had given up on him long ago. The annual Christmas card was the extent of their contact. But not Dad. He never gave up. He didn't want to go to his grave thinking his prodigal dropout son was living hand to mouth in New York as an appliance repairman.

I've probably got more socked away than you do, Dad.

He winced as he remembered their last conversation.

You've got to see this place, Jack. It's growing like crazy—a gold mine for someone like you. You establish yourself here as a reliable repair service and in no time you'll have a fleet of trucks all over the county.

Be still my heart, he thought. A fleet of trucks, and maybe, if I play my cards right, the cover of *Entrepreneur* magazine.

Jack had been begging off, hoping Dad would get the message, but obviously he hadn't. When Jack called back, he was going to have to tell his father point blank: No way was he leaving New York. The Jets would be wearing Super Bowl rings before he moved to Florida.

Then again, if work didn't pick up, maybe he'd have to rethink that.

He'd just checked the answering machine in the drop on Tenth Avenue. Nothing there. Business had been kind of slow lately. He was getting bored.

And when he got bored, he bought things. He'd picked up his latest treasure from his Post Office box just this morning.

He stood and rubbed his eyes. The computer screen tended to bother them. He removed the clock from its packing to admire it again.

A genuine Shmoo pendulette alarm clock. In beautiful condition. He ran his fingers over its smooth, white, unmarred ceramic surface, touching the eyes and whiskers on the creature's smiling face. It had come in its original box and looked brand new. The eBay seller hadn't exaggerated.

Now seemed as good a time as any to hang it on the wall. But where? They were already crowded with framed official membership certificates in The Shadow and Doc Savage fan clubs, Captain America's Sentinels of Liberty, The Junior Justice Society of America, the David Harding Counter-Spy Junior Agents Club, and the Don Winslow Creed.

What can I say? he thought. I'm a joiner.

His apartment was crowded with wavy-grained Victorian golden oak furniture. The wall shelves sagged under the weight of the neat stuff he'd accumulated over the years, and every horizontal surface on the hutch, the secretary, the claw-and-ball-footed end tables was cluttered as well.

And then he saw where the clock could go: right above the pink Shmoo planter... which still didn't have anything planted in it.

He was just about to look for his hammer when the phone rang again.

Dad, give me a break, will you?

But it wasn't his father.

"Jack? It's Gia. You there?"

Something in her voice... Jack snatched up the handset.

"Always here for you. What's up?"

"I'm waiting for a cab. Just wanted to make sure you were in."

"Something wrong?"

"I'll tell you when I get there."

And then a click.

Slowly, Jack replaced the handset. Definitely upset. He wondered what was wrong. Nothing with Vicky, he hoped. But she would have told him that.

Well, he'd find out soon enough. The West Village to the Upper West Side wasn't too bad a trip this time of day. No matter what the circumstance, an unexpected visit from Gia was a treat.

He thought back on their stormy, off-again, on-again relationship. He'd been crushed and thought it was off forever when she'd found out how he earned his living—or thought she had. She'd concluded that he was some sort of hit man, which was as wrong as could be, but even after she'd learned what he really did, even after he'd used those skills to save Vicky's life, she still didn't approve.

But at least she'd come back to him. Jack didn't know where he'd be without Gia and Vicky.

A short while later, he heard her footsteps on the stairs leading to his third-floor apartment. He turned the knob that retracted the four-way bolt system, and opened the door.

The sight of Gia standing on the landing started that warm funny twitch he got deep inside every time he saw her. Her short blond hair, her perfect skin, her blue eyes— Jack felt he could stand and stare at her face for hours.

But right now her features were strained, her usual tight composure seemed to be slipping, her normally flawless complexion looked blotchy.

"Gia," Jack said, wincing at the pain in her eyes as he pulled her inside. "What is it?"

And then she was clinging to him, loosing a torrent about Christmas toys being stolen from the AIDS kids. She was sobbing by the time she finished.

"Hey, hey." Jack tightened his arms around her. "It'll be all right."

He knew Gia wasn't much for emotional displays. Yeah, she was Italian, but Northern Italian—the blood running in her veins was probably more Swiss than anything else. For her to be sobbing like this... she had to be hurting something fierce.

"It's just the *heartlessness* of it," she said, sniffing. "How could somebody *do* such a thing? And how can you be so damn *calm* about it!"

Uh-oh.

"I hear anger looking for a target. I know this has really cut you deep, Gia, but I'm not the bad guy here."

"Oh, I know, I know. It's just—you've never been down there. Never seen these kids. Never held them. Jack, they've got nothing. Not even a parent who cares, let alone a future. We were collecting those toys so they'd have a nice Christmas, a *great* Christmas—the last Christmas for a lot of them. And now–"

Another sob.

Jeez, this was awful. He had to say something, do something, anything so she wouldn't feel like this.

"Do you know what the presents were? I mean do you have some sort of a list. Because if you do, just give it to me and I'll replace–"

She pushed back and stared at him. "They were donations, Jack. Most of them all wrapped up and ready for giving. Replacing them's not important. Getting them *back* is. Understand?"

"Yes...and no."

"Somebody's got to find these guys—the ones who did this—and teach them a lesson... make an example of them... a very public example. Know what I mean?"

Jack fought to suppress a grin. "I think so. You mean, make it so that the next creep who gets the same idea will think twice, maybe three times before he decides to go through with it."

"Exactly. *Exactly.*"

With exaggerated innocence—and still fighting a smile—he said, "And um, just who could we be thinking of to make such an example?"

"You know damn well who," she said, fixing him with those eyes.

"Moi?" And now he had to grin. "But I thought you didn't approve of that sort of thing."

"I don't. And I never will. But just this once..."

"...you could live with it."

"Yes." She began wandering around his living room, aimlessly tracing her fingers across the golden oak hutch, the rolltop desk where he kept his computer. "But just this once."

"But Gia—"

"Please," she said, raising her hand. "I know what you're going to say. *Please* don't start pressing me for some sort of moral and philosophical consistency between not marrying you because of what you do and then coming to you when there's a problem that looks like it can only be solved by your kind of tactics. I've been battling that all morning—I mean, trying to decide whether I should even *mention* it to you. Even in the cab, I was ready to tell him to turn onto Fifty-ninth and forget the whole thing–"

"Oh, great. That hurts. Since when is it that you can't come to me for *anything?*"

She stopped and looked at him. "You know what I mean. How many times have I mouthed off about this 'Repairman Jack' thing?"

"About a million." More like three million, he thought, but what's a couple of million between friends? "But the 'Repairman' thing was Abe's coin."

"Right. Whatever. I know I've gone off on how it's stupid and dangerous and violent and dangerous and how if you don't end up dead you're going wind up in jail for the rest of your life. And I haven't changed my opinion one bit. So you can imagine how this thing must have got to me if I'm asking you to fix it."

"All right. I won't say another word about it."

"Maybe not now, but I know you will later."

Jack raised two fingers. "I won't. Scout's honor."

"I think that takes three fingers, Jack."

"Whatever. I promise I won't." He reached for her hand. "Come on over here."

632

She took his hand and he pulled her onto his lap. She settled on his thighs, light as a feather, and they kissed— not a long one, but long enough to warm him up.

"There. That's better. Now... let's get down to practicalities. Who's hiring me?"

"I spoke to Doctor Clayton—she's the acting director."

Jack felt his insides tighten. "You told her you know me?"

He'd warned Gia about that. *Never let on you know me— to anyone. Even your best friend.* He'd made too many enemies over the years. And if one of them thought he could get back at him through Gia...or Vicky...

He shuddered.

"No. I said I knew *of* someone who might be able to help get the toys back. Didn't mention any names. Just said I'd try to contact him and see if he was available."

Jack relaxed. "I guess that's okay."

Still, if he got involved in this, it would leave a link—at least in this Dr. Clayton's mind—between Gia and a guy named Jack who "fixed" something. Probably be okay, but he didn't like it.

"Well?"

"Well what?"

"Are you available?"

"I don't know."

"How can you not know?"

"Well, there's a problem. I mean, the Center can't hire me, because I can't work for a legit business. They've got to account for their expenses and I don't exactly take checks."

He didn't even have a Social Security number.

"Don't worry about it. I'll pay you."

"Oh, right. Like I'll take money from you."

"No, I mean it, Jack. This is my idea. I want this. What's your usual and customary fee?"

"Forget it."

"No, I'm serious. Tell me."

"You don't want to know."

"*Please?*"

"Oh, all right." He told her.

She gaped at him. "You charge *that* much?"

"Well, as you said, 'it's stupid and dangerous and violent and dangerous' and if I don't end up dead I'm going wind up in jail for the rest of my life. So yeah, that's what I charge." He kissed her. "And I'm worth every penny."

"I'm sure you are. Okay. It's a deal."

"No, it's not. Told you: I'm not taking money from you."

"But you've told me you never do freebies. It's against your religion or something."

"It's just a policy. But let's forget about money for now. Let's first see if this is something I can deliver on."

"Fair enough." She was staring at the TV screen. "Why do I know that actor?"

"He's Dwight Frye. You've seen him before."

"Didn't he play that guy in 'Dracula' who was always eating flies?"

"Until he graduated to 'big, juicy spiders.' Yeah. He played Renfield."

Gia buried her face in his shoulder. "I can't believe I know that. I've been hanging around you much too long."

"And getting educated in the process. Now... where can I meet this Doctor Clayton?"

"In her office."

"When?"

"This afternoon at four."

"How do you know she'll be there?"

She smiled that smile. "Because you have an appointment with her then."

Jack laughed. "You were that sure?"

"Of course. And I'll be there with Vicky to introduce you."

He frowned. "Do you think that's wise?"

"Introducing you?"

"No. Taking Vicky down there."

"Are you kidding? She loves helping with those kids."

"Yeah, but they've got...AIDS."

"No, they've got HIV. There's a big difference. And you can't catch HIV by holding a baby in your arms. How many times have I told you that?"

"Lots. But I still..."

"When you see, you'll understand. And you'll see at four o'clock, right?"

"Right."

They kissed, but Jack felt a chill. His list of things that scared him was a short one, but the HIV virus was top on the list.

Chapter 3

Jack took a walk over to Amsterdam Avenue.

Gentrification continued its relentless progression on the Upper West Side. New brownstone renovations, new condos, and of course, new eateries. In a few hours the streets and the host of new restaurants, trattorias, and bistros would be crowded with yuppies and dinks out for their Friday night fling to initiate the weekend's respite from buying and selling.

As individuals, Jack didn't have anything against them. Yeah, they could be empty-headed when it came to one-upsmanship in the conspicuous consumption arena and the endless panting after trends, and as a group they tended to suck the color out the neighborhoods they invaded. But they weren't evil. At least most of them weren't.

Jack checked his watch. Getting near three. Abe would be ready for a mid-afternoon snack just about now. He stopped in at Nick's Nook, a mom-and-pop grocery—a vanishing breed in these parts—and picked up a little treat.

Next stop was the Isher Sports Shop. The iron grate was pulled back, exposing the blurry windows. Beyond them, an array of faded cardboard placards, dusty footballs, tennis balls, racquets, basketball hoops, backboards, Rollerblades, and other good-time sundries basked in the sunny display space.

Inside was not much better organized. Bikes hanging from the ceiling, weight benches over here, SCUBA gear over there, narrow aisles winding past sagging shelves. ESPN meets *Twister*.

As Jack entered, Abe Grossman was just finishing with a customer—or rather, a customer was finishing with him.

Abe's age was on the far side of fifty and his weight was in calling distance of an eighth-of-a-ton, which wouldn't have been bad if he were on the right side of five-eight. He was dressed in his uniform—black pants and a white half-sleeved shirt. A frown marred his usually jovial round face, a face made all the rounder by the relentless retreat of his gray hair toward the top of his head.

"Hooks?" Abe was saying. "Why should you want hooks? Can you imagine how that must hurt a fish when it bites into it? And those barbs. Oy! You've got to rip them out! Such damage to the tender mouth tissues. Stick a fish hook in your own tongue sometime and see how you like it."

The customer, a sandy-haired thirty-something in a faded Izod stared at Abe in wonder. He made one false start at a reply, then tried again.

"You're kidding, right?"

Abe leaned over the counter—at least as far as his considerable gut would allow—and spoke in a fatherly fashion.

"It's an ethical position. Baiting a hook, or using those flashing little spinners to catch fish, it's deceitful. Think about it. You're dressing up a nasty little hook to look like food, like sustenance. A fish comes along, thinks it's found lunch, and *wham!* It's hooked and pulled out of the water. Is that fair? You're proud of such a thing?" He straightened and fixed the guy with his dark brown eyes. "I should be a party to such a so-called sport based on treachery and deceit? No. I cannot."

"You're serious!" the guy said, backing away. "You're really serious!"

"I should be a comedian? This place looks like the Improv to you maybe? No. I sell sporting goods. *Sporting.* That means something to me. A net is sporting. You wait for the fish to come along and then scoop it up with a net. The fastest one wins. *That's* a sport. A net, I'll sell you. But hooks? Uh-Uh. You'll get no hooks from me."

The guy turned away and headed for the door. "Get out while you can," he said as he hurried past Jack. "This fucker is nuts!"

"Really?" Jack said. "What makes you think so?"

As the door slammed, Jack stepped up to the counter. Abe had positioned himself, sitting like a toad on the high stool that was his perch for most of his workday. He sat with his hands on his spread thighs, a middle-aged Humpty Dumpty.

Jack placed his offering on the counter.

"Entenmann's brownies?" Abe hopped off the stool with surprising agility. "Jack, you shouldn't have."

"I figured your stomach would be rumbling about now."

"No, but really you shouldn't have. My diet, you know."

"Yeah, but they're fat free."

Abe touched the yellow sticker that said just that. "So they are." He grinned. "Well, in that case, maybe just a bisel."

His short chubby fingers were surprisingly nimble as they zipped open the box. A knife appeared and carved out a huge section which went directly into his mouth.

"Mmmm," he said, closing his eyes and swallowing. "Who could believe this is fat free? Too bad it's not calorie free." He pointed the knife at Jack. "You're having?"

"Nah. Had a late lunch."

"You should try. All this food you bring me and I never see you eat."

"That because I bring it for you. Enjoy."

Abe promptly did just that with another piece.

"Where's Parabellum?"

Abe spoke around a mouthful. "Sleeping.'

For some reason Jack could not fathom, Abe had bought a little blue parakeet and become paternally attached to it.

"He doesn't like chocolate anyway." He wiped his hands on his shirt. Brown smears joined similar yellow smudges that looked like mustard. "Hey. You want to see will power? Watch."

He closed the top and pushed the box to the side.

"I'm impressed. First time I ever saw you do that."

"I'll be thin as you before you know it." He found a crumb on the counter and popped it into his mouth, then looked longingly at the brownie box. "Yessir. Before you know it."

In what Jack knew was a prodigious act of will, Abe pushed away from the counter and shrugged. "Nu?"

"Need a few things."

"Let's go."

Abe locked the front door, turned a "Closed For Lunch" sign toward the street and, navigating aisles just wide enough to allow his bulk to pass, led the way toward the back, into a rear closet, and down to the cellar. The neon sign that overhung the stone steps flickered but never quite came to life.

"Got a sick sign there, Abe."

"I know, but it's too much trouble to get fixed."

He hit the switch that illuminated the cellar's miniature armory. Abe moved among his stock, adjusting the pistols and rifles in their racks, straightening the boxes of ammo on their shelves. Everything neatly arranged down here, in sharp contrast to the floor just above them.

"Restocking or something new?"

"New," Jack said. "Need a pair of weighted gloves."

"You lost the last pair you bought?"

"No, but I need a white pair."

Abe's eyebrows lifted. "White? I never heard of such a thing. Black, of course. Brown, maybe. But white?"

"See if you can find me any."

"I should go asking for white leather gloves with half a pound of fine steel shot packed into the knuckles? You want this in a lady's size perhaps?"

"No, it's for me. To go with formal wear."

Abe sighed. "And I should have it for you when?"

"Tonight if you can, but by early tomorrow at the latest. And listen for any noise about someone with a whole bunch of kids' Christmas gifts to sell... cheap... already wrapped, most likely. I told Julio to put his ears on too. You hear about someone like that, get word to the guy that you know a buyer. Someone who'll take his whole stock."

Abe's curiosity surged to the fore. "Just what is it you're getting into this time?"

"Something I probably shouldn't be involved with. But to do it right, it looks like I'm going to have to do something stupid."

Abe stared and Jack knew he wanted to know just how stupid. But Abe wouldn't ask, knowing Jack would tell him about it afterward.

He looked around and spotted something hanging on a rack in the corner. And that gave him an idea.

"You know what? Maybe I could use one more thing..."

Chapter 4

Jack took the D train downtown and emerged into the bustling Third World bazaar that was 14th Street. He threaded his way among deadlocked Dominicans, turbaned Sikhs, saried Indians, suited Koreans, Pakistanis, Puerto

Ricans, Jamaicans, and an occasional European mixing in the chill air on sidewalks flanked with signs in half a dozen languages.

He arrived early at the Seventh Avenue address Gia had given him. A little placard on the door was the only indication that this nondescript storefront had anything to do with AIDS.

He probably could have started hunting the stolen Christmas gifts without coming down here, but he figured a quick look at the scene wouldn't hurt. Might even give him a handle on the thieves.

"I have a four o'clock with Doctor Clayton, I believe?" he told the slim, attractive black woman at the reception desk. The nameplate read simply, *Tiffany*.

"Name, sir?"

"Jack."

"Jack what?"

He wanted to tell her, *Just Jack*, but that inevitably led to more questions, and further refusal tended to brand his identity in a person's mind. He preferred to slide off people's memories without a trace.

He smiled and fished for a name beginning with "N." He'd used Meyers last time he'd been asked, and since he liked to proceed in alphabetical order...

"Niedermeyer. Jack Niedermeyer."

"Fine, Mr. Niedermeyer. Doctor Clayton is still in another meeting right now. A reporter. We had a robbery here last night, you know."

"Really? What did they take?"

"All the donated Christmas toys."

"Get out!"

"It's true. The police are on it right now. I think they should—oh, there's Doctor Clayton now. Looks like she's finishing up."

Jack saw a slim brunette in a white coat walking his way with a guy who looked more like a delivery man than a reporter. She escorted him to the door, then scanned the street outside as if looking for something. Whatever it was, when she turned back Jack's way, she didn't look as if she'd found it. Or maybe she had. Either way, she didn't seem happy.

"Doctor Clayton, this is your four o'clock: Mr. Niedermeyer.

Dr. Alicia Clayton was better looking close up, but still kind of... plain. She had fine, angular features—a thin, sharp nose, sharply etched lips—neither too fine nor too full—and blue-gray eyes. Her hair was fine too, bobbed to chin length, and a deep, deep black—not black-dye black like a Goth, but a genuine, rich, glossy black.

And no make-up. Someone who took such good care of their hair, you'd think they'd want to enhance their other assets. But not, apparently, Dr. Clayton.

Well, if nothing else, the lack of make-up gave her a clean, scrubbed look, which Jack supposed was a good thing for a doctor.

But her eyes... something hiding there. Fear? Anger? A little of both, maybe?

She thrust out her hand. "Welcome, Mister Niedermeyer."

She had a good grip.

"Just call me Jack."

"You'll want to see the scene of the crime, I imagine."

"I was going to suggest that."

No wasting time. All business. Jack liked that.

The Center wasn't at all what he'd expected. The halls were bright, painted cheery shades yellow and orange.

"You're a pediatrician?" he said as they walked along.

She nodded. "Subspecialty in infectious diseases."

"My sister's a pediatrician."

"Really? Where's she practice?"

Jack kicked mentally himself. Why the hell had he said that? He never thought about his sister the doctor. Or his brother the judge. Must be those calls from Dad.

"I'm really not sure. We don't keep in touch."

Dr. Clayton gave him a strange look.

Yeah, he thought. Sounds pretty lame, I know, but my sister's far better off not being linked to me.

As they passed open doorways he peeked through and saw rooms filled with toddlers laughing and playing and running around. They didn't look sick.

"That's the daycare area," Dr. Clayton said. "Where HIV-positive kids can play with other HIV-positive kids, and no one has to worry about passing on the infection."

A little boy ran out of one of the rooms and skidded to a stop before them.

"Doctor Alith!" he cried. "Look at my hair! I got a buthcut!"

"Very nice, Hector. But you know you're supposed to stay in the playroom."

Hector was all of four years old and maybe thirty pounds, with ultra-short light brown hair about the same shade as his skin. He looked pale under his pigment, but his grin was a winner.

"Feel my head! It'th a buthcut."

A heavyset woman in a flowered smock appeared at the door of the playroom, filling it.

"C'mon back, Hector. It's your turn at the light box."

"No. I want Doctor Alith to feel my buthcut!"

The woman said, "He just got that haircut and he's been driving us all nuts about it."

Dr. Clayton smiled and brushed her hand over Hector's stubbled head. "Okay, Hector, I'll check out you buzzcut, but then—"

Her smile faded and she pressed her hand to his forehead. "I think you feel a little warm."

"He's been running around like a little madman—'Feel my buzzcut! Feel my buzzcut!' I'm sure he's just overheated."

"Could be, Gladys, but bring him by my office before he goes home, okay?"

Hector jumped in front of Jack and angled the top of his head toward him. "Feel my buthcut, mithter!"

Jack hesitated. Hector was a cute little guy, but he was a cute little guy with HIV.

"C'mon, mithter!"

Jack gave the bristly top of Hector's head a quick rub. He didn't like himself for how quickly he pulled his hand away.

"Ithn't it mad cool?"

"The maddest."

Gladys scooted Hector back to his playroom and they moved on to the next area, which wasn't so pleasant. Jack peeked through a window in a door and saw a room full of kids hooked up to IV's.

"This is the clinic area. Kids come in here for outpatient therapy—we infuse them, monitor their progress, then send them home."

Then they came to a huge plate-glass window that stretched from waist level to the ceiling.

"We board the homeless or abandoned infants in there. We have volunteers to hold them and comfort them. The crack babies need a *lot* of comforting."

Jack spotted Gia cradling a baby in her arms on the far side of the glass, but he didn't pause. He didn't want her to spot him.

"You do a lot here," he said as they moved on.

"Yeah, we've had to become a clinic, a nursery, a daycare center, and a foster home."

"And all because of a single virus."

"But we have to deal with more than the virus. So many of these kids aren't born merely HIV positive—as if 'merely' can somehow be used with 'HIV'—but addicted to crack or heroin as well. They hit the world screaming like any other baby at the insult of being ejected from that warm cozy womb, but then they keep on screaming as the agonies of cold-turkey withdrawal set in."

"A double whammy." Poor kids.

"Yes. Some parents leave their kinds an inheritance, some leave hidden scars, these kids were left a virtual death sentence."

Jack sensed something very personal in that last sentence but couldn't latch onto what it might have been.

"Perhaps 'death sentence' is overstating it," she added. "We can do a lot for these kids now. The survival rate is way up, but still... once they get through withdrawal, they still have the aftereffects of addiction. Crack and heroin burn out parts of the nervous system. I won't bore you with a lecture about dopamine receptors, but the result is fried circuits in the pleasure centers. Which leaves our little crack babies edgy and irritable, unable to take solace in the simple things that comfort normal infants. So they cry. Endlessly. Until the strung-out junkie mothers who made them this way beat them to shut them up."

Jack realized she probably gave this spiel to all the visitors, but he wished she'd stop. He was getting the urge to go hurt somebody.

"The lucky ones"—she cleared her throat harshly—"try to imagine a lucky HIV-positive crack baby—wind up here."

She stopped before a windowless door.

"Here's the storeroom where the toys were kept."

She showed him the space, empty but for some scotch tape and wrapping paper.

"The toys will be wrapped in this paper?" he said, memorizing the pattern.

"Most, but not all."

He pulled open the door to the alley and checked the alley itself. Easy to see how it had been done. The outer door frame and the surface around the latch were deeply gouged and warped. Looked like the work of a long pry bar in the hands of someone with the finesse of an orangutan.

He saw Dr. Clayton shiver in the cold wash from the open door. She rubbed the sleeves of her white coat. She was very thin—no insulation.

"How are you going to handle this?" she said as Jack closed the door.

"Not here. Can we talk in your office?"

"Follow me."

On the way to her office, Dr. Clayton stopped at the front door and peered out at the street. He saw her stiffen, as if she'd seen something that frightened her.

Chapter 5

A chill rippled over Alicia's skin and collected at the base of her spine as she watched a gray car double-parked across the street. It idled there, slightly uptown from her vantage point, its motor running.

The same car as this morning? She couldn't be sure. Was it watching the door of the Center or waiting for someone in one of those stores? How could she know? Hell, between the sun glare and the tinted windows, she couldn't even tell how many people were in it.

She forced herself to turn away and led Jack Niedermeyer back to her office. Maybe it was just her imagination. Why would anybody follow her? What was the point? She did the same thing every day: from her apartment in the Village to the Center, from the Center to her apartment. A model of predictability.

Relax. You're making yourself crazy.

"Have a seat," she said as they entered her office.

Raymond stopped by to drop off some papers. She introduced them but said nothing about why Mr. Niedermeyer was here.

When Raymond was gone and they were seated, facing each other, she took a good look at this mid-thirtyish man in jeans and a reddish flannel shirt. He stood about five-eleven, had a tight wiry build, dark brown hair, lips on the thin side, and mild brown eyes. The very definition of average.

This is the guy who's going to get the toys back? Oh, I doubt that. I doubt that very much.

"Now, Mister Niedermeyer–"

"Just call me Jack."

"Okay, Just Jack." *And you can call me Doctor Clayton.* No, she wouldn't say that. "Ms. DiLauro told me you might be able to help. Are you a friend of hers?"

"Not really. I did some work for her aunt once." He leaned forward. "I believe the subject is missing toys?"

A tiny flash of intensity there. Well hidden, but Alicia had spotted it. *Something personal between these two? Or simply none of my business?*

When he'd leaned forward he'd put his hands on her desk. Alicia was struck by the length of his thumbnails. His hands were clean, his nails well trimmed... all except for the thumbs. Their nails jutted a good quarter inch or more beyond the tips. She wanted to ask him about them but didn't see how she could do so with any grace.

"I wasn't prying. I'm simply curious as to how one man could possibly find those toys ahead of the whole New York City Police Department."

Jack shrugged. "First off, it won't be the 'whole' department. Maybe one or two robbery detectives—if you're lucky."

Alicia nodded. He was right.

"Second, I think it's a safe bet that the guys who ripped you off aren't family men stocking up for their own kids' Christmases. And from the look of that door, they weren't pros. I smell a quickie, spur-of-the-moment heist. I'll bet they don't have a fence in place to dump their loot, which means they'll be looking for one. I know people..."

He left that hanging. *What people? People who buy stolen Christmas gifts? Was he some sort of criminal himself?*

She looked at him and realized that his mild brown eyes revealed nothing... absolutely nothing.

"So... you 'know people'... people, I assume, who might lead you to the thieves. And then what?"

"And then I will prevail upon them to return the gifts."

"And if you can't 'prevail?' What then? Call in the police?"

He shook his head. "No. That's one of the conditions of my involvement: no contact with officialdom. If the police recover the gifts, fine. All's well that ends well. If *I* return them, it's a wonderful occurrence, a Christmas miracle. You don't know who's responsible, but God bless 'em. You've never seen me, never even heard of me. As far as you know, I don't exist."

Alicia tensed. Was this some sort of scam? Rob the gifts, then charge a fee to "find" them. Maybe even collect a reward?

But no. Gia DiLauro would never have anything to do with something like that. Her anger this morning had been too real.

But this man, this "Just Jack"... he might have involved Gia without her knowledge.

"I see. And what would you charge for–?"

"It's taken care of."

"I don't understand. Did Gia–?"

"Don't worry about it. All taken care of."

"There'll be a reward."

She'd had calls—businesses and individuals offering to contribute to a reward fund for the arrest of the perpetrators. The total was mounting.

"Keep it. Spend it on the kids."

Alicia relaxed. All right. So it wasn't a scam.

"What I need is some information about the gifts—anything distinctive that'll help me make sure I'm on the right track."

"Well, for one thing, they were all wrapped. We only accepted new toys or clothing—all of it *un*wrapped—and then we wrapped them ourselves as they came in. You saw the kind of paper we used. Other than that, what can I say? It was a real hodgepodge of gifts, a beautiful, generous assortment..."

Alicia felt her throat begin to lock with rage.

And they're all *gone!*

The man rose and extended his hand across her desk. "I'll see what I can do."

Alicia gripped his hand and held it. "What are our chances? The truth. Don't think you have to make me feel good."

"The truth? Chances for recovery are zip if they've already fenced the toys. Slim if they haven't. If they're not recovered, say, by Sunday, I'd say they're gone for good."

"I'm sorry I asked." She sighed. "But that's the way it goes around here, I guess. These kids are born under a dark cloud. I don't know why I should expect they'll get a break this time."

He gave her hand a little extra squeeze, then released her.

"You never know, Doctor Clayton." He gave her a crooked smile. "Even the worst losers get lucky once in a while."

Maybe it was the smile that did it. It dropped his shields. Alicia saw into this Jack for an instant—a nanosecond, really—and suddenly she had hope. If it was at all possible to find and return those gifts, this man believed he could pull it off.

And now Alicia was beginning to believe it too.

Chapter 6

Instead of heading for the front after leaving the doctor's office, Jack ducked to the left and returned to the infant area. He stepped back into the relative shadow of a doorway across from the big plate glass window and watched.

Gia sat half facing him, but all her attention was on the blanket-wrapped bundle in her arms. She rocked, smiled, cooed, and looked down at that bundle as if it were the most precious child in the world. Someone else's baby, but no one looking at Gia now would know it. Her eyes were aglow with a light Jack had never seen before. And her expression... beatific was the only word for it.

And then Vicky hopped into the picture, an eight-year-old slip of a thing; her dark brown braids bouncing as she hurried a bottle of formula to her mother. Jack smiled. He had to smile every time he saw Vicky. She was a doll and he loved her like a daughter.

He'd never met Vicky's father and, from what he'd heard about the late, not-so-great Richard Westphalen, he was glad. Jack had it on excellent authority that the Brit bastard was dead—he knew the where, when, and how of his death—but the remains would never be found. So it would be years before Richard Westphalen was declared legally dead. Gia had taken back her maiden name after the divorce, although Vicky remained a Westphalen—the last of the line.

Vicky didn't seem to miss her father. Why should she? She'd hardly known him when he was alive, and now Jack had more than taken his place. Or at least he hoped so.

He watched a few minutes longer, unable to take his eyes off the two most important people in his life. It worried him no end that they were both in an enclosed room with HIV-positive infants.

Right, right, right. He knew all the facts and figures about how safe they were, and all that. And that was all fine and good for other people. But this was Gia and Vicky. And the threat was a virus, something you couldn't see, and not just any virus. This was HIV.

Jack felt he could protect those two people in there against just about anything. But not a virus. And they were putting themselves right in its way.

If either one of them should catch it... he didn't know what he'd do.

HIV was something he could not fix.

He pulled himself away and walked back the way he had come.

He saw the heavyset Gladys leading a line of preschoolers down the hall. She smiled and nodded as she passed, a huge goose with her goslings. He spotted Hector bringing up the rear.

"Hey," he said, pointing. "Who's that kid with the mad buzzcut?"

Jack had expected another offer to "feel my buthcut," or a smile at least, but Hector's eyes were dull when he looked up at Jack. And then he staggered against the wall and dropped to his knees. Before Jack could react, Hector vomited.

"Whoa!" Jack yelled. "Trouble here!"

Gladys was there in a second. "Stay back," she said as she pulled on latex gloves that seemed to appear from nowhere.

She picked up a hall phone, spoke a few words, then knelt beside Hector. Jack couldn't hear what she said, but he saw Hector shake his head.

And then Raymond appeared—he too was wearing latex gloves. He gathered Hector up in his arms and carried him back the hall. As Gladys directed the other children back into their playroom, a janitor appeared and began mopping up the mess with a solution that reeked of antiseptic.

Jack moved on. He'd been a frozen observer, not knowing what to do. The staff here had its own set of rules and protocols that he was not privy to. He felt like a stranger in a foreign country, with no knowledge of the language or the culture.

He quickened his pace. Hector had been smiling and bubbling less than an hour ago, and just now he'd looked like a little rag doll with all its stuffing vacuumed out.

The happy sounds of the children in the daycare rooms attacked Jack as he moved. Each shout felt like a shot, each laugh a knife thrust. Death hovered over every one of them, a fatal infection lurked around every corner, but they didn't know. And just as well. They were kids, and they should be happy while they could be.

Especially the crack babies. Their short lives had been full of pain from day one, while a virus chewed away at their immune systems.

And now someone had stolen their toys.

Jack felt his jaw muscles bunch. Don't worry kids... Uncle Jack may not know how what to do when you're sick, but he's not quite as useless as he looked a few minutes ago. He's going to get your toys back. And in the process he sincerely intends to have a heart-to-heart chat with the oxygen waster who took them.

Life really sucked sometimes.

But it didn't have to suck *all* the time. Sometimes things could be fixed.

Saturday

The Nail sat behind the wheel of his truck and rubbed his hands together for warmth. Cold as shit out tonight, man. Cold as *shit!*

But not for long. An hour from now, maybe less if the buyer didn't try to Jew him down too much, he'd be flush and warm in his crib, sucking on some rock instead of this piss-poor excuse for a joint.

The Nail took a deep toke and held it. He wiped the condensation off his windshield and wished the heater in this damn truck worked. He flicked his Bic to check the dashboard clock. The buyer had said like eleven-thirty. Just about that now.

He'd floated the word that if anyone wanted a deep discount on a bunch of new Xmas toys, wrapped and ready to go, the Nail was the man. Word had floated back that a fence who was a friend of a friend of a friend wanted the whole truck load. Yes!

He exhaled and peered down the alley, looking for headlights. Lots of wheels rolling by out there, heading for the nearby Manhattan Bridge. He wished the right set would roll in here so he could get this deal done.

His contact hadn't said so, but The Nail figured the fence was bringing his own truck. Had to be. How else was he going to cart the stuff out of here?

Better not have any ideas about taking *this* truck, man. He patted the little .32 automatic in his belt. Better not be thinking of anything beyond passing the cash and off-loading the stash.

Hey, that rhymes.

Passin' the green and splittin' the scene.

The Nail smiled and took another toke. Too bad he wasn't with the band anymore. Maybe him and the drummer could've like worked that up into a song or something. That'd be cool.

He missed Polio. Best damn punk thrasher band in the world, man, and he'd played bass for them. Well, for a few months, anyway. Until they kicked him out for not showing up.

But it'd been a good few months. That was when he'd picked up the name The Nail. Well, not picked up, actually. That was when he'd started calling himself The Nail. You needed a name like The Nail if you was playing for Polio. Like who'd want a bass player named Joey DeCiglia?

And The Nail was *such* a cool name, having like a double meaning and all.

But even with a handle like The Nail and having gigged with Polio, there wasn't no work out there. Least not for him. Shit, yeah, he got auditions just by name-dropping Polio, and everybody was real interested in hearing him... until they heard him.

Then it was like, don't call us, man...

Yeah, well, like fuck you too.

He sucked the joint down to his fingertips and tossed the roach out the window. Not worth saving, man.

After a bunch of wasted auditions, The Nail said goodbye to the music scene. He had his pride, man. As a lark, he started boosting stuff and selling it off. Wound up making more that way than from what he'd've been paid by any of the nowhere, no-name thrasher bands that never called back.

But then Tina goes and gets herself knocked up and tries to tell him the kid's his. Sure. Right. Like with the way she jumps on anything upright and hard, he's gonna believe that shit? No fucking way.

Then she gets all fucked up in the head and won't have an abortion. Nah. She's gonna have the kid and be a mommy.

Right. Mommy Tina. Sure.

But surprise, surprise. She's goes through with it. And of course the kid's born like totally wasted. And then the word comes down that it's got fucking AIDS, man. *AIDS!*

That meant Tina had the bug, and *that* blew The Nail's mind. Fuck, he could have it too, what with screwing Tina all the time and sharing needles. He should've gotten tested right then, but he was too scared, man. Like he didn't want to *know*.

But for Tina, it was like she wasn't even sick and like the kid wasn't sick either. Her head was royally fucked. So she was all broke up when they took the baby away from her.

And she kept telling him it was *his* kid. Kept saying how it looked just like him. So one day last week she finally hounded him into going over to this place where they keep the kid and look after it. The Nail didn't know what had gotten into him—maybe that Ceylonese brown they'd been using had got him over-mellowed—but he was glad he'd given in. Because as he was hanging around the place he saw people carrying a bunch of Christmas gifts through this doorway. He took a peek figuring he might be able to make off with something small, but he saw a whole room *filled* with toys. Whoa.

Merry Christmas to me.

He did the place two nights later.

And the coolest part of the whole thing was the news coverage. Shit, man, last night you couldn't turn on a radio or TV without hearing about "the AIDS baby Christmas toy theft." He'd spent hours hopping from channel to channel, one news show after the other, grinning like a total asshole.

That was him they was talking about. The Nail.

The only bad thing was, he couldn't tell anyone. At least not until he'd sold off the stuff. After that he could talk all he wanted because the toys would be gone and no one could prove nothing.

The only thing he didn't get was how pissed off and disgusted all the news geeks acted. Like it really mattered to them. Bull*shit*. Everybody knew how stupid it was to waste presents on those AIDS kids. Really, how long were they gonna live anyway? Weren't gonna be around long enough to appreciate them. Total waste, man.

Leave it to The Nail to put the stuff to good use.

And it'd been so fucking simple. All he'd had to do was–

The Nail jumped as he heard a *skree-eek* behind him. He twisted in his seat. That sounded like–

It was! Shit, some asshole had opened one of the truck's back doors. And now he was flashing a light inside.

His first thought was cops, but he hadn't seen a fuzzmobile pull up. And The Nail knew cops had to follow certain rules about searches.

The buyer? Maybe, but he didn't think so. More likely some strung-out junking trying to boost *his* stuff.

The Nail pulled out the automatic and chambered a round. He'd put an end to that shit *real* quick.

He jumped out and ran around to the back of the truck.

"Hey, man. What the fuck you think–?"

Nobody there. And both rear doors closed. The Nail scanned the alley up and down: not a fucking soul in sight.

He couldn't have imagined it. The weed hadn't been *that* strong. And he'd heard the noise. He'd *seen* the light.

Better check to see if anything was missing.

But as The Nail reached for the handle, the door sprang open and slammed into him, knocking him flat. He landed on his back, rolled, and popped to his feet, the gun stuck out ahead of him. He saw the open door of the truck, but no one there.

And then he heard a deep voice.

"Ho-ho-ho!"

The Nail looked up and saw this fat guy with a white beard in a red suit standing on top of the truck.

The guy did his ho-ho-ho thing again, then shouted, "So *you're* the one who stole the toys I was putting aside for the AIDS babies! No one steals Santa's toys and gets away with it!"

Aw, man. This asshole thinks he's Santa Claus!

The Nail raised the pistol and plugged a round into his heart.

Santa fucking Claus flew backward off the top of the truck like someone had yanked a leash wrapped around his neck.

No one steals Santa's toys and gets away with it?

Shit, yeah. *I* steal *anybody's* fucking toys and do what I damn well fucking please, asshole!

The Nail hurried around the side of the truck. Time to put another slug in Santa Hole...

But he wasn't there.

"What the fuck?" The Nail said aloud.

And then something red and white popped up from the shadows behind a garbage can and slammed a white-gloved fist into his face.

The Nail had heard about seeing stars, but he'd never believed it. Now he did. He heard his nose go *crunch* as his face erupted in a star-studded explosion of pain. He staggered back, caught the heel of his shoe on some alley shit, and felt himself falling backward.

He windmilled his arms, trying to keep his balance, but he was out of control. He went down hard.

And when he looked up, Santa was leaning over him.

"You think you can stop Santa Claus with a bullet? A mere *bullet*? Think again, sonny!"

The voice wasn't quite as deep and strong as it had been a moment ago, but the guy was still standing. And there, not two feet from Nail's face, was a bullet hole in the red fabric of his suit. Right over his heart.

Shit! What was going down here? The fucker should be dead, man.

Unless of course he really *was* Santa Claus.

But that was crazy.

But so was the guy in the red suit. The Nail saw his eyes gleaming between his white beard and the furry brim of his hat. Whoever he was—hell, maybe he really was Santa Claus—he was pissed. *Royally* pissed.

The Nail started to raise the pistol for another shot, but Santa stomped a foot down on his arm.

"Don't bother trying again, sonny! You can't kill Santa Claus!"

The Nail levered himself up and reached across, trying to grab the gun with his free hand, but Santa clocked him again with a brain-jarring right, rocking his head back against the pavement.

Santa had a punch like a fucking mule kick.

The Nail felt the gun ripped from his hand, heard it skitter across the asphalt. After that, things got fuzzy.

And painful.

The Nail remembered getting flipped over onto his belly, grabbed by his collar and his waistband, and hauled off the ground.

"I checked my list," Santa said. "Checked it twice, in fact. It says you've been naughty, sonny. *Very* naughty!"

Then Santa started using him like a battering ram.

Slam! Head first against the bumper of the truck.

"Know what happens when you steal from Santa Claus? *This!*"

Slam! Head first into a bunch of trash cans lining the alley.

"If I decide to let you live, spread the word: Don't mess with Santa Claus."

The Nail was spun around and flung face first against one of the alley's brick walls.

He let out a puny groan of agony as he slid down the wall, feeling like a splattered egg oozing toward the ground.

But it wasn't over. Not by a long shot. The Nail felt his consciousness fading over the next ten minutes as Santa used him like some sort of rag to wipe up the alley.

Finally Santa released him. The Nail dropped to the ground, a puddle of agony on the broken pavement. He felt his breath bubbling through his bloody mouth. He was sure his jaw was broken. And his ribs—every breath was a dozen stab wounds. Was it over? He hoped so. He *prayed* it was over.

Just leave me be, he thought. Just take the toys, take the whole damn truck and go. Hitch your fucking reindeer to the bumper and you and Rudolph take off. Just don't mess me up anymore. Please.

But just as he finished the thought, he felt hands go under his armpits and lift him.

"No," he managed to groan past his shattered teeth. "Please... no more."

"Should have thought of that before, sonny. Stealing from defenseless little sick kids puts you on Santa's ultra-naughty list."

"I'm sorry." It came out a faint whine. Totally wimpy.

"Well, good. I'm glad to hear it. And I'll take that into consideration next Christmas. But you complicated things by trying to kill Santa. That's *very* naughty. Santa doesn't like to be shot. It makes him cranky. *Very* cranky."

"Oh, no..."

Something rough and long slithered past The Nail's cheek, and true panic set in. *Rope!* Oh, fuck no. Santa was going to string him up!

But then he felt the rope snake under his arms instead of around his neck. That was a relief. Of sorts. It still hurt like all hell when the rope tightened around his shattered ribs. He was lifted and seated on the truck's rickety front bumper, then tied there.

"Wha–?"

"Quiet, sonny," Santa said in a low voice that had lost all its heartiness. "*Don't* say another word."

The Nail looked up. Everything—Santa, the alley, the whole fucking *world*—was mostly a blur... except for Santa's eyes. He'd always thought Santa had blue eyes, but these were brown, and The Nail shriveled up inside when he saw the rage bubbling behind them.

Santa wasn't just pissed. Santa was bugfuck nuts.

The Nail closed his eyes while Santa taped something to his head. By the time it squeezed through to his battered brain that he shouldn't let Santa—even this homicidal psycho Santa—tie him to the front of a truck, it was too late. He tried to wriggle free but the rope that lashed him to the grille crisscrossed his body around the shoulders and between the legs. His legs and his arms were free, but all the knots were somewhere behind him.

With a cold sick certainty, The Nail realized he wasn't going nowhere. Not under his own steam, anyway.

He stiffened as he heard the old engine rumble and shudder to life against his back. He began to blubber as the truck lurched into motion.

Santa was going to run him into the wall!

But no. The truck bounced out of the alley onto the street. After that it was a nightmare ride through the Lower East Side with people staring, pointing, some even laughing, then crosstown on Fourteenth with the truck swerving from lane to lane, running lights, screeching to a halt inches—*inches!*—from rear bumpers and fenders, then roaring into motion again.

All that was bad enough, man, but when the westbound lanes weren't moving fast enough, the truck swerved into the oncoming traffic and played chicken with a banged-up yellow cab. The Nail knew fuck sure ol' Santa wasn't going to back down, and for the few screaming, terror-filled heartbeats it looked like the cab wasn't going to either, The Nail lost it. Literally. Warm liquid spilled down his left leg.

But the cab lunged out of the way at the last second and the truck got back on the right side of the street and began accelerating.

A cop! The Nail had never dreamed he'd be in any situation when he'd want to see a cop on his tail, but here it was. And where were they? Why wasn't there ever a fucking cop around when you needed one?

The truck fishtailed into a wide, screeching turn onto what The Nail thought might be Seventh Avenue, but he couldn't be sure because he closed his eyes as they scooted within a hair of a horn-blaring bus. Then the truck jumped the curb and scattered terrified pedestrians before skidding to a halt on the sidewalk.

As the engine cut out, The Nail whimpered and waited in terror to see what Santa had planned for him next. But Santa said nothing, did nothing. The Nail twisted and looked through the windshield. Santa was gone.

But The Nail wasn't alone. A crowd of gawkers was gathering, forming a semicircle around him and the truck, staring, pointing at his bloody face, his pee-stained pants, and whatever it was Santa had taped to his head. Someone laughed. Others joined in.

The Nail wanted to die.

And then he heard the sirens.

Sunday

"Oh, no," Alicia said as she rounded the corner and saw the police cars in front of the Center. "What now?"

She had her donut and coffee from the hospital caf in one hand, the fat Sunday *Times* in the other. She usually spent the rest of Sunday morning at the Center. They still had kids coming in for their treatments, just like every other day, but it was lot less intense than the rest of the week—nowhere near as many phone calls, for one thing—so she used it to catch up on her paperwork.

But now...

Just inside the front door she nearly collided with two cops, one white, one black, talking to Raymond. *Raymond.* He was devoted to the Center but he rarely if ever showed up on Sunday.

"Oh, Alicia!" he said. "There you are! Isn't it wonderful?"

"Isn't what wonderful?"

"Didn't anyone tell you? The toys! The *toys* are back!"

Suddenly Alicia wanted to cry. She turned to the pair of policemen. Raymond introduced her. She wanted to hug them.

"You found them? Already? That's... that's wonderful!" Better than wonderful—fantastic was the word.

"I guess you could say we found them," the black cop said, scratching his bald head. His name tag read, *Pomus.* "If you can call opening up a truck parked on the sidewalk by your front door 'finding' them."

"Wait a minute. Back up just a bit. What truck?"

"A panel truck, Alicia," Raymond said. "Filled with the toys. The police think it was the same one used to haul them away. Someone drove it up on the sidewalk last night and left it there."

"Any idea who?" she asked, although she had a pretty good idea.

The white cop—*Schwartz* on his tag—grinned. "According to the guy tied to the bumper, it was Santa Claus himself."

"Guy tied to *what?*"

They went on to explain about the man they'd found lashed to the front of the toy-filled truck. Someone had "knocked the crap out of him," as Officer Pomus put it, and taped some rubber antlers to his head. The battered man admitted to the theft and swore that his assailant had been Santa Claus—even admitted to shooting Santa, rambling on about shooting him in the heart without killing him.

"But of course, you can't kill Santa," Officer Schwartz said, grinning.

"He's obviously a user and he sounds like an EDP, so we don't know what to believe," Officer Pomus added. "We've got him up on Bellevue's flight deck now, under observation."

"Flight deck?"

"You know—the psych ward. Sooner or later, we'll get the straight story out of him."

"And throw the book at him, I hope."

"Oh, yeah," Pomus said. "No question about that. But he's already had worse than a book thrown at him." He grinned. "A *lot* worse."

"Yeah," Schwartz said. "Someone worked him over *real* good before dropping him here. The creep seemed almost glad to be arrested."

After they were gone, Alicia and Raymond went to the storeroom and inspected the gifts. Except for a little wrinkling of the paper and an occasional bumped corner, most were in the same condition as before the theft. She told Raymond to get hold of a locksmith—she didn't care that it was Sunday—and have him secure that door, even if it meant putting a bar across it.

Then she went to her office and sipped her coffee, lukewarm by now, and thought about that nothing-special looking man named Jack—"Just Jack" Niedermeyer.

On Friday afternoon he'd said he'd see what he could do. Thirty-six hours later, the gifts were back and the thief in custody.

A man who could do that just might be able to solve her other problem.

Alicia looked up a number in her computer's directory and began dialing...

A FAMILY CHRISTMAS TERROR

Dan set the book down. "Certainly nothing like *our* Jack. That guy had balls. *God.*" He stared into the fire. "Why are my kids such losers? What did we do wrong?"

"You can only do what you can do. I know how you feel."

"What's *that* supposed to mean?"

"Take it for what it is. Your mother and I tried, but there comes a point..."

"*Fuck* you, old man. You're lucky we let you live here all these years. We could've just shipped you off to some old folks' home years ago." He hurled the book at his father's feet. "There. You can finish the book. I'm fucking done with this shit!" He left the old man with the book at his feet.

"Dan..." Grandpa's face held pure disappointment. He got up to follow, but only took a couple of steps. He looked down at the book. "I need to finish it." He went back to the chair and picked up the book. "*The Boy and His Backpack...*"

THE BOY AND THE BACKPACK

JON LAND

The boy entered the bar dragging the storm behind him. The cold wind chased him all the way inside, drawing a shudder from the few patrons closest to the door before it swung closed. The boy flipped back his hooded sweatshirt to reveal long brown floppy hair stained dark at the tips by melting snow. His faded, frayed jeans, too, were storm blackened in splotches, and his worn motorcycle boots featured a broken buckle that dragged along the floor like a Christmas bell.

Fitting, thought Ray Dunwoodie from his customary spot in a back booth between sips of house scotch, since this, after all, was Christmas Eve. Rare for Dunwoodie to look up from the BlackBerry that sat next to his glass, daring the ring of condensation to reach it. Rarer still for him to notice anyone entering or leaving the bar he frequented every night. He could tell you the man passed out at a center table beneath a perpetually flickering light bulb drank away his monthly welfare check, but that was about it.

Except for a single plain wreath hung outside the entrance, the old bar showed no signs of the season. It had been a much more central haunt when this part of the city had been home to industry and hope now lost behind buildings awash in FOR SALE signs. One of these hung not far from the wreath, its letters cracked and storm-blasted while inside four patrons who called themselves regulars sat amidst peeling paint and rotting floorboards.

The boy's boots clacked atop these as he strode beneath the dull, dusty lighting for the bar and took a stool. His shoulders sagged from the weight of a backpack that seemed ready to pull him over at any moment. The jacket that covered his gray sweatshirt had once been black leather before much of what was black, and leather, were lost to age and too many storms like the one that had descended on the city tonight. He swept the bangs of his matted hair from his forehead and it swept right back.

"You got an ID?" Celia the bartender asked him, hefty arms crossed menacingly before her. She might have been a woman, but the baseball bat kept always within reach knew no gender. Her dingy fell hair limply past her shoulders, and she smelled of dishwasher solvent and stale beer.

"Oh." The boy smiled. "I'm not drinking."

And with that, he unslung a backpack, so overstuffed the seams looked to be tearing from his shoulders. It looked frightfully old and tattered; wisps of fabric sticking up in some places, thinning patches in others, and downright rips in still more. Looked as if it might burst as soon as he set it down, but it didn't.

"This is a bar, son," Celia noted in a far from motherly fashion. "That's what people do here. Drink."

"Give the kid a break, Ceil," came a voice from the far end of a bar. It belonged to a man named Hank Waggoner, unlit cigarette dangling in his hand even though he'd quit smoking a dozen years back. "Can't you see he's hungry?"

Celia regarded the boy again. He looked no more than sixteen, seventeen at the most, and was practically licking his chops now. On the bar's scratchy television, *It's a Wonderful Life* was playing for the millionth time, Jimmy Stewart dancing through Bedford Falls having recovered his will to live. No one was watching.

"That true, kid?" Celia the bartender asked.

The boy looked at her with wide, puppy dog eyes. "Starved, actually."

"Cook went home. But if you wait a bit, I'll see what I can fix you up."

"That be great. Got a remote?" the boy asked, following Jimmy Stewart's prance down Main Street.

"Got a name?"

"Guess."

"Guess?"

"Guess."

The bartender sneered but answered anyway. "Okay. Trevor."

The boy slapped the bar with a palm. "See, you guessed right."

Celia laid her two flabby hands down on the counter, wondering how exactly she'd come up with that name. "Well, the remote's been missing for a month now. Last time the channel was changed was the night before Thanksgiving."

"Then it's a good thing I brought you a gift," Trevor said, leaning low enough off his stool to reach down and unzip his bulging backpack. After a few tries it finally opened with a slight tearing sound. "Here you go."

Spoken as he sat back up with a small, neatly wrapped and bowed present he handed to Celia. She eyed it suspiciously at first, then set to stripping the paper off while never once taking her eyes off the boy until she'd finished the task.

"You kidding me?" she said, the open box revealing a universal television remote control, sleek and black.

"Batteries installed and already programmed."

Celia was too busy flipping through the channels to ask how the boy had managed that. Something made her stop on an old nostalgia station that was playing an ancient Andy Williams Christmas special, Andy just breaking into *White Christmas* as fake snow with the texture of cardboard rained down upon him.

"Roget Ellis hates that dang song," came a voice four stools down from the boy, belonging to an old black man with white hair that looked like thick cotton woven to his scalp.

675

"Who's Roget Ellis?" Trevor asked.

"Him," said Hank Waggoner from the other side of the bar. "Old Roget likes to talk about himself in the third person."

"It's Ro-jay," the old man corrected. He pointed at the screen as Andy Williams cruised into the chorus. "Bing Crosby sang it for the first time Christmas Day 1941 on his NBC radio show *The Kraft Music Hall*. But the recording was lost forever. Know how Roget Ellis knows that? 'Cause he was there." Ellis was focusing on the boy now with droopy, bloodshot eyes suddenly bursting with intensity. "Part of the band. Played the saxophone and man, was Roget good. His very last gig until he shipped out to boot camp at Fort Dix. Came back from the war with this ..." Here, the old man used his left hand to help raise his right, pretty much a gnarled and useless appendage with two of the fingers missing. "Land mine killed Roget's arm and his career on May 29, 1942, the same day Crosby recorded 'White Christmas' with the John Scott Trotter Orchestra. Oh well," he said, plopping his dead arm down and lifting a glass of whiskey in its place, "least Roget Ellis got his memories."

Saying nothing, the boy dropped down from his stool and fished a second present from his still unzipped backpack. This one was flat, rectangular and thin, but equally well wrapped. He walked down to Roget Ellis and handed it to him.

"Merry Christmas, Mr. Ellis."

The old man took it with a suspicious smile, the boy already back on his stool by the time he finished peeling off the wrapping with his one good hand to reveal an unmarked sleeve and pristine record. "What is..."

"Turns out that original recording of *White Christmas* wasn't lost at all," Trevor told him. "Just missing for a while."

The old man used his good hand to slip an old 78-rpm recording disc from the album sleeve. His eyes misted up, holding the record in disbelief.

"Tell Roget this is what he thinks it is! Tell him that!"

Trevor grinned broadly. "I'm a sucker for a sax, sir."

And as Roget Ellis clutched the record like it was a newborn babe, the boy ducked his hand back into his seemingly bottomless backpack. "And I've got something for you too, Mr. Waggoner."

"Ain't had nothing to mattered to me since longer than I can remember," Waggoner said, studying the knobby fingers of his workingman hands. "I don't give up the smoke when I do, maybe I'm dead now." He gazed at the unlit cigarette as if it were a lost love. "Guess maybe I never should've quit."

Trevor used the new remote to switch the channel again, this time in a swift motion to the Major League Baseball channel that was showing World Series highlights held forever in grainy black and white. Waggoner's eyes widened as Trevor slid a small, equally well-wrapped box his way.

"Merry Christmas, Mr. Waggoner."

Waggoner resisted at first, trying to place exactly when he'd told the kid his name, then yanked at the small box with feigned disinterest until its contents were revealed. "Topps Baseball Cards. Why this looks just like ..." His eyes snapped outright, seeking the boy out with suspicion. "How'd you know? Who told you?"

"Told me what?"

"My baseball card collection," he continued, opening the box as if something might jump out. "My dad and I, we collected them together. Then he died and I was so angry and bitter I tossed them all out. Still remember chasing the garbage truck down the street after I changed my mind, but I never did catch ...Oh my," he said suddenly, flipping through the box's pristine contents. "Mickey Mantle, Willy Mays, Stan Musial, *Ted Williams*!" His grateful gaze sought out Trevor anew. "They're all here, all brand spanking new! How did you, how could you ..." Again Waggoner's words drifted off, attention returned to his bounty.

"Whatcha got in there for me, punk?" an angry voice demanded. "Gotta be something in there for me!"

"Oh boy," muttered Ray Dunwoodie, recalling that the nameless man who drank away his welfare check was prone to fits that had drawn Celia on more than one occasion to take baseball bat in hand.

"There is," Trevor replied, holding a small box as his boots click-clacked toward the man.

The man's eyes looked red and wild in the light flickering over him, his hair a thinning mess of tangles and ringlets aimed in all directions at once. Dunwoodie could almost smell the stench washing over him. Closest thing the man had to a shower was a soaking rainstorm few and far between this time of year. Funding deficits had forced off the hot water in the shelter where he lived.

"Better be, I say, better be!" he blared, rising to his full height, which looked enormous in the shadows but barely passed for average.

Trevor extended the box toward him and didn't so much as flinch when the homeless man tore it from his grasp. He went at the wrapping like a piranha, emerging with a prepaid cell phone.

"This some kind of joke?" the homeless man shouted at the boy. "That what it is? Like I got someone to call?"

"You do?"

"Huh?"

"Your son," Trevor told him.

The man's face got red, his teeth starting to bare enough for Celia to remember the baseball bat. Then he simply sighed, all the air seeming to drain out of him. "Like I know where he is."

Trevor looked unruffled, the flickering light making his features seem more liquid than solid. His eyes aimed toward the box the homeless man still held in his grubby hands. "His number's preprogrammed. Just turn the phone on and press '1.'"

"But how could ...

That's as far as the homeless man got, his shoulders sagging to make him look very small and not nearly as scary. No one seemed to notice that the light over him had stopped flickering. Behind the bar, Celia took her hand off the knob of the bat, unable to similarly take her eyes off the boy. She wanted to say something, couldn't.

The whole room, in fact, had gone dead quiet. The television was back on the old Christmas special, Andy Williams singing *Silent Night* now. Everyone's eyes rotated between the various gifts Trevor had come bearing and the boy himself. Paying them little heed, Trevor zipped his backpack back up and shouldered it.

"Guess I won't be needing that meal," he told Celia. "But thanks all the same."

He retraced his steps down the center of the bar. Almost to the door before he turned and took a few steps toward Ray Dunwoodie.

"Unless there's a publishing contract in there, don't bother, kid."

"Thought I recognized you," Trevor told him. "Raymond Dunwoodie. I've seen your books. How come you stopped writing?"

"I didn't. Publisher stopped buying."

"Sorry."

"Perfect word to describe my sales, kid," Dunwoodie said, seemingly unfazed by all he had just seen. His eyes fastened on the kid's backpack. "Wouldn't happen to be carrying around a great story in there, would you? Something original that I could sell for sure?"

The boy eyed the backpack slung behind him. "In this? No."

"Well, if you find one in your travels, you know where to find me."

"I'm headed south. Little place just like this, only with warmer weather." Trevor pulled a scrunched-up piece of paper from the pocket of his jeans and handed it to Dunwoodie. "Give them a call. Tomorrow, maybe the day after. Ask for me."

Dunwoodie held the paper without straightening it, as Trevor flashed his gleaming smile, straightened his shoulders and aimed himself for the door again.

"Merry Christmas, everyone."

For a time anyway, the backpack had seemed thinner. As Trevor slid back into the storm, though, it suddenly looked as crammed and stuffed as ever.

"Merry Christmas," five voices said back to the boy, but the night had already reclaimed him.

*

The kid wasn't dressed for the weather, not wearing a bulky jacket and sweatshirt on the warmest Christmas Eve on record, the bartender thought as he watched the floppy-haired boy take a seat at the bar.

"You better have an ID, son."

"Oh," the boy said, pulling an overstuffed backpack from his shoulders, "I'm not drinking."

A FAMILY CHRISTMAS TERROR

CHAPTER 23

Grandpa read the last words and closed the book. He felt an odd sense of relief, but not enjoyable one. He stared at the cover, pondering.

"What did you do to us? You're not a gift... you're a curse."

He went to the fireplace and threw the book in.

He watched the corners of the book darken and heard the pop as the glue caught fire. The flames flickered and red glints of embers floated up.

"And to all a good night, indeed," he muttered. With that, he slowly turned and walked to the stairs, not noticing the one stray ember that floated out and up from the fireplace.

Nor did he see the ember land in a pile of discarded Christmas paper.

*

"So what do you think happened here?" Rick Turnbill asked his partner Frank Bates as the two firemen slogged their way through the sodden rubble of the building.

"I don't know. It's weird. I mean, it's seems like there was some kind of accelerant used. Five bodies charred beyond recognition. The whole place burned to the ground. How long was it burning before anyone noticed? I mean, there's *nothing* left. I've never seen a house fire like this."

"It's Christmas. They probably had candles burning, paper by an outlet, dry tree. Maybe they left a fire burning in the fireplace."

They walked over to the bricks; the only part of the house that didn't seem to have burned. Frank kicked at the ashes there. "Well, it wasn't a lit fireplace."

"How do you know?"

"Look."

Rick looked down into the ashes Frank had kicked away. "What the hell?"

Frank bent over and reached down. "It's a book. Perfectly clean. Not a mark on it." He turned it back and forth. "How is that possible?"

"You got me. Maybe the ashes protected it?"

"Yeah, right," Frank studied the cover, then turned it over and read. *Never Fear—Christmas Terrors.* Twenty-two tales of terror."

"It sure was a tale of terror for this family," Rick said.

"Now this is strange." Frank had flipped to the table of contents. "The cover says there are twenty-two stories, but in the beginning here there are twenty-*three* listed. The last one's called: *A Family Christmas Terror.*" He frowned. "You don't think this story has—"

"Don't be stupid. Throw it out."

"Naw, I think I'll keep it. Bridget and I are going to Cancun for New Year's." He held up the book in his hand. "I can read it on the plane."

"Whatever. Let's get back to the station."

CHRISTMAS TERRORS

ABOUT THE AUTHORS

13Thirty Books is now **Invoke Books**
Find more information on our Authors and Books at:

WWW.INVOKEBOOKS.COM

Author Collective includes:

New York Times, USA Today, Publishers Weekly, Amazon Top Ten bestselling and award-winning authors, as well as new, unique and upcoming writers.

Pick up your copy of:

Never Fear

Never Fear - Phobias

Never Fear - Tarot

Never Fear - The Apocalypse